Bestselling rural crime author Fleur McDonald has always had a strong affinity with the land and the vast Australian outback. Raised in Orroroo, South Australia, Fleur loves the open roads, red dust and magical sunsets. With twenty-four fiction novels and more than 850,000 book sales to her name, Fleur has built a strong following of loyal readers with an insatiable appetite for her craft and characters, most notably Detective Dave Burrows.

She spends much of her year behind the wheel, traversing our big country, scouting inspiration and potential storylines for future books and appearing as a guest speaker at a range of events, including country shows, ladies' days and writers' festivals. A trailblazer in all aspects of her life, Fleur has been a jillaroo farming the land for more than twenty years, founded DVassist to help regional dwellers access crucial support for family and domestic violence, and raised two children with developmental and speech delays, teaching them Makaton sign language to communicate.

These days, in between putting out two books a year, she has her sights set on learning to fly a plane. Fleur now lives in Esperance, Western Australia with her two children, Rochelle and Hayden, and fur child, border collie Shadow.

Also by Fleur McDonald

Contemporary Detective Dave Burrows series
Red Dust
Blue Skies
Purple Roads
Silver Clouds
Crimson Dawn
Emerald Springs
Indigo Storm
Sapphire Falls
The Missing Pieces of Us
Suddenly One Summer
Where the River Runs
Starting From Now
The Shearer's Wife
Deception Creek
Broad River Station
Voices in the Dark
Out in Nowhere

Young Detective Dave Burrows series
Fool's Gold
Without a Doubt
Red Dirt Country
Something to Hide
Rising Dust
Into the Night
Shock Waves

THE
PROSPECT

THE PROSPECT

FLEUR McDONALD

HarperCollins*Publishers*

HarperCollins*Publishers*

Australia • Brazil • Canada • France • Germany • Holland • India
Italy • Japan • Mexico • New Zealand • Poland • Spain • Sweden
Switzerland • United Kingdom • United States of America

HarperCollins acknowledges the Traditional Custodians
of the lands upon which we live and work, and pays respect
to Elders past and present.

First published on Gadigal Country in Australia in 2025
by HarperCollins*Publishers* Australia Pty Limited
ABN 36 009 913 517
harpercollins.com.au

A catalogue record for this book is available from the National Library of Australia

ISBN 978 1 4607 6688 0 (paperback)
ISBN 978 1 4607 1810 0 (ebook)
ISBN 978 1 4607 3211 3 (audiobook)

Cover design by Hazel Lam, HarperCollins Design Studio
Cover image by istockphoto.com
Author photo by Anna Hill
Typeset in Bembo Std by Kelli Lonergan
Printed and bound in Australia by McPherson's Printing Group

MIX
Paper | Supporting
responsible forestry
FSC
www.fsc.org   FSC® C001695

To Mike and Donna who tried to make me a local
by taking me to every restaurant in Kalgoorlie

and

To those who are precious

CHAPTER ONE

Trespassers prosecuted or shot.
Whichever comes first.

Zara Ellison stared at the hand-written words on the corrugated iron-tin. The two-wheel dirt track she'd been nosing her four-wheel drive down was overgrown with spiky bushes and branches, and it was hard to see what lay ahead. Tall blackbutt trees towered above her, long pieces of bark peeling from their trunks, swinging sideways in the breeze.

The sign wasn't particularly friendly, but she decided to ignore it and keep heading towards Ted Upton's camp.

And perhaps towards her own death-by-shooting.

She took a breath then put the dual cab back into gear.

Hopefully Ted was a listening type of fella, rather than the type who let his gun do the talking first.

She really needed to talk to him.

On the ute's passenger seat, her computer and notebook bounced up and down in time with the potholes.

Was the need to write a story for the newspaper important enough to lose her life?

Apparently so. She needed to prove it to herself, and to show her new colleagues that she was a good journalist. The Kalgoorlie rumour mill was awash with speculation that *The Prospector* was about to shut down. Zara wasn't ready to believe she'd been sent to a newspaper on its last legs and was hedging her bets both ways. No one had said anything to her directly, but she'd heard the whispers around the lunchroom and noticed the anxious lines in Joanna Fiddler's face. As the youngest journalist, Joanna might be the first one let go. Or maybe it would be a longer employed journo with more experience. They were the expensive ones. Either way, she was concerned.

No one in the Kalgoorlie office had been happy when Zara arrived. After the court case, she knew she wasn't welcome at any newspaper. Journalists never give up their sources, and Zara hadn't – not really. But her evidence had provided enough clues for people to work out who had been feeding information to her and now the CFO of a national accounting firm was under investigation for breaching confidentiality.

Every time Zara thought about the courtroom and the things she'd said, her body flushed with shame. Her heart rate would pick up and nausea flooded through her.

God, she wished she could change her testimony.

Still, as Jack had told her: 'You just have to move on and accept what's happened.'

Easier said than done. He hadn't stuffed up his entire career and been banished to the backblocks. He had, however, given up his job as a detective and gone back into uniform so he could move to Western Australia with her. That was worth a lot to Zara.

Back in Adelaide her colleagues used to greet her with easy smiles and respect. But in Kalgoorlie, the editor, Bruce, and the other journalists dropped their heads to avoid her eyes. They had ignored her for three weeks in a row – not offering her coffee when they went on their four-times-a-day cafe run and not inviting her to join them at the bar down the street each night.

Yet why would they? She was tarnished in a way a journo never wanted to be.

The office this morning had been as silent and cold as the bush on a winter's eve.

So she'd gone to the Tatts bar and talked to some of the locals, trying to find a story. Something to redeem herself. One of the men she'd met, Vince, had sent her to Ted and now she was driving down this potholed road with shrubby bushes reaching their long tentacles towards her and scratching the sides of the car.

She wound the window down and rested her elbow on the ledge, the thrum of the engine vibrating as she listened and watched carefully.

No shotgun blasts yet.

Tiny birds, no bigger than a fist, trilled, their green wings blurring as they flitted from tree to tree.

Running parallel with the track, a ridge with layers of white rock rose against the sapphire-coloured sky. Deep crevices pushing back underneath the rock. The thought of going down them made Zara want to claw at the imagined darkness. Underground always smelt musty and decaying to her. It also smelt like fear, but she wasn't sure how, considering being terrified wasn't a smell. But it did.

In a distant age, branches had been used to build up the entrances around mine shafts and then driven into the sides to brace the walls. Now they were crumbly and rotten, a death trap to those who braved exploring them, hidden within the landscape.

Vince had warned her about the mine shafts and the catacombs of tunnels. The ground could give way and swallow her, at any moment. Some were fenced off and others, in the middle of the landscape, looked lonely and abandoned.

Zara shook as the weight of history landed on her shoulders. The bush opened to a clearing, a barbed-wire fence across the road and another friendly notice. This time each word was written in red paint that trailed to the bottom of the sheet of tin.

FUCK OFF. GET OUT OF HERE.

Zara looked again at the red letters, imagining for a moment it wasn't red paint but the blood of some earlier trespasser who hadn't heeded the warnings.

She turned off her car.

Tick, tick, tick. There were a few dead tree stumps in front of her too, and pink pigface flowers smiled cheerfully, radiant in among the grey-green of the bush.

An unnerving silence swirled through the ute. Zara's stomach tightened.

Ted wouldn't really shoot her, would he?

Surely Vince wouldn't have sent her out here to visit some crazy. He had seemed like a decent bloke.

Maybe it wasn't a good idea to assume. He'd been a stranger

until she'd introduced herself to him at the bar and offered to buy him a handle of his choice of beer.

But in the few weeks since she'd arrived in Kalgoorlie, she'd noticed that people here did what they wanted, when they wanted, regardless of the law. It really was the wild west.

Zara could hear her own breath. Quick and sharp.

The bush outside was unusually silent. Normally there'd be birds singing or branches cracking. Perhaps the rustle of leaves against each other. Sometimes even the distant thump of kangaroos or whinnying of brumbies, along with the ever-present flies. Not that they made much of a noise until they got inside your ear canal, which seemed to be their favourite place to hide!

All comforting sounds she could tune into.

Not today, however. Today the bush was songless. Not even the constant clanging of mines and rumbling of machinery could be heard.

There was only the engine tick and the rustle of her puffer jacket sleeves against her body.

She focused on a small bunch of waving purple wildflowers, which seemed out of place in this jarring landscape.

'Get a grip,' she told herself as she grabbed her notebook from the passenger's seat.

She got out of the car, her feet sinking a few centimetres into the soft, rusty red earth, then walked to the barbed-wire fence, putting her hands on it. The hum of the tightly strung wires bounced around her.

The land felt uninhabited, as if she was the first person who had set foot on this piece of Australia in a long time. She knew it wasn't true, but that was how this country north of Kalgoorlie felt. Empty, isolated, lonely.

A little like her since she'd stuffed up back in Adelaide.

'Hello?' Swivelling on the heels of her feet, she searched the bush for a house, a shack, any type of living quarters. 'Hello?'

She had to squint against the glare, even with the heavy cloud cover.

Silence.

'My name's Zara Ellison. I'm a journ—' She broke off. Maybe announcing she was a journalist wasn't the best move right now.

She pushed the wire down, intending to climb over, when she saw a rusted, small gate behind a shrub. A COD – carry or drag gate – but a gate nonetheless. Perhaps she was in the right place after all.

When she carried it open, dry hinges protested loudly. It was a crude security alarm and seemed out of place next to the well-maintained fence. In the Flinders Ranges, where Zara was from, the galahs and white cockatoos would have left the giant gum trees in a cloud of white, grey and pink, squealing in protest at the high-pitched creaking, but not here. The empty bush absorbed the noise, right down into the depths of the hidden mine shafts.

Now her eyes had adjusted, Zara realised that the dead tree stumps were in fact branches laid across the ground, outlining a pathway leading to a partially hidden caravan.

It looked as if it had been swallowed by the landscape. Trees pressed their branches over the roof, enveloping it in a hug, while shoulder-high scrub hid the entry. Zara clocked a small tank hooked up with PVC pipe. An agricultural-looking rainwater catchment from the roof to the tank lay covered in dirt and dust, yet a raised garden bed, made out of another tank cutoff, was overflowing with green plant tendrils. Potatoes maybe.

Despite the thriving plants, the caravan looked unlived in, desolate. An empty chair was next to the door and a bed with an untidy pile of covers lay underneath a verandah, which was nothing but a piece of shade cloth, roughly fastened from the van to a tree.

Vince had said Ted was a gold prospector. All the locals out here were. 'No one living out there in the bush could be anything but half mad.' He'd paused. 'From gold fever.'

Amateur prospectors hunting for gold left a trail, even if they were careful. Little holes, small piles of dirt next to them. That was their calling card.

Professional prospectors, like Vince had said Ted was, created sunken crevices or shafts as well as digging holes. They could read the ground like a book and even though alluvial gold was much harder to find these days, a sixth sense seemed to help them.

Behind the trees, there could be dingoes, wild dogs, brumbies, another human. A mine shaft she couldn't see.

Zara took a few steps down the makeshift pathway, towards the brave succulents that were growing on either side of the path. There was so much pigface out in the bush, it had to be native, but she wasn't sure. There were many houses in town with it in their front yards too.

'Hello, I'm looking for Ted,' she called out again.

As if in slow motion a figure rose from the bed. The shade was so dark she couldn't make out the face, but this must be him.

Zara smiled her I'm-a-journalist-there's-nothing-to-be-worried-about grin.

'Oh, hello, are you Ted? I'm—'

The person looked around as if confused and then held up something.

'Get the fuck off my property!'

A loud blast echoed around the bush.

Letting out a squeal and hitting the ground with her hands over her head, she called out: 'I'm Zara Ellison!' Her words coming in such a hurry they tripped over each other. 'From *The Prospector*! I'm not here to cause any trouble.'

Another blast and her ears started to ring.

'You got no business here! Get the hell out.'

Uncrumpling herself from the foetal position, Zara brought her head up.

Anger flickered inside her and she stood. Defiant. 'I'm here to talk to you. If you're Ted. I'm looking for Ted,' she repeated. 'I was told he might talk to me.' Her frightened fury spurred her on. 'Though you obviously haven't read the country protocol about welcoming visitors.'

'Trespassers will be shot!'

Risking another burst of gunfire, she took a step forward. 'Are you Ted?'

In response, the person flopped heavily onto the bed and seemed to bounce a few times then was still.

Zara stared in confused horror. 'Oh my god, do you need help?' A few more hesitant steps then she asked: 'Can I—'

'Stop where you are. Trespassers aren't welcome. Turn around and go back the way you came. Get the fuck off my land.'

This time the words circled around her and Zara looked around to see where they were coming from.

Then she felt something push against the back of her neck and heard the click of a handgun. She froze and slowly put her hands in the air.

'Just looking for Ted,' she squeaked over the sound of her own frantic heartbeat.

'And who the fuck might you be?'

CHAPTER TWO

'Jesus, Jayne, will you get a move on? We're gonna be late.'
Barry walked around the caravan again, touching the tyres.
He wasn't really sure what he was checking for, but he'd seen
other caravanners do it so it seemed like a good idea. He
made sure he'd stowed the step properly. Driving off with it
dragging on the ground was a rookie mistake and he didn't
want anyone to think he was green. A successful lawyer,
deal-closer and financial wizard was how Barry wanted to
be known.

'Jayne!' Frustration made him yell louder than he'd intended.
Where the bloody hell was that woman?

A few moments later, he saw his wife laughing with another
camper near the entry into the Gwalia Mine Museum. The
same woman whose ear she'd been chewing off during last
night's dinner. They'd spent a week following this couple,
crisscrossing down the Goldfields Highway, always running
into them at a caravan park or a service station.

Jayne caught his eye and gave a wave, and signalled she
wouldn't be long.

Barry clenched his teeth. After fifty years together, her

chitchat was bloody irritating and on top of that, always made them run late. Today was clearly going to be no exception.

Barry abhorred tardiness.

Plus, he wanted to get to Kalgoorlie, set up camp and get the TV working because the footy was on in four hours and the new lad was making his debut for the Crows today.

Barry and his golfing mates on the WhatsApp group would compare notes on the game and place some bets. If everyone showed up, that could amount to nine or ten thousand dollars.

'Nice van.'

Barry turned at the voice and saw a woman leaning against his caravan. She was the one who'd been camped three caravans down last night. What was her name again? She'd been sitting next to him at dinner. Or had she?

'Thanks.' He frowned, annoyed she was leaning against the spare tyre. 'You know that's my van?'

'And it's a beauty. In a hurry?' she asked.

'There's always places to be.' Barry tried to attract Jayne's attention again.

'I thought you were retired.' The woman gave a bright smile and ran her hand over the spare tyre. 'Taking life slowly is the motto of the road. Unless you're a truckie.'

Barry gave a self-deprecating smile. 'It takes time to teach old dogs new tricks. Guess I still have to learn how to relax.'

The woman pulled her beanie down over her ears. 'We wear our busyness like a badge, don't we?' she said with a soft smile, the air so cold, her breath turned white as she spoke.

Barry felt a flicker of anger. Who was she to judge what he did or didn't do?

'The busier we are, the more successful we'll be,' she continued, 'and that means more money, more things, more ...'

She shrugged. 'Whatever you want. But it's less life, isn't it?' She indicated towards the mine they were camped near. 'Mines run twenty-four seven in the search for riches, but what do they get out of it?'

'Riches,' Barry said, glancing over to the open-cut scar on the earth. 'I wouldn't say no to some of what they find.'

The mine was cavernous. Someone had said it was around 1660 metres deep, the open pit carved deep into the landscape. When Barry had peeked over the edge, the yawning hole was large enough that the huge mining machines were only specks at the bottom. The sight gave him vertigo.

'Are you heading anywhere today, ah ...' Barry shook the door of the van to make sure it was locked and wouldn't come open.

'I think so. Probably north. Or maybe south.' She shrugged. 'Wherever the mood takes me.'

'We came from up north,' Barry said. 'If your husband wants to know about the roads, I can tell him how we found them.'

'Husband? Oh no, I don't have one of those.' She smiled. 'I'm alone.'

Barry frowned again. He had a hard time understanding all these women who just took off by themselves and travelled the Outback. Didn't they have responsibilities at home? Families at the very least? What about security? Didn't they get frightened?

'I thought you were in that huge van over there.' He pointed towards a black and grey van, with the curtains drawn and the windscreen protector still on the dash. Envy whirred in his stomach. He'd wanted that model but it was far more expensive than the one he'd bought. That one had a separate shower and toilet; in Barry and Jayne's, the shower was over the loo. Barry found it unsuitable for his ample frame and, well, wet.

The woman just smiled at him.

'I'd better go check on my wife,' he said, keen to get away from this pesky, self-opinionated woman. Giving her a brief nod, Barry headed quickly towards Jayne. When he looked back, the woman was still leaning against his van. She gave him a little wave – wiggling fingers and everything.

His scowl deepened. Maybe she hadn't been at the dinner last night. Whatever her name was, had she even told him? Jayne would know. Well, she was bending down now and looking under his van! Inspecting the tyres and axles.

Rude.

'Hey!' he called. 'Hey.'

That was another thing he disliked about other travellers. They were always checking out other people's vans. He was about to walk back and ask what she was doing, but then he remembered another couple from yesterday. The husband had spent a good ten minutes checking the chassis of Barry's van, comparing it to his. 'I like to check out other van's frames,' he'd told Barry. 'Good to know if there's any improvements with the new ones so I know when it's time to upgrade.'

Although, as if that woman would know if there was anything new or wrong with his van.

And the wife, a bossy, fussy woman, had ooh-ed and ahh-ed over the solar panel that he had on the roof. 'Really, you have one that big?' she'd asked. 'I could use my hairdryer, the voltage is so high.'

He decided not to bother with that woman again. She'd probably just ask whether he wanted to smoke a peace pipe or something ridiculous. He stomped over and stood next to his wife.

'I know,' Jayne said, seemingly agreeing with her new friend. 'Have you read the latest book in the series?' She smiled at Barry. 'Hello, love.'

The other woman grinned too. 'Are you a reader like your lovely wife, Barry?' she asked. 'Who's your favourite author?'

'What?' Barry asked. He really didn't understand this caravanning life. Everyone was on go-slow mode, too friendly with people they'd never met and too willing to overshare.

And there were flies.

Way too many flies.

Every morning was less than ten degrees and yet those bastards clustered right around his nose and mouth so every time he took a breath, he swallowed some. It made him want to puke.

But Jayne seemed to be enjoying their time on the road.

'Do you like to read?' the woman repeated.

'Only legal documents,' he replied curtly. He caught Jayne rolling her eyes. 'Come on,' he told her, 'we need to head off or we'll be late.'

'To where?' the woman asked.

'We're headed to Kalgoorlie,' his wife answered. She and the woman agreed to catch up there and then Jayne linked her arm through his. 'You need to relax, love.' She squeezed his arm as they headed back to their van. 'You *wanted* to stop working, remember? Get away from all that stress.'

But there was a whole lot of different, confusing stress out here.

'Have you met that woman anywhere before?' he asked, tipping his head towards their camping spot, but the woman was gone. Whatever the hell her name was, seemed to have moved on. Probably passing on her do-gooder advice on a subject that had nothing to do with her to another unsuspecting soul. Barry huffed.

'Carol? The one I was talking to just now?' Jayne pulled her arm away and Barry felt her coolness. 'Come on, Barry, you've met her numerous times now. Don't be rude.'

'No, the one checking out our van. Her jeans were covered in red dirt and looked like they needed washing. She kept looking over our van and spouting some new-age bullshit.'

Jayne's annoyance evaporated as she laughed. Barry felt her repeat the arm squeeze. 'You've described every woman on the road. Can you point her out?'

Barry checked the camp site again. 'No.' He turned to Jayne, holding her arm tightly now, so she couldn't escape. 'Let's go before you start yakking to someone else.'

'Barry,' she drew out his name.

'What? Let's just get on the road, okay?' He opened the car door and waved her in.

'Seriously, what's the hurry, love?'

'I want to watch the Crows match in Kalgoorlie. Come on.' He looked around for the woman again, but she seemed to have disappeared into thin air. 'She said she was travelling alone, but I don't remember seeing anyone by themselves last night, did you?'

'Oh, love, I don't think I was even looking. I was just enjoying.'

This time, he glared at her.

'Maybe she arrived this morning,' she said hurriedly. 'A LandCruiser pulled up at the entrance earlier.'

Someone beeped their horn as another van headed out towards the road. Jayne raised her hand to wave. 'Travel safe,' she called.

Barry stalked off to open the driver's door of the new Ram they'd bought to go with the new caravan so they could join the 'Joneses' and do the *big lap*.

Jayne seemed to slip in among these people like she'd been travelling for years and yet he, the King of the Courtroom, was floundering like an upside-down turtle.

'Come on,' he said more sharply than he intended. 'It's time to go.'

'Love, it's only ten am. Let's have morning tea before we go. A real coffee would be such a treat.'

Jayne's eyes begged him to stay, but Barry was already seeing the opening bounce of the game, feeling the cold beer in his hand and licking his lips at the money he could win if he made the right bet. Would the new full forward kick the first goal? Maybe he could lay a bet on that happening.

'No, we're leaving now. There's no way I'll get set up in time, the way you've been wasting time today.'

Jayne's face fell and Barry felt a twinge of regret. The big lap had been his idea and now, only two months in, he was being a prick and he knew it.

'We should be making the most of all these opportunities, Barry,' she said, still not getting in the ute. 'Not just racing through every place we stop. We'll miss the small things. The best things. I'm sure we won't be here again.'

'God, now you sound like that bloody woman.' He made his voice high, imitating her. '*We wear our busyness like a badge. Or whatever shit she was yabbering on about.*'

'Sounds like a smart woman to me.' Jayne didn't make

any move to get into the vehicle. 'Look,' her voice softened. 'Carol and Jim are staying for morning tea and then heading to Kalgoorlie too. Why don't we go in convoy with them? And I'd really love to see inside the museum – there's a whole heap of mining machinery just inside the gate and Hoover House is a bit further up. You find history interesting, Barry. Or you used to. Have you forgotten? Carol and Jim are nice people.'

He ignored the pleading in her voice. 'I told the others I'd be on the WhatsApp group this afternoon. We always message each other as soon as the game starts, you know that. Now, hop in. You haven't left anything in the laundry, have you?'

Jayne threw a look at him as she got into the ute. Her white sandshoes were covered in sticky red mud from the heavy dew the night before and it left a trail on the floor mat. He itched to ask her to shake it out but managed to control himself.

Dirt, dust, flies. Everything out here made his skin crawl.

Jayne slammed the door shut and clicked her seatbelt into place. She was annoyed with him, and with good reason. He should apologise, but he just breathed out relief. Finally they were ready.

Checking the mirrors, he eased the car and van out onto the road.

'Look at that little mining village they've done up,' Jayne said with her nose glued to the window. 'They lived hard back then, didn't they? Temperatures would have been so extreme. Boiling in summer and how cold has it been this morning? Winter would have been awful. No insulation and dirt floors and no air con.'

'Probably not as hot as now, with climate change and all that,' Barry said as he waited to turn on to the Goldfields

Highway, heading south. A triple road train thundered past, and he felt the ute being buffeted under the wind drag. 'God, they're huge,' he muttered, checking again to make sure the road was clear. There was another truck coming but he had time to pull out.

He floored the accelerator and the ute jumped forward.

'Shit,' Barry muttered, forgetting how powerful it was. He glanced in the rear-vision mirror and saw the truck driver flashing his lights at him.

He set the cruise control at one hundred kilometres an hour, the exact same speed the truck behind him should be driving and settled back in his seat. He didn't care, the truck would slow down.

Jayne turned in her seat. 'Barry, love.'

He sighed at the determined look on his wife's face. He should listen, but he'd heard the spiel she was about to deliver so many times that it was easier to zone out.

'You're going to have to chill out a bit,' she said. 'We're not going to have any fun if you keep moving on so quickly and don't talk to the others who are doing the exact same thing as we are. You wanted to make this trip. To do something different. Sitting in front of the TV watching footy isn't different.'

Pressing his lips together, Barry checked the temperature, and every other gauge on the dash, and ignored his wife.

'Love? What's wrong?'

'Nothing's wrong.' Heat flooded his face, and he pushed his foot down on the accelerator despite the cruise control. Admitting that this trip was nothing like he imagined would show weakness. He wasn't about to do that. Instead, he reacted angrily. 'How about you just shut up for a while. Give a man some peace.'

Jayne looked as if she'd been slapped, but she sat back in her seat. Barry threw her one final glance and focused back on the road.

'Got a copy on the two-way radio there, Barry and Jayne,' a tinny voice asked as the two-way spluttered to life.

Barry didn't pick up the microphone but checked the side mirrors and saw a LandCruiser coming up behind them.

Jayne was the one who'd insisted they get their names turned into stickers and put on the back of the van with the two-way channel they were going to monitor.

'Channel forty, like all the truckies.' Jayne had laughed when they'd stood behind the van looking at the outcome. 'We'll be able to hear everything that's going on. Whether the police are around or if there are any speed cameras. Even if there's an accident – and I reckon that would be good to know, in case there's a road closure or something.'

Barry had grunted and privately thought they'd be able to find out anything they needed to know without it.

'Got a copy there, Barry and Jayne,' the voice persisted. A female voice.

The LandCruiser pulled out to pass them, blinker flashing.

Snatching up the mic, Barry answered. 'Got a copy,' he said, pretending he was just like a truckie and knew exactly what to say.

'Where you headed?' The voice was friendly, but Barry's brow deepened as she spoke.

'Why does everyone need to know what we're doing?' he asked without depressing the transmit button.

Jayne looked at him in horror, thinking he'd sent the words over the airwaves.

He held up the mic, then pressed the button so she could see.

'Into Kalgoorlie. You?'

As the LandCruiser drew level with the driver's door, Barry could make out a hand waving through the dark tint. He stared straight ahead, hands on the steering wheel.

'Same,' the voice said as the ute pulled away to the front. 'How about we catch up for a drink when we get there?'

'Do we know these people?' he asked Jayne.

'Who knows,' she said. 'They've probably stayed in the same caravan park as we have at some stage and recognise our names on the back of the van. Wouldn't hurt you to say yes.' She crossed her arms.

'Let's see how we go,' Barry answered the two-way and put the mic back in the holder. The LandCruiser moved off ahead of them.

A low roar reached their ears. 'What?' Barry checked all the gauges again and lifted his foot slightly.

'Oh my god, look!' Jayne pointed to the rear-view mirror, just as Barry glanced down.

'What the hell is—'

'Barry,' Jayne's voice was calm. 'You're crossing the white line. Barry!'

Looking to the road, he yanked the steering wheel back to the left, just as a group of motorbikes roared past them.

His lips parted slightly as one rider rode alongside the ute and gave him the finger for a few seconds, then roared off.

'What in god's name?'

'Bikies,' Jayne said uneasily. 'Are they the real ones?'

'How the hell would I know?' His heart was beating wildly. Last time he'd had anything to do with a bikie, it had been a court case he'd lost. One of the members went down for a long stint behind bars. The sergeant-at-arms had leaned in close and told him to watch his back. Was this a message from them? How long ago had that case been?

He already knew the answer. It had been the last one he'd tried and part of the reason he'd wanted to get away.

The car slowed on a long, straight stretch of road as he lifted his foot and willed his heart to slow down.

Jayne was still staring after the disappearing group of bikes. 'Wow.'

Words, it seemed, didn't come to either of them.

'Look at this,' Barry said a few moments later. 'There's a truck coming up behind like a freight train. Seriously, what's his problem? Looks as if he wants to pass.' As he spoke, he realised he'd slowed to eighty kilometres an hour.

Behind them a horn sounded.

Get out of the way!

'Pull over or slow down,' Jayne said. 'Let them by. It's not like we're in a hurry.'

'But we are,' he said, pushing his foot down again, watching his speedo creep back up to one hundred. 'I really want— Geez, look at this idiot, he's going to overtake.'

He watched in the rear-vision mirror as a monster-sized truck pulled out and gained on them.

'Barry, watch the road!' Jayne told him.

Again, he jerked the wheel back, still seeing the middle finger encased in a black leather glove, stuck up in his face.

One hundred and four tyres and two hundred tonnes of iron ore and truck was suddenly pulling out on the wrong side of the road to pass their little caravan.

Stubbornly, Barry continued at his speed. If the truck wanted to pass him, it would have to go fast.

As the back trailer reached the front of their ute, the blinker flashed and the entire truck started to move back into their lane.

'Barry!' Jayne sounded alarmed.

'It's fine,' he said, maintaining his speed, but the truck's last trailer was swaying close to the shiny silver bonnet of their ute.

'Barry, slow down!'

Too late. The corner of the last trailer clipped the bull bar.

He was going so fast, there was no time to hit the brakes. No time to think.

Only Jayne's screams made Barry realise that the ute had started to tip. Rolling over and over and over while the truck kept driving towards Kalgoorlie.

CHAPTER THREE

'How do you feel about being back in uniform?' Senior Sergeant Martin Rogers leaned back in his chair and looked at Jack over his glasses.

Feeling his face flush, Jack looked away to the photo of the senior sergeant's graduation on the wall behind his chair. Twenty-four fresh-faced constables. He wondered how many were still in the force.

There were only five remaining from Jack's intake year. Suicide had taken some and others had retired with PTSD, while a few had decided policing wasn't for them.

How did he feel?

Frustrated. Pissed off. Resentful even. Rearranging his thoughts, he crossed his legs stalling for time, to get his anger under control.

'I'm looking forward to it, sir,' he lied.

Martin linked his hands over his stomach and stared at Jack. 'Are you?'

He squirmed. Could the senior sergeant see the turmoil inside him? His bitterness at having to leave his dream job?

Outside the office, other police officers were talking and phones were ringing. It was almost as busy as the Adelaide Central Police Station, where he'd worked as a detective.

Now he was back in uniform. He could argue all he liked, but every which way Jack looked at it, following Zara to Kalgoorlie had caused him to be demoted. Even if it was by his own choice.

Moving interstate had meant he'd now have to work his way back up the ranks, after completing the transition course that was mandatory for an officer moving states.

The radio on his belt came to life, and he leaned slightly towards it.

'Ignore that for the moment,' Martin told him. 'You're in a meeting with me.'

'Sir.' Jack did as he was asked.

'And cut the sir crap. Kalgoorlie has never stood on airs or protocol. Coffee?'

Unsure of how to answer, Jack looked around to see if there was someone who was going to make the coffee. He half stood. 'Where do I make it?'

'Are you always so jumpy? Calm your farm.' Martin stood and walked over to a cupboard on the wall then opened the door. He pulled out a shelf that had a coffee machine on it and a fridge underneath. 'Always thought the hotel designers were clever the way they could hide their machines, so I had a crack at it. Try to do a bit of handiwork during my days off. You know what it's like, you've got to have something that helps you relax and forget about the job. We see so damn much that the public don't.' He dropped a pod into the slot and cranked the handle over.

The machine whirred to life. 'What do you do to relax, Jack?'

Martin handed over a cup that had a chip out of the edge.

'Cheers.' Jack took the teaspoon that was also being held out. He stirred his coffee, watching the milk blend in with the black liquid and thought about the question.

Over the last six months, when he wasn't working, he was either cleaning the house or cooking meals because Zara had been tied up with that bloody court case she'd been called to testify in. She had just about lived at the courthouse and her office, then one day she turned up and said she was being sent to Kalgoorlie and was he coming with her?

Some days he wished he'd thought more about his answer and the ramifications on his life before he'd said yes.

'I run,' Jack told him. 'Every day, rain, hail or shine.'

'That'll come in handy if you have a foot chase. What made you come to Kalgoorlie?' Martin asked, leaning back in his chair.

'Not much to tell really. I've completed the six-week transition course and here I am. Ready and willing.' He gave Martin a smile, while he tried to swallow the bubble of resentment towards Zara. Still, this really wasn't her fault, was it? Now he was here, in his new senior sergeant's office, he realised it was time to take a breath and suck it up. But that was hard.

'But why have you gone back into uniform, Jack? That's confusing me. You were a good investigator in South Australia. Got results in a couple of murders and a tricky drug case. Didn't have a breakdown, did you?'

'I'm just looking for something new,' Jack said, glad he'd rehearsed his speech.

'Are you?' Martin put down his mug and locked eyes with him. 'A successful detective throwing it all in to come and work out in the backblocks of Kalgoorlie? Seems strange to me.'

'I've heard that policing over here can be eventful,' Jack said. 'I used to work with a bloke who was stationed nearby, and he talked about gold stealing and other unusual things. It sounded like something I wanted to put on my resume.' He shrugged. 'I'm not sure what else you want to know.'

'That's investigative work, yet here you are back in uniform.'

Jack leaned forward. 'Look, Martin, I know what I've done seems strange, but Kalgoorlie is the last frontier. I've heard this place gets under your skin. I just wanted to try it out. See how things work here. Get some different experiences.' He placed his cup on the desk. 'Something new. I'm hoping there'll be a vacancy in the detectives soon. I mean, you've got a few different squads, haven't you? As soon as there's a position I'll be applying, but the rules state I must get up to speed again being in uniform, so that's what I'll do.' He paused. 'I'm not afraid to do the work to get back as an investigator, Sir, ah, Martin.'

The senior sergeant observed him for a moment, his fingers steepled in front of his lips. Then he took a breath and sat up straight. 'You got a missus? Gone through a breakup or something? No shame in that, god knows police officers have one of the highest divorce rates in the country.'

Jack wasn't ready to talk about Zara yet. 'No, no divorce or breakup.'

Martin looked as if he was going to push on that subject but seemed to decide against it. 'Okay then.' He looked at the file on his desk. 'Well, welcome to Kalgoorlie. Even with your experience it will be a big learning curve. Policing here forces you outside of any comfort zone you've created. There are no other stations to rely on, like there are in the city. It's Kal and our officers, and only us. Our policing district is over one million square kilometres and we're the biggest area in the world. Perth is a six-and-a-half-hour drive away. There're many pressure points. Domestic violence, youth crime, break and enters, gold theft, drugs, bikies. You name it, you'll find it here. By the time you leave, nothing will surprise you.'

Jack nodded, listening intently.

'I've been stationed here for nearly fifteen years,' Martin continued. 'Seen lots of officers come and go. Some go quicker than others because the isolation is too much for them, but many come back. Something about this red dirt and country gets under everyone's skin, like you said.'

'Not just your skin,' Jack said. 'The dust gets into everything. You should see my car.'

Martin let out a roar of laughter. 'Too true, too true,' he said. 'Any questions?'

'Who am I being paired with?'

'You and Constable Aiden Scott are going to be working together this week. Another senior connie. He's a good bloke and better copper. I think you'll get on well. And if you don't, you'll have to sort yourselves out.'

CHAPTER FOUR

'Turn around.'

Heart still racing and hands in the air, Zara began turning slowly towards the voice.

There was no point in screaming. No one would hear. Over one hundred kilometres away from Kalgoorlie and the main drag north, she was alone and deep in the bush. Jack wouldn't even know where to start looking if she didn't turn up tonight. There hadn't been any need to tell him what her plan had been. Maybe today was going to be her biggest mistake, not the court case. This could be the end of her. Shot and tossed down a mine shaft!

Hadn't that happened to a couple a few years back? Somewhere north-west of here. The man's body was discovered at the bottom of a mine and the wife was never found. Neither was their dog. Police were still looking.

A lot of disappearances. People, dead or alive, missing.

She was about to become a statistic.

'You haven't told me who you are.'

Zara finished turning very slowly to face the person holding the handgun. This was not the time to mention she had said her name numerous times since the gun had been pulled on her. She brought her head up defiantly.

Then her eyes widened.

'Oh my god!' Shocked adrenalin ran through her. 'Are you Ted?' Then a bubble of excitement and she leaned forward to put her hands on her knees, quickly straightening again, hands back above her head.

'No need to bow.' The line was delivered with an annoyed expression and without humour.

Her hands fell slightly. 'Hello, I'm Zara Ellison. A journalist. From Kalgoorlie. You're a woman.' She felt ridiculous for stating the obvious.

A woman with wild grey hair pulled back into a long ponytail, clear blue eyes and a leather-like face stared back, her gaze locked on Zara's.

The pistol hadn't changed position – it was still aimed at Zara's heart. There was another gun on the woman's belt. Oversized jeans and a thick grey jacket dwarfed her frame, yet despite her tininess, she was clearly not frightened of Zara.

'And?' The gun didn't waver.

'I thought Ted was a man. I supposed, well, you know, it's pretty harsh out here. I just assumed …' Her voice trailed off.

'You assumed wrong.'

A silence sat between them and Zara risked looking behind her to the other person who had been upright.

She could only see the bed covered with a heap of crumpled blankets and sleeping bags. A bulge underneath. *How* … There had been someone there only moments before. Someone yelling at her.

Perhaps the echoes of the woman's voice had bounced off the caravan and back at Zara making her think there was more than one person.

'So,' the woman said, waving the gun in a talk-now-or-I'll-lose-my-patience gesture, 'why is a journalist trespassing on my land?'

'Oh, Vince.' Zara refocused. 'You must know him? Old bloke with snow-white hair and a cheeky face. Has red cheeks, although that might have been because it was late in the evening when I was talking to him, and he'd had a few.' She was babbling. 'He sits at the right-hand side of the bar in the Tatts, with a couple of mates, Scribbly and Marigold. I'm sure they were the names I was told. Never worked out if they were having me on, or not.

'Anyhow, I was asking around, trying to find a story, and Vince said you might talk to me. He said you were the most interesting person in Kalgoorlie.' Zara looked around and jerked her head back towards the caravan. 'So here I am. And I have to say –' she flashed a smile '– it appears he's right.' Flattery almost always worked when she was looking for information.

Silence.

'Where has that person gone?' Zara jerked a thumb towards the van.

More silence.

Zara should just keep quiet. She knew that. People also talked when there was silence because they needed to fill the space, but she couldn't do that now. The situation was too disconcerting.

She didn't trust the woman – and the woman, despite being unafraid, didn't trust her. Zara would fix that if she was given the chance.

The woman blinked and something flashed in her eyes. Indecision?

The gun lowered.

'Vince, eh? Old bastard wouldn't know fool's gold from the real stuff. He sent you, did he?'

Taking in a calming breath, Zara let herself relax momentarily, hoping Vince was a good guy.

Clicking the safety back on, the woman shoved the pistol into the holster on her hip. She stepped around Zara and strode towards the caravan, taking very large steps for such a small person.

Zara had to take off at a jog to keep up with her. Her stomach was fizzing. Imagine writing the story of a wild woman, living in the middle of nowhere, searching for gold. She could already see the headline: *Searching While Surviving Solo*. Or *Solitary Searcher Surviving Solo*. *Wild Woman Waits* … Even *Going for Gold*. Still, this wasn't the Olympics.

Her love of alliteration had never been shared by the editors.

The woman stopped in front of a dead campfire and reached down to pick up a few leaves and sticks from the pile next to it, tossing them onto the dead ash. Instantly a fizzing sounded then a thin wisp of smoke furled upwards and reached towards the open blue sky.

Zara drew in a breath. She'd been sure that fire was out. No visible coals, only grey ash. This woman could win *Alone Australia*. Maybe she'd be the next big thing and Zara would have discovered her! Reputation restored. All past misdemeanours forgotten.

Oh god, yes please!

'You'd better give me some information,' the woman said, filling a tin with water from the tank. 'Who are you and what the hell do you want?'

Make it good, Zara, make it good.

'Well, like I said, Vince told me about you. I'm a reporter and I'm very keen to understand mining and gold from a personal point of view, not a company's perspective.' She took a breath. 'I'm new to Kalgoorlie and I thought talking to a real-life prospector who is a local might be the best way I could get an authentic story.'

'Real-life prospector,' the woman mocked.

Embarrassed, Zara realised her description sounded ridiculous to this woman who could slay an intruder at five paces. She waited, keeping silent. Sometimes the best way to dig yourself out of a hole was to say nothing.

'There's a difference between prospecting and mining, you know.' The woman didn't expand on that statement. Instead, she asked, 'Not local? Where're you from?'

'Ah.' Zara wondered if she shouldn't admit she was from Adelaide in case the woman googled her and found out the story behind her banishment. Then she sniggered at herself. The woman probably didn't own a phone, let alone know what googling was. 'I'm from South Australia. Just moved across the Nullarbor.'

'Crow-eater?' Surprise. 'What the hell are you doing over here?'

'Learning to barrack for the Eagles. Or the Dockers. I haven't made up my mind yet.' Her own words took her aback. How could she be so flippant when only moments before a gun had been pointed at her?

Fear and adrenalin will do that.

'No point in giving either the time of day,' the woman said. 'Too commercialised. Ridiculous to think that men –' she cocked an eyebrow as she looked at Zara '– and now women run around chasing a ball and get paid for it. There's much better places for that sponsorship money to be spent. Accommodation for the homeless for a start.'

Opening a folding chair, she plonked it in front of Zara and indicated for her to sit, then opened a second chair and gave it a hearty thump. Dust rose from the fabric and a few leaves that had been stuck underneath the seat drifted to the ground. 'Got to keep them folded up and under the van,' she said. 'The dew is always heavy this time of year and the material gets wet. I spend enough time with a cold arse when I'm mining, don't need a wet one too. Chilblains are uncomfortable.'

The fire was now throwing a few flames around the kindling.

'Didn't think the fire was alight,' Zara said. 'Didn't take long.'

'Fire never goes out in this camp. What'd you say your name was?'

'Zara Ellison.'

'Nice to meet you.' She held out a filthy hand. Chocolate-coloured earth was ingrained around her fingernails, while soot was smeared across the top. The woman's skin was dry and her calluses rough as they shook hands.

'And you are ... Ted?' She had to ask, because she wasn't going to be told.

'Edwina, but most people call me Ted,' the woman confirmed. 'Cuppa?' She fished around and brought out two enamel cups, both with blue chipped handles. Running the hem of her jacket inside the first one, she waved it at Zara.

'Sure.'

'Sugar?'

'No sugar, but a splash of milk would be great.'

Ted scoffed. 'Don't have milk out here, love. It'll have to be black and sweet.'

'Oh, that's okay.'

Ted upended two tablespoons of sugar into the mug and tapped the billy that was now sitting on the coals.

She obviously spent most of her time out here with very few people to talk to, so she was very comfortable with silence. No point in trying the 'fill the silence' journalist tactic then.

A few minutes later the billy boiled and Ted hooked a stick under the handle, drawing it off the coals to let it rest next to the fire, while she wiggled her hands into some welding gloves.

Then tapping the side of the billy with her foot, she suddenly snatched the can up and whizzed it around in circles next to her body, the can upside down as it whipped past her ears. Round and round. Fast.

Zara leaned back, fascinated, half expecting the boiling water to pour all over Ted, but when the other woman finally slowed her arm, nothing happened.

'Sends the tea leaves to the bottom,' Ted said before Zara could ask why. 'You can pour the tea without getting too many in the cup.' She smirked and added: 'No tea leaf readings out here. Gravity keeps the water in the billy, in case you're wondering.'

For someone who had grown up on a farm and had regularly gone camping with her family before her father and brother had died, swinging a billy in circles was new to Zara. *A trick?* she wondered. Was Ted a bit of a show pony? That would make for an even better story. Questions bubbled just the way the billy had only moments before.

Amber liquid poured from the blackened can and Zara took the mug she was offered. As promised, there was hardly any grit floating in the mug.

Ted squatted down next to the fire and poked at it, stick in one hand and mug in the other.

'Where'd the other person go? The one who fired the first shot at me?' Zara asked.

'Only me here,' Ted answered.

Shooting a disbelieving look at her, Zara got up and walked towards the caravan.

She had intended to fling the covers back, exposing whoever was under there. But Ted's gun came to mind and she thought better of it.

'Didn't sound like you were alone,' she said, turning back.

Ted didn't answer.

'Look, sorry if I should've warned you I was coming,' Zara said, sitting back down. 'Vince didn't give me a number to contact you. Only directions.'

Ted got up and moved the billy back under the van then sat back down, her heavy boot resting over her knee. Her fingers tapped to an unheard rhythm.

Zara felt her scrutiny.

Finally, Ted gave a bit of a scoff, which might have been a laugh. 'Should have seen your face. Got to hand it to you – you're a bit harder to scare than most people. That's impressive. Some of the others ...' She waved her cup around as if to underline her point. 'Nothing but lightweights. Run at the slightest noise.' She sighed as if disappointed with every person who had been scared by her.

Zara guessed she'd passed a test. She relaxed slightly.

'Got a bit of a security set-up,' Ted continued. 'Never know who might wander through these days. Bloody amateur prospectors turn up with their flash, expensive Minelab detectors, ignoring the fact that I lease this tenement and they're trespassing.' Ted smiled, showing a straight set of teeth. There was a hint of ruthlessness behind her smirk. 'So, I got me a gas cannon.'

'A gas cannon?' Zara looked around again, expecting to see a large, heavy cannonball flying through the air. Nothing would surprise her now.

'Supposed to be for scaring birds, but they scare the shit outta unsuspecting humans too.' Ted laughed and took another sip of tea. 'Then there's the intruders you can't see, they're the ones you should be frightened of.'

Zara's heart fluttered at the warning in Ted's low voice, and she followed her gaze to the sky.

'The ones you can't see?' The bush seemed to crackle with tension.

'Yeah. The ones you can't see.' Ted dropped her voice. 'But they're there alright.'

The fire gave a sharp crack of sparks towards the sky and Zara jumped. She grappled for another question.

'But the voice ...'

'Haven't you ever heard of a tape recorder?' Ted's tone changed. She cackled again, but this time raised her mug towards Zara. 'Got to look after yourself out here. A woman more so than most, unfortunately.'

Zara snorted. 'You recorded a message to scare intruders? Does it run on a timer or something?'

'Works, don't it?' Ted got up from next to the fire then

moved her chair until it was level with Zara and sat down. 'Now, Zara Ellison from South Australia, what's this story you want to write?'

'I was hoping to write an interest piece on mining gold.'

Ted swilled her tea around in the mug. She peered inside, investigating the bottom deeply, as if the non-existent tea leaves would give her the location of her next find. 'Who's interested in gold?'

'Who's inter— Ha! Only everyone. Gold holds some kind of intrigue. People are fascinated by it. With the lifestyle, how it's mined, where it is, the individuals who are prospecting, what their stories are. You'd be surprised; there's so much interest! There's even TV shows about gold hunting now. Bit like being a detective and investigating homicides. Everyone wants to know the ins and outs of how it's done.'

'Must be a slow news day.' Ted looked up at Zara, her elbows resting on her knees. 'And I know about those TV shows. Stupid, if you ask me. Completely unrealistic. Do you know that the TV stations buy the nuggets that the prospectors find? Ridiculous. People have been poking around out here over the last few years. Encroaching on those of us who are out here trying to make a living. Ending up in places they shouldn't. Nothing but a menace.'

'Maybe you could talk about the trespassing. Explain why it's not on.' Zara looked around at the small camp area. There didn't seem to be anything of value: a couple of chairs, the van, an old table with chunks taken out of the legs. Still, it was the gold that was the value, not the minimalist lifestyle. 'Seems you know about a bit about that.'

Ted didn't answer and Zara inwardly sighed, pulling out a safe question. 'How long have you lived here for?'

Ted frowned and tapped the cup on her thigh. 'Well, now. I guess ... What year is it again?'

Zara wanted to laugh but caught herself in time. Was Ted serious?

'It's 2025.'

'Well, I came out here when I was twenty-one and I was born in 1975.'

Zara did some quick calculations. 'You bought this land in 1986? Have you found much gold?'

'Leased it, yeah. Can't own this land, it's leased from the government for a set time frame. And eighty-six sounds about right. Mum fell off the perch the year before and I was a bit lost for a while. Wasn't really sure what to do with myself. Tried town for a couple of years. Didn't like that one bit. Turned up here and liked it, so I stayed.' She stared off into the distance. 'Well, there you go. Nearly forty years. Who would've thought.' Her voice was soft, full of memories.

Zara evaluated Ted again. Her skin was deeply tanned, dirt deeply engrained under her fingernails. She seemed thoroughly at home in the bush, yet her voice was cultured, even though she tried to hide it, and her comments about the footy earlier had been said with thought. There was a lot more to Ted than her general appearance.

Zara repeated her previous question. 'Have you found much gold?'

A warning look passed over Ted's face as she answered. 'I find enough.'

'What does that mean? What's enough?'

'Enough is just that. Enough. There's an unwritten rule out here: we don't talk about our finds. Only makes thieves out of men.'

'What do you mean?'

'I mean that the unscrupulous will raid the area if it's known you've had a big discovery.' Ted's voice was edgy.

'Do you have any neighbours?' Zara was firing questions at her because she was frightened that if she stopped talking, this woman of the bush might refuse to answer any more.

'Hope not. I don't like people much.'

'But do you see anyone? Don't you get lonely?' Zara wrapped her cold fingers around the mug and took a two-handed sip. The liquid burned her throat, and the sweetness made her want to screw her eyes up. *Don't react, don't react. She's your ticket back to the world of real journalism.*

'Same as the gold, I see enough.' Ted leaned back in her chair and regarded Zara. 'You're bloody nosy.'

Zara flashed a quick smile. 'No more than the next journo.' She stopped, finally picking up the signals Ted had been throwing her.

Most people's favourite subject was themselves. Ted wasn't like that.

This interview was going to be a slow burn.

'I'll tell you this for nothing. Since time began, humans have had an unhealthy relationship with wealth. Gold indicates wealth. Especially in this environment, it's worth a shitload of money per ounce. It's a currency used by criminals and honest people because it's tangible, yet in raw form, untraceable. That is why some of us live out here and search for it. Others live out here because they like the peace and quiet.' Ted gave Zara a hard stare. 'There are also some who are hiding. From the law, from family, from life. Everyone out here has a different story, but we're connected by one thing.'

'Gold,' Zara said.

'The thrill of the hunt and the ecstasy of the find.'

'God, you're fascinating.'

Ted snorted and raised her mug to her mouth.

'I'm curious, though, can you help me understand the why? Why do you choose to live out here? To prospect?'

Ted stared into the fire, ignoring the question.

'Are you just waiting for a big find, is that it?'

'Gold is like a unicorn – you can chase it, search for it all your life but you never catch it. Not really. The gold catches us, rather than the other way around.'

The flames reflected in the older woman's eyes.

Zara didn't really understand. 'But surely you've found some? How else do you support yourself? And what do you mean "catches us"?'

'We've all found some. I guess that's why it draws us back, takes a hold of us.'

'It pulls you in?' Zara asked. 'It sounds a bit like quicksand – once you're in, you can't get out.'

Ted locked eyes with Zara now. 'No matter how much or how little you find, you will never, ever own the gold; it will always own you.'

CHAPTER FIVE

'Siri, call Jack.'

Zara couldn't wait to tell him everything. He'd find Ted as fascinating as she did.

Ted was remarkable. Strange. Intelligent. And definitely interesting.

A woman living in the middle of the bush, all alone. Independent, without fear.

After their cup of tea, they had walked out to the part of Ted's lease where she kept the machinery. Ted demonstrated how the backhoe operated, dug out soil and told Zara about the difference between a shaker table and a water-processing plant.

Ted reminded Zara of her farmer mother, how easily she handled the machinery. Her skills were seriously impressive and Zara had begun to feel envious. How liberating to trust and believe in yourself so much.

What she wouldn't give to feel like that.

Then they had walked beneath a granite overhang, Ted pointing out the head of an old pick, horseshoes, equipment from a bygone mining era embedded in the soil. But the most exciting part had been the tiny hole in the rock.

They'd been walking next to each other and Ted had told her to wait as she'd scrambled down a small hill. During the minute amount of time in which she'd turned to look out across the land, Ted had disappeared.

She'd called her name with no response and Zara was just beginning to feel uneasy when Ted's head appeared unexpectedly from the ground. It had been the only time during the day that Zara had screamed. Ted had laughed. Then invited her down the mine shaft, which had been dug by hand back in the late 1800s apparently.

Later, Ted had shown her tracks across the sand: a goanna, a kangaroo, an emu print.

'No snakes this time of the year,' Ted had told her. 'Too freaking cold. By the time the sun has warmed them up enough to move, they'd have to be looking for their burrow again. Summer is a different story. Gotta keep your eyes peeled. There are so many stories of old-timers being bitten. The cemeteries are full of people killed by snake bites. The miners and their women and littlies too. Those king browns love to crawl into cribs. So it's not just rock falls out here you need to be worried about.' Ted had laughed at Zara's quick look of horror before she'd schooled her face back to neutral.

Ted clearly liked to shock. She'd delighted in telling the story of the Mulga snake she'd found in her caravan. 'Just draped over the table like a strand of Christmas tinsel. See, Zara, even though snakes are partial to the warmth of late spring and early summer, they don't like extreme heat. That's when they're looking for a cooler place and that's usually down a mine shaft, under a shrubby bush or inside a building or piece of machinery.'

'What did you do?'

'Nothing.' Ted raised an eyebrow. 'Opened the door and waited until it found its way out. What did you think I'd do?'

Zara tapped the steering wheel now, thinking about the first line of her story.

To the north of Kalgoorlie, deep in the bush, gold isn't the only thing of value.

She screwed up her nose then realised Siri hadn't answered her.

'Dammit. Siri, call Jack!' The phone didn't connect again and when Zara glanced down she saw there wasn't any mobile range. Moving to a new town meant she had to find where all the black spots were – she knew them by heart in South Australia and often avoided driving those routes when there were important phone calls to make or receive.

Out here, there wasn't a choice. One main road to the north, one to the east, another to the south and the last one to the west. That was it. No interconnecting main road networks.

Oh, there were little two-wheel tracks, or well-formed roads off into cattle station country or mines, but they were private roads or only for adventure seekers. They didn't lead anywhere except out bush.

She went over the conversation with Ted in her head, trying to find the headline.

Gold is like a unicorn – you can chase it, search for it all your life but you never catch it.

Eye-catching, but too long. And what did those words really mean? No matter how much gold Ted found, she'd always be searching for more. In that way, prospecting was like gambling. Every bit, even the smallest piece, would renew the hope that a bigger piece could be found next time. And the next, and the time after that.

Gold is like a unicorn.

Nope, without the rest of the sentence it didn't have the same impact. Or make sense.

She'd have to think on it some more.

A few caravans and trucks passed her, heading north. There were puddles alongside the road from the storm that had come through two nights ago. Most of the wildflower buds beside the road were still tightly closed, holding the promise that purple, green and white blooms would soon be vibrant against the harsh red of the earth. Birds had come in droves to enjoy the puddles, budgies chirping and twittering, their flights as jaunty as their song. White cockies screeching, bathing themselves in the surface water. Roos were lying sleepily under trees right near pools, so they didn't have far to go for a drink. The road verges held the sweetest green grasses to eat.

The bush was popping with colour and life.

That's why there were so many caravanners on the road here at this time of year. To see nature in all her glory.

Zara made a mental note of the distance she was from Kalgoorlie, so she would remember this dead spot.

So much to tell Jack. She had that familiar itchy feeling when she needed to do something *now*, rather than wait until the right time.

Patience was a virtue everywhere, but especially on the road, sitting behind a caravan or truck. Not twenty minutes ago, a group of motorbike riders had passed her with a roar. She'd been lost in thought then too, and had started as they'd pulled out and passed her, their eyes focused on the road ahead.

Zara wondered if they were from the local bikie chapter, The Untouchables. She'd scrawled a note on her window with a whiteboard marker to remind herself to ask a few questions about them. Who the president and sergeant-at-arms were. Information like that was always useful.

Heaving a sigh, she thought: *When will I get some contacts in this town!*

'Got a copy white dual-cab ute, southbound?'

Zara flinched at the two-way squelch hitting her ears. She checked her mirrors and saw a truck bearing down on her. Assuming the call was for her, she answered in the affirmative.

'Got any oncoming traffic?' the driver asked.

Zara lifted her foot. 'You're clear. I'll slow it down for you.'

'Cheers.'

The truck pulled out on the right-hand side of the road and passed her, so closely she could hear the chains clanking against the bins as it hit a rough spot in the road.

She decelerated even further to let it pass safely, wondering how quick trucks were allowed to go out here. Supposedly not faster than a hundred, same as caravans and any vehicle pulling a trailer. Zara couldn't quite remember the speed differences between here and South Australia. Her own speedo showed eighty, so the truck had to be going faster ... Unless her gauge wasn't accurate.

Still, no doubt it would be back in the other lane soon to overtake the caravanners she had seen just ahead of her, with their cheery note on the back of the van telling everyone that Barry and Jayne were keen to have a chat on channel 40.

That note had made Zara think of her mum, Lynda, who was out on the road with her partner, vanning it. Last she'd heard they were in Queensland. Her mum had refused to have their names or channel numbers on the back of their van. 'All that'll do is annoy the truckies,' she'd said. 'They don't like it when caravanners start yapping on their channel. Channel forty is there to make sure everyone on the road is safe.'

'Channel forty,' Zara said aloud, even though the caravanners couldn't hear her, 'is not about you lot chatting to each other about where you stopped for coffee or to check out the best wildflower display.'

Zara ran her fingers through her hair and stared moodily ahead, watching as the truck pulled back into the right lane to overtake Barry and Jayne.

She rested her head against the window, feeling the vibrations from the road run through her cheek and down into her chest. Comforting after the adrenalin, fear and exhilaration of the morning.

What would Jack say when she told him about Ted's gun? She giggled at the idea. His expression would be a mixture of shock, disbelief and that stern don't-break-the-law look she knew so well. Then it would change to the softer are-you-alright look he got when Zara had done something crazy.

Of the two of them, she had always been the wild one. Jack was steady and dependable, responsible, which made him a good police officer. As for Zara – her dear friend Lizzie from the newspaper in Adelaide had always said she was a free spirit.

In Zara's imagination, free spirit meant she was floating around the sky, chasing shooting stars and trying to catch moon beams. Instead, she chased stories and pushed boundaries trying to get information. Rolled her sleeves up and got dirty to find the best news she could.

Jack was the sort of fella who followed flatpack instructions to the tee, while Zara winged it, then got infuriated when there were bolts and screws left over and the item didn't look like the photo or wasn't as sturdy as it should be.

If he'd been with her today, Jack would be annoyed that the caravanners in front of her weren't paying enough attention and drifting over the white line, then back again.

'Drop back,' Zara muttered. 'What *are* you doing?'

The words had barely left her mouth when a side mirror from the car in front of her appeared, hurtling through the air, and smashing onto the road. She turned the wheel sharply to avoid it.

'Wha—'

Then she watched in horror as the ute began to tip and roll off the road, pulling the van with it.

Zara jammed her foot on the brake.

'Oh my god!'

The vehicles in front of her slid over the road and smashed into the table drain, then kept crashing through bushes and branches, leaving behind a trail of debris.

There had to be so much noise; screeching and tearing as the steel, glass and aluminium crumpled. Yet for the second time that day Zara couldn't hear anything except her heavy breathing and her heart trying to escape her chest.

'Oh no, no, no,' she muttered, pulling up to the side of the road. Grabbing her phone, she dialled triple zero, but the call didn't connect.

No range, still! What type of hellhole was she living in? This was 2025 and everywhere should have decent, constant and reliable communications!

Throwing open her door, she ran towards the wreckage.

She glanced towards the road, hoping the truck had slowed to a stop too, but the highway was empty.

The truck driver must have clipped the ute when it pulled back into the left lane, and probably didn't even notice.

'Hello!' she called as she ran towards the ute. 'Don't worry. There's help coming.'

That was a lie.

'Stay calm,' she yelled, her puffer jacket flapping around her arms as they pumped harder. 'I'm coming!'

Pushing bushes out of the way, Zara sprinted as if her own life depended on making sure Barry and Jayne were okay.

The ute had slammed straight into a large salmon gum tree, the branches were still shuddering and creaking. Heavy drops of dew were pinging onto the wreckage and thumping into the earth.

A window shattered.

'Jesus.' Zara glanced at the phone in her hand, but the four bars remained greyed out.

Her breath was ragged and hot in her throat as she assessed the carnage, gasping for air.

Zara didn't hold a lot of hope for either Barry or Jayne. The front of the ute was caved back on itself and the driver's side buckled around the tree.

'Hello,' she called, taking a few unsteady steps towards it. 'I'm Zara. Are you okay?'

A waterfall of glass tinkled to the ground and an eerie silence fell over the land.

'Oh, shit, oh shit,' she whimpered. She was having flashes back to her father's car accident. The dark night and the back end of the ute, still looking perfect when the police found him. There hadn't even been a scratch on the paint.

The damage had been to the front, the nose embedded deep in a ditch. He hadn't stood a chance.

Zara made herself take a few steps forward. God, she didn't want to. But there wasn't a choice.

She peered around the corner of the crumpled caravan, her heart pounding. The driver's door. A man ... Well, the top half of a human hanging from the window. The arms were stretched down towards the ground, swinging slightly from the force of slamming into the tree, while the head swayed from side to side. Zara didn't need to see the face or feel for a pulse to know the eyes had lost all the life they'd held only minutes before.

Nausea crept up in her stomach and she took another few unsteady breaths. They didn't help. Bending over, hands on her knees, she vomited.

'Help.'

The word was so quiet, so feeble that Zara wasn't sure she'd heard it. Wiping her mouth, she walked unsteadily to the passenger's side, holding the side of the vehicle so she didn't fall.

'Hello? Is anyone ...'

The words were so faint.

Cupping her hands against the shattered passenger's window, Zara saw her.

Jayne.

'I'm here, I'm here,' she called loudly, and yanked on the door handle. It didn't open. She yanked again. It opened just enough this time for her to get her fingers into the gap and put her foot onto the back door. Using her whole body weight, she pulled and grunted, scrabbling to get to the woman inside.

A loud screech and the gap widened and she could insert her body into the space.

Oh no, no, no. Zara looked at the woman and thought immediately of her mum. Jayne and Lynda were probably about the same age. This accident could have happened just as easily to her mother, who was happily holidaying and pulling a caravan.

Zara cleared her throat and then her mind, concentrating on what was in front of her.

The dash was pushed up against Jayne's chest. Her pale and pleading face was covered in blood.

'Where's Barry?' Whispered words. She licked her lips and tried again. 'Have you seen Barry?'

'Barry, he's your husband?' she asked, reaching for Jayne's hand, which was lying useless against her side.

'Yeah. He was … he was driving.' Beseeching eyes searched Zara's face. The woman seemed to be unable to move her head, pinned in behind the dash. 'Barry, is he …' Jayne tried to clear her throat. 'Okay?'

Zara took a breath and stared desperately towards the road, screaming in her mind for help. Then she pressed her lips together and felt for the woman's pulse.

A weak beating met her fingers. Zara tried to pull the seatbelt from Jayne's neck, to give her space to breathe, knowing in her heart it was futile. There were going to be two fatalities here today.

'Is Barry …'

'I saw Barry, he's out of the vehicle.' Zara said the words before she had time to think. She reached into her pocket and brought out a tissue, dabbing helplessly at the blood on the corner of Jayne's mouth.

Jayne tried to smile. 'Good. Good. I thought … When we hit the tree …' Her voice trailed off and she coughed.

Zara saw blood on her lips. She fought the urge to run away and tried to stay calm. Jack did this stuff all the time. If he could, so could she.

Get it together, she told herself, touching the tissue to the fresh blood and recalling the first-aid course she'd completed many years ago. She should keep Jayne talking.

'Are you Jayne?' Zara asked. She smiled, forcing her eyes to stay on the dying woman and not slide over in the direction of Barry's body. 'I saw names on the back of the van. Barry and Jayne.'

'Jayne. Barry. Barry.' Her eyes flickered but she rallied and gripped Zara's hand with gentle pressure. 'Tell him ... to come here.'

'The doctor needs to see him before he can do that,' Zara lied again, hating herself.

Jayne smiled. 'He's a good ... man ... is my Barry.' Her eyelids flickered. 'Sometimes ... gets a bit ... cranky.'

'Don't all men,' Zara tried to joke.

There wasn't an answer.

Zara checked Jayne's pulse again. Barely even butterfly wings against her fingers and now the woman's eyes were closed.

'Stay with me, Jayne, don't go to sleep,' Zara said, her voice kicking up a notch. She squeezed the woman's arm, not wanting to touch anywhere else in case she hurt her. 'Jayne! You've got to stay awake until help comes.'

'As long ... as Barry's safe ...' It was an effort for Jayne to speak.

In the distance, Zara heard an engine. How could she run out to flag down the traffic?

There was no way she could leave her.

Jayne's fingers tightened with a slight touch.

'He's safe.' Zara reached up and smoothed Jayne's hair back from her forehead.

'Very tired,' she mumbled.

'Stay with me, Jayne,' Zara said. 'Have you got children?' She heard a vehicle pull to a stop and a car door slam.

Thank, god! Zara wanted to sag in relief.

'Mmm, two ...' Jayne's words were becoming hard to understand. 'They're. Lovely.'

'What the hell happened?' a voice called out from the edge of the road. 'Are you all right?'

Still holding Jayne's hand, Zara stood and waved her other arm above her head.

'Call triple zero,' she yelled. 'We need an ambulance!' Surely it was bloody obvious what had happened.

'I've called the mine via my two-way, they're on it.'

'Barry?' Jayne's eyes flicked open.

Zara rubbed Jayne's hand. Her fingers were cold. 'I'm here,' she said, searching the dying woman's features. 'I'm here.'

Jayne's body was colourless. Translucent in her face, her arms, everywhere.

Someone pushed in next to Zara.

'You okay, love?' The man who had been on the road was alongside her.

Zara couldn't answer him. Instead, she kept murmuring to Jayne, holding her hand and smoothing her hair. Doing all the things her own mother had done for her when she was young and needed comfort.

'She's gone.' The man told her gently. He leaned over Zara's shoulder and ran his hand over Jayne's face, closing her eyes.

Zara stroked Jayne's hair again.

'Love? She's gone.'

'I know.'

She let go of Jayne's hand.

CHAPTER SIX

'Good to meet you, Jack.' Aiden held out his hand and Jack took it, assessing him. So this was the senior constable he'd be working with for a month, until the rosters changed and he'd be paired with someone else.

Aiden seemed about his age, maybe a bit younger, and moved with the energy Martin had been speaking about. They were almost the same height too. The only difference Jack could see in their physiques was that Aiden clearly spent a lot of time at the gym.

Jack didn't. His vice was running. After every shift, night or day, as soon as he got home, he stripped off his work clothes and pulled on shorts and a T-shirt and went running. Four, five, six kilometres. Sometimes more. That was how he dealt with the stresses of the job.

He'd been trying to talk Zara into becoming his running partner, but her exercise was walking or swimming. Mostly the former, while talking on the phone and waving her hands around.

'Good to meet you, Aiden. Been in Kalgoorlie long?'

'On and off my whole life. Had my first crack at policing here when I was twenty-three but I had to move back to Perth after a bit of trouble with the girlfriend.' His mouth tightened.

'Oh yeah.' Jack let the question go unspoken.

'Long-distance, you know how it is. She wasn't prepared to move out here, but then the whole thing fell apart anyway, and I hightailed it back. Been back two years, met someone else.' He paused. 'Come on, let's grab a coffee and then I'll show you around.'

Warmth, coffee beans and the smell of toast met Jack's nose as they walked in through the door of the cafe across the road.

'What would you like?' Aiden asked, cracking open his wallet. 'This is the coppers' watering hole. For caffeine.'

'Flat white, no sugar,' Jack told the woman behind the counter. 'Thanks.'

'No trouble, love. You're new over the road? I'm Nellie.'

'Hi, Nellie,' he said and was about to introduce himself when Aiden spoke over the top of them.

'I'll have my usual,' he said and handed over a hundred-dollar note.

'Got anything smaller, Aiden? You'll run me out of change so early in the morning.'

Aiden looked in his wallet again and this time held out a fifty.

'Better, thanks.'

Moments later two coffees were handed over and Nellie waved them off. 'Make sure you come back. We'll look after you here.'

'Thanks very much. I'll look forward to that.'

The door closed behind them and Aiden nodded towards the squad car. 'Let's go for a spin.'

'Sounds good.'

Jack was about to get into the driver's side when he stopped. This wasn't his gig. He was the new bloke on the block.

Moving quickly to the passenger door, he hoped Aiden hadn't noticed.

'What's the best thing about Kalgoorlie?' he asked once they were on the road.

Digging into his pocket, Aiden brought out a crumpled Juicy Fruit packet and offered it to Jack, who shook his head. Aiden threw one into his mouth and brought his teeth down on it a couple of times, then drove for a few minutes before answering.

'I don't know,' he said, finally. 'All I know is I enjoy it. It feels like home and nowhere else I've lived has. Maybe it's because I was born here.'

Jack nodded. 'When I worked in Barker, in the Flinders Ranges, I enjoyed the town, even though it was small. Moving to Adelaide was different; a bit enclosing after all the wide-open spaces.' He paused and thought about his mentor and friend, Detective Dave Burrows, and felt the familiar ache in the space around his heart. He missed working with him. Their laughs, the way they always knew how each other would react, the advice that Dave always gave – whether it had been asked for or not. Their jokes. 'I reckon it's the people who make a place feel like home, rather than the town itself. I might be wrong, but that's how it works for me.'

'Yeah, could be right.' Aiden nodded his head towards a bright pink building, sitting close to the edge of the street. 'Now, this is the only operating brothel left in Kalgoorlie.' He cruised past slowly.

'I've heard about it. Didn't the tours put Kalgoorlie on the map?' The building, clad in Colorbond, boasted a huge sign:

QUESTA CASA

A sandwich board on the street gave a telephone number to ring and the time the next tour started.

BOOKINGS ESSENTIAL

Aiden's jaw worked overtime as he pulled into a parking bay and rested his elbow on the window while gesturing towards the brothel. 'The Pink House,' he said.

'Fairly obvious name,' Jack replied.

Aiden sniggered. 'And this, my friend, has been in operation for a hundred and twenty years plus. Apparently born out of necessity. Too many blokes turning up to town by themselves. With needs.' Aiden gave a loud laugh. 'Don't think much has changed. It's pretty much just the same now.' He was in full tour-guide flight. 'Back in the seventies, there were three sex houses in town. Large operations. Each had about twenty to thirty girls working there, but then the sex industry was deregulated and ...' He held up his hands. 'Buggered it for everyone.'

'Buggered? How?'

Aiden wound down his window and hoicked the chewie out of his mouth, replacing it immediately with a new piece. 'A brothel's number-one concern is for their girls and their customers. Mandatory health checks and a safe place for everyone to do business. The employees have a madam to look after their interests, other people around in case someone gets a bit too rough or doesn't want to pay. You get the picture. Anyhow, Hay Street is the only place they operated back in the day. It's different now, they can operate from anywhere. And the girls who are operating from "everywhere" –' he made quotation marks with his fingers '– aren't health checked and protected like the ones in the brothels. And the clients aren't either.'

Surely Aiden's jaw was aching from the pressure he was putting on that chewie.

'No rules around putting something on social media or in the paper advertising massage with full service and price on application.' He pointed towards the brothel. 'Girls can come in from overseas, book into a hotel and offer their services from there.'

'It's the same anywhere.'

'If you want the full rundown on brothels, Carmel is the Madam at the Pink House and she runs tours. The stories are ones you won't hear anywhere else. Kal's a special place in that way.' Aiden put the patrol car into reverse and checked his mirrors, still chewing. 'There's a life-size Bundy Bear handcuffed to one of the beds. Whips and mirrors on the walls and ceiling, and some of those high heels – shit, they should be classed as weapons.' He gave a laugh. 'Bit outta place with all the steelcap boots around.'

'What are those little yards for? Out the front. They look like small stables.'

'They're the starting stalls. The girls used to stand out there, all dolled up and looking the part. A bloke could choose the one he wanted, then ask for her when he went inside.'

'And this still happens?'

'No, not anymore, and it's nothing you wouldn't see at beach on a hot day.'

Aiden gave Jack a sideways glance. 'The bars are full of skimpies. Not just Friday and Saturday nights, but every night. Most of the pubs have them. I'll show you the ones you need to stay away from because they have links to bikies. Some of these girls are flown in from Queensland, do their shifts for a couple of weeks, then head home. I had to get a witness statement from one about an assault in a bar a few months back. She said the work pays her uni fees. She's not having sex, the men don't touch and she's serving drinks like any person working behind a bar. Only difference to the normal barmaid is she's wearing barely nothing.' Aiden gave a laugh. 'Tits but no nipples, and a lotta arse. If you're ever free on a Sunday, the two-up ring is just out of town. Great atmosphere and it's fun yarning with the old-timers.'

'Isn't two-up only legal on Anzac Day?'

'Haven't you realised that Kal is different from the rest of the state?' Aiden grinned as he spoke. 'To the rest of Australia? Kalgoorlie runs to its own rules. They have a licence from the Gaming and Liquor Department for every Sunday. It's all above board.'

'I'll check it out, sounds interesting.'

'And there's the races too, if you're partial to a bit of a flutter. Yours truly can give you a few tips, if you want to make a few extra folding ones.'

There wasn't a chance to answer as Aiden drove down an isolated street and pulled up a short way from a high fence, with barbed wire on the top. He waved a discreet finger towards a tin shed inside the unwelcoming perimeter. 'This is The Untouchables.' His voice was low.

Jack leaned back in his seat, understanding he was looking at the chapter of an outlaw motorcycle group or, because the coppers loved acronyms, an OLMG.

On the fence a sign said trespassers would be prosecuted. Heavy netted gates were padlocked and Jack could immediately see four security cameras.

'Looks friendly,' he said.

'The Pres is a pretty wealthy bloke,' Aiden said, pushing out another piece of chewing gum from the packet and tossing it in his mouth. 'Never would guess he's a bikie. Clean shaven, nicely dressed, well spoken, all that sort of shit. Got his own business and, funnily enough, no record. But we watch him closely.' He tapped his fingers on the steering wheel now. 'The sergeant-at-arms, now he's a bit of a prick. Never likes to cooperate with us when we turn up for a chat.' As he spoke, the steel door of the clubhouse flew open and a beefy, bald-headed man walked out. He stopped, arms crossed, legs spread wide, and glared in their direction.

For a tiny second, Jack's stomach dropped. Didn't matter how many times he came face to face with bikies, adrenalin always hit him. Only for a moment but it was enough. He'd seen what OLMGs could do to people.

Jack had worked a case once where the only part of a body that had ever been recovered was an ear. Sliced off with a sharp blade in one swipe. They'd managed to charge a bikie from an interstate chapter, after a stake-out, which had resolved in a gun fight.

An ear didn't need a very big coffin.

'Speak of the devil,' Aiden said. 'The serge here is one of the friendliest. Watch this.' He wound down the window and waved.

The serge returned a middle-finger salute. There was a spiderweb tattoo on his hand and others up his arm.

Aiden put his pointer finger to his forehead and flicked it out quickly. A short wave of sorts.

The serge glared a bit longer, his finger still in the air, before deciding they weren't after anything and were wasting his time.

Jack let his breath out as the bikie turned to go back into the clubhouse. Then a strangled laugh combined with a gasp left his mouth, while next to him Aiden chuckled.

The serge had turned, dropped his shorts and bent over in a full moon salute. He slapped his bare, white-as-a-lily arse cheeks, gave a little shake and stayed like that for a few seconds more. Then he straightened, pulled up his pants and went inside without glancing back. The whole building seemed to shake as he slammed the door behind him, locking the outside world outside.

'Ha,' Aiden said with a snort. 'Told you.'

'He should take a little more care when he's wiping next time,' Jack said. 'Do you think we should tell him?'

Aiden choked on his chewie as he tried to let out a bark of laughter. 'What the fuck?'

'Well ...' Jack said.

Aiden, trying to get his breath back, still coughing, eased the brake out and started to move away. When he recovered, he said: 'Bikies are always so bloody hostile. I don't reckon they realise we've got better things to do with our time than annoy the shit out of them.'

'Didn't you know the world revolves around them?'

Aiden grunted.

'Who is the serge when he's at home? Any history?'

'His real name is Lionel Watts.'

They drove down to the end of the no-through road and Aiden swung the patrol car in a U-turn.

Passing the headquarters at a very slow pace, Jack could imagine Sarge inside, leaning against the bar, or sitting astride his bike, watching them on security cameras. It gave him a strange feeling.

'I reckon I'd change my name too,' Jack said. 'The Serge sounds more formidable.' He noticed two guard dogs, sitting straight up, under the shade of a lean-to off the end of the shed. They weren't moving but staring straight at the car, their ears on alert.

'Yeah. He has all the normal shit. There's a VRO against him, from his ex-wife. He's been done for blowing over, but he got his licence back. That was a while ago now. Martin threatened to charge him with obstructing last year, but that didn't go anywhere.' He pushed his arms back from the steering wheel and stretched, still chewing. 'Actually, now I think about it, they've been keeping a low profile recently. Makes me think they could be up to something.'

'Might have turned over a new leaf,' Jack said.

'You really don't think that.' Accelerating down the road, Aiden took a few quick turns and ended up on another street. He pointed at a weatherboard house that was painted in a soft green. The curtains were drawn and the front door closed. 'Know what this is?'

'Drug house,' Jack said.

'Spot on. There's four of these in town. We raid them periodically, clear everything out, charge the offenders. They go to court and get a slap on the wrist, or do three months behind bars, get out and start up again. Gives me the shits, but what can you do?'

'It's the same in SA,' Jack said. 'We used to work our arses off to make sure the charges stuck only to have them get a fine and then they're shunted back out on the streets. Got any links to The Untouchables?'

'They're too clever. I'm sure they take some and shift it, but they can make money in areas that carry a lot less penalties and are more profitable. We caught the bastards trafficking reptiles a few years back.'

'To overseas?'

'Yeah, they're worth a shitload on the black market.'

'I worked on a similar case a few years ago. This old couple who lived way out in the Flinders Ranges were transporting reptiles over east so they could be packaged up and freighted through the mail. Locked them up and threw away the key.'

'What is it about small country towns? They're like the underbelly of the crime world where you least expect it.'

'Ain't that the truth! That town had car jackings, elder abuse; we even had a school principal blow up his family home. Turned out he was a paedophile and a murderer.'

'Dirty fucker,' Aiden said.

'Yeah. I think small towns are popular hiding places for people who are trying to avoid the law. The police numbers have been cut back so there's not as many of us out in the bush and it's an easy place to hide.'

'True story.'

The radio clicked to life. 'All units, vehicle accident, Goldfields Highway. Required on scene. Two fatalities.' The voice went on to give GPS coordinates.

Jack froze. As the passenger, he was supposed to answer the call, but he couldn't think of what to say. How to answer. It had been so long since he was in uniform.

Aiden picked up the mic and told Comms that their unit was responding. As he flicked on the lights and headed to the highway, heat flooded through Jack's face.

CHAPTER SEVEN

'Priority two,' the radio operator told Jack, who was now holding the mic.

'Roger,' he answered and watched as Aiden increased his speed once they reached the highway.

'Get many fatalities out here?' Jack asked as other cars edged away from them.

Grimacing, Aiden nodded. 'This time of the year, we can. Or at least we get bad accidents. Don't know if you've noticed the number of grey nomads in town? They're the troublemakers. Not in the real sense of the word, but they give us grief because some of them are very inexperienced.'

'I've noticed a few getting around.'

Aiden shook his head in frustration. 'I find it hard to understand why people who have never driven anything bigger than a Toyota Corolla most of their lives decide that when they retire they have to buy a large vehicle. Suddenly they're driving a rig that's higher and longer than anything they've driven before. They're pulling more weight, loading the vans incorrectly and going on roads they've never been on, all at a hundred kilometres an hour. What could possibly go wrong?' He chewed extra hard.

'I don't want to laugh but you're right,' Jack said. 'In the Flinders Ranges, there were always a large contingent of caravanners. If I had a dollar for every time I saw arguments between husbands and wives when they were trying to park or reverse into a camping spot, I'd be richer than Elon Musk! I reckon they should make towing courses mandatory.'

'Agreed,' Aiden said.

The car filled with silence.

Jack shifted in his seat, running his sweaty palms up and down his pants. This wouldn't be the first motor vehicle accident he had attended, yet he always felt apprehensive until he arrived. The unknown was a horrible thing.

When he'd worked out bush, he'd attended every accident. Not when he was in Adelaide, though. There was a dedicated Major Crash Unit and the Uniforms for that.

Now, Jack was one of those uniforms again and the murky, unascertained details made for unease.

Once he was there it was easy to flick the switch and become the police officer who dealt with what was in front of him, clinically and without emotion, but until he saw the scene, he worried about what carnage there would be, what lives had been changed forever, what damage had occurred to the people who had been living, breathing, laughing, loving … until suddenly they weren't.

Aiden finally spoke. 'It's all good,' he said. 'Until it's not.'

The countryside was passing in a flash of red, grey and muted green.

Mountains of dirt towered behind high fences on the western side of the road, while virgin bush stretched out on the other. Utes emblazoned with the logo of the mine crisscrossed over makeshift roads. Machinery moved soil from one place to another, upending massive bucketfuls into the back of tip trucks. Jack watched as a humongous bucketful of dirt was emptied into the tray of a truck, that was four sizes larger than he'd ever seen before. The machine bounced up on its springs as the weight hit the bottom. It bobbed, steadied, then they did it all over again until it was full.

Further down the road, he could just make out some buildings. Gates guarded the entrance to them, with signs saying only approved personnel were allowed any further.

'See all those huts,' Aiden asked as he squeezed another piece of chewie from the packet. 'That joint is like a mini town. The FIFO blokes who live on site have everything they could want. Get their meals cooked for them, there's a gym. It's like living in a retirement village, except they're at work.'

'Got any idea how many live in town and how many are FIFO?'

'Lots of both,' he said after giving the question a moment of thought.

A few kilometres further on, a large stretch of tall blackbutts were scattered over the land. Underneath their canopy, there were shrubby bushes, ironstone and litter. So much litter.

Crushed beer cans, McDonald's paper bags and chip buckets. Toilet paper, glass bottles. Crumpled newspapers.

Even so far from town, humans were having a devastating effect on this beautiful area.

The patrol car ate up the bitumen, passing another mine, this one closed. There were young saplings and bushes out the front, along with native grasses planted in rows.

Aiden pointed, without taking his eyes from the road. 'This was the Hillview Gold Mine, decommissioned about seven years ago. They've been working on rehabilitating the land.'

'Is it a requirement?'

'Yeah, the mining companies around here have a pretty responsible outlook. I know there's been a few bungles with mines up north, but here? Different story.'

A sign came into view telling them that the town of Menzies was seventy kilometres in front of them.

'You play any sport, Jack?'

Jack smiled. He'd been waiting for the questions to start. Getting to know a colleague, learning to trust them, was imperative. The only way to get to that stage was to ask questions, hang out and talk.

He had some of his own queries, but until Aiden started, he had been going to keep quiet. Sometimes silence made it easier to get information.

'Back when I was younger and didn't pinch a nerve just by blinking an eye, I used to play cricket,' he said. 'Loved it. Now all I do is run. I get a bit nervous about moving the old bod too quickly. How about you?'

Aiden's glance slid across to Jack then back to the road. 'Are you younger than me?'

'Dunno, I'm thirty-two.'

'Not far apart. Twenty-nine.' Aiden tightened his hand around the steering wheel and looked over at Jack. 'Holy crap!'

Jack looked around, startled. 'What?' They were still doing a hundred and thirty kilometres an hour. Outside of the car, Jack couldn't see anything amiss.

'What the hell happens to your body in three years that makes you pinch a nerve while you're blinking?' He looked ahead, but his jaw was moving.

Jack laughed. 'I wish I knew. It only gets worse apparently. You play anything?'

'Proud member of one of the veteran footy clubs in town. We're the Dazzlers! Stupid name, but we like it. Between all of us, there's enough who work in different parts of the gold industry to make us dazzle.'

Jack crinkled his forehead in a mixture of amusement and confusion. 'The Dazzlers. Are you sure? Makes me think of glittery costumes and tapdancing, not footy.'

'I know.' Aiden glanced down at the dash and checked his gauges. 'All a bit of fun. And no, before you ask, we're not all gay. Just a couple.'

Jack held up his hands, smiling at the laughter in his partner's voice. 'Hey! No judgement here,' he said.

Aiden paused. 'The team's been together for about two years now and we believe –' he glanced at Jack '– there's every chance this year that we might get up the ladder a bit.'

'How far up the ladder?' Jack leaned back and crossed his arms as he checked the rear-vision mirror for other patrol cars and an ambulance.

Nothing yet.

'Not sure,' Aiden said, seeming to give the question due consideration. 'Getting off the bottom would be a good start.'

Jack snorted. 'I'd offer to play but I wouldn't want to upset that well-oiled machine.'

'No way, we don't want you. You might blink!'

The radio crackled to life, telling them the road had been closed at the edge of Kalgoorlie and at the township of Menzies.

'Good,' Aiden said. 'We won't have to worry about any busybodies. That really shits me, people wanting to see the accident. Just stay away and let us do our job. They wouldn't be so inquisitive if they knew what crappy things we see.'

'Agreed,' Jack said.

Aiden shot him an apologetic look. 'I can be a bit opinionated sometimes. Boss says I need to try and pare that back a bit. So, where'd you grow up?'

'Adelaide. Or rather in the Adelaide Hills. Do you know it at all?'

'Nothing except they've got a couple of footy teams that sometimes upset us.'

Jack huffed. 'Depends on what season you get them on. They're not exactly reliable.'

Nodding, Aiden checked his mirrors.

'Anyhow, we had a few acres just outside of Hahndorf. Good place to live as a kid. Lots of space and freedom. Dad used to go down to the cattle sales and buy a few of the poddy calves from the farmers and we'd feed and raise them. Didn't have enough space to have too many, but there were always three or four. All went to shit when Dad died. I was fifteen and the work on the block was too much for us to keep up with, so we sold the land and moved into suburbia.'

Aiden glanced over at him. 'Shit, mate, your old man carked it when you were fifteen? That must've been hard.'

Jack shrugged. The numb pit in his stomach had never left him, it just wavered in intensity. He vividly remembered the moment he'd come home from school and his mum had met him at the front door trying to hold herself together.

I'm sorry, honey, Dad has had a bleed on the brain. That was all she had managed before dissolving into tears.

'It is what it is.' Jack gave a humourless laugh. 'I hate that saying, but it's true. I was old enough to help Mum out a bit and she turned herself inside out to make sure my sister and I had everything we needed.' He smiled, remembering his mother's words. "'Everything you need, Jack. Not everything you want." That's what she used to tell us. What about you?'

'Couple of sisters over east,' Aiden replied. 'And there's a brother. Mum and Dad are in Perth, and I see them every chance I get. I try to go up to the footy once a month. I'm a die-hard Eagles supporter. Up the blue and gold!' He raised his fist in an air punch. Then his face fell and Jack felt the car begin to slow. 'Jesus, look at that.'

Debris was strewn over the road. Chunks of a silver and black caravan. There was a man in a high-vis jacket, setting out witches' hats. He looked up and raised his hand.

'Who's that?' Jack asked. 'He's not one of ours.'

'One of the mine's emergency responders. They've got first-aid vehicles so if they're closer to an incident we call them. Makes sense to use them when they might only be five minutes away and we're an hour.' He jerked his thumb over his shoulder. 'See if there's another couple of patrol vehicles behind us.'

'Not yet.'

Aiden brought the car to a stop, lights still flashing. He looked around and sighed heavily, then sat bolt upright. 'What the fuck?'

Searching the scene, Jack couldn't see what had upset him. The accident looked pretty standard for a vehicle rollover and, at this point, they couldn't see the deceased. 'What's wrong?'

'That fucking journalist is here already. How would she have known? Shit!'

Jack's stomach dropped as he searched the faces of the few people walking around, seemingly dazed. Their high-vis gear reflected in the flashing lights and their expressions told him none of them had seen carnage like this before.

'Shit, have you seen Zara?' he asked. A bead of sweat broke out on his forehead.

Aiden's head swivelled around. 'Who's Zara?'

'What journalist?' Jack's voice was more urgent this time. He yanked the door open.

'What the hell are you doing?' Aiden asked as Jack half staggered out of the car.

'You said there was a journalist. Was it Zara?' His voice was louder now.

Jack took a few steps towards the wreckage and then back to the patrol car.

'I don't know what her name is. That bloody one who's been sniffing around the station recently,' Aiden was saying. 'I know she's been trying to suck up to Renee, the court reporter. I bet she's already taken photos of the crash site and put something online, and we don't even know who the victims ...'

Jack continued to search the crash site, not hearing Aiden's voice anymore.

A white dual-cab ute with South Australian numberplates, two spotlights and a light bar across the bull bar was sitting at an erratic angle across the deep drain.

The rushing in Jack's head was so loud it took him a moment to understand what was in front of him, then realisation came down on him like a tonne of bricks.

'No,' he whispered. He swung around, wildly now. 'Zara?' he yelled. He looked back to the police car. 'Aiden, where did you see her?'

He tried to control his breathing, but his heart was hammering too fast.

'Mate, what the hell is going on?' Aiden was at Jack's side, his hand gripping his arm. 'I saw her get into that ute over there.'

Jack ran towards the ute, his eyes searching … And then he saw her.

'Zara, are you okay?' He pulled her to him, wrapping his arms around her. 'What happened?' His hands came away red. Blood. He pulled back. 'Jesus, you're covered in blood. Are you hurt?'

'Jack …' She gave a small shudder.

'Oh, honey, it's okay,' he whispered, stroking her hair before gently checking her arms, head and neck, feeling for injuries.

'Jack?' A different voice and the word sounded like a blow from a hammer on steel.

Jack looked over his shoulder. Aiden's face was set in a stony expression, his arms crossed over his chest.

'Aiden, this is Zara,' Jack said, his voice deep with emotion. 'She's my partner.' He glanced at Zara who didn't seem to be able to even raise her hand.

A heartbeat passed and then Aiden took a step backwards, shock crossing his face. 'Your partner?'

'Yeah. She's the reason I'm in Kalgoorlie.'

'Jesus, mate.' Aiden's voice was full of incredulity and anger. 'How the hell were you even allowed in the force?' He turned and stomped towards the wreckage.

Jack felt Zara stiffen and he turned his back on Aiden, knowing he'd probably stuffed up that relationship without even getting off the front foot.

He looked into her face. 'You're not hurt? There's a lot of blood on you.'

'I'm not hurt,' she said. 'I think it's from Jayne. Jesus, it happened right in front of me. I tried to help. The driver.' She took a breath and ran her hands over her face. 'Jayne wanted to know if Barry was okay. I told her he was out of the car. I *lied* to her.'

'Sometimes that's the kindest thing to do,' Jack told her. He felt his heart rate return to normal. 'Just stay here and keep warm. You're in shock. I'll come back for you as soon as I can. We'll need a statement from you. Don't go anywhere.'

What he didn't say was that he didn't want her wandering around in case Aiden and the other police officers decided she was going to write a story and things turned nasty.

'Jack?' Aiden called out. 'Come and do your bloody job. Now.'

Zara put her hand on Jack's wrist, tears spilling down her cheeks. 'She died while I was with her. I should ...'

'You shouldn't be doing anything right now,' he said. 'You're distressed. There's nothing that can be changed. Okay?'

No answer.

'Okay?' he asked again. 'Look, I've got to go, but I'll be back.' He started to move away.

'Jack,' Zara called out after him, her voice steadier now.

'I found this. It was attached to a part of the van that had been ripped off. It was buried in the dirt.' She held out a dome-shaped disc about the size of a twenty-cent piece. 'I've never seen a van with one of these attached to it.'

Jack looked down at her outstretched hand and his eyes widened. 'That's a GPS tracking unit. What the hell was that doing there?'

CHAPTER EIGHT

'Aiden, come and have a look at this.' Jack motioned his partner over to the caravan. He wanted a second opinion.

Aiden was walking back from outlining the yaw marks on the road with yellow spray paint. The black skids slid from one side of the road to the other, and where they hit the dirt, they became deep, wide ruts.

The sky was thankfully still clear, though the forecast had mentioned the possibility of rain later in the week. Even without the environmental influences, the dirt part of the evidence would deteriorate quickly, with cars zipping along the road.

Jack was having trouble keeping his mind off the 'what if?' of Zara's involvement.

What if it had been her vehicle?

What if it had been her body he was helping haul out of the wreckage?

What if, what if, what if?

Zara was still tucked in the ute, safely away from the rest of the police officers, but it hadn't taken long for word to spread around the scene. Other officers he'd met that morning were now throwing him sidelong glances before their gaze flicked over to where Zara was sitting.

Talk about the elephant in the room.

He frowned as he snapped a few more photos of the underside of the caravan. The whole axle was caked in dirt from the slide, which was why Jack had almost missed it.

'What have you got?' Aiden stood back slightly, his arms crossed.

The animosity projecting from his partner was going to create a reckoning as soon as they were alone.

'See this,' Jack said, bending down again.

Aiden didn't answer.

Punching him would be pure joy.

Well, bring it on, Jack thought. *I've never had any trouble with having a journalist as a partner before, I don't know why there'd be a problem now.*

'See here,' Jack said, pointing this time.

Aiden squinted at the axle. It was covered in wet dirt. 'The box, you mean?'

'Yeah. Attached very solidly to the axle.'

Bending in close, Aiden inspected the site.

Jack had already chipped away part of the dirt; just enough around from the circumference of the box to show what it was. Magnetic. Heavy duty. Nothing was going to shift this baby.

'Don't reckon that means anything. I mean, it's probably where they kept the spare keys. Leave it with me and I'll get it opened and admitted into evidence. Although this is a pretty standard vehicle accident so there won't be much evidence to collect.'

'Hmm, I don't think so,' Jack mused, thinking hard. 'It's too thin for a car key or a bunch of house keys. What would they need to hide under their van?' He straightened up.

Aiden bristled. 'Why would you think you know better? You've just arrived in town and don't even know how to answer a radio call.'

'Is that right?' Jack snapped back.

'I know you were a detective when you were in South Australia,' Aiden continued, 'but you're in WA now and you're in uniform, so you don't get to pull rank. If you think there's something suspicious then call the dees and get them to look at this, not you. Though you're wasting your time.'

'We both know your attitude isn't about the scene,' Jack replied. 'Want to do this here?' He stared at Aiden. 'Get everything off your chest in front of everyone?' He took a step forward. 'Or do you think we should just do our job and sort it out when we're finished? I understand you're pissed off, but as you mentioned when we first arrived, we've got work to do.'

Finally, Aiden inclined his head. 'What are you wanting me to say? That I think the box is strange? Well, I don't.'

'You don't think it's suspicious that a caravan would have a lockbox hidden underneath it?'

'No.' Aiden stared at Jack, then he shrugged as if to concede. 'Might be nothing. Could be something.'

'If it's *something*, what would it be? Drugs?' Jack asked. 'What's your *local knowledge* tell you?' Jack made his tone heavy on 'local knowledge'. Every cop knew their area best, he understood. Just as every cop could smell when something was off.

This lockbox was rotten.

Aiden looked down at the axle and rocked on his heels, hands deep in his pockets and away from the biting wind. 'Drugs would be the most obvious thing they're transporting, but I haven't heard anything on the grapevine about grey nomads being used as mules.'

'Anyone can be a mule,' Jack said. He paused and indicated for another police officer to come over. 'You've logged the GPS I gave you into evidence?' he asked.

'Yep, and I've taken Zara's statement,' Sally answered.

'Let's have a look.'

'What GPS?' Aiden asked. With his phone in his hand, he looked at the screen, then swore, before returning it to his pocket. He turned and glared towards where Zara was still in the ute, staring into space.

Jack filled him in as they headed towards the patrol car. 'Zara picked up a piece of the van that had a GPS tracker attached to it. It was half-covered in dirt, and she picked it up so it wouldn't get overlooked.' He held up his hand. 'Yes, I know she shouldn't have touched it. Normally, she wouldn't have. But what she's just been through is an exceptional situation, wouldn't you agree? Not thinking straight would be understandable.'

'Don't have to justify her actions to me,' Aiden said, clearly thinking the opposite.

'Here.' Sally held out the evidence bag and Jack took it. Inside was a piece of aluminium with jagged edges and a black, plastic dome with dirt in its cracks and crevices.

'You think it came off the van or vehicle?' Aiden asked, leaning in to look.

'From the material it looks like the van. Be very odd for there to be a GPS tracker lying randomly in the dirt,' Jack answered. 'Especially one still working.' He pointed to the tiny solid blue light on the top of the casing.

In his hand, Jack felt his mobile phone vibrate. He frowned, knowing there wasn't any reception.

Aiden's hand crept down to his pocket at the same time.

'It's trying to pair to my phone,' he said to Aiden. 'Yours too?'

Aiden nodded, turning his phone around to show Jack. 'Must be satellite based. There's no mobile reception here so it's not using the towers.'

Jack tapped the screen and opened the Bluetooth app. The dots were blinking – one, two, three and back to none.

Aiden put his phone back in his pocket.

'Do we know who these people are?' Sally asked.

'Their IDs were in the car, and I've got Comms running checks,' Aiden said. 'I'll get them to run their names through all the systems and see if they're known to us.'

'Good idea,' Jack said. 'Right-oh, well, let's get the whole she-bang back to the station. Looks like our day just got a whole lot more interesting.'

Aiden's face flushed as he waved over the tow truck that had arrived a few minutes beforehand. 'Not for us it hasn't. I'll report this to the Drug Squad,' he said above the noise of the reversing alarm.

—

Fury made Aiden's eyes glitter as he got out of the car. He slammed the door, looking at Jack over the roof. His fingers tapped on the car, while he waited for what Jack guessed was an explanation. The drive back to the station had been quiet, neither speaking unless to answer a phone call.

Now Jack just returned the stare.

The darkening sky should have meant the shithouse day was ending, but there was more to come.

'You should have told me,' Aiden spat.

'That my partner was Zara, or that she was a journalist?'

'That your *partner* is a *journalist!*'

'And?' Jack took a step towards Aiden.

'Police and journalists are not friends.'

'Old-school view,' Jack said dismissively. 'Also, as far as I'm aware, who I spend my private time with isn't your concern.'

'Mate, you're not getting it. How can we trust you? How do we know that you're not going to get your cock sucked after you've given her intel? Or before.'

Jack didn't even think. He swung an open hand and slapped Aiden across the face.

Aiden stumbled back and his hand flew to his cheek, which was already turning red, his eyes watering.

'Haven't you got *any* manners?' Jack asked, on his toes, waiting for Aiden's response.

Jack wasn't disappointed. Aiden's hands had formed fists at his side.

'Hey!' The call came from the door of the police station. A group of police officers were finishing their shift and heading home. 'What's going on here?'

An officer appeared at Aiden's side and made to grab his arm, but he shoved them away. Sally stood in between the two men, holding her hands up. 'Guys,' she warned. 'Enough.'

'What the hell?' Another officer asked in an incredulous voice.

Aiden didn't drop his stance. 'Ask him,' he snarled. 'He's the one fucking a journalist.'

Jack gave a short bark of laughter. His knuckles clenched in anger. 'So? What the hell has it got to do with you?'

'That's enough.' A male officer now had a firm hold of Aiden, with another jogging towards them.

'It's everything to do with me if I'm working with you.' Spit flew from Aiden's mouth, landing on Sally's hand. She rubbed it on her uniform and brought her hands back up to keep the men apart. 'Seriously, fellas, stop it now. Before the boss comes out.'

'And not out here,' the other one said. 'Jesus!'

Aiden and Jack were surrounded by other police officers, trying to defuse the situation, but neither took their eyes from one another as they moved in a circle around Sally.

'Everyone needs to know—'

'Aiden!' The word was like a bullet. 'Stand down.'

Aiden's eyes slid across to the door where Martin was standing, his face red and furious.

'I will not tolerate this at my station. Aiden, wait in the change rooms. I'll be in to see you shortly. Jack, my office. What are you? Teenagers?' He looked at them both with disgust. 'And out here where everyone can see you. What a great example to the public.'

'This isn't finished yet,' Aiden hissed as he adjusted his shirt and belt and started to head inside.

'Careful, you might end up with a matching cheek.'

'I'd like to see you try. You won't fit in here, *mate*.' Aiden stalked off towards the change rooms.

All the other police officers looked at each other, then their gazes returned to Jack.

'All good?' one asked Jack.

What a stupid question. Giving a short nod, Jack adjusted his sleeve cuffs.

'Guess you've all got jobs to do,' he said, then felt for his collar and made sure it was sitting correctly. Clearing his throat, he headed into Martin's office.

His boss was pacing the carpet behind his desk.

'What's this I'm hearing, Jack?'

Jack didn't answer. He stood tall and straight, waiting for more.

Realising he wasn't going to get an answer, Martin ploughed on. 'Right then. What's your story? I'm all ears. You and this journalist. In our conversation this morning you implied you weren't in a relationship and now I'm hearing you're living with this ...' He waved his hand around.

'Zara,' Jack supplied.

'Zara.' Martin shook his head. 'I asked you this morning if you had a partner.'

'You asked if I moved to Kalgoorlie because of a breakup and I said it was nothing like that. There wasn't the option to explain further.' Jack stood tall and looked Martin in the eye.

'Fuck me dead, boy, that's splitting hairs, and you know it. Don't play games. It's imperative I know this type of information. If you have to testify in court you could be seen as being compromised, whether you are or not. How can I make sure everything is above board if I don't know this shit?' He pointed a finger at Jack. 'You're new and you've got to build relationships with your colleagues. Jesus, surely you know this stuff. How you've acted is not the way to win the trust of all the other officers in this station.

'I run a tight ship. I told you that this morning. The boys and girls I've trained here will not allow you to treat them like this. Openness and honesty – that's what this police station runs on.' Martin stopped pacing and put his hands on the desk.

He looked at Jack. 'What did Aiden say to you to make that happen?'

'I won't be repeating what he said, sir, but he insulted my partner.'

'Who is a journalist.'

'Correct.'

'So ...' Martin started to wave his hand, indicating for Jack to speak. He leaned forward and waited.

Jack tapped his hand against his thighs and took a breath.

'Zara is an investigative journalist. She works, or rather used to work, for a national paper. Unfortunately, during a court case she gave enough information for people to work out who her source was. She wasn't sacked but demoted to a rural paper.' He spread his arms out. 'And here we are.'

Short, sharp and to the point.

Even though Martin didn't speak, the room wasn't silent. The noise of phones ringing outside, conversations and radio chatter came through the closed door.

Jack waited.

'You gave up being a detective to come to Kalgoorlie?'

'No. I gave it up so I could be with Zara.'

Tapping his two pointer fingers on the desk, Martin suddenly stepped away and clasped his hands in front of his waist. 'That's commendable.'

'I guess that depends on who you ask.'

'Have any of the brass cautioned you on this relationship?'

'It's never been a problem. We don't speak about my work or anything that is confidential in hers.'

'Ha.' Martin rocked on his heels now, indecisive. 'That sounds hard.'

'Not really. We both love our jobs and take them seriously.

We understand the consequences if either of us breached any confidentiality or privacy issues. She doesn't expect information from me, and if she comes by something I don't expect her to give it to me.'

'Can't imagine your pillow talk.'

Jack decided not to comment.

Martin sighed. 'Well, you've got your work cut out for you. I'm sure you'll have plenty of colleagues regard you with suspicion. A police officer and a journalist are –' Martin searched for a word '– an unusual combination and not usually recommended. I think you'd find that our brass in Western Australia would've strongly advised against this relationship.' He thought for a moment. 'I suggest that you google the detective who found that little girl, in the north of the state, a couple of years ago and take on board what happened to him after he leaked information.' He paused and connected with Jack's eyes once more. 'And, Jack, I will be watching you as close as a dog sniffing sausages. Let me make this clear. If any intelligence is leaked, you'll be the first one I haul into my office, so you'd better make sure you have the whole station eating out of your hand, so no one else does it just so you get the blame. I'll talk to Aiden, but if he wants to push the fact you slapped him, you'll be in a world of hurt.'

'I understand that.'

'Good, now get the hell out of here.'

CHAPTER NINE

It was the top of the hour and the ABC news jingle sounded through the car stereo speakers.

Jim pushed his arms back on the steering wheel, checked his mirrors to make sure the caravan was pulling straight behind him and groaned. 'Must almost be time for a break. Some lunch?'

'You can't really want lunch after all those scones?' Carol looked over at him, then gave a cheeky grin and patted his stomach. 'Careful, Mr Bethall.'

Jim rubbed his hand over Carol's and grinned. 'Always, love, always. But scones with jam and cream are a bit of a favourite of mine.'

'You surprise me!' She pulled her hand away and pushed her hair away from her eyes. In the side mirror, Carol caught her own eye and got a shock as she always did. When had her blonde hair started giving in to streaks of grey?

'Bit of a shame Jayne and Barry and Irene and Ritchie didn't want to stay and sample the wares. Coffee was good there too.'

Carol let out a peal of laughter and dropped her hand. 'How funny was it when the police car arrived just in time for morning tea? I bet they do it every day.' She'd been admiring the roses and bougainvillea bushes covering the verandah at Hoover House in Gwalia when the police had pulled in and parked, apparently 'accidentally' hitting the flashing lights for a couple of seconds before they got out of the car and headed for the cafe.

'I reckon I would stop too,' Jim said, 'if I was passing. Even if you put the scones aside, their time chatting to us tourists so we know the police are on the road was a good strategy. Clever community policing, I believe that's called.'

'Oh, is that what it is? I thought they were just getting something nice to eat.'

The jingle finished and a deep, mellow voice spoke to them from the depths of the radio.

'The No Mines political party has announced new candidates for the Kalgoorlie electorate – good afternoon, this is Tony Carr with the ABC radio news.'

'God, we've arrived in the middle of an election campaign. I can't think of anything worse.' Carol reached forward to turn down the radio.

'Hang on, they're talking about Kalgoorlie. We might get the lowdown on what's happening there.'

'Can't see how that's going to affect us, love,' Carol said, but she stopped talking as the news continued.

'Ms Janelle Salter is the new No Mines candidate for the seat of Kalgoorlie,' the newsreader said. 'Ms Salter told ABC News that she would be working hard to see the mines in Kalgoorlie and surrounding areas closed by 2030.'

The report switched to a woman's voice. 'People need to realise what damage this industry is doing – not only to the land, but also to the employees of these hellholes. The companies who own the mines are headed up by communists and capitalists and we cannot allow them to pillage our resources and sell the product overseas, nor make our loved ones ill.'

Carol raised her eyebrows. 'Sounds extreme,' she said. 'Can't think she'd get too many votes around here.'

'What do you expect from a party that's called No Mines?' Jim asked with a laugh. 'Anyhow, you're right, it won't affect us. I thought it might be something important. Hello, what's happening here?'

In the distance a line of cars, trucks and caravans were parked either side of the road. A car with orange flashing lights was angled across the white line, blocking the road.

'God, is that an accident?' Carol leaned forward, trying to see further ahead.

'I hope not.' Jim lifted his foot and started to slow their vehicle. 'We really need to redo our first-aid course. Maybe we can see if there's one we can do while we're in Kalgoorlie. Better to help out than watch on when something's wrong.'

'You've said that for a while.' Carol glanced across at her husband fondly. 'You're always trying to help people. I'm not sure I'd be able to hold myself together if we came across an accident and people were badly hurt. Even thinking about it makes me feel sick.'

Jim took his hand from the steering wheel to squeeze hers. 'So many people say that, and when they're confronted with a problem, they just act. I think you'd be like that, even though you get a bit anxious from time to time. Anyhow, wouldn't you like to know what to do if I had a heart attack?' He gave her a sideways glance.

'God, don't even talk like that, love.' Carol looked troubled. 'Just don't. Okay?' She squeezed his hand back.

Jim flicked the blinker on and followed the five caravans in front of them that were being directed off the road by the traffic controller. The orange flashing lights were reflected in puddles along the edge of the road and a low, heavy grey cloud gave the whole area an eerie feeling.

Even though it was midafternoon, it felt later, and darker. Ominous.

People had left their cars and were standing in huddles, hands shoved in their heavy jackets, talking to each other.

No one was smiling. Occasionally someone looked at the sky and held out a hand as if they were checking for rain.

A couple were walking towards the traffic controller, while a truck driver paced the length of his trailers back and forth, talking on the phone, waving his hands around as if very annoyed.

'There was nothing on the radio news,' Carol said, reaching for her mobile phone to check the news app.

'Must've just happened,' Jim answered. 'Look, there's Irene and Ritchie. They left about an hour before us.' He motioned towards the other couple standing nearby. 'Maybe they know something.'

He unclipped his seatbelt and got out, leaving the car still running and Carol tapping at her screen. When she looked up, Jim was lifting his hand to Irene and Ritchie.

'G'day, you two,' he called out. 'Looks like there's a bit of a hold-up.'

Ritchie strolled towards their van, hands shoved in his jeans pockets, his beanie askew on his head. 'Sounds like we're going to be here for a time,' he answered. 'I've spoken to the bloke over there.' He pointed to a man sitting in the traffic control vehicle. 'Single-vehicle rollover. Fair way in front of us but they've closed the road here, where there's room for us to park. Pretty nasty accident, by all reports. Couple of fatalities.'

'Oh no.' Carol joined them, her phone still in her hand. 'That's terrible. Hopefully you're wrong.'

'That would be nice, but I don't think so. The police flew through here about half an hour ago, lights flashing, no sirens. That's never good. Fella over there says that's the second cop car from Leonora. Ambulances and more police came from Kalgoorlie too.'

'Have you been here long?' Carol had reached over and turned off the engine. She leaned against the front now, spreading her hands over the warm bonnet. 'We saw the police at Gwalia having morning tea but they left before we got on the road.'

'About an hour. The road's been shut for a while now.' Ritchie rocked on his heels. 'Bad business,' he said gravely. 'Very bad business.'

'There was already a big line-up when we arrived,' Irene put in. 'Some people have been here for a lot longer than us. There's not much information.' She pointed to the traffic controller in conversation with the couple they'd seen walking towards him. He was shaking his head and holding his hands up. 'Poor bloke is here to make sure no one drives through, so he hasn't got anything to tell us. Or at least, he's not handing out much info.'

'Probably can't, love.'

'They should be able to convey to everyone who's stopped what's actually happening and how long we might be stuck for,' Ritchie said, shaking his head. 'Some people don't have caravans and will have to go back to a hotel or where they stayed before.'

'The authorities mightn't have any information yet,' Jim said. 'Might take a while to work through what they need to do.'

'God, even the thought of an accident is …' Carol shook her head, unable to find words to communicate her anxiety. 'I hate the thought of what could have happened.' She turned and looked towards the road closed sign.

'What type of vehicle, did he say?' Jim asked.

'Nope. Nothing except they are hoping to open the road by about five, but it'll be dark by then and, if they run into any problems clearing the road or shifting the bodies, it'll be later.' Ritchie looked around. 'Could be anything, couldn't it? I mean look at the variety of vehicles lined up here. Truck, car, caravan, motorbike. They could have hit a camel or a cow or rolled.'

'The truckies are pretty unhappy about the hold-up,' Irene chimed in. 'That driver over there was ranting and raving when we got here. Something about how he's got six hours until he has to stop again, according to his logbook, so he'd rather be driving now than stopping.'

'That bloke handing out directions told him he wasn't going anywhere for a while, so he might as well go to bed and get some more driving hours up his sleeve by sleeping now and not later,' Ritchie finished.

Carol huffed. 'What about the poor people who have lost their lives? Aren't they more important than where that man has to be?'

'Everyone is always in a hurry,' Jim said. 'And no one likes a hold-up. The trucking companies are on tight schedules. But roads are roads, and you never know what could happen. Look at Barry and Jayne this morning. He was in a hurry, not wanting anything to stop him.'

Carol's stomach was rolling with concern. Perhaps it was the thought of deceased people being within such close proximity, or that they might have been caravanners just like them. Even if they weren't, they were still someone's family, someone's loved ones. She swallowed hard, continuing to keep her fingers near the warmth of the bonnet.

'Well, Jayne and Barry should've got through this given how fast he was going this morning,' Ritchie said. 'Reckon he would've left before himself, if that was possible.'

Irene laughed. 'That man needs a time machine not a caravan! I think there might have been trouble if he didn't get to set up the TV and watch the game, don't you?'

'Silly bugger's on holidays.' Carol shook her head.

They heard a horn blaring in one continuous sound and turned to look. A vehicle was coming from the north, with its lights flashing.

'What the ...' Ritchie's words stopped as the four-wheel drive stopped with a jerk in front of the roadblock and a person wrapped in a heavy jacket and beanie almost fell out of the driver's seat.

'I need to get through. I *need* to get through.'

'Look at that,' Jim said shaking his head. 'There's always one.'

The traffic controller waved his hand and shook his head, then talked into his radio a bit more.

'But I have to! It's an emergency.'

'Should we go and help?' Irene asked. All four of them were turned towards the commotion now.

'Best we stay the hell out of it,' Ritchie said. But he didn't turn away from the spectacle.

'That poor person,' Carol said. 'They must have a terrible emergency to be yelling like that.' Then she gasped. 'Oh my god, what if they're related to the people who died in the accident? They might have just found out.'

There didn't seem to be anything to say to that.

'Jesus fucking Christ. I won't …' The words were drowned out by the roaring of another engine, coming from the opposite direction.

Red and blue flashing lights reflected from the clouds as the police car came into view from the southern side.

'Called in the reinforcements,' Jim commented.

'I hope you rot in hell!' The person stormed back to their car and slammed the door shut, before the police had time to stop and talk to them. A screech of tyres echoed over the bush as the car took off back towards Gwalia.

The couple who had been talking to the traffic controller before the interruption now walked towards them. 'Some people just think there's one rule for them and another for others, don't they?' The man shook his head. 'Anyhow, sounds like we're stuck overnight,' he said, self-importance written all over his face.

'You've got more info?' Jim asked.

The man nodded. 'Yeah, they're talking seven pm now. I don't know about you, but I'm not keen on driving these roads at night towing a van. Too many things could go wrong. Blow a tyre, hit a roo.' He shrugged. 'I don't want to be another statistic, like those people up ahead, so we're going to set up camp for the night.' He looked down the empty road. 'Especially now it looks like the crazies have gone.'

'Right-oh,' Ritchie replied with a nod. 'Thanks for the information.' He glanced at his watch as the couple walked away, then looked at Irene. 'Not a bad plan. We should probably set up for the night too, don't you think?'

Irene nodded. 'I guess so, unless you want to go back to Gwalia?' There was a slight pleading note to her voice.

Ritchie shook his head. 'We've already over halfway to Kalgoorlie. Let's stay here.' He looked towards the bush. 'Might get the detector out and go for a swing. Never know, love, it might be fate we pulled up here for the night if I find a lump of gold.'

Carol was looking at her phone, a concerned expression on her face. 'I'm trying to ring Jayne to let her know about the road closure.'

'They watching the game?' Jim turned back to their van and began assessing where they'd parked.

'It's going through to voicemail.'

'Leave a message. They'll ring back.' Jim rubbed his hands over the tyres, checking for wear, before walking around the van. 'Barry has probably told her to keep her phone on silent so he can hear the commentary.'

Carol's brow crinkled. 'Jayne told me she never turns her phone off or puts it on silent because her daughter has epilepsy and she's an emergency contact for the grandkids, in case they can't get hold of their dad.'

Jim straightened up and faced Carol, putting his hand on her shoulder. 'Maybe there's no mobile range.'

Unconvinced Carol put her phone back in her pocket. 'Maybe.'

'Carol, will you come and collect some wood with me?' Irene called. 'I know we're not supposed to, but I'm sure no one will dob us in if we get a few sticks tonight.'

'Sure. Nothing cheerier than an open fire.' Carol checked the back seat of the car for her gloves. 'I'll be back shortly,' she told Jim, who patted her on the bum as she walked by him.

A warm glow spread through her body, and she turned back and kissed him. 'You're alright, you know that?'

'Not bad yourself,' he answered, kissing her back. 'Get on with you.'

Another smile and she followed Irene, who was already at the fence, pushing the top wire down.

Then Carol stopped and looked back at the long line of vehicles and trucks. People had begun to go back into their own cars and open up rooftop tents. A few had brought camp chairs out of their caravans, already with beers in hand. Three cars had turned and headed back towards Gwalia, obviously hoping Hoover House wasn't booked out that night.

'Maybe we should try to get everyone to come together for a communal tea tonight. It's a sombre feeling here, isn't it?'

Cracking a few thin sticks off a dead tree, Irene followed her gaze. 'I don't know, Carol. Perhaps leave everyone to themselves. Some are going to care, and others won't. It's horrible knowing we're only a few kilometres away from a fatal accident, but maybe others don't feel that way.'

Carol pulled out her phone and tried Jayne's number again.

Hi, you've called Jayne, please leave a message, or if it's urgent, Barry's number is ...

'Have you got your phone there?' she asked Irene. 'Can you try to call Barry?'

Dropping the sticks at her feet, Irene stood up. 'He was awful, Carol, don't you think? He was always bossing Jayne around. All I heard at Gwalia was him picking on everything she did.'

'I thought he was a know-it-all idiot too, but Jayne is lovely, and we had a bit in common.' Carol dialled Jayne's number again. 'I thought they might want to get together to have drinks or share information on the caravan parks. That sort of thing. Sometimes it's nice to have an idea of what a place is going to be like before you get there.'

'Yes, she's lovely,' Irene murmured as Jayne's voice recited Barry's phone number and she keyed it into her phone.

Leave a message.

Barry's voice was clipped and to the point.

'Sounds like him, doesn't it? Short and sharp. Why do lovely, warm women marry men like him?'

'And the other way around,' Carol said. 'So many nice men marry rottweilers.'

Irene looked at Carol with a bemused expression. 'Sounds like you're speaking from experience.'

Carol snapped a few more branches off and cradled them in the crook of her arm. 'My brother.'

'Oh. Families.'

'Tell me about it.' She thought she could feel her mobile vibrating in her back pocket, but when she pulled it out, the screen remained empty.

'Maybe they got a flat tyre and had to pull up in a spot out of range,' Irene said.

The women looked at each other, knowing neither believed what they were saying.

'Do you think …'

'I don't know. I hope not.'

They collected the wood silently, hoping inside their hearts they were wrong.

CHAPTER TEN

The front door of Jack's was ajar.

Light was peeping through the crack and he clocked the beam before he stepped inside the front gate.

He stopped and listened carefully.

Silence.

Taking the steps two at a time, he paused at the top to assess the door. Force of habit.

It hadn't been jimmied.

Did Zara leave it open?

He pushed it open further, putting his keys on the hallway table, then poked his head through the living room door. He took a sad breath in through his nose.

Zara was on the couch, doona wrapped around her and wineglass on the table. Just as he had thought.

Shrugging off his jacket he wiggled down onto the couch, making sure he didn't sit on her legs. 'Hey,' he said.

She clutched the top of the doona and peered at him. 'Hey.'

Jack leaned forward and kissed her, leaving his lips on hers a little longer than normal.

He picked up the wineglass sitting on the coffee table. White wine filled half the glass, and he took a sip. 'Nice.'

Zara folded her fingers around his hand and held on. 'Probably shouldn't have opened it so early, but it's been a hell of a day.'

'Master of understatement.' Jack squeezed her hand. 'I might get myself a beer.'

In the kitchen, he checked what was in the fridge. It was empty except for the barbecue chicken he'd bought yesterday, a litre of milk and some butter. Chook and a bit of bread would do for tea, but he suspected neither of them would want much to eat.

The window above the sink mirrored his image and he stared at himself for a long time, watching as his reflection took a swig of his beer, then another.

Aiden's red face, clenched fists and twisted mouth were front and centre in his thoughts.

Politics at the station was going to be a disaster now.

'Jack?'

He yanked the curtains closed and shut his eyes.

'Coming,' he called back. He looked down at his hands; his knuckles were white as he clenched his beer.

Another breath and then another. He straightened his shoulders. Being angry with Zara for her career choice or her stuff-up in court wasn't going to help anything.

You're not angry, he chanted silently. *You are not angry.*

He concentrated instead on the anticipation of running a new case. He'd only been on the job for a day and he'd caught a very interesting investigation …

Gut punch.

No, he hadn't.

Constable Jack Higgins was back in the humdrum of uniform life, patrolling the highway and pointing the radar gun at speeding cars.

He took another breath, grabbed some peanuts and poured them into a glass bowl.

Aiden's reaction was on him, not on Zara.

The shift to Kal is on Zara, though, he thought unwillingly. He upended the beer and put the empty bottle down on the bench heavily, trying to shift his agitation.

Her mistake was just that, a mistake. Everyone made those.

Opening the fridge, he grabbed another beer and told himself once more: *You're not angry.*

Zara looked up when he returned. 'When did you get back to the station?'

'Not long after you left,' he said, filling up her glass and handing it to her. Jack sat down next to her and leaned back, dropping his head on the back of the couch. It was easier to keep his eyes shut because when he looked at her right now, he didn't see the love of his life. Jack saw the reactive, unpredictable and impulsive Zara. The one who had made a huge mistake and was paying the price for it. The one who had made him pay a price too.

He also saw a person who had been caught up in a terrible accident. And, despite everything, he loved her.

They sat without talking, listening to the outside noise of cars, kids yelling from two backyards across and the occasional siren, a long way away.

His mobile phone beeped, and he ignored it, squeezing her fingers. 'There anything you want to talk about?' he asked, opening his eyes and turning his head to look at her.

She took another sip of wine, and he noticed her hands shaking as she placed the glass back on the table. 'Nothing.' Tears welled in her eyes. She glanced away as if she didn't want him to see.

Jack thought his heart was going squeeze so hard it would burst. He opened his arms and they both moved so Zara could bury her face in his chest.

'What a fucking horrible day.' Her words were muffled.

Kissing the top of her head, Jack nodded in agreement.

There was nothing he could say to make it better.

Zara would have to put this to bed by herself.

'Jayne could have been my mum.'

'But she wasn't.'

'I lied to a dying person,' Zara whispered. She'd turned her head, so her ear rested on his heart. 'That feels so wrong.'

Jack let out a heavy breath and started rubbing slow, soothing circles on her back. 'You did what you had to do. There was no point telling her something that would break her heart just before she died.'

Zara wiped her nose with the sleeve of her shirt.

'Maybe,' she answered, after a few moments, 'but I still lied. I know it was for good – I *know* it was for a good reason, but it was a lie.'

He watched her eyes.

'I held Jayne's hand as she died,' Zara continued. 'She just … stopped talking.' She looked down. 'And then her whole body went limp. Spaghetti like.'

'It's a horrible experience, sweetheart. It changes you.' Jack's voice was heavy. He'd been a witness to the moment of death more than once. 'I've had training in dealing with these types of situations. You haven't, yet everything you did was right.'

'Would you have told Jayne that Barry was okay?'

'Absolutely.' He pumped her hands up and down gently to emphasise his words. 'I would have stayed with her, just like you did. A lot of people would have run in the opposite direction, but not you!' He smiled at her. 'You, my brave girl, did what you always do and tackled the situation head-on. No one could ask for more than that.'

'They've got kids,' Zara said. She sat back, pulling the doona around her. 'Who will get in contact with them?'

'Their local police would have notified them.'

'Will they come here?'

Jack raised one shoulder. 'Who knows? Sometimes families want to see where it happened, sometimes they don't. Depends on the ones left behind.'

Zara nodded slowly. 'What happens to … uh …' She looked down at the fingers which were stroking the edge of the doona for comfort. 'To their bodies.'

As a reporter, Zara knew all of this but he understood she needed him to tell her about the process and that Jayne and Barry were going to be well cared for.

'The funeral director came out after you left and we finished processing the scene and picked them up. Jayne and Barry will be at the funeral home now. After that, it's up to the family.' Leaning in, he kissed her. 'Right now, they are being cared for by the people who look after the deceased the best.'

'Well, that's that then.' Her fists clenched around the doona. Then she let go. 'Actually it's not. Did that connie tell you about the bikies?'

'Bikies?' Jack turned to look at her.

'Yeah, there was a group of them that rode past, I don't know, maybe ten minutes before the accident. They would have had to have passed Barry and Jayne. Not that they could've caused it. That was Barry's godawful driving, swaying all over the road. Then the truck …' Her voice faded.

'Did you put that in your statement?'

'Yeah.'

'Good.'

'Did you give them the GPS?'

'Yeah, that's all been documented.'

'Don't you think that's weird? A GPS on a caravan. I mean I could understand if it was on the ute, but …'

Jack leaned forward and kissed her, stopping her words.

'It must have been tracking the van …' she said around his lips.

'Shh.'

Jack put a finger over her lips, set his drink down and took off his shoes. He put his arms around her and held her as tightly as he could, hoping this would be the end of it.

'I want to understand why this happened.'

'Sometimes, there aren't answers. Accidents are called that for a reason, honey.'

The mind was powerful, and Zara was clever, quick and kind-hearted. She'd been through much trauma already in her life so he knew there was no way the accident or her questions would be buried easily.

CHAPTER ELEVEN

The sound of loud, mechanical buzzing made Zara open her eyes. They were crusty from sleep and crying, and the dull thud of a headache confirmed what she already knew. She had a hangover.

There had been a few tears last night. Some had been from sadness and others from anger. *Why do women always cry when they're angry?* she'd wondered.

In the deep of the night, when the alcohol had started to wear off, she'd tossed and turned.

Memories of the accident, yes, thoughts of her mum as she set off in her caravan, yes, but also Aiden's furious face as he'd accused Jack of lying to him. In the blur of the shock, Zara could still remember the wildness in the cop's eyes.

The heaviness in Jack's shoulders when he'd walked through the door – that hadn't been all about the accident. That had been to do with the decision they'd made, after her fuck-up in court.

'Shut up,' she muttered as the engine noise outside became louder. A lawnmower most likely. Pulling a pillow over her head and groaning, she reached out for Jack's side of the bed but found it was empty. Zara tried to stop her mind from replaying the slow-motion footage of the vehicles rolling, rolling, then sliding across the dirt and into the tree.

She tried not to remember the explosion of debris that rose into the air like a flock of birds and scattered across the land. Mirrors, lights, glass, pieces of the van. Despite her efforts to repress it, the noise and horror of the accident flooded through her body. She tossed the pillow onto the floor and swung her legs to the side of the bed and sat there, running her hands through her hair. The green glow of her watch hands told her it was eight thirty in the morning.

'Shit, I'm late.'

Throwing the curtains open, she found herself staring at a man dressed in high-vis orange, a yellow hard hat and protection glasses. Grass was flying up in a small tornado as he ran a whipper snipper along the edge of the kerbing. He looked up and gave Zara a wave.

'Oh god!' She clutched her hand to her braless chest and yanked the curtain back into place.

In the bathroom, she turned on the taps and listened to the water gurgle down the drain before putting her hand under the spray for a second. Goose bumps spread over her skin.

'Come on,' she told the water, frustrated that it was taking so long. Leaving the stream running, Zara headed for the kitchen, flicked on the kettle and saw a piece of paper on the bench with Jack's writing scrawled across it.

I've rung the paper. You don't have to go in today if you don't want to. Don't be a hero. Stay home and eat crap if you need to. Love you. See you tonight. Xxx

God, she hoped Jack still did love her. What chaos she'd created with only a few words in that courtroom.

Zara held the note to her chest for a couple of breaths until she remembered the shower was still running. She raced back to the bathroom tearing her T-shirt off as she went.

Underneath the hot spray, she scrubbed at her face and her arms. Her limbs felt like they had yesterday: crusty with dried blood, dirty with soil and leaf litter.

When she'd washed after the accident, the dirt and blood had mingled on the shower floor, combined, until Zara couldn't tell the difference. Red blood and red dirt had become one until they had circled the drain and disappeared. Just as the light in Jayne's eyes had.

Holding out her arms now, she turned them in different directions, searching for any spot of blood or smear of dirt that had been missed during her frantic scouring the previous day.

Her skin was white and freckled as normal. All that remained from yesterday were the dried scratches and cuts she'd sustained from the shattered glass and sticks as she'd run through the bush.

No one could possibly know that barely twenty-four hours before she'd been holding a dying woman's hand. And lying to her.

Lady Macbeth kept washing her hands, trying to get rid of blood that wasn't there, she thought. *Come on, you're being dramatic as usual. Keep busy.*

Busy.

Reaching out around the shower glass, she took the whiteboard marker she kept next to her toothbrush and wrote *Road toll* on the mirror.

How many had died this year? Was it up or down on last year? Were the roads worse, driving skills lacking, people hurrying? What was the root cause of road accidents and, therefore, deaths?

Zara massaged shampoo through her hair.

'Yes!' she whispered to herself. 'An article on road deaths. Interviews with the people left behind. I could pitch that to TV as well as radio.'

She rinsed out the suds, letting her thoughts percolate.

Turning off the shower, she stepped out and grabbed her towel. Catching her own eyes in the mirror, she watched herself, trying to see into her own soul.

'Jayne doesn't need to have died in vain,' she told her eyes. 'You can make a difference. That's what you do, tell stories, bring things to people's attention. That is who you are, Zara. Do your job. You've got an extra reason now. Maybe you can save someone else's life by writing about the road toll or at least make some noise about the appalling mobile coverage.'

Pep talk done, she walked through the house. With the remote, she flicked on the TV and made sure the twenty-four-hour news channel was on so she could get up-to-date with what had happened overnight. Finally, she made a coffee and settled at the kitchen table.

The lawn outside was covered in ice.

'Jack Frost has been to visit,' her mother used to say when Zara and her brother, Will, had been children. 'Run outside and leave your footprints!'

Images of the last night Will had been alive ran rampant in her memory. Lying in his childhood bedroom, unable to get out of bed without help. Her mum waking her to say Will had taken his last breath. Her mum tooting the horn as she and her new partner, the doctor who had cared for Will, drove out of the farm driveway for the last time.

The man telling her Jayne had gone.

Zara had to get her mind busy to forget, and her body moving so she could function.

If she didn't feel or stop, just focused on work, she would be okay.

You've been here before, she reminded herself as she got dressed for the office. *After Will, after Dad. Come on, keep busy, think about something else and you'll get through. Ring the Department of Transport. Major Crash Unit. Is there one in Perth?*

As she was about to wash her cup and lock the house, a sweeping breeze came through the open window and tossed Jack's note onto the floor. Zara picked it up and read it again.

Don't be a hero.

A pause as she digested the words, but then she shook her head.

Work was definitely where she needed to be.

—

The office was only four blocks away and Zara counted her steps as she walked, her hands jammed into her pockets and chin tucked into the scarf wrapped tightly around her neck.

'Fifty-two, fifty-three, fifty-four, fifty ...' Her mind went blank as to what number she was on. She started again. 'One, two, three ...'

Then she was pulling the door open into the office and smiling as broadly as she could at Kimberly who was on the front desk.

'Heard about yesterday,' Kimberly said, not returning the smile. 'Didn't expect to see you this morning.'

Zara's foot caught on the mat. 'Oh.' Her mobile phone vibrated in her pocket. 'Thanks.' What was she thanking the testy Kimberly for? 'Sorry, have to take this.'

'Boss wants to see you ASAP. Now that you're here.'

Sighing, she put the phone back in her pocket. 'Sure, thanks.'

Inside the newsroom, Zara walked with her head high, ignoring the other journalists at their desks who still turned away from her. Except for Joanna, the young journo who was in her first year of a cadetship. She gave her a quick smile.

Her return expression was tight and worried, and Zara remembered with a jolt about the swirling rumours of closure. Not before she'd written her piece on road safety, she hoped.

Changing direction, she walked over to Joanna's desk, which was in the corner, away from the others.

'Hey, you okay, Jo?' Zara asked putting her bag on the edge of the desk. 'You look a bit … anxious.'

Jo looked around, then leaned forward. 'I think the paper is really shutting down. Have you heard anything?'

Fishing back into her pocket, Zara found her phone and tapped on the email icon. She scanned the inbox for any correspondence from HR or her editor. 'No, not a word. How did you hear that?'

'Bruce was on the phone when I got here. I don't think he saw me come in. I was always told eavesdroppers never hear anything good about themselves.'

Jo looked so downcast, Zara felt sorry for her. Huffing a small laugh, she gave Jo a rueful smile. 'Newsrooms are like colanders,' she said. 'Very leaky.'

'What will all of us do if it shuts?'

'I hope you've been keeping your eyes open and applying for other jobs. You're not really getting the benefit of any mentoring here. There are better places to do a cadetship. Trust me.'

Zara indicated to the tired, washed-out walls that weren't white anymore, old filing cabinets lining the wall and filthy windows looking out over Hannan Street. The door into the lunchroom revealed unwashed mugs and dirty benchtops, while the archive room, which she had checked out on her first day, was a dust-filled, chaotic mess with past papers tossed in haphazardly.

There was even an obligatory dead indoor plant on the windowsill.

Jo could never have the same excitement and experience Zara had had working under Lachie as a newbie.

'What are you going to work on?' Jo asked. 'Should I still be doing what Bruce told me to?'

'I'd be looking for another job, if I were you,' Zara told her bluntly. 'Oh, hang on, I've had an idea. Let me ring someone and …' She turned away, and looked at the missed call on her phone – it was from Liz.

Liz would be sitting at her desk with her feet up until another journalist or editor came along and pushed them off. Her laptop would be on her lap, defying the frenetic working pace of a newsroom.

'Zara!' Her friend answered on the first ring. 'How are you? How are things?'

'Fine. Quiet but fine.'

'Quiet? What do you mean? Newspaper offices are never quiet. They're supposed to be loud and raucous. There's always people yelling. God, can you hear Lachie in the background?' Liz didn't wait for an answer. 'TVs blaring, keyboards tapping. The bloody editors telling us something isn't good enough. What's wrong with yours?' Finally, she took a breath.

'It's broken,' Zara answered. 'Well, maybe that's not strictly true. Perhaps I bring down the tone.'

'What? Don't be ridiculous.'

'It's deserved and you know it.'

'Zara.' Liz's tone held a warning not to go there.

In the silence of the newsroom she wanted to admit she'd expected this treatment. Would it make any difference to her colleagues whether they were in Kalgoorlie or back in Adelaide, if she told them how she'd tried to word her answer differently when she'd been in the witness box, but the pressure and fiery accusations from the lawyer had tripped her up.

Then she wanted to issue a challenge to them: see how you fair under such conditions.

'Look, you want to hear my honest thoughts?' Liz didn't give Zara a chance to answer. 'You're better off where you are, even if they're all giving you the cold shoulder. Over here, well, you know how catty this joint can be, and people are still talking about what happened. They're calling it the "Zara Effect".' Liz sighed. 'Sorry to be the one to tell you. Truly, you're better off not seeing this stuff.'

Zara swallowed hard, trying to dislodge the lump in her throat. All the journalists in that building had been her friends. Or so she'd thought.

'I want to talk to you about something else,' Zara said, needing to change the subject.

'Hmm, what's that?'

'Have you heard of any cadetships going?'

'Why?'

'One of my colleagues here is doing hers and there are better places for her to be. Rumour has it this newspaper is going down and I'd like to help her find another spot.'

'So many questions right there,' Liz said. 'What's her experience?'

'I'll put her on to you.'

Before Liz could respond, Zara explained to Jo who Liz was and gave the phone to her.

'Give it your best shot,' she said.

At her desk, she pulled out her laptop and opened it, waiting for emails to download.

Not long ago, she'd have got twenty or thirty emails overnight. Sources giving her information, other journalists asking her advice, people she had written stories on. Now she'd be lucky if there were ten and most of them were news subscriptions.

'It's a pretty slow news day here in Kalgoorlie,' she said brightly to her new editor, Bruce, as he walked up to her desk and slammed down a piece of paper. 'Sorry, I was just coming to find you.'

'You can cover this,' he growled.

'Please and thank you,' Zara said, turning over the sheet. 'This looks interesting.' She scanned the page and slumped. 'A media release from the No Mines party. Well, that should be a riveting interview. Cheers, Bruce.'

'Give it your best shot,' he said and walked away.

Zara's eyes narrowed as she followed Bruce's path. Was this repetition of her words his way of telling her he'd overheard her conversation with Liz?

She shrugged, not caring. He was the worst editor she'd ever worked for.

Bruce went into his office and shut the door.

'No Mines, in a mining town?'

'I can't tell you how much irony there is in this town,' Jo said as she handed Zara's phone back to her.

'Very true,' Zara replied, putting her laptop back into her briefcase, along with the media release. 'How'd you go?'

Jo's face broke into a smile. 'You really didn't have to do that.' She took a breath. 'Liz is going to ask around and give me a call tonight.'

'You won't get anyone better than Liz. Keep her on your side. Now you'd better get back to whatever you're supposed to be doing. Good luck!' Zara walked towards the door.

'Where are you going?' Bruce yelled from the doorway.

The atmosphere in the newsroom dropped a few degrees and Zara realised she had two options. One was to respond like a young, inexperienced journalist and not stand up to him, or two, set an example and show Jo that no one needed to take shit from anyone.

Slowly she turned around. The room was silent except for Bruce who was now standing in the doorway to his office. A rotund man, wearing a dirty green open-neck shirt with jeans and thongs. It was freezing and he was wearing thongs. To work.

Her gaze slid around the room.

'I'm going to find a story,' she said.

Jo had disappeared back to her tiny corner, where she was invisible to everyone.

One of the other journalists looked up, his face war weary, but a vague interest in his eyes.

'I just gave you one,' Bruce said.

Zara cocked her head to one side. 'You don't want me to go and interview this woman at her office?'

'Ring her up. You don't need to see her face to face. Why spend money on fuel or coffee to do an interview with her?'

'Sure, no worries. Why would I want her to trust me or open up so in time she might give me a scoop? Can't make that happen if I'm talking to her on the phone.'

Bruce sniggered. 'Darl, this is a political candidate who's running for a position in the federal government. One she's not going to win. She won't be making too many friends with her No Mines party in a town that lives on mining. Let's not go making more out of this than what there is, alright?'

The war-weary journalist dropped his eyes and moved his mouse around to wake his screen. Jo peered out from around the corner, her face a mixture of horror and glee.

Zara wanted to scream. Bruce needed to wake himself up. Find the stories. Interesting ones, ones that people cared about. Shit, he could interview her on what happened yesterday! They were the stories that sold newspapers.

Bruce could save this paper single-handedly if he wanted to.

'Guess I won't know unless I go and eyeball this woman. I've always found the personal touch is the only way to get the best out of someone.' She paused and then added: 'Darl.'

CHAPTER TWELVE

Heavy frost had greeted Jack three hours ago, when he'd walked out of his house to his car. Ice on the grass, on the windscreen of his car. He'd even slipped on a light layer of it on the road.

The sky was still dark, with a smudge of deep blue and crimson on the horizon that told him the sun would rise in minutes. The station was only four blocks away, so he had decided to walk, even though it was frosty.

A clear head and fresh outlook would be worthwhile. And hopefully Aiden would have calmed down overnight.

In the short time he'd been in Kalgoorlie Jack had learned that the streets were abandoned at this time of the morning. The mines collected their employees in buses between 4 and 5 am and the streets were filled with utes and buses and the coffee line was long. Later, at about eight thirty, the streets would once again fill with people, as the above-ground working day got going.

It would take Jack a few months to understand the rhythm of the town, but he'd get there.

His steps clipped the bitumen as he walked briskly, thinking about some of the things Sally had told him last night, while he finished up the last of the paperwork. The young constable's friendly face had been a relief after Aiden's cold shoulder and she'd been keen to share some of her observations of Kal.

Kal. People said it like it was a woman's name. Jack had heard both Martin and Aiden call the town by the same nickname, but it had felt strange when he'd tried to use it – as if he hadn't been here long enough.

'You wait until tomorrow, Jack,' Sally had said. 'It's supposed to be the first frost of winter. You won't know what's hit you!'

But he did know. The frigid mornings were not unusual in inland Australia, and he was certainly used to them after living in the Flinders Ranges for many years.

It wasn't any different here – the dry, cold air turned his breath into white puffs. It made his nose run and turn red, and he had to keep his hands deep in his pockets so he didn't get that burning-cold feeling.

There were a few stragglers outside the station when he arrived. People being let out of the cells from the night before; police officers finishing their shift.

Jack nodded to a face he didn't know and followed the officer in uniform inside, grateful as the heating hit his face. Cupping his hands to his lips he blew and the man next to him laughed.

'This isn't cold yet, mate. Wait until about August when there's clear night after clear night! Sunny days but nights colder than a roomful of ex-wives.'

Jack barked out surprised laughter. 'That sounds … icy.'

'You betcha. I'm JP.' He held out his hand. 'Guessing you're the new bloke. Heard there was a bit of a stir last night.'

Jack nodded and shook JP's hand. 'Unfortunately.'

'Well, you can't say you haven't had a welcome to Kalgoorlie Police Station. Coffee? Through here.' JP nodded and walked in the direction of the lunchroom.

'What's on the go today?' Jack asked, keeping up with JP's long strides.

'Who knows. We'll get our briefing shortly. One thing I can tell you is there's always something happening. Not a night goes by when there isn't an incident we have to follow up on the next day. Morning, fellas. You all met Jack? New kid on the block.'

A cluster of officers at the coffee machine looked around. Aiden was in the middle of them. He nodded good morning. Jack eyed him warily, trying to work out how the day might unfold. Aiden gave him little.

There were murmurs from the rest of the blokes, some still bleary-eyed, their hands wrapped around warm mugs.

'Here we go again, fellas, we've got a big day today,' Martin told them as he came into the room. 'Couple of drug busts overnight and the late-night boys caught some young blokes leaving a premises that wasn't theirs. We've got five in the lockup.'

He issued instructions to the four other two-officer teams and then turned to Aiden and Jack.

'You two can get in the patrol car and run some vehicle and rego checks and keep an eye on speeding vehicles. Head west on the highway, okay?' He eyed both men, giving them a warning. *Don't fuck around.*

'No trouble, boss,' Jack said, while Aiden nodded.

Outside, Jack could've sworn the temperature had dipped even further than when he'd arrived. Vapour trailed out of the exhaust pipe as Aiden started the car and slammed his door, all without speaking.

Heaving a sigh, Jack got in and stared straight ahead.

Neither man moved and Aiden didn't put the car into gear. He kept his hands on the steering wheel.

Jack followed his lead and stayed silent.

A few moments later, Aiden pulled out of the parking lot and started to drive towards the western highway.

Jack rubbed his eyes. The shift was going to be a long one.

On the outskirts of Kal, without discussion, Aiden pulled into a car park where there was a coffee van and hopped out. It was surrounded by people and Aiden slapped a couple of blokes on the back as he walked by.

The baristas joked with him while he gave his order and then he walked away to speak to some other men standing under some trees, leaving Jack to put his own order in and pay for both.

Jack got the message; this was Aiden's town and he was liked and respected.

'You new?' the barista asked.

'Sure am,' he told her. 'Jack.'

'I'll remember,' she said, giving him a swift smile before handing over the cups.

Jack turned and assessed the crowd of people. High-vis shirts, pants with reflector bands across the legs. Beards, tattoos, hair pulled back into manbuns and ponytails.

Did Kalgoorlie even have a hairdresser? The town could do with one from what he saw. It would be hard to tell the hardcore bikies from a law-abiding citizen in this group.

He could hear Aiden was talking about the horse races that had been on the previous weekend. One heavily tattooed, well-muscled man told Aiden to 'Be good, and if you can't be good, don't get caught.' They all laughed.

'Hey, Boof, do you know my footy jumper number?' Aiden asked.

The man frowned, but before he had a chance to answer, Aiden spoke again. 'If you don't, you'll know it well enough by the time Saturday's game's over. You're gonna be watching my back while I'm kicking all the goals.'

'In your dreams,' the man replied, with a laugh.

Jack was starting to get an idea of what a blokey world Kalgoorlie was.

If Zara had heard the comments he had, she would burst a blood vessel.

They hopped back in the car and kept driving. Aiden had the speed control set on a hundred and ten kilometres an hour. Steady driving, which Jack was relieved about, after Aiden had driven away from the coffee van with a shriek of tyres.

Their coffee cups were empty, and the radio announcer was telling them that the temperature in Kalgoorlie was only one degree and without any cloud cover so the minimum temperature wasn't going to get any warmer overnight.

Mining trucks, utes and cars whooshed by in the opposite direction. Not one had been speeding when Jack checked the display screen of the radar gun.

'Have you done some driving education?' he asked Aiden. 'Not going to top up the brass's bank balance the way we're going this morning.'

'Nothing more than usual,' Aiden answered, the end of his words clipped. 'Daily patrols help more than education. Drivers know they're going to see us on the road.'

'South Australian police were stepping up their patrols as I left,' Jack replied. 'Oh, though this bloke is in trouble,' he said as a motorbike passed them. 'One thirty.'

Aiden didn't answer. He checked his mirrors and slowed, as Jack hit the lights.

The U-turn was sharp and fast, throwing Jack against the door. He held his tongue as Aiden floored the accelerator.

Checking the speedo, Jack saw they were doing one thirty, then one forty, yet the bike remained out of sight. Too fast for coppers, even if they were on a chase. They were only allowed to go one hundred and thirty, tops.

'Call it?' he asked, when the needle reached one fifty.

Aiden lifted his foot just as a motorbike appeared, driving in the opposite direction.

'Did he turn around?' Jack asked. 'Is that him?'

'These bastards play all sorts of games. Did you get the numberplate?'

'Nah.'

As they slowed, Jack checked the bike for a numberplate while the rider casually lifted the middle finger in greeting.

'Bastards,' Aiden said. 'I should just pull him over.'

'No point in exciting the natives,' Jack said. 'He's dead on one hundred.'

'Get a licence check.'

Jack lifted the radio handset and asked for a numberplate check. While they waited, a blue Ram ute and caravan pulled out from a parking bay.

The vehicle made Jack think of the crash yesterday and Zara hunched over in the passenger's seat of the mine ute afterwards. Her eyes full of pain and grief, and how she'd clutched at his hand.

Clearing his throat, he rubbed his hands along his trousers. A habit he realised he had created since he'd been back in uniform.

'Clear.' The radio operator's voice broke into his thoughts. Jack signed off. Nothing to be done to the rider. His thoughts returned to Zara.

She had been curled in a ball, asleep, when he'd left this morning. She was so much more fragile than she ever let on. Many years had passed since he'd seen her in that position. Not since the months after Will's death, as she'd grieved her brother.

'Any word about yesterday's accident?' Jack asked, needing to change up his thoughts.

'Only that forensics were going through the wreck. Haven't heard anything about the lockbox. Probably won't. Not our gig anymore. The dees have taken it over, like they should have in the first place.'

Jack stared straight ahead, then turned quickly in his seat. 'Mate, if you've got a problem, which clearly you do, how about we have it out now? I can't work alongside you if you're not going to talk to me.'

Jack knew his words had hit the mark because Aiden's knuckles tightened around the steering wheel.

They drove on a few more kilometres.

After another car drove by, his partner turned briefly towards him and then back to the road. 'Look, I'm sorry about yesterday. Shouldn't have said the stuff I did. I was out of line. Got a bit of stuff going on, but that shouldn't matter.'

'Forget it,' Jack said. 'It was a pity I didn't get to let you know about Zara earlier, but the timing hadn't been right.' Jack went quiet. 'Gotta say, it was a fair shock to find her at that accident. Shit, I didn't even know she was out of town! Anyhow, don't think I hadn't mentioned it because Zara's job's a secret. Country towns don't work like that, last time

I looked. Everyone knows everyone, so there'd be no point trying to hide her career choice.'

'Yeah, I get it. Guess I was … surprised that an officer would even think about teaming up with a journo, but you can't control who you fall in love with. I just don't like them.' Aiden looked uncomfortable and moved to change the subject, but Jack had more questions.

'Did you get burned by a journo at some stage?'

Aiden's glance slid over to Jack then straight back on the road. 'Why lie down with dogs when you could get fleas?' he finally replied.

Jack took a sharp breath. 'Meaning?'

'You're setting yourself up. If there's a leak, everyone is always going to be looking at you. I don't get why you'd do that.' Aiden gave a snort. 'Most police stations can be like leaky boats. Some time or another, a piece of information gets out into the public when it shouldn't. Anyway, your reputation is squeaky clean.' Aiden paused, his eyes sliding to Jack again, then back to the road. 'I checked.' Another silence to let that sink in. 'But if I was Martin and something got out of my station, you'd be the first officer I looked at.'

'Fair call. Surely, though, my reputation and my previous conduct and performance would speak for itself.'

Aiden looked at Jack for longer this time.

'People's circumstances change, though. Something might've happened to make a person want or need to leak information. The rewards might be greater than they can resist. I've seen it happen before with officers I've worked with.'

Jack raised his eyebrows. 'That's true,' he said slowly. He turned in his seat and regarded Aiden as he drove. 'Not sure if you know why I came to Kal, but I'll tell you in case it makes a difference. Zara was reassigned over here. We didn't want to be apart, so I decided to come too. The only way I could stay in the police was to go back into uniform. It's a step down from where I was, but I was happy to do it for her. Policing is important to me, and hopefully I've proved that by taking the demotion.'

Aiden flicked on his blinker and cruised off the road.

For a second, Jack wondered if his partner was going to get out and flog him, but Aiden turned and held out his hand.

'Reckon we got off on the wrong foot. Sorry 'bout that. All good?'

'All good.' Jack shook Aiden's hand, relief sweeping through him.

—

'Jack! Jack, over here.'

People were milling around at the back of the station when Jack and Aiden walked in after their speed checks. Jack looked around for the voice.

'There,' Aiden said with a nod towards Martin's office. 'Looks like the big fella wants you.' He clapped Jack's back. 'Good luck. See you afterwards.'

For a second, fear skittered through Jack. He'd taken Aiden's change of direction on face value, but now the boss was calling for him. Clenching his jaw and hoping he hadn't been taken for a fool, Jack reluctantly headed for Martin's office.

'Morning again,' he said, standing tall in front of Martin.

'Ah, Jack. Come in, come in, I've got someone I want you to meet.' He ushered Jack inside and motioned to a detective standing in the office.

'Jack, this is Detective Jett Black. And skip all the jokes about his name, he's heard them before.' Martin sat down behind his desk and indicated for the other two men to take a seat.

Jack felt a laugh start in his throat, but he swallowed it quickly. Instead, he offered his hand.

Jett held out his own. 'It's a typical Australian opposite joke. I was born with white-blond hair and a mop of it apparently,' he said.

Jack sat and rubbed his hands over his pants. Then cursed himself. He had to stop that.

'I've unexpectedly found I need another detective,' Jett began. 'ASAP. No time to fly anyone in and there's no one available anyhow. Martin told me you've just started so I've spoken to your old colleagues in South Australia. Seems you're a thorough and highly regarded detective.'

Jack gave a sharp nod.

'Now, Martin tells me why you've come to Kalgoorlie, and I have to be upfront and tell you that your relationship is a concern, but –' Jett's feet jiggled up and down '– I'm not able to let that affect my decision. We are damn short on detectives.'

Martin leaned forward and stared Jack down. 'Normally I wouldn't let you go straight into the detectives, but given the current issues on your team, I think a few weeks there might help cool things down.'

Straightening, Jack looked directly at Martin. He should tell him that Aiden and he had put their differences to rest this morning.

'Well, what do you want to do, Jack? Stay here or go over to the dees?'

'If the opportunity is there, I'd love to take it.'

Does a bear shit in the woods?

'Right.' Martin nodded to Jett.

'The vehicle accident yesterday has raised some issues,' Jett said. 'I know one of the witnesses to the accident, Zara Ellison, gave you some material that was consistent with the caravan cladding, which had a GPS attached. I'm told she found it on the ground. Half buried?' He looked at Jack expectantly.

'That is correct. And I should mention that Zara is my partner.'

'I'm aware. You also found a lockbox under the chassis of the caravan.'

'That's also correct.'

'On further inspection we found another identical box attached underneath the front of the van. Both boxes had a GPS inside. From further forensic examination of the van, we suspect the GPS your partner found was attached to the outside of the roof so it must've peeled off when the accident occurred. There's paint stuck to the device which matches the caravan.'

The words hung in the air and Jack felt the bubble of excitement he felt at the start of every case. The first time he had experienced it was when he'd gone undercover during a case involving an animal activist. The feeling was addictive, even to a methodical dee like him.

'That's strange there are so many GPS units in such a small area,' Jack said. 'Do you have any idea why?'

'Clearly someone really needed to know where that caravan was.' Jett referred to his notes and then leaned forward, closer to Jack. 'Obviously it was imperative we found out what was inside those lockboxes. Might have been something normal, like a spare set of keys to the caravan. But we're usually a bit more suspicious and naturally the first thing we assumed was drugs.' He cocked his head giving Jack the opportunity to respond.

'That would be my assumption too.' If he was being tested, Jack would give them the answers they were looking for.

'Well, we busted them open and there weren't any drugs inside.'

Jack frowned. He quickly thought back to the moment Martin introduced him to the detective. He hadn't told him which squad Black was with. Jack leaned forward. 'What was in there?'

'Gold. Two bars. One in each lockbox, each weighing in at around five hundred grams. Together, one kilo.' Jett looked from Martin to Jack. 'Worth about one million dollars on today's market.'

CHAPTER THIRTEEN

The moment she was out of the newspaper office and back on the main street, Zara took a few deep breaths, then stomped towards the nearest cafe, fuming. Where did that jerk get off speaking to her like that. Speaking to *anyone* like that.

Bruce was such a cliché.

An invisible red mist of anger was blurring her thoughts so much that at first she didn't hear her name being called.

'Zara! Zara!'

She stopped and looked behind her. Jo was jogging down the street, a grin on her face.

'OMG, you were awesome back there. Someone should have cut Bruce down to size ages ago. He's a—'

'Wanker,' Zara supplied.

'Yeah.'

'Tell me something, Jo. It's so weird here – no one seems to get off their bum and chase a story. That's what we were taught to do as cadets. If it was a slow news day, we'd go and find something to put in the paper. There are some great stories out here. I got put on to an incredible woman who lives out in the bush by herself and mines her own land. My god, the stories she could tell. I'm going to go back and interview her again. Why aren't the rest of you doing that?'

'Oh, wow, who is she? Isn't it dangerous for her being there by herself?'

'She's got the security side of things sorted,' Zara said dryly, remembering the pistol pressed to her back. 'I can't be sure but it doesn't sound like she's ever had a partner, romantic or otherwise. She's just lived out there alone looking for gold since 1986.'

'Woah, how old is she?'

'She's one of those women who could be forty or seventy. Ageless. But I think she's around sixty. I want to get to know her more. I reckon she's sitting on a wealth of stories. I might even be able to get one of the TV channels interested in her.'

Zara's steps started to bounce at the thought. She imagined sitting around the fire, talking to Ted, while a cameraman filmed. Flames reflecting in her eyes. She might even be able to find a love story gone wrong that then goes right, because everyone loves a happy ending.

Her mind buzzed with ideas. Then she remembered Jo was keeping up with her step by step.

'Being at *The Prospector* is so different,' she told her young colleague. 'That's why you'd be better off somewhere else.'

'I like Kal, though,' Jo said, spreading her arm out at the main street. 'Did you know these were designed to allow the camel trains to turn around in the early years of mining.' Giving a self-conscious smile, Jo lowered her voice. 'Can't you just hear the clank of the chains from the camel trains and the clip-clop and whinnying of the horses as they drew out bucketfuls of dirt, looking for that prize of gold? Life back then must've been so difficult.'

Zara saw passion for the first time on the young woman's face and stopped to look around, trying to see what Jo saw.

On the day Zara and Jack had arrived, they had wandered up and down the streets, getting to know their new home. Majestic, two-storey pubs, the town hall and a golden dome on the top of the clock tower, which sat above the courthouse.

The streets whispered of history; tragic and tough lives.

Gold. Just like on the dome that was glinting at her now. Gold plated ... in real gold!

'It doesn't feel like a city,' Jo continued. 'Although it is officially one because of the number of people who live here. It's not sleepy. The weekends are full of things to do. It's family-orientated despite the single-man vibe it likes to give out. Don't you *feel* it?'

Zara smiled at Jo's enthusiasm. The young woman reminded her of herself, when she'd first started working. The thirst for stories had been insatiable.

'I feel it.' She pointed to a sign that hung from a wooden rafter, holding up a verandah. 'Geez, I haven't seen a pawn shop in years! There'll be some stories in there for sure.'

A couple of First Nations people crossed the road, their dog pulling on its lead. Three purple scooters were parked underneath a pub verandah and a young boy was bent over one, reading the instructions.

'Have you been on the brothel tour?' Jo asked. 'Sooo interesting.'

'How is it there's prostitutes here making sure the men are looked after,' Zara responded, 'but I haven't managed to find a gigolo for the ladies who work on the mines. That's the irony of Kal, you mentioned before. There are loads of women working on the mines here.'

Jo stopped and gasped. 'Maybe that's my next career, since it looks like I won't have a job in a few days. Running a brothel for women.'

Instead of finding her comments funny, Zara's stomach turned as she remembered the humiliation of the courtroom again. She took a breath and kept her tone light, to match the conversation.

'Nah, the women have more business sense than that, Jo. They'll go to the pub and pick up there. Or get on Tinder. Either way, they won't have to pay. See, women have the brains.'

'Yeah, you're probably right,' Jo said, deflating slightly. 'I guess the brothel is only catering for the blokes who can't pick up women in the pub.'

'That brings me to my next question. Have you been in here?' Zara asked pointing at the pawn shop.

'Ha, you're funny. I don't think he sells X-rated vids.'

'Why would he? They're available online for free.' Zara laughed. 'This industry is a pretty resilient one. Bit like libraries, they've had to revamp themselves to move with the times. So, have you been in here?'

'Nope.'

'Why not? The sign says he buys and sells gold.' Zara noted down the name, address and telephone number, then cupped her hands and peered in through the glass.

The interior of the shop was dark and gloomy, but she could see a silver tea set inside a cabinet towards the back of the shop.

'Bruce has never suggested it,' Jo said, 'but I get what you're saying about finding stories.'

A white ute with an orange light and two aerials on the bull bar pulled in on a sharp angle and a woman in high-vis and sturdy boots got out. She locked the door, nodded to Zara and Jo and went into the chemist.

'Zara,' Jo was suddenly serious. 'Have you heard of other papers being shut down?'

Zara huffed and moved on down the street, trying to keep warm. 'That's been going on for years. Especially after Covid. News available online. Not a large-enough readership or not selling enough copies to pay the journos' wages. *Darl* should have been talking with you all about the possibility of a closure if that's the case.' Zara grinned remembering her earlier sassiness. 'Oops, I meant Bruce, our editor.' His name brought a scowl to her brow, and she kept up a brisk pace. Bruce's unprofessionalism was in-your-face and because of that she didn't trust him.

A cold breeze skittered a bunch of leaves down the path as a ute and caravan pulled up, taking over seven parking bays. Zara gave it a cursory glance, checking for her mum, even though she was in another state, then did a double take.

The van was black and grey outside with two spare tyres attached to the back. Orange trim. It looked exactly like the one Barry and Jayne had been towing yesterday, but then she saw the sign on the back of the van: Carol and Jim, channel 32.

'Zara? What's up?'

'Huh?' She put her head down and started to walk. 'Oh, nothing.'

'Doesn't look like nothing.'

That pulled her up. She stopped so quickly that Jo, who'd been trying to catch up, bumped into her back. Zara swivelled on her heels, back towards the caravanners.

A car door slammed, and a short woman with curly grey hair got out. A man appeared from the driver's side and stood next to her and they both looked around as if they weren't sure what to do next.

Zara continued to walk towards them, a smile fixed on her face.

'Good morning,' she said, in friendly passing. 'Cold one, today.'

'Hello love.' The woman answered. 'Can you tell us where the best coffee is? I always think it's best to get recommendations from the locals.'

The woman's smile was warm, and Zara realised an opportunity had landed in her lap.

'I'm Zara,' she said. 'And this is Jo. We were just on our way to get a coffee, weren't we, Jo. You can come with us if you like?'

'How wonderful. I'm Carol and this is Jim.'

'Lead the way,' Jim told her in a jovial tone.

'Where have you come from today?' Zara asked.

'Gwalia,' Carol said. 'We were supposed to be here last night but ended up camped on the side of the road because the road was closed.'

'Oh,' the word left Zara's lips involuntarily.

'Have you heard anything about it?' Carol asked, as they walked in through the doors of the cafe and were hit with a blast of warm air. 'We had friends we were supposed to meet up with here, but we haven't been able to reach them. We were worried they might have got caught up in the road closures too.'

'That's better,' Jim said rubbing his hands together. 'Coffee, love?'

'Please. What about you girls?'

Jo put in her coffee order and gave him Zara's order too.

Carol sat down and looked expectantly at Zara and Jo. Her smile dropped when she saw Zara's face. 'Are you alright, pet?'

Zara shook her head. 'Yeah, thanks. I was first on scene at that accident and it was a bit of a shock.'

'Oh, you poor love.' Carol looked over at Jim, who was ordering at the counter, and seemed to wrestle with her thoughts. When she spoke again her voice was tentative. 'Do you know who they were?'

Zara swallowed. 'A couple called Barry and Jayne. Did you know—'

'Nooo!' Carol's face drained of colour. 'Jim, it was them!' She half stood then sat down.

Jim was putting his wallet back into his jeans pocket and looked over at her words. 'Who?'

'Barry and Jayne. They were in the accident.'

Jim darted back to their table. 'What? Are you sure?'

'Their names were on the back of a van just like yours,' Zara told him.

Jim reached his hand over to grab Carol's. 'Ah shite.' A dawning on his face. 'Oh, those poor buggers.' He was silent and Carol's eyes watered.

A waitress arrived with four coffees and put them down, oblivious to the emotions circling the table. 'Anything else?'

No one answered. She looked from one face to another and left.

Carol and Jim were staring at each other, shock etched in their expressions. After a minute, she put her hand to her chest. 'I knew it,' Carol said heavily. 'I had a feeling. Somehow, I had a feeling it was them.'

'You knew Jayne and Barry?' Zara asked.

'Not well, but we'd crisscrossed at some camp sites,' Jim said, slipping his arm around Carol.

'I couldn't get Jayne to answer her mobile when I phoned,' Carol began. There was a pause. 'She was lovely.' She picked up her coffee and took a sip, hands shaking slightly.

Two people entered the cafe and Zara glanced up as they walked to the counter.

'Jack!' she called out. Motioning him over, she tried to smile.

'Zara. Hi, honey. Are you okay?' He put his hand on her shoulder, and she covered it with hers.

'This is, um, Carol and Jim. They knew Jayne and Barry. From the accident yesterday. And this is Jo, from the paper.'

'Sorry for your loss,' Jack said to Carol and Jim. His eyes flicked from the couple to Zara. 'Gosh, that's a bit of a coincidence for you to run into each other.' His eyes checked hers for an explanation.

She stared back and squeezed his hand. 'Fate.'

Jack gave Jo a short nod, then turned his attention back to the couple. 'Did you know Barry and Jayne well?'

Jim repeated what he'd told Zara.

'I think they'd been on the road for a few months,' Carol added. 'Jayne told me Barry had wanted to spend a couple of years travelling around Australia, but it sounded like he wasn't enjoying it as much as he had expected to.'

A woman joined them, holding two takeaway cups of coffee. She held one out to Jack.

'Thanks Kirsty,' Jack said. 'Kirsty, this is my partner, Zara.'

The cop held out her hand. 'Nice to meet you.' She looked like she wanted to ask more, but her gaze went to the others sitting at the table and she closed her mouth. There would be time later.

Zara turned her attention back to Carol and Jim, something tugging in her mind.

'So Jayne and Barry were doing the big lap?' Jack asked, pulling up a chair and sitting down. 'They didn't have any set place to be?'

'Barry was desperate to get to Kalgoorlie yesterday,' Jim said. 'He was going to be here come hell or high water.'

'Any reason?'

'Yeah, he wanted to watch a footy game,' Jim replied.

'Did he like prospecting?'

Zara narrowed her eyes at Jack's question and sat a little straighter.

'Prospecting?' Carol replied, and gave a humourless laugh. 'Barry wasn't into anything that was uncomfortable. Being outside meant it would be cold, and there would be flies and dust.'

'Not even the pull of gold could get him out there?' Jack gave a friendly smile.

'Not on your nellie,' she said.

'Funny,' Kirsty said. 'So many caravanners have metal detectors on board. Do you guys like to have a bit of a swing?'

Carol blinked. 'Ah ...' She glanced at Jim. 'Swing? As in ...'

Zara snorted with laughter, while Jack flushed.

'Swing, prospecting. They use that word because the detector swings across the ground.'

'Oh.' Carol looked like she wanted to laugh but the seriousness of the discussion wouldn't let her.

Jim had taken a large gulp of coffee. 'Oh no,' he said. 'We are on the road for the pure pleasure of travel and seeing places we haven't been before. Nothing else.'

Zara saw Kirsty exchange a look with Jack. He gave her a small nod.

'Carol, Jim, I'm a detective and we're looking into yesterday's crash,' he said. 'It's quite fortuitous that we've run into you because we've actually got some questions about Jayne and Barry. I wonder if you wouldn't mind answering a few for us at the station?'

Zara held her breath, then glanced over at Jo to see if she'd picked up anything strange. Her colleague was taking a sip of her coffee.

'What do we need to come to the station for?' Jim was asking.

'We always look into road crashes,' Jack answered.

No, you don't, Zara thought. *And when did you become a detective again?*

CHAPTER FOURTEEN

'Did you notice Jack's questions?' Zara asked Jo when the others had left the cafe. 'There's something going on.'

'I noticed something, but I wasn't sure what it was,' Jo said. 'Do police usually put the Gold Squad on a car crash?'

Zara's head snapped around. 'Gold Squad?'

'Yeah. Kirsty plays netball with me. She's in the Gold Squad.'

'And Jack was asking about prospecting,' Zara said, the adrenalin of a story starting to bubble in her stomach. 'Okay, let's think about this.' She explained to Jo about the GPS. 'That's unusual, right? Most people would get a GPS on their car but not on a van, which must mean they were more interested in what's in the van than the car.'

Jo's eyes began to sparkle. 'Do you think the detectives found gold somewhere they shouldn't?'

Zara smiled at her excitement. 'I'd say that's exactly what they found, but there's no way they'd confirm that if we asked. We better find out who Jayne and Barry really were and then see if we can get Carol and Jim to talk to us too.' She picked up her cup and drained it, screwing up her nose as the cold coffee hit her tongue. 'But first, I need to go and interview Janelle from the No Mines party. Do you know anyone in the coppers other than Kirsty?'

'A few of the younger ones,' Jo said. 'Don't know them well, though.'

'Would they answer any of your questions about the accident yesterday?'

'Ha, do coppers ever answer enquiries from journalists?'

'Let's grab a couple of coffees and we'll see if we can bribe our way into getting the police to talk to us.' Zara nodded her head towards the counter, then brought out her phone.

—

'I'm ready to commit bribery and corruption,' Jo said holding two cups of takeaway coffee.

'Right,' Zara said, pocketing her phone. 'Let's give it a go!'

She led the way outside. 'Do you want to interview Janelle Salter with me after we've done this?' she asked as they waited for the lights to change to walk.

'I can't,' Jo said. 'I've got a doctor's appointment. Do you know it takes six weeks to get seen by a GP in Kal?'

'See, there you are. Another story. There aren't enough doctors in rural areas. Okay, I'll interview Janelle and we can meet back at the office later.'

They'd reached the sliding doors of the police station now and went inside. Zara touched Jo's arm and nodded to her. Jo took a deep breath and went over to the constable on the desk, fixing her most winning smile to her face.

'Is Sally around?' she asked.

The constable pushed his glasses down his nose. 'If you're looking for anything to do with the newspaper, you've got to go to Media Relations,' he told her.

Jo held up the coffee and wiggled it. 'I've brought her a coffee. You know what it's like out here in the bush. You should always bring something when you're going to catch up with someone.'

Good play! Jo's tone implied Sally had asked for one. And everyone knew cops lived on adrenalin and caffeine.

The constable fixed Jo with a look and slowly picked up the phone, lowering his voice so they couldn't catch his words.

Letting her breath out, Zara watched as Jo placed the two coffees on the counter and waited.

A sneer spread over the constable's face as he put the phone down. 'Seems Sally didn't know about your catch-up. She's out.' He put his elbows on the desk and leaned his chin on them. 'Media Relations, okay?'

Jo smiled and held up the extra cup to him. 'Here, this might help brighten your day.'

'I don't take carrots,' he answered and turned back to his computer.

'Thanks anyway.' Jo picked up the cups.

Zara fell into step next to her as they left. 'Good try,' she encouraged. 'I'll go find Janelle and I'll see you back at the office. Oh, can I take Sally's coffee?'

'Sure.' Jo swivelled on her heel and walked towards the newspaper car park.

Coffee in hand, Zara continued towards the main street. The pawn shop was calling to her again. She couldn't walk by this time.

As she pushed open the door, an angry voice reached her.

'I'm a good customer,' a man said loudly. He was standing at the counter, fingers wrapped around the Perspex security screen that shielded the pawnbroker from the public.

Above Zara, the small brass bell had tinkled, alerting the man to her presence.

He whipped around and gave her a stare before turning back towards the small man behind the counter, and continued to yell. 'You should be treating me with a lot more respect! Your offer is too low. I know that. You know that.'

The high-vis reflector band around his shirt flashed in Zara's eyes as she slid in behind the first lot of shelving.

'I understand you're disappointed,' the pawnbroker said, 'but, mate, there's nothing more I can do. Your watch isn't worth what you think it is.'

'You're right,' the man growled. 'It's worth much more.'

Zara shifted herself behind a shelf where neither man could see her and inspected the goods on display. The silver teapot she'd seen earlier had an eye-watering price tag attached to the handle and next to it were some gold-rimmed white teacups, saucers and cake plates. They were from a different time and only someone with a keen interest would be seduced by them.

'I'm happy to up it by fifty dollars to *buy* the watch, mate, but it won't be a loan. You'd have to buy it back, it'll be a sale. You understand what I'm saying?' The man behind the Perspex screen made his voice a little louder, as if he thought the customer was hard of hearing or a little dense.

'Ah, you're full of shit.'

The pawnbroker shrugged and turned his attention from his customer to a computer screen.

There was a loud, frustrated groan and the clattering of boots on wooden floorboards and then the bell rang again.

The angry man disappeared outside, shoving his hand in his pocket as he went.

Whether he was putting the money in there or he'd snatched back the watch, Zara couldn't tell.

She turned her attention to another glass display cabinet and looked at the watches and jewellery inside. Nestled against plush maroon and deep sapphire-blue padding, rings studded with diamonds and gemstones, mostly set in gold, twinkled alongside necklaces.

Another cabinet held coins, and towards the back of the shop were larger, more unusual items. A guitar caught Zara's attention, and she walked over to it. Running her fingers over the soft, velvety maple wood, she was transfixed. A long time ago, in another life, she'd played the guitar. If she placed her fingers on the neck or fretboard, would they remember the strings and frets?

This was a beautiful instrument, worth a lot of money. No one would have given this instrument up without a very good reason. Running her thumb over the strings, she wished she knew why the owner had not yet come back for it. Every object in here had a story. Next to it was a hand-carved wooden chess set. Someone had spent a lot of time carving those pieces with so much love.

The bell tinkled again, and Zara peeped over the top of the shelves. Two police officers in uniform.

She ducked back behind the shelves. From where she was standing, they wouldn't be able to see her, but she could hear them.

'What can I do for you, fellas?' The pawnbroker didn't sound pleased to see them.

'G'day, Percy, run off your feet today, I see?' There was a certain amount of sarcasm in the woman's tone.

'Always busy. Too busy for you lot, for sure.'

'Ah, come on now, we're happy to see you.'

Percy didn't answer, but Zara heard heavy thumping. She wanted to peer over the crammed shelves again but didn't risk it. Sometimes loitering and listening were the best ways to find things out.

'Percy, we need to talk,' the female voice said.

'We're breaking up? I can't tell you how happy I am. I hope you'll have a wonderful life.'

'Look, we've been in before to ask you nicely. We understand you're new to town and things would have been done differently in Sydney, but, mate, you've got to work with us. Buying stolen jewellery isn't doing that.'

'Stolen jewellery? I don't know what you're talking about?'

'Really?' The woman sounded bored now.

'If someone comes in with a piece, I'll either loan 'em money against it, or buy it off them,' Percy said. 'Not my business how they come by it. I show you all my books, as required, and that proves I never break the law.'

'There's rules …' This was a male officer.

'Is there?' Percy sounded surprised, then his tone hardened. 'What did I just say?'

The shop fell silent and then Zara heard another thump – it sounded like hands hitting the counter. Her mind skittered to the man who had just left. Had his watch been stolen?

'You know what I wanna know, Percy,' the male voice continued. 'Why'd you leave Sydney? Did someone run you out of town? I can find out, you know, but it would be better

139

if you told me. How about it?' The challenge in his voice was unmistakeable and Zara made a note to follow up on Percy the pawnbroker and gold buyer from Sydney. The police officer's question was valid. What a major move, Sydney to the wild west.

'Wanted a change.' Percy's voice broke across her thoughts.

'Couldn't get more changeable than Kal.'

'Look, I don't know why you're hounding me. I do everything the law asks of me. I've been in this industry a long time and I know how it works.'

'We're doing our best to lock up all the perps who are executing the B and Es. You, my friend, are making it difficult for us because they can sell their stash in town. If you didn't accept it, they'd steal less from around here, because they'd have to go to Perth to move what their sticky fingers have taken. Now, we worked with old Terry before you. He was happy enough to not buy anything from the known crims. It's not like we don't know who they are, is it? We've already provided you a list of known, repeat offenders.'

Zara had managed to sneak herself around to the edge of a shelf, and if she tipped her head slightly, she could see Percy's face. He was still sitting down on the office chair, his arms crossed, looking unimpressed at his visitors.

'You might have, but I'm new to town as you just pointed out, so how could I know who's who at the zoo? I'm not sure I remember a list.' Now he upended his palms and gave them a sorrowful smile. 'I'm terribly sorry, officers, I don't think I can help you.'

The silence was broken only by the rustling of the police officers' uniforms as they considered their next option.

'Well, that's disappointing. We're invested in working with the community and business owners for better outcomes for the town. Shame you don't want to be a part of that.'

Percy lifted his hands and gave a few slow claps. 'Wonderful performance and toeing of the company line, officers. I'll keep it in mind next time someone comes in wanting to sell me a bracelet or ring. Okay? Was that all?'

'No, actually.' The female officer, who Zara now recognised as Sally, took her phone out of her pocket and tapped at the screen. 'Anyone brought anything like this to you, trying to sell it in, say, the last week? Or have you ever had anyone trying to sell something like this?'

Percy leaned forward and stared, then let out a long whistle, clearly impressed. 'Nice ingot,' he said.

'So have they?' she asked again.

'Let me tell you something for free,' Percy said. 'If someone walked in here with that – and from the untrained eye, the bar looks like about a five hundred grammer – I'd have to go to the bank and withdraw the cash. I don't keep that amount in the safe.'

'Is that a no?' the other constable asked.

'Take it as you will.'

'Well, we need you to let us know if something like this comes to you. Otherwise we're going to charge you with obstructing an investigation. Are you listening?'

'My ears aren't just painted on, officers.'

A battle of wills made for a long silence, until the police decided they'd had enough.

'Well, thanks for your time,' Sally said and made the universal hand signal for a phone. 'We'll be waiting for your call. We're a very friendly bunch here in Kal.'

Zara ducked down to inspect a couple of electric typewriters that were on the bottom shelf.

After the tinkling of the bell above the door had died away, she stood and fished in her pocket for her business card, took a breath and went around the shelf.

'Hi,' she said with a smile.

Percy jumped then looked towards the door. 'Where did you come from?'

'Oh, just behind the shelf over there. Do the cops always give you such a hard time?'

'Bloody pigs,' Percy grumbled. 'Always sticking their nose in. Not usually uniform, though. More the Gold Squad. They're always on my case.'

'What's the reason for them doing that?'

'Who knows? Maybe they like to think they've got a handle on every part of the town. I haven't been here long, but I know that's not the case. There are regulations about pawning or selling stolen jewellery – whatever story the seller comes up with, they seem to forget I've heard it all before. They might think they're being original, but they're not. Easy to spot stolen goods a mile off. I keep my nose clean, no matter what the cops think.' He sat up straighter in his chair. 'Anyway, enough of that. How can I help you? Are you someone who has broken and entered a house and has stolen goods for me to buy?' He looked her up and down. 'You look like you could have a bad streak about you.'

Zara laughed. 'Was the watch that the gentleman just tried to hock stolen?'

'As if I'm going to tell you.'

Her mobile phone rang. 'Excuse me,' she said and dug it out of her pocket.

Bruce.

Not a chance of her answering that.

'Sorry,' she said. 'I'm Zara. A journalist at *The Prospector*. I saw your sign and thought your shop looked intriguing. Looks like a shop of stories.'

Percy leaned back in his chair. 'A journalist? I don't talk to you lot.'

Zara cocked her head to one side. 'I hear that more than you realise,' she said. 'I'm not here to pump you for information, but I am trying to get a few public interest stories to run in the paper. Seems to me that the paper is lacking a bit of ... oomph and maybe a good fun story, or a tearjerker, will help change that.'

'Well, you'll have to do that without my assistance. Sorry. Not something I'm into.'

'Sure. If you change your mind, though, this is my card.' She slid it through the gap in the Perspex and then tapped on the screen. 'Is this because of Covid or because you have to keep safe?'

Percy stared at her. 'You're new to town, aren't you?'

'Probably newer than you,' Zara said with a smile.

'Once you've been here a while, you'll work out the answer.'

CHAPTER FIFTEEN

On the iPad screen, Barry and Jayne came to life for Gold Squad detectives Jett, Lucas, Kirsty and Jack.

Have you found anything, love? Jayne's voice from behind the camera.

Not yet, there's a lot of beeps in my headset. Barry looked up at Jayne, his face creased into a smile. *It's hard to work out which one means I've found something!*

Practice for when we get to the gold.

Hey! I reckon I've found … Barry dropped to his knees, throwing the detector aside and digging into the sand with his hands.

The vision became bumpy as Jayne ran closer. *What have you got?*

Not sure … Barry was running his fingers through the sand now. *How do you tell where it is?*

I don't know! There was laughter in Jayne's voice, and Jack imagined a smile etched into her face.

Oh, what? Barry stopped digging as his hands closed around something deep in the sand.

What is it?

Barry slumped in disappointment as his hand came into shot, holding up a bottle top.

Jayne let out a peal of laughter and her arm came into view as she put her hand on his shoulder, and everyone in the detective room was given a bird's-eye view of the sand granules in the kids play area.

There was a scratching and more wind, then they heard Jayne say: *Oh, this thing is still recording, how do I turn it—*

The video finished.

A heavy silence settled in the room.

'Well, he was trying to learn how to prospect for gold,' Jett said.

'I don't know about you,' Jack said, 'but either he's had a hell of a lot of beginner's luck or those couple of bars aren't theirs. Would they even know that they could have the gold melted down and turned into bars?'

'I doubt it,' Jett said. 'Jack and Kirsty, you can hit up some of the buyers in town. I've had uniform ask at Percy's pawn shop already. Also, you can head over to forensics and go over that ute and caravan with your own eyes. Lucas, you can get on the blower and ring around to Barry and Jayne's friends and ask a few questions. Let's get them ruled in or out ASAP.'

Jett moved to the corkboard where photos of the crash were pinned. 'Jack, we're lacking funding so our offices are a bit primitive. You'll have to get used to what we use.'

'Just like every police station I've ever been in,' Jack said, standing up. He looked over at Kirsty who was gathering her things. 'Lead the way,' he said.

They walked through the smoko room, heading towards the car park.

Aiden was standing at the coffee machine. Jack nodded to him, and inwardly sighed as Aiden made a beeline towards them.

'Back in the dees, Jack,' he said with a smile. 'Congratulations. You'll be happy there.'

'Yeah,' Jack said, slowing his stride only momentarily. 'Busy?'

'Just heading out again. What are you two up to?'

Kirsty was a few steps ahead and turned back. 'You got anything you need to tell us about that accident yesterday?'

Aiden shook his head. 'Nah, pretty standard MVA. Except for those lockboxes, I guess. You know what was in them yet?'

'Still investigating,' Jack said.

'I guess that GPS was weird, now I think about it,' Aiden said, his brow furrowed. 'Are you able to get into the information on the tracker? To see where the car has been?'

'Yeah, we're on it,' Kirsty said. 'Cheers, see you later.'

'Sure.' Aiden gave a two-fingered salute and went back to the coffee machine, his jaw moving up and down as he bit down into the ever-present chewie.

Out on the street, Jack asked: 'How many gold buyers are there in Kalgoorlie?'

'We call them dealers,' Kirsty replied. 'There's four above-board ones but we know there are others who aren't registered. Gold has a very healthy black market.'

Jack looked around and saw Zara and another woman deep in conversation, some distance away. She looked like she was coping well today, despite the shock of the accident. Her face was animated and in very Zara-like fashion her hands were flying around as quickly as her words came out.

'Over here,' Kirsty pointed to a nondescript shed at the back of the station.

Jack refocused.

'This is where the vehicle will be.' She led the way into the high-fenced yard and held the shed door open for Jack.

The ute and caravan were in the middle of the shed, bright lights angled onto the crumpled frames. Someone, suited up from head to toe in a disposable protective suit, was peering under the caravan.

'Hi Jesse,' Kirsty called out.

The figure responded by waving an iPad in a greeting.

Putting his hands behind his back, Jack inspected the wreckage from a few feet back.

'This is where the lockboxes were attached,' Jesse's muffled voice said from behind the mask. 'One fastened to the front and one closer to the back. Both boxes contained a gold bar each, along with a GPS unit.' He pointed to a spot on the axle. 'See how the paint has disappeared here – and here? The magnet has moved very slightly and rubbed the paint away.'

Jack leaned in. 'Where's the gold?'

'Locked in the safe. You want to see it?' Jesse took a step back and ripped the mask off, revealing a whiskery chin and eyes that were chocolate brown. 'Come this way.'

Jack was keen. He'd never seen a gold bar before.

After entering the code into the keypad on the safe, Jesse opened the door and pulled out two evidence bags. He handed one to Jack. 'Careful, they're—'

'Heavy,' Kirsty said, taking the other one.

Jack turned it around in his hand, looking at it through the clear packaging. 'Geez, that's a hell of a lot heavier and looks nothing like I thought it would,' he said. 'It's not even shiny.'

Jesse laughed. 'Yeah, not like the buffed, shiny jewellery in the shops, is it. This hasn't been buffed, so it's still dull, rather than having that gleam the polished rings and bracelets have.'

Dull as it was, the bar was also imperfect. It had dents and dimples in the surface of the metal and Jack was sure there was red dirt ingrained in it too. That shit got everywhere!

'This is what is called a dore bar, Jack,' Kirsty said. 'It needs further refinement before it's pure. It hasn't had the minerals and impurities refined out.'

Jack made a note.

'We had to get a jimmy bar to prise the boxes off the frame,' Jessie said. 'These babies weren't moving. Which leads me to think this isn't the first time gold has been moved like this. Perhaps they've trialled it.'

'That goes without saying,' Kirsty said, handing the bar back to him.

Taking one last look at the top and bottom, Jack handed his back too and Jesse safely stowed them back in the strong box.

'Now, the third GPS was attached to the roof of the van,' Jesse said. 'Three! So, whoever was tracking the gold was keen to know where it was at all times.'

'As would you if you were carting a million dollars around,' Jack said.

'Especially if you'd gone to the trouble of stealing it,' Jesse replied. He picked up a GPS unit from the evidence table and handed to Jack. 'Serial number is on the bottom.'

Jack pulled out his notebook and wrote down the number.

'We're going to send the gold off for DNA testing—'

'DNA?' interrupted Jack. 'You can do that with gold? How does that work?'

'I scratch off a speck from these bars and send it to a fella called Cameron Scadding. His company conducts tests to find its origin.'

'What are they testing for?'

'Analysing what content of minerals is in the gold. Once we know that, we can trace it back to other mine sites and see which it matches.'

'Each mine has different gold?' Jack asked.

'Well, different properties. For example, mines further north have more nickel in their gold than around this area, so if we find that these two bars have a high nickel content, then we'll look at some of the mines about four hundred odd kilometres north. Around the town of Leinster.'

'Do you have a data base on each mine in Western Australia?'

'Not yet,' Kirsty said. She was circling the ute, taking photos on her phone. 'That's something we're working on. You'd think it'd be easy, wouldn't you. Just grab a speck of gold from each mine, test it and Bob's your uncle. Upload everything onto the computer. I wish it was that simple.' She pointed inside the vehicle, where the dash was nearly touching the passenger's seat. 'What was in the glove box?'

'Normal stuff. Panadol, car maintenance records. That's all here.'

'And in the van?'

'I'm nearly finished in there. Nothing that has piqued my interest. They liked to read, and drink coffee. There's lots of capsules in the pantry. There's also an epi pen in both the console between the two seats in the ute and in the drawer next to the bed.'

'Okay, thanks. So, just to clarify – no more gold? Only those two bars?'

'Only those two bars, two lockboxes with heavy duty magnets attached and three GPS units.'

'Right.' Jack made another note.

'Anything else you need?' Jesse asked, as his hands went to his hood.

Jack took one last walk around, while Kirsty inspected the goods on the table.

'I reckon that's us,' she said. 'Thanks, mate.'

Jesse nodded. 'I'll let you know if I find anything of interest.'

They waved their goodbyes and headed out onto the street. Jack was immediately swishing flies away from his face, even though the day was cold. 'Bloody hell, I thought I could cope with flies after living in the Flinders Ranges, but you've got them on the next level,' he said.

'You can't go bush without a net in October. Sometimes November too. Drives us all mad,' Kirsty said. She stopped and flipped through her notebook, looking for something.

'What's up?'

'Checking my notes. Both of these bars are half a kilo, so worth approximately five hundred thousand each in the current market, right? Probably a bit more. Any sale over ten grand will trigger an alert with Austrac.'

'What's Austrac?' Jack asked, concentrating on not swallowing any flies.

'A government agency. Every transaction of ten thousand dollars and over must be reported to them. Doesn't matter if it's gold or something else. It could be ten thousand in cash made from gambling, the bookies would need to report that payout.'

'Can you make two deposits of five K each and not be reported?'

Kirsty shook her head. 'No, if a prospector went to a dealer over two different days and sold ten thousand in differing amounts, it would still trigger an alert and they would need to be informed. Doesn't necessarily mean that the ATO is going to come looking for the person. There's a loophole in the taxation office which means someone who has a hobby *without* the intention of making a profit is allowed to earn any monetary limit without paying a cent of tax.

'Austrac is different. They use any financial information that comes through to look for criminal activities. Terrorism, money laundering, organised crime, child exploitation. They do check for tax evasion. But again, if a prospector is out doing what he or she loves most in the world, trying to unearth gold, then ...' She raised a shoulder. 'But look, we take this seriously, because there are certain people in our community who have come to Kal to work and send money back to their families overseas. Sex work is something we keep a close eye on, and if gold is being stolen or mined for criminal activities then we have to check for laundering. Cash industries. We have to be sure that money isn't funding illegal activities overseas. Or here in Australia.' She pointed to a shop window emblazoned with *We buy GOLD!* 'This is the main buyer in town. There's that pawn shop on the main street, but Kendall, being off the main drag, is the one most people go to. She's honest, which is helpful. Not sure about that Percy in the pawn shop. There's something off there, but we haven't been able to pin anything on him yet. Let's go in.'

Jack nodded. 'Give me two secs,' he said, writing down *Austrac* and *10 K* in his notebook. He had certainly heard about the regulator, but he'd never had call to understand much about them.

'Right?'

'Let's do it,' Jack said, pocketing his notebook.

CHAPTER SIXTEEN

A flutter of angry butterflies battered their wings against Zara's stomach wall. Bruce had just called again and demanded she return to the office as soon as her interview with Janelle Salter was wrapped up. She could guess what this was all about.

But she couldn't focus on that right now. As she walked towards Janelle Salter's office, she glanced over the Google search results.

The No Mines Political Party was formed in 2023 when founder Janelle Salter decided that mining was a divisive and unsafe industry which needed to be halted ...

The excited feeling from the pawn shop was fading. Politics had never really been her thing. She read on.

'*We need to be brave enough to stand up to the mainstream industries, which are killing our people and land. We need to stand against these monstrous businesses. One person becomes two, then two becomes three and so on. That's how we stop this. Join me!*'

'Look out!'

Zara's head jerked up at the panicked voice to see a purple scooter tearing towards her, a young boy holding on for dear life.

'Look out,' he yelled again, his dark fringe pulled back by the drag of the wind.

'Shit!' Zara took a couple of steps to the left, the boy reefing on the handlebars to make sure he missed her. She gasped, pivoting on her heels to see him disappear around a corner.

He hadn't zoomed past with an apology or even a cheeky grin, only a look of determination on his face. Thankfully there hadn't been a yell from around the corner so she figured no one had been run over.

Zara tapped the voice memo app on her phone and recorded a note to see if the hospital would talk to her about the number of injuries caused by scooters, taking up valuable resources and the time of nurses and doctors.

The media release was still in her hand, so Zara read through Janelle Salter's biography. Love of family, hatred of mining. Grew up in Kalgoorlie, moved, came back.

'Riveting,' she muttered to herself. Still, perhaps if she dug around, there might be something interesting to find. She tapped on the voice memo app again. 'But what is the why? Why is she back in Kal, and why is she trying to shut down mining here when that's what keeps the town afloat? That's where the story will be.'

Further down the street, a sign swayed in the wind. It announced Janelle Salter's office in large white letters with a purple background. Purple was an interesting choice of colour for a political party.

'What's the why?' she whispered again. Fossicking in her handbag, she made sure she had her ID, pen and notebook.

An electronic buzzer sounded as she walked through the door and a few pamphlets fluttered under a paperweight on a low table, which also held a vase of purple flowers.

Zara bet Janelle Salter had a florist on the payroll who delivered a fresh bouquet once a week.

A framed photo of Janelle Salter was hung on the left-hand wall; her welcoming smile made Zara want to grin back, despite feeling awfully peevish that she was even in the office. *No Mines* was scrawled under the picture. The wall behind the photo was purple, but the rest of the office was painted off-white, with classic furnishings showing elegance and wealth. How unusual.

Zara's once-over of the office was interrupted by a voice that gave her a fright. She hadn't noticed anyone behind the desk in front of her.

'Can I help you?'

Another glance showed a blonde-haired woman, wearing a beige pant suit and coat. No wonder she was invisible; she blended in with the décor of the office.

Giving her practised smile, Zara walked to the desk, taking in the receptionist's name tag – Lou – pinned to her blazer. Zara was impressed; well-dressed, professional-looking employees were few and far between in Kalgoorlie. High-vis, jeans, T-shirts and steelcap boots were mostly the order of the day. To fit in, Zara had started dressing down since moving here, even though it wasn't how she liked to present herself. Still, when in Rome …

'Hello, I'm Zara from *The Prospector*,' she said to Lou. 'I'm here to speak to Janelle Salter, please.'

'Do you have an appointment?' Lou asked.

'Ah no, but I have this.' She waved the media release in the air. 'I'd like to interview Ms Salter about why she's running a No Mine campaign in … Kalgoorlie.'

'Ah, yes, thanks for showing some interest. I'll check with

Ms Salter and see if she's free sometime this afternoon,' Lou told her, fingers tapping at the keyboard. 'I might ...'

An email pinged into her inbox and Zara watched Lou's eyes flick across the screen and then back to Zara. She indicated towards the door behind her. 'You're in luck. Ms Salter will see you, but before she does, could you please sign the visitors' book.'

The door behind her desk opened and a woman, who looked nothing like the photo on the media release or the photo on the wall, stood there, hand outstretched.

'Hello, I'm Janelle, please, come through.'

Zara took her hand, giving it a firm shake and introduced herself. 'I was given your media release this morning, so I decided to walk over here and try my luck.'

'I'm glad you did. Come, sit.' She stepped back and let Zara into her office, indicating towards a plump, overstuffed chair. 'Obviously my main policy isn't popular in the Kalgoorlie electorate, so I'm not gaining a lot of traction.' She gave a soft laugh. 'Nor am I winning a lot of friends. Would you like a coffee?'

Zara sat down. The chair had no give and she wiggled to find a comfortable spot. 'Yes, I imagine that's the case. Maybe we could start with why you are even considering doing this? From my point of view, what you're trying to achieve feels like political suicide. Your media release says you want to stop all mining, yet there are, according to my research, twenty-seven active mines in the Esperance Goldfields area. Those companies must employ tens of thousands of people. I wonder how you could possibly think you'd sell your idea to the people who would lose their jobs if you were, in fact, successful.'

Janelle sat down at her desk, crossing her legs and fixing a smile to her lips. 'No coffee?'

Shaking her head, Zara waited. Her foot twitched slightly, a sure sign she was already too caffeinated.

How far she'd fallen, Zara thought as she tried to look interested in Janelle's reply. The glitz and glamour from the night of the Walkley Awards presentation, the night she'd *won*, was nowhere to be seen now.

'All true, of course,' Janelle was saying. 'But what irritates me enough to want to shut these mines down is the safety aspect. No life should ever be lost at work, and even though the losses are small, they are there. All risks need to be taken out of mining and the only way to do that —' she paused dramatically '— is to not mine.'

The only way to do that is to not mine.

The woman had a screw loose.

Zara's phone vibrated in her pocket, reminding her she hadn't asked permission to record the interview. She pulled it out and waved it around, glancing quickly at the screen, then flicking away the missed call notification. 'Are you agreeable to having this interview recorded? I like to conduct interviews with a recording to make sure I don't quote you incorrectly.'

'Of course.'

'Could you repeat your previous comment for the recording, Ms Salter?'

'All risks need to be taken out of mining and the only way to do that is to not mine.'

'Thank you. If the mining companies were able to guarantee one hundred per cent safety for their employees, would you still be opposed?'

'Of course. Because there are the other aspects as well. The damage done to the land, the harvesting of precious metals that aren't ours to harvest.'

'Whose are they?'

'Well, that's my point. They don't belong to anyone and should stay in the ground. Our government didn't bury them, gold and iron ore doesn't grow like crops, so why should anyone profit from something which occurs naturally?'

Zara sat back in the chair and looked around the office. The desk was a deep oak colour, with thick legs and top; again, money seemed to be no problem.

The bookshelf held three books: *Australia's History of Mining*, *The Goldrush in Western Australia* and a small, thin volume called *Heads and Tails: The story of the Kalgoorlie two-up school*.

A university diploma hung on the wall, proclaiming Janelle Salter had passed the University of Western Australia's Master of Fine Arts course.

Zara indicated to the framed certificate. 'Not really anything to do with mining – or politics.'

'No, it isn't.' Janelle ran a hand across her skirt, flicking something unseen from the material and looked at Zara, clearly waiting for the next question.

Taking her time, Zara formed her words with care. 'Without being disrespectful, Ms Salter, to run for parliament takes a lot of money. You only get reimbursement from the electoral commission if you receive four per cent of the first preference votes. You need an army of people to drop pamphlets, brochures. Then there's a car, fuel, money for wages ...' Zara let her silence ask the unformed question.

Janelle uncrossed and recrossed her legs.

A small smile played around Zara's mouth. *Okay, well, if that's the way you want to play it.*

'Tell me,' Zara said, leaning forward and placing the phone on the table in front of her. She kept her elbows resting on her knees. 'How do you think the hundreds of thousands of people who will be out of work, if your policies get through, are going to live? Pay their mortgages, send their kids to school? Where do you think the employment would be for those people, for the families.'

'They will find new employment. Better jobs that ensure they'll be home every night with their loved ones. They won't be living in a town that isn't family focused – and we might find that if that's the case, our society will change. Back to what it was like when you and I were growing up, Zara. When there was little family or domestic violence, when women and men, parents, were respected and children were disciplined, not allowed to run free.

'You see, our families have been eroded over the generations and the fly-in fly-out mentality has a lot to do with this, as do the big wages. More money has allowed for disposable income. Drugs, fast cars, whatever.' Janelle shook her head in disgust. 'We really need to return to the old ways to save our society. We are imploding.'

If Zara sifted through what Janelle had told her, there was sense in some of her words.

'Also, high interest rates are caused by high inflation, which is caused by spending. If the mining pay packets are reduced, spending on frivolous things and luxuries won't be as easy, so inflation will come down, as will interest rates. I'm sure you understand the theory, Zara. A woman of the world such as you are.'

Eyeing Janelle, Zara tried to work out if this woman knew something about her. If she knew about the court case and her banishment. She wanted to run but instead frowned.

'I beg to differ on the family and domestic violence,' Zara countered. 'It just wasn't talked about as much in earlier years as it is now.'

'We'll have to agree to disagree. Did you know that in 2022/23 one woman was killed every *eleven* days. Eleven! And one man was murdered every ninety-one days. That's all by intimate partners. If you can show the same statistics from the 1980s perhaps, I'd be interested to see them.'

'I don't think those sort of statistics were kept back then. So you're wanting better outcomes for families, which includes lower interest rates and fewer cases of domestic violence, and you think stopping mining will help that? Because the issues you're raising have been around since time began.'

'Of course it will help. I've just told you how.'

Zara nodded and wrote the words *family/interest rates/inflation* on her notepad, then put a ring around them.

'You wouldn't class yourself as a radical greenie?'

'A greenie, yes. Radical? No.'

'And when did you decide to run for this election?' she asked.

'This political party has been years in the making. We have expanded into the Northern Territory, Queensland and South Australia. States where mining is a big industry and have candidates being onboarded as we speak. Of course, it's a large undertaking, but we are determined to make sure people realise that mining is unhealthy for the country and community and should cease immediately.'

'I understand.' Zara nodded. 'And you decided to run – when?'

'I've wanted to do this my whole life,' Janelle told her, with a wide smile.

Her smile, Zara thought, could be wild, not wide. 'How many other candidates from your party will be contesting this election across the nation? It must be hard to attract people to your party given the sheer amount of mining in Australia and people who are employed by the industry.'

Janelle tucked one ankle behind the other. 'We'll have candidates in every state, as I said.'

'One candidate in each state? Two?'

'We're still working through that process.'

'Do you have any experience in politics, Ms Salter?'

'The best experience comes from life.'

It was Zara's turn to smile. 'That may be true, but learning on your feet in this type of game is hard work. What about a mentor? Is there someone on your team who understands this strange game of politics, who is helping you?'

'Zara, I've never been one to shy away from a challenge and what I've set out to do here is certainly that. I've researched other politicians and, from what I see, there doesn't need to be previous experience. You must believe deeply in what you are trying to achieve, and I do. Sometimes practical learning is the best learning.'

Yep, if you want to get eaten up and spat out, Zara thought. She changed tack. 'You said yourself, you're not winning many friends. Are people making their disagreements with you obvious? Have you had threats made against you?'

'Nothing we can't handle.' Janelle waved her words away with a flick of her hand. 'Look, we, I, my party, understand that what we're supporting and what we stand for will be disliked. I don't know any politician who has had the indulgence of being popular during their whole time in parliament. I'm prepared for some unpleasantness, and what has happened recently is piffle really. Nothing we weren't expecting.'

'What sort of problems have you had?'

'Oh, you know, just the normal. Eggs on the windows, nasty letters under the door. Nothing that's frightened me.'

'Have you reported them to the police? Surely that's harassment?'

'It's under control.'

'Right.' Again, Zara quickly changed tack. 'Yesterday I was on the Goldfields Highway and witnessed a car accident. There wasn't any mobile phone coverage out there and we had to wait until another passerby arrived, one with a two-way, to be able to call a mine for help, and get them to call the emergency services. My question, do you think that's good enough in 2025?'

Janelle leaned forward and reached out her hand as if to touch Zara, then seemed to think better of it. 'I'm so sorry you went through that.'

Zara impatiently shook her head. Sympathy wasn't required here. 'Do you think that is good enough for 2025?'

'Of course not. I wasn't aware there was such a problem. I can look into that for you and see if there are any telcos who plan to put up mobile phone towers in that area. Tell Lou exactly where the area is when you leave.'

'What action can you take?'

'As soon as I'm elected I can raise it in parliament. Look, we know here in regional, rural and remote areas that telecommunications are vital—'

'Did you know that mines help fund some of these towers?' Zara asked.

Janelle seemed to stumble. 'As I said, I can ask questions, but I don't have the information at my fingertips.'

'If there weren't any mines, perhaps there would be even less coverage than there is now.'

'That may be so, but I can't help but wonder if they would even be needed if there weren't any mines in such isolated areas.'

'The couple who died yesterday were tourists. Needing help from the mines. This area, as you would know, is really popular with tourists during the wildflower season. Tourists still need coverage.'

'I'll certainly do some research on this issue and get back to you.'

The wind-up was obvious.

Zara's phone vibrated on the table.

Bruce. Again.

She ignored it and looked up at Janelle. 'I'll look forward to reporting what you find out.'

'Absolutely. Now, Zara –' Janelle flashed another smile '– if you could just let everyone know I'm here. My door is open and I'm not going anywhere and if anyone has any issues they'd like to bring to me that fit in with my ethics and vision, I'm happy to take them on board.'

'Thanks for seeing me.' Zara snapped her notebook shut and grabbed her phone. 'I'll let you get back to your day. Hopefully this will be in next week's newspaper.'

In the front office she gave the required information to Lou and signed out, then stepped out into the cold air. It was a relief after the stuffiness of Janelle's office. How could someone work in an office that didn't have windows?

Looking towards the newspaper office, Zara prepared herself for Bruce.

CHAPTER SEVENTEEN

Kendall was nothing like Jack had expected. Although to be truthful he didn't really know what to expect anywhere he went in Kalgoorlie. It was a place everyone could be themselves without judgement. A fella could walk down the street in a high-vis tutu and no one would turn a hair.

The woman behind the counter would have been seventy, if not older. Her long hair was dyed purple and swept up in a knot on top of her head. Her jeans were bright red and her shirt matched her hair. Jack didn't miss the long gold earrings and gold-rimmed glasses. He wondered if the gold was real.

'Hi Kendall,' Kirsty said, walking to the counter.

Following his partner, Jack assessed the plain room. Wooden floorboards that creaked as he walked, a simple counter and a TV on the wall with outstretched, galloping horses on the screen, jockeys whipping their rumps. TAB signs and white posts.

'Officers.' Kendall didn't move from her seat behind the counter. Smiling pleasantly, her eyes darted from the TV screen to their faces. Jack clocked her curiosity towards him.

'How's business?' Kirsty asked. 'Got to use these lately?' She touched the old-style scales and made them wiggle up and down.

'I should smack your hands,' Kendall told her mildly. 'Where are your manners? Introduce me to your friend.'

Kirsty did the honours.

'I had a mate who lived in Adelaide, a long time ago,' Kendall said. 'Nice town and he was a lovely man, but he liked the roulette tables more than me, so I had to fuck him off.'

Jack's mouth twitched. 'Sorry to hear that,' he said.

Kendall adjusted her glasses. 'Well, his loss. Now, how can I help you? I'm sure you're not here on a social visit.'

Leaning her hip against the counter, Kirsty crossed her arms and looked Kendall in the eye. 'We're following something big, Kendall,' she told the older woman. 'Have you had anyone come in recently looking to sell a bar?'

'A bar? How big?'

'Well, in the proximity of five hundred grams and up.'

'Any prospector would be stupid to bring a bar that big to me. They should be selling it in the pure form. Wouldn't raise as many eyebrows that way. Nah, just wouldn't happen.'

'Hmm, we're thinking they aren't prospectors.' Kirsty straightened up again and glanced at the TV, then back again, while Jack continued to check out the shop. He couldn't find one thing to ask a question about, except the scales.

'These are amazing,' he told Kendall. 'Have they been restored?'

Kirsty frowned at him. Jack had interrupted her flow.

Kendall smiled. 'These were my great-grandfather's. He had a lease about fifty kays east of here. Did alright, until he got put away for murder.' Her whisky-rough voice faded away.

The black frame, which held up the brass weighing plates by linked chain, was polished and the long needle, which pointed to the weight, was shiny.

'Murder?' Jack asked.

'He didn't mean to kill the poor bastard. Got time to hear the story?'

Kirsty casually looked towards Jack and gave a wink, telling him she'd heard the story a few times before.

'I do,' Jack said.

'Well, Great-granddad, he'd found a few good nuggets, and they were burning a hole in his pocket, so he decided to saddle up his horse, which was as old as he was. He wanted to get into Kalgoorlie to cash in. Was only about five mile out when a drunk miner ran onto the road, trying to wave him down.

'Granddad wasn't stopping for no one with his loot, so he kicked the horse into a bit of a gallop, but then another bloke came out of the bush, and another, so Granddad reckons they're after his gold, right? He lets fly with a few rounds. Everyone always carried a pistol back then. Got one of the blokes fair and square in the chest.' She heaved a theatrical sigh, which Jack knew she'd done many times before and he wasn't convinced the story she was telling was completely factual.

'Anyhow, he did time and when he got out, he cashed in the last few nuggets he had stashed away and bought these scales. To him, they represented hope. And let me tell you, if a gold miner doesn't have hope, he or she doesn't have anything.'

Jack touched the scales. 'Did he find much after he got out?'

'Nah, nothing,' Kendall said. 'He was too old. A few months later, they found him down one of the shafts, dead. Must've had a heart attack or something down there. He was half decomposed, so they couldn't tell much.'

'That's a hell of a weighty story for a set of scales,' Jack said.

Kirsty looked at him, her top lip curled slightly. 'That wasn't even funny,' she said.

Jack gave a one-shoulder shrug and looked back to Kendall. 'Do you use them to weigh the gold you buy?'

Kendall reached under the counter and brought out a set of digital scales and plonked them on the top. 'Nothing romantic about these. Don't get me wrong, Granddad's weigh perfectly, and I sometimes use them as a second opinion or just for a bit of show, but everyone can read the screen easily on these and can see I'm not diddling them. More's the pity. I love these – and Granddad was right, they are hope. Everyone is crossing their fingers their gold weighs more than they think, when they walk through that door.' She put the digital scales away and looked at Kirsty. 'Anyhow, you didn't come to talk about scales. You came to talk about gold bars, so talk away.'

'You hear about that car accident yesterday?' Kirsty asked.

'The one up north? Yeah, bad business that. Gee, I feel sorry for the families.'

'Well, we found two large bars in the van.'

Kendall pursed her lips, her eyebrows lifting skywards. 'That's not a casual prospector,' she said.

'What makes you say that?' Jack asked.

Throwing him a pitying look, she gave a sorrowful smile. 'Ah you really are green, aren't you? Well, in all my years around here, casual prospectors don't find a million dollars' worth of gold in a few hours. You'd have to go at it all day every day for years and years. Then you might be lucky enough. Then there's the breakdowns and fuel, that always costs money. The days of finding a million bucks lying on top of the ground have gone.'

'What if you're wrong?' Jack challenged.

'I'm not,' Kendall told him. 'Back a hundred years ago, before the joint had been pillaged, sure.' She put her hands on her hips and leaned forward. 'If there was that type of gold lying around out there, we'd be more overrun than we already are.'

'Who has this type of gold?' Kirsty asked.

'Reckon you'd be looking at someone who's pulling it off a mine site.'

'Stealing?' Jack replied.

'Mate, you're exceptionally quick for a detective,' Kendall told him.

'Have you heard about any of that going on?'

Kendall crossed her arms and gave a laugh. 'Love, this is Kalgoorlie. What do you think? Everyone who works on a mine would be tempted at some point. Not like there's much security on the sites. I know that many people who've walked out with flakes in their lunch box or dust in their cigarette packet. Come on!'

'Not much security?'

'Nah, got me beat why they don't install some of the metal scanner thingies like they have at the airport, but, no, they just put cameras in the gold pour rooms and forget to clean the lens, along with relying on the security checks.' She leaned forward. 'If you wanted to take some, it's really not that hard. And you,' she turned to Kirsty, 'your lot know that, but you just don't seem to be able to do anything about it.'

CHAPTER EIGHTEEN

Ted pulled up the backhoe at the edge of the pit and shifted the levers forward and back, digging deeply into the dirt with the five-tine ripper. The engine groaned as it struck rock and skittered up and sideways, trying to avoid the obstruction.

Reefing on the hydraulic lever, she lifted the tines from deep within the earth and whirled the machine around to dig out a couple more bucketfuls of dirt.

The mounds would be ready for processing through the wet plant tomorrow, when she was ready to get started.

She turned off the loud, rattling machine and looked at the gouged pile. Wouldn't hurt to run the detector over that and see if there was any alluvial gold. An easy find to finish off the day.

'Thank god for that,' she muttered, ripping the earmuffs off her head and rubbing where they had been sitting most of the day. She stretched, then let her body sag and relax like a rag doll.

In the unpleasantly springy seat, she took a moment to let herself adjust to the silence and stillness. After hours with the engine roaring, she was always left with a high-pitched ringing inside her head and her hands feeling as if they were still holding the buzzing levers. Her back was as tight as a drum and the rest of her body felt as if the machine was still running, vibrating through her.

She grabbed the water bottle at her feet and unscrewed the lid. The cold moisture on her lips and in her throat was sheer bliss; the cab in the backhoe wasn't air conditioned or heated and it didn't matter how cool it was outside, the windows heated up the cab to an uncomfortable temperature. Still, she had to be thankful for a cab with windows because the first machine she'd owned hadn't had them at all.

Instead of using the steps, Ted jumped down, landing on heavy, damp soil. When her feet thudded into the ground it sounded deep and hollow.

Underneath could well be hollow, she thought; the mineshafts were dug straight down, deep into the ground, while the tunnels stretched out like catacombs winding under the earth. There were many no one knew existed. Not unless a present-day miner found them in their own search for the elusive reef of gold.

At the front of the machine, the pile of dirt was as tall as Ted, times two.

'So, what have we got in here,' she said aloud.

She walked around, occasionally bending down to assess the soil, burying her hand in it and letting it trickle through her fingers.

This was normally when Zero would stick his nose under her arm and push his boofhead through, looking for a pat.

Even three months after his death, Ted still braced her body, expecting his cold nose and hot breath on her skin. Some prick – the shire council or some government department – had laid dog baits and Zero had picked one up when they'd been out walking.

No warning, no notice, nothing to let them know there had been a baiting program. If there had been, she wouldn't have let Zero follow her free range, as he had done for all of his life.

Ted wanted to weep again as she remembered her friend taking his last agitated and painful breath in her arms. Then the awful job of digging his grave. She still visited it every week, sat under the large gum tree and talked to him.

She'd gone there yesterday afternoon and told Zero about the journalist who'd arrived unannounced that morning.

'God, you should have seen her face, Zero, it was priceless. These chicks from the city, they've got no idea.' Ted had been sitting cross-legged in the dirt, scratching at the surface with a stick as she'd talked to him. 'Still, I think that woman might have a bit more nous than most. She seems a bit more worldly and at home in the bush. Can you believe Vince sent her? Stupid old bastard. Fancy sending her out here, he knows better. Not like I go looking for company. People – just by being human – cause drama and I'm not into drama or problems. I like a peaceful life and I thought Vince understood.'

The bush had spoken back to her then.

A strong wind had lifted her hair and the leaves of the tree, as a Southern Boobook owl called its two-note cry, sounding more like a frog than an owl. A lazy, laid-back noise.

Boo-book. Boo-book.

Until there was danger and then it was a fast *bo-bo-bo-boook!*

Their hoot had always made Zero howl.

Zero's blue eyes and white and grey coat had set him apart from any other dog that might have wandered into her camp.

His howl would rival a dingo's or even the Nullarbor Nymph's, if you believed in her.

His size and ferocious bark had been enough to deter any unwanted visitors. She liked her security out here. Needed it.

She cleared her throat a few times and pushed Zero from her mind. There were things to do.

Reaching into the troopy, she pulled out her flynet and put it on.

Flies could carry you away out here, Vince used to say.

This year, they seemed worse than normal. Or maybe they just forgot from year to year how awful they were.

She hooked the Minelab detector onto her arm, before swinging the base over the pile of earth. The scanner's notification system stayed silent as she methodically checked the surface area of the dirt. The familiar hope and anticipation that always sat in her body faded with the lengthening silence.

Suddenly a series of low-pitched squeals blasted through the air and turned to high-pitched shrieks. Ted moved the detector back over the dirt, back and forth, back and forth.

Squeal, squelch, shriek. Silence as she overshot the mark.

There was enough of a sound there to think there could be a small nugget of gold. Unhooking the small trowel from her belt, she knelt, carefully shovelling through the dirt. A few scoops later, she passed the detector over what she'd pulled out from the pile.

No noise.

'It's still in there,' she told herself quietly, concentrating hard.

The sun had slipped behind the range and the dusk light was beginning to swallow the landscape now, the long shadows from the hills making it darker than it should have been at this time of the day, and the temperature had plummeted. Ted grabbed her woollen hat out of her back pocket and switched her head torch on.

Shovel, check, shovel, check.

Finally, there was a loud squelch from what Ted had shovelled to the side. Only then did she allow a small smile.

'It's out.' Out of the pile or dirt or whatever ... That was the miner's language. Gold was either still in the ground or out where they could get at it.

Even if it didn't turn out to be a nugget, there was a satisfaction in narrowing down the huge pile of earth to a small shovel-load.

Searching for a needle in a haystack was easier than trying to find gold in among all the millions of hectares out here in the middle of Western Australia. Along with all the cast-aside horseshoes, lost coins, bullet shells, pieces of wire and every other tiny thing that would set a detector off!

Carefully, she trowelled the dirt into a sieve. Soft showers of soil hit the ground. Each time the filter emptied, Ted put in a few more trowelfuls. Sift, trowel, sift, trowel.

'What have we got here?'

A small lump, covered in mud, lay in the bottom of the screen.

With filthy fingers, she picked it up and examined it. 'See, now this is why I don't get excited,' she told herself. She switched off the detector and stood up with a groan, stretching her back out again.

'Well, that's it. I'm calling it for today.' She dropped the crushed bullet shell into a container in the back of the troopy. 'Wonder if I'll ever get too old for this?' Looking skyward, she saw a cloud floating along in the wind. 'What will happen to me then?'

Ted often spoke out loud to herself. Just to make sure her voice still worked, and words were remembered.

First sign of going mad, Vince had said once, when he'd come to visit, *talking to yourself.*

You'd know, she'd tossed back quickly and pushed down her embarrassment.

Maybe she'd been out here by herself too long.

Not that she would ever change it now.

Ted slowly drove back to the caravan, through the trees, bushes and other diggings she'd done over the years. Really, she must've been a termite in another life, because the piles that had been dug and filled back in could have looked like the ant hill mounds that you'd find driving into Onslow in the north of the state or scattered throughout the national parks.

A glimmer of discontentment flickered through her as she thought about her tenement. There really wasn't much left unturned after being out here since '86. Might be time to drag out the map and reassess where she was looking. Perhaps there was some more country that she could peg when a lease came due. No one knew, including Ted, how much gold she'd found over the thirty-nine years, but her last statement said her balance was seven point six million. A high percentage of that had been found in the first ten years.

Even with rising costs, she assumed that much would see her out. Might even be a bit of change left over. She guessed the people she would leave that excess to would grab it before she was even cold in her grave.

Eighty-six? How had time gone so fast? Surely it was only a few months ago she'd lit her fire for the first time.

Every morning since, Ted had got up, made sure the fire was crackling and had a cup of tea. Made her breakfast *and* her bed – there was a lot to be said for doing that one chore, even if you didn't manage to do anything else for the day. Threw together a bit of lunch and headed out to search.

Every evening, she stoked the fire to life, had a cup of tea, made a snack and either listened to the radio, read a book or, depending on how bad the midges and mozzies were, watched the stars.

Her routine rarely varied. Perhaps that's how come the days disappeared so quickly.

Only when her cupboards ran out of food and her library books were due back would she make the long trip into Kal. That was only once every couple of months and more than enough for her.

Unless someone lived in mostly silence, as she did, it would be hard to understand how the noises of a town – even a quiet one like Kal – bounced around inside her head, her body. How they reached a crescendo by the end of the day, making her crave nothing but the crackle of the fire, the screeches of the galahs. Even the buzz of a mozzie would be better to hear than the horn of a car or shout from a kid on the street.

And the smells, well, some of them she didn't even recognise these days. Not since the fast-food chains had come to town. Never once, not even at Vince's insistence, had she eaten a piece of food from *those* restaurants.

The supermarket, the library and the bank were the only places she called in to. Oh, and perhaps Vince's place, if they were talking at the time.

During a visit to the bank, the manager, Donna, had told her the safe deposit boxes inside that particular bank were the last ones operating in Australia.

'Make sure you keep paying the yearly fee, Ted,' she'd said in her Canadian accent. 'Don't want whatever goodies you have in there to go to the government, do you?'

'Not on your nellie,' Ted had answered as she slipped another nugget into the box while Donna had her back turned.

That had been three years ago.

Three years since she'd found a decent amount of gold. It wasn't ideal, but it wasn't the end of the world. Ted owned the lease on the tenement, her cost of living was minute, although fuel prices were certainly going up. And there was enough to buy more land if she wanted.

Things, really, were pretty good. Especially with those seven big ones in her bank account.

Back at the caravan, Ted threw a few sticks on the fire and watched with satisfaction as flames sprang to life. She lugged the largest billy can she owned (and could lift) – the one she boiled her bath water in – over the coals and put it on to heat.

While she was waiting, she turned on the battery-operated radio and listened to the news. Boat people in the north; China roughing up ships in the South China Sea. She turned it off again. History repeating itself. What was the point in spoiling the evening's peace?

She poured a few bucketfuls of cold water into a steel tub and sat on the ground, waiting for the billy to boil. Normally she would be feeding Zero and getting dinner ready, but tonight, she wanted to sit and think and feel.

'Eighty-six, huh?' she said to the closest tree. 'That's a long time to be out here.' How old did that make her then? So long ago, she'd stopped counting the years, the decades, because if she did then she'd have to remember all the anniversaries that came and went. The birthdays, the deaths. Her losses were too great.

Steam rose from the billy on the fire.

A cup of Epsom salts later and she was stripping off her sweat-soaked shirt and jeans and lowering her aching body into the warm water. A contented sigh slipped from her lips before they lifted in a smile.

Tipping her head back she looked at the stars that were starting to peek through the twilight sky. Thin wisps of cloud streaked the sky, turned pink by the setting sun. Different from the day before when the heavy, mottled grey had blocked out the sun and blue.

People – or so advertising told her – paid big dollars to have a bath under the open sky like this.

That gave her a good belly laugh. She doubted they'd like to do it for more than a couple of days in a row.

She reached into the water and scooped some up in her hand, dribbling it behind her neck. She pulled out the hair band holding her hair in a ponytail and slid down in the tub.

The tub was half the size of a normal bath, so she hung her legs over the edge as she lathered her hair, then rinsed it and slid back to sitting on her bum.

The fire crackled alongside her, but the cold air was beginning to nip at the exposed parts of her skin.

Flapping her hands around her ears, she shooed away the mosquito that was making its presence known.

Except, as the water from her hand splashed over her, she realised it wasn't a mozzie.

It was a different sound.

Not one she knew.

She froze and listened hard.

Grabbing a towel hanging over the back of her chair, she stepped out of the tub onto a wooden pallet. Best way to not get her feet muddy.

She pulled on her dirty jeans, shirt and jacket, then dried between her toes and put on her socks. Boots, beanie and pistol. She walked further from the fire, on high alert.

Four years before, when the world was beginning to open again after Covid and the WA premier wouldn't let anyone in or out of the state, people had come to the Goldfields in droves, driving over and camping on lease tenements. Leaving their rubbish behind and sometimes even vandalising the permanent shacks where miners lived. Trespassing, caring little for the locals.

Zero had been handy when that had been going on, his growl enough to stop any trespasser in their tracks. She wished he was by her side now.

The resident Boobook owl gave a few hoots and, from a long way away, another answered. It was a comforting, recognisable sound.

Not like this electric whirring behind her. Ted swung around. The country was crowded with trees and bushes. Scrubland. Impenetrable.

Ted's fear often turned into anger. Her emotions had worked that way since she was a small girl. Fear turned to anger, and anger became fury.

Fury was what she was feeling now.

This was Ted's tenement, and she knew her land's symphony.

Just like she recognised the landscape, every dip, hollow tree and bush. This was her home.

The buzzing was a constant drone. Continuing above, behind and circling around her. Far enough away that Ted felt it didn't know she was there.

Unease and apprehension swirled through her stomach. What the hell was it?

Ted took up a position underneath a heavily leafed tree, scanning the sky.

She cocked her gun.

CHAPTER NINETEEN

Zara stomped down the street, heading back to the office. Bruce's phone calls had changed to text messages, demanding to know when she would be back in the office.

Ten minutes, had been her reply.

Further up the block, Percy came out of the pawn shop and looked up and down the street before stretching out his back. He looked as tired and pissed off as she was.

A slow smile spread across her face, and she raised her hand in greeting. There was more than one way to skin a cat, she thought.

He caught her eye and his expression didn't change, except he hunched his shoulders and went back inside, shutting the door tightly.

Being nice to someone when they're not nice to you only confuses them. Something her mum would have said. *Try it and see what happens.*

Walking inside the cafe, she asked the young girl behind the counter what Percy's favourite drink was.

'I'm not sure,' she answered, then turned and yelled over her shoulder. 'Nellie, what's Percy normally order?'

Nellie came out wiping her hands on a tea towel. She smiled at Zara, but there was a question on her face.

'I'm Zara, and you're ...'

'Nellie. Welcome. I saw you in here this morning.' Her smile was like a sunflower and Zara instantly liked her.

'Only this morning? Seems like days ago,' Zara said. 'You make great coffee, by the way.'

Nellie grinned. 'Thank you,' she said. 'Percy?'

'I thought I might take him a cuppa. He looks a bit fraught.'

'He's a cantankerous old bastard, that's what he is,' Nellie said affectionately. A glance to the clock showed it was nearly five. 'Take him a large hot chocolate. It's too early for a whiskey and too late for a coffee. Reckon hot choccy's your safest bet.' She gave Zara a sidelong glance. 'You softening him up for something?'

'Just being nice,' Zara said with a wink.

'Don't expect too much in return,' Nellie said over the noise of the milk frother.

Takeaway cup in hand, Zara opened the door of the pawn shop, making the bell tinkle.

'I told you before—' Percy began when he looked up and saw her.

'Thought you might like a cuppa,' Zara said, speaking over the top of his words. 'Must be difficult working on your own and not being able to get out to grab something to eat or have a loo break.' She put the cup down and walked away from Percy's stunned expression, smiling to herself.

Her phone beeped again. This time it was Jo.

Something's going down, you'd better get back here quick as.

Zara started to run.

A few minutes later, she threw open the office door.

Kimberly was dabbing a tissue to her eyes, while distraught expressions greeted her from the other journalists.

Bruce was stomping around his office, pulling open drawers then slamming them shut again.

Zara swept the room for Jo. She couldn't see her.

'What's going on?' Zara asked.

'Ah, nice of you to turn up.' Bruce stood up straight. 'I was going to wait until we were all here, but you were dragging your feet or ignoring my calls.'

'I was conducting the interview you told me to do,' Zara snapped.

'No, I told you to ring, not visit in person. Anyway, it won't make any difference,' Bruce said. 'Get your story written, then pack up your gear. The paper is done. Finished. Tonight is the last edition.'

Zara glanced around the room. Desks were almost already packed up. Jason wiped his nose with his sleeve and had a shellshocked expression on his face.

'This is on you,' Zara told Bruce.

He looked startled. 'What?'

'The closure. That's on you. These journos losing their jobs, that's on you too.' She took a few steps towards him.

Bruce turned purple. He stuttered a few words but the only one Zara heard was 'Why?'

'Because you didn't lead. You didn't chase the story and that's what all good journos do – chase stories. The news you've been printing is uninteresting and unprofessional.'

'You can't talk to me about being unprofessional,' Bruce retorted. 'Look at why you're here. Now write that last story and pack up. There's paperwork here for you to sign, so you can get four weeks' worth of wages.'

Zara's heart thumped as she remembered the lawyer pumping her for information, Jayne and Barry's car rolling, rolling, rolling. Her brother smiled at her from inside her mind and merged with Jayne's bloody hands and face.

'We all make mistakes, Bruce,' she said. 'Hopefully the ones we make don't affect other people too much. Your mistakes here have affected a lot of people and so did mine. But at least my mistakes weren't through sheer laziness.' She picked up her bag and stood tall. 'Don't worry about my wages, and you won't have to worry about me resigning, because I quit. I owe you nothing and you won't get the Janelle Salter story from me.' She leaned in. 'Oh, what a juicy, newsworthy story you've missed out on there. But don't worry, I'm sure there'll be a national paper interested.'

She gave him a wink and, with her heart trying to escape her chest, she turned on her heel and walked out the door.

Zara got outside before she sagged against the wall and tried to catch her breath.

God, that had felt good. Liberating!

But what would Jack say? They were here because of her.

Footsteps pounded behind her and Jo appeared, holding her backpack to her chest.

'Zara!' she called. 'Are you okay? Oh my god, you were awesome. How do you have the confidence to speak to him that way? I wish I could've done that.' Jo drew a breath and sagged alongside her. 'Bruce's always whingeing and whining about the company and he's late with his own deadlines. Plus, I've seen him talking with some bikies over the time I've been here, so I've never really known about his loyalties.'

'I know,' Zara said. 'I saw it the moment I arrived and when you've got an editor who doesn't pull the team together, that makes it hard for the journos. Trust is a big thing and Bruce isn't trustworthy – only in the sense that he doesn't do what he asks of us.'

Jo's next question was in a small voice. 'What are we going to do?'

Straightening up, Zara looked her squarely in the eye. 'Do?' she echoed, realising she had the answer. 'We're going to do what good journalists do. Find the newsworthy stories and tell them. We might start off small, but we'll get bigger. There's enough people in Kal to have a paper, despite what the hierarchy think, and they deserve to be able to read the news. We might have to go online for a while, until we get sorted and have enough advertising to pay our wages and get a paper printed, but that, Jo, is what we are going to do. Come on, we've got work to do. Unless you've got another idea?'

Looking at her in awe, Jo shook her head.

Jo followed Zara's purposeful steps. 'What do you mean exactly?'

'We're starting our own newspaper. I'll pitch some stories nationally, to see if we can get a bit of money. We'll have to get advertising to cover a website design and so on, but as journalists, we have a responsibility to connect the people of Kal with anything important, no matter how small. So we'll do just that.'

Zara couldn't let Jo in on the myriad emotions she was feeling. She wouldn't show weakness. After all, words and stories were her purpose in life.

She stopped in the middle of the street and looked at Jo. 'Are you in?'

'Without a doubt.'

'Good.' Zara took a breath. She needed to think. 'We'll catch up in the morning. Make a plan from there.' She paused. 'This is going to be good, I promise. Just think about a name for the paper, okay?'

'Sure,' Jo said with a giggle. 'God, I'm nervous.'

'That's good! Anything that matters should make you nervous because of just that. It matters. I've told you before, this place is full of news, we've just got to get off our bums and find it.' She gave Jo a confident smile and squeezed her arm, then headed down the street towards their house, hoping Jack would be there already.

Her watch told her it was only 5.30 pm so she doubted he would be. Instead, she pulled out her phone.

'Hello, my friend,' Liz answered. The background noise was the hum of a car.

'Driving home?' Zara asked.

'No, to Ceduna. Just a casual seven-hour drive for the sake of a news item.' Liz laughed. 'What about you?'

'Well, you were right, the paper *is* shutting down.'

'Can't say I'm surprised.'

'Me either. Anyhow, I've decided to open an online paper for Kalgoorlie. I need to make it work here. I can't have Jack upending his life for me and then this happening.'

Liz gave a soft laugh. 'Ah, Zara, if anyone can do it, you can. Your young journo could learn a lot from you.'

'So, why are you driving to Ceduna?'

Two buses carrying mine workers drove past her. One man waved at her. Zara automatically lifted her hand and waved back.

'There's a weird story,' Liz said. 'Bloke's been found outside his caravan – dead. Official word from the cops is he died of natural causes, but the caravan park owner rang me. I know him from way back. He reckons there were ligature marks around the dead guy's neck. And some of the neighbours reported a yell and bumps in the night. They reckon the police aren't telling them everything.'

'Slow day in Adelaide?'

'No,' Liz drew the word out slowly. 'Not sure but I think there's more to this. Buddy wouldn't have rung me otherwise.'

'Well, drive carefully,' Zara told her.

A man dressed in a singlet and shorts rounded the corner, making Zara jump. A smile spread over her face.

'Jack's here,' she told Liz, 'so I'd better go.' She put the phone back in her pocket and watched Jack jog towards her. 'Not sure about you,' she called out, 'but I'm liking the view.'

Jack slowed to a walk and wiped his forehead, dragging in deep breaths. 'Finished for the day?'

'And what a day it's been,' she told him.

'Can't be worse than yesterday.'

'In a different way. You nearly finished?'

'I can walk back with you now.' He swiped at the sweat on his forehead.

The streetlights came on as they walked back towards their house. Smells of dinner wafted around them and they heard the occasional scream from a child not wanting a bath.

'The paper's done,' Zara told Jack.

His head whipped around. 'What the hell, are you kidding?'

'Wish I was, but don't worry, I've got an idea. I'm going to start my own newspaper and Jo's going to help.'

Jack raised his eyebrows. 'Trust you to have something up your sleeve, but you've only ever written the articles. What do you know about running a newspaper?'

'Well, nothing,' she said, ignoring the fizz of annoyance at his lack of support. 'But I can learn.'

'There'll be much more to it than you imagine.'

Zara changed the subject. 'I spoke to Liz a couple of times today.'

'How was she?'

'Talking ninety words to the minute as usual.'

'Lots to get through in a very short space of time,' he said as he unlocked their front door, 'if I know anything about her calls.'

'Yep, just like that.' Zara went inside after him. 'She said that all the journos in the office are calling my stuff-up the "Zara Effect".'

'Doesn't matter. You can't see or hear them.' He paused. 'Liz shouldn't have told you.'

'Hmm, I think I'd rather know.'

'Do you?' Jack was untying his shoelaces but he looked up at her, searching her face.

Zara thought about the office, the journos sitting at the desk, casting glances her way. The whispers in the lunchroom. Sometimes journalists were like kids at school. Cruel and mean.

Their reactions would always keep Zara on her toes, remind her of her indiscretion. That way, she would never, ever stuff up again.

'I think so.' Another pause. 'I almost told her to come across to Kal. She's driving to Ceduna to talk to some of the police over there. It's not too far from Ceduna to Kal, you know. Maybe I could get the spare room done up and suggest it to her?'

Jack let out a laugh. 'Are you serious? It's another fourteen or fifteen hours to drive!'

'Yeah, but in the scheme of things, Ceduna is halfway.'

Jack pulled off his shoes and walked back to her, dropping a kiss on her head. She shifted her face, so he connected with her lips.

'Only you would think a fourteen-hour drive isn't far. Do you want a drink?'

'Yes please.'

She watched him go into the kitchen, thinking how nice it was to see him in his shorts and T-shirt, rather than the uniform. It hadn't suited him.

Hang on. There was something about his posture; his back was taut and his walk rigid, his arms weren't flowing around the side of his body as they usually did.

'You haven't said anything about work,' she said, following him into the kitchen. 'You got taken over to the dees?'

'Yeah, how good is that? I thought it might take twelve months or so. Not just one day!'

'Are they needing extra manpower?'

Jack pulled out two glasses from the cupboard and poured wine into each, then chugged back a glass of water. 'Something like that.'

She was about to ask him about it but his phone rang, just as police sirens sounded in the distance.

'G'day, Lucas,' he said and then listened. 'Sure, I'm coming now.' Tucking the phone back into his pocket, the tension in his shoulders ramped up. 'I gotta go.'

CHAPTER TWENTY

Jack ran towards the noise. He arrived just as the street shook with a second explosion. Glass blew out onto the road and he quickly turned his back and shielded his eyes with his hands.

Screams came from across the street as more people from the pub ran outside. Questions and loud voices tangled with each other in the air.

'Get back, get back!' Voices of authority came through as the police cars slowly moved through the crowd, lights flashing, and started to cordon off the area.

Glass, brick and pieces of a sign were scattered all over the footpath. In the distance, black smoke snaked out from a shop, while the firies tried to extinguish the few flames that could be seen from the road. There was a lot more smoke than fire.

In the distance, Jack thought he heard a female voice yelling, but his ears were ringing from the blast and the sirens. They were now silent, thank god. He made his way towards the first of the cars.

Bystanders were gathering a few blocks down, some had their phones out videoing, while others were yelling out to the officers.

'Someone get rid of them,' he yelled at the uniforms, gesturing towards the crowd. 'Or at least stop them from using their phones. We need to shift them back further.'

'We're on it,' Martin said, appearing out of the haze. Lucas was with him.

'Okay, people, there's nothing to see here,' an officer yelled as he walked towards the crowd. 'You need to move along. Go home.'

'Holy shit,' Lucas muttered. 'That's a bit of a bloody mess.'

Another senior constable, Kane Burgess, came over to them, dirt covering his jeans and face.

'Was there anyone inside?' Lucas asked him.

'Not that we are aware of,' he answered, dusting off his hands. 'Firies are checking, to be on the safe side.'

'Explosion?'

'Yep. We need to get inside and have a proper look.' He pointed to a few shops further down the block. 'As you can see there's not really much damage. The bombs were only small. Probably a letter bomb pushed through the door, or something of the like. Just enough to send a message, although I can't work out if they wanted to hurt people as well. What is it?' He turned his wrist to look at his watch. 'Hmm, quarter past six. I guess whoever was the culprit wasn't expecting the office to be occupied. They would have timed it for during the day if that's what they were aiming for.'

Jack wriggled his hands into gloves he kept in his pocket and picked up a piece of purple plaster, turning it over in his hands. There were white loops on it. A word or a symbol he wasn't sure. He indicated for another officer to come over and log the evidence.

'Whose office is this?' he asked.

'Janelle Salter,' Kane replied. 'Independent politician running for a seat in the federal election. To be honest, I'm surprised it hasn't happened before now. She's trying to get the mines shut down.'

Jack's eyebrows shot up in surprise, then he frowned. 'Sorry? Shut the mines down? Here? In Kalgoorlie?'

'Yep.'

That seemed like an improbable task.

'Yeah, crazy, isn't it?' Lucas added. 'Why would you want to stop mining in a mining town? It's madness. Not like there'd be any anger about that.'

Jack shook his head. 'She's really doing that here?'

'Only trying. She hasn't been elected. Won't be elected.'

'Well, it should narrow down the list of suspects.'

Lucas huffed a laugh. 'True. So, what've we got, Kane?'

'Triple zero reported numerous calls, but the first one came from the pub over the road. I've got a couple of officers over there. We got here quickly. No one around on the street. The alarm was going off and the security company have come and turned it off. The firies were on it quickly and there's no problem there. They're just securing the building and making sure it's safe for us to go in. Not sure we'll even have to put in a call to the Bomb Squad. But if we do, they'll take twelve to twenty-four hours so let's work this like it's only us. Got it?'

Other officers Jack hadn't met were combing the road with torches, looking for evidence, while others were setting up spotlights to flood the street with light. Sally, the officer he'd met the day before, was starting to stretch out the crime-scene tape.

He searched the crowd for faces he knew. So many strangers.

Then he came across a familiar one, the well-muscled man from the coffee van yesterday.

Jack recognised the tatts. What was his name? Boo? Boof? Something like that. He was walking along the street, holding his phone up.

'Stop that bloke there,' Jack told a uniform officer who was walking by. 'Get any footage he's taken, please.'

A fire-fighter came out of the smoke and stood for a moment, looking disorientated. Finally, she saw Martin and walked over. Her face and hands were covered in soot. Her hard hat sat crookedly on her head.

'All clear from us,' she told him, with a solemn expression, as she blinked to clear her eyes.

'Thanks, Celia,' he said. 'Anything you can tell us?'

'The blast has come from the back of the building. There's an office behind the reception area. There's a bit of damage to the wall but really not much else has sustained any large amount. Lots of smoke, without fire, so there's blackening of the walls and carpets. No one inside. You're good to start your investigation.' She paused. 'Look, I can't say too much without really looking into the blast, but I think the point of origin might be a wall. There's a small blast hole right behind the desk at about knee level.'

'As in the height of where someone might store a handbag or similar?'

'Yeah, that type of height. What I do know is that it hasn't been thrown in the window or started in the front office, despite the damage there.' She shook her head. 'What the fuck, though? We shouldn't be having this type of shit here.'

'True,' Martin said. 'But you know as well as I do, what *should* happen and what *does* are two different things.'

'Fuck me sideways,' Celia said. 'We're a community not a warzone.'

'Who owns the building?' Jack asked.

'We'll look up council records,' Martin told him. 'Let you know as soon as we find out.'

'Certainly a bit of excitement for the night,' Lucas said. He rocked back on his heels, looking down the street at the crowd gathered at the tape, trying to see what was happening. 'Anyone found Janelle Salter?'

'There's no bodies in there, if that's what you're asking,' Celia said.

'Reckon that's her down the way a bit,' Kane answered with a tip of his head.

Across the road, two women leaned against the wall of the pub, their arms crossed over their chests, watching proceedings.

'Right-oh, we'll have a chat,' Lucas said. 'Coming, Jack?'

'Yep. Right behind you.' Jack inspected the blackened cement path as he followed Lucas, lifting the tape and ducking under. He walked backwards for a few steps, assessing the building, and was surprised there wasn't more fire. Usually when a bomb was detonated, destruction was caused not only by the blast but also by electrical wires clashing together or gas pipes exploding. This was either very well planned not to cause a large fire or something along the lines of complete luck.

'Is Ms Salter known to the police at all?' Jack asked Lucas. 'And why are we here?'

'All hands on deck during an event like this, mate. Even if it's something small. Janelle Salter, well, her name doesn't ring any bells.'

'She hasn't made any complaints previously?'

'Not that've come across my desk. Here we go.'

Jack heard Lucas pull a deep breath into his lungs.

Both women were dressed for home rather than the office: trackies and jumpers. One of them was wearing a beanie and both had sneakers on.

'Janelle Salter?' Lucas asked, getting out his notebook.

'That's me,' the blonde woman said, raising her hand.

'What a night,' Lucas said. 'You both okay?' He gave her a friendly smile and Jack followed suit.

'Just a bit shocked,' Janelle replied, 'but we weren't in the office so no harm done. There was nothing in there that can't be replaced. You know, I felt the explosion, but I didn't take any notice straightaway. I thought it was the mine blasting again.'

'I'm Detective Lucas McEwin and this is Detective Jack Higgins. We wanted a quick chat with you. Nothing hard. Only to establish a few things. Do you think you're up to that?'

'Sure,' Janelle answered.

Lucas looked towards the other woman, who was huddling deep inside her jacket. 'And you are?'

A small hand reached out to shake both Jack's and Lucas's. 'I'm Lou. Louise Halter. I work for Janelle at front of house.'

'Janelle, you just said you thought you felt the blast. Do you live near here?'

'Not really. I'm about eight streets away over towards the oval.'

'You were together when you heard the news?'

Janelle shook her head. 'No, I rang Lou on the way here.'

'And how did you hear about the explosion?' Jack asked. He too had his notebook out. He noticed Janelle's hands were shaking.

'Well, I felt the floor shake to begin with, like can sometimes happen when the mines are blasting, but it wasn't until I heard the voices outside and some doors slamming that I realised something wasn't right. When I got here, I could see it was my office.'

'We understand you're campaigning on a policy that mightn't be that popular here in Kalgoorlie. Have you had anything like this happen before? Has anyone made any threats towards you?'

'Not open threats,' Janelle replied. 'There's been a few mornings we've arrived and there's been a little present for us.' She turned her eyes to Lou. 'Hasn't there?'

'Yeah, the windows have been egged, or someone has slipped a note under the front door telling us to leave town. Nothing that wouldn't be expected considering what Janelle is trying to do.' Lou shoved her hands in her pockets and stared at the blackened building. 'Bastards.'

Janelle gave a tiny shrug and thin-lipped smile. 'It's okay, we'll just start again.'

'No threatening phone calls or intimidating visits?' Jack asked.

'No, nothing like that.'

'Do you have copies of the notes that you were sent?'

'We didn't keep them,' Lou answered.

'What about reporting the incidents?'

Both women shook their heads.

'What was the point?' Janelle suddenly asked, her voice strong. 'I knew my party wasn't going to be welcomed with open arms here, but I had to try. Campaigning in another seat where the land wasn't being decimated by humans would be as ridiculous as trying to get votes here. It wouldn't mean anything to them. The only option I have is to open the eyes of the people who are inside this industry because that's the only way to get it shut down. Where both the numbers and the power are.'

'That's right,' Lou said, reaching out to put her hand on Janelle's arm. 'You're committed and so am I. We'll make an impact yet. We'll just start again, like you said.'

'Do you ever work late at night, Janelle? Or you, Lou? Could the person who did this have been expecting that you might have been there?'

'No,' Janelle and Lou said at the same time.

'The latest we're ever at the office is six and that's only if I have a meeting that goes over,' Janelle said. 'It's more likely we'll come in early. The eastern states seem to forget Western Australia is on a different time zone and often schedule meetings before seven in the morning, our time.'

Both Lucas and Jack made a note.

'Who else has access to your office? Cleaners or …?'

'No, we do everything ourselves,' Janelle said.

'Could anyone have been inside your office, Janelle, without you knowing?'

'Lou goes back there but she'd be the only one.'

Jack turned to look at the other woman. 'Lou?'

'They've got to get past me first and I haven't let anyone in unless Janelle has been there.'

'Okay. Do you know who owns the building?' Jack asked.

'Ah, no. We lease it from a real-estate company. I'd have to check the lease documents,' Lou answered. 'That's easy enough to do. I have them on my laptop.' She looked over the road to the damaged building. 'Thankfully I took it home with me tonight.'

'No worries, we can find that out,' Lucas said. 'Is there anything else you want to tell us? Even the smallest thing might help in this circumstance. Has anyone been hanging around outside, or have you received threatening phone calls?'

Both women were silent, as they looked over at each other. A few moments later, Janelle shook her head. 'No, I don't think so. Well, I can't think of anything straightaway.'

'How long has the office been open for?'

'Oh, over twelve months but it's only been the last three months we've started putting signage up. It costs money to run a campaign.'

'I imagine it does. Where do you get your funding from?'

'Donations mostly. People who believe in what we're trying to do.'

'We'd like to see a list of names.'

'Sure.'

'Okay, well, thanks, Janelle, Lou,' Lucas said. 'We'll be in contact over the next day or so and one of our constables will be around to take your statement in the next few hours. If you want to go home, just leave your address with Kane, over there. I'll let him know you might go home.'

'Okay,' Janelle's voice was slightly weaker than before. As if the shock was setting in.

Kane waved them over. While Lucas filled him in, Jack turned to survey the street again and saw Zara, trying to talk to Sally at the edge of the crime scene. She was smiling, her head to one side, using the charm he'd seen her use time and time again. Mostly it worked, when she was using it on the public. But he'd never known a time when Zara's charisma had worked on *coppers*. Not the ones he worked with anyway.

Jack was used to her being at a crime scene, so acted as he always did. Instead of making eye contact, he heaved a deep breath and got on with his job. He couldn't help but wonder if Lucas had noticed her, but then remembered Lucas hadn't met Zara yet.

They headed across the road and down the street to the pub on the corner. A couple of patrons were sitting at some tables outside, and inside, the bar was subdued, the only noise coming from the TV screens. One had reruns of *Friends* and a few of the others were showing horse races from the previous day. The last two, which were hung closer to the bar, showed an international soccer game.

'Hey, mate,' the barman held up his hand in greeting. 'What a sight, hey?'

'Not good,' Lucas responded. 'What did you see?'

'Nothing, bro. Not a thing. Only heard it. Everyone went running out to have a gander, but I stayed here. Last time I left the bar, a few of the customers poured their own. Figured if it was life threatening, someone would let me know.'

Jack shook his head in bemusement. Laid-back Kalgoorlie. Normal people would have run a mile and not given a shit about what mess they left behind!

He glanced around the bar, looking for people to talk to. His eyes settled on another familiar face.

Aiden Scott. He had his head in his hands, staring at the table, an untouched beer in front of him, looking like he had the weight of the world on his shoulders.

Jack walked over. 'Mate, you alright?'

Aiden looked up. 'What? Oh, Jack. G'day.' He tried to smile. 'Bit going on out there.'

'Yeah,' Jack agreed. 'Bit busy.'

'Must've gone off with a bang,' Lucas said as he pulled up a chair and sat down, picking up a coaster and tapping it on the table. Jack took the other empty seat.

'The windows shook,' Aiden said, his hands on his beer. 'But it was only a big-enough bang to get attention. It's not like the windows blew out or anything.'

'They shattered,' Jack said.

'Yeah, but they didn't blow out the way a big explosion would make them. This was more like a pfft, rather than a smash, bang, crash.'

Jack understood what he meant.

'Did you want to go out for a look?'

'I did, for a few minutes, but I could see it wasn't too bad. You guys were all on your way. I could hear the sirens, so I left you all to it. I'm off duty.'

Jack assessed Aiden closely. There was something not right with him.

Lucas checked his phone and sent a text. 'We should ask for people to send that footage through,' he commented.

'Don't suppose you saw anything beforehand?' Jack asked. 'Noticed anyone hanging around?'

'I'd like to be able to say yes, but I can't. Had a few bets on the horses earlier in the evening and ordered tea.' He ran his hands over his face and Jack noticed tiredness in his eyes along with a five o'clock shadow. 'No point in going home now the missus has packed up and fucked off, so I decided I'd stay here until closing. People to talk to here.'

'Oh.' Jack's heart squeezed in sorrow, and a mixture of emotions he couldn't explain sparked in his stomach.

Lucas caught Jack's eye, giving a minute shake of his head. He hadn't known either. Silence stretched out between all three men.

'Sorry to hear that, mate. You okay?'

'What sort of a fucked-up question is that?' Aiden replied without any heat in his voice. Only desolation.

Lucas pursed his lips and gave a grimace. 'Yeah. Sorry. Didn't think.'

Aiden looked into his beer as if he was going to find an answer in the amber liquid. 'You know, the missus and I used to go camping a lot. That's part of the reason I came back here. Grew up in the bush and it got under my skin, you know?'

Jack was thrown by the change in subject. He glanced at Lucas.

'Look, mate, we'll get someone to come and run you home, okay?' Lucas said, getting up. 'Give us a yell if you need anything.'

Lucas sent another text and Jack assumed it was organising a ride for Aiden.

This Aiden, the one who looked as if he'd had the guts kicked out of him tonight, was so different from the one spitting anger and words at Jack just the day before.

Jack tried to put himself in his place, wondering how he would feel. The deep anger he'd felt when Aiden had first made the crack at him about Zara was still there, as was the resentment he'd had to upend everything for her. He shook his head. Now wasn't the night to think about how he might feel if Zara walked out because he might come to the conclusion it would be a good idea.

CHAPTER TWENTY-ONE

'Do you know what's happened?' Zara pushed her way through the throng of people who were gathering at the end of the street. 'Can anyone tell me what's going on?'

The streetlights were shining in spheres of light, casting out only small domes. In between, the light was dim and it was easy to step back into the darkness.

'Haven't you got any eyes?' someone muttered next to her.

Zara ignored them, darting a glance to the street corners, looking for anyone who might be lurking, watching. How many times had she reported on a case in which the person who had committed the crime had been there watching; she'd even interviewed them, taking them for bystanders.

Zara's sources within the police department had usually managed to get her a list of witnesses, and she'd tracked them down with the determination of someone who was frightened of failing.

She didn't have any informants in Kalgoorlie yet and she suspected they were going to be a lot harder to make, considering it was a smaller station. Also it was the only one in town, rather than Adelaide's many across the city. She needed Jo. She'd been here longer than Zara and knew more people. What she lacked in experience she made up for with local knowledge.

'Does anyone know what happened?' she asked again.

'Sounds like there was a blast,' the woman replied. Her tone came close to suggesting Zara was a dunce.

'Anyone know why? Or who did it?'

A man turned sideways to look at her. 'What are ya? A reporter?' He muttered something under his breath as he turned back to watch the happenings.

She kept her eyes on the man for a second, then realised there wasn't any point in confirming his suspicions.

She turned to the person next to her. 'Were you here when it happened?'

This time, she received a glare, before a shoulder blocked her view.

Heaving a sigh, she edged along the crowd, wondering if there was a back street that wasn't taped off. Maybe she could duck down and 'just' end up right near the shop that had been damaged.

She took out her phone and jotted down some notes; time, date and a basic outline of what she could see had happened.

When she looked up next, police officers were walking towards the barriers, asking people to put their phones away and move on.

'Excuse me. Excuse me!' Zara was the only one trying to attract the cops' attention. The rest of the crowd were melting into the darkness, waiting to reappear like moths to light as soon as the police were distracted.

'Could you move back please?' It was a woman's voice. 'This isn't a circus. No sightseers, thanks. You need to head off now.' The words were said with authority.

'Yes, I understand you don't want onlookers,' Zara said quickly. 'But I'm not here to gawp. I'm a journalist with—'

'We have nothing to say to journalists. Come on, you know that.' The tone was mocking. 'If you wait until the morning, I'm sure there will be a statement from our media department.'

The woman was backlit from the lights that had been erected near the damaged shop. Zara couldn't see her face clearly.

'Of course, I'll look forward to receiving that, but could you just give me the basics? So I can mock up a frame for the story and fill in everything when the media release comes through. You won't need to give me anything I can't see for myself, Constable ...' She looked down at the woman's uniform, and shielded her eyes. 'Sally?' Her voice rose in a question. 'Sally? You're the one who drove me home from the caravan accident? The two fatalities. Out on the highway.'

'Zara?' Sally moved until she could see her face. 'Is that you? How are you?' She reached out to touch Zara's arm.

'I'm ... fine. Maybe still a bit wobbly. Just trying to keep busy, you know.' She indicated towards the commotion. 'What's going on here? It looks like a right ruckus!'

'I can't tell you anything, Zara.' There was regret in her voice.

'Sure. I don't want you to get into any strife.' Zara made her tone understanding and not in the least demanding.

A few young people on the other side of the street edged forward, pushing over the crime-scene tape.

'Stay here,' Sally said and stepped purposely towards them. Their phones were held outstretched, and Zara assumed they were zoomed in on the chaos. She'd seen plenty of kids who filmed videos and posted to their social media pages. Young adults spent a lot of their time in FOMO mode and to post to their socials gave them a reward of the opposite.

Searching hashtags related to incidents was always helpful. Sometimes she found videos on their socials before the police did and downloaded them to her phone. Once she'd even found a witness that the police hadn't.

Zara tapped on the voice memo app and recorded herself saying, 'Video/social media.'

'Delete that,' she heard Sally call out to the kids. 'Right now, turn your phone around and show me you've deleted it. Come on. *Now!*'

Dammit, Zara thought, *maybe there won't be videos to look at afterwards.*

'Zara, sorry about that.' Sally was back.

'Are you sure you can't tell me anything? Off the record, of course.'

'I can't.' Sally shook her head. 'But if you walk around that way,' she jerked her head to the left and lowered her voice, 'you'll probably find Janelle and her receptionist. They might talk to you.'

'Was it Janelle's office?' Zara blinked. 'She told me they'd had some problems.'

'Did they? Well, let's hope this is the last one. We don't like incidents like this.'

'Who does? Hey, I don't suppose you've seen anyone else from the paper here?'

'Ah, nope, don't think so.' Sally looked behind her. 'If you know something, we'll probably want to speak to you.'

'Nothing firsthand. Just what Janelle communicated to me today, during a short interview. Her office has been egged … Once I think.' It was important to return favours if a journalist was trying to engage a source. She smiled at Sally. 'That's all I know, but I can send you a copy of the story when I write it, if you like.'

Sally nodded, and wrote Zara's name down. 'I'll let the dees know. Anyhow, I'd better get back. Martin will haul me over the coals if he thinks I'm talking to you.'

'Why?'

'Because you're a journo, why do you think?' She turned to leave. 'Hey, how's Jack coping? That shit that went down between him and Aiden was pretty rough. You should've seen Aiden's face after Jack slapped him.'

What?

'Sally?' Another police officer waved her over.

'Better go, good to see you, Zara. And I really do hope you're feeling okay after yesterday. It's traumatic, being first on scene, especially an accident like that one.'

'Wait!' The word shot out of Zara's mouth before she could stop it.

Sally stopped.

'Sally! Come on.' The police officer was standing with his hands on his hips now.

'Sorry, Zara, gotta go.'

Her hand slipped to her belt with the seven kilos of equipment, gripping it tightly as she broke into a run back towards the activity, leaving Zara staring after her.

You should've seen Aiden's face after Jack slapped him.

Zara thought about Jack's rigid walk and unbending posture just hours before. Then his immediate secondment to the dees.

'Idiot,' she hissed. Caught up in her own worry and torment, she'd missed seeing Jack's. He was probably getting roasted because of her and she hadn't even noticed or offered any support. Self-loathing made her lips curl up.

Hey, her mind told her. *He didn't tell you and you did ask.*

Zara stood still, then as if a light switch had turned on, she flicked her hair back and straightened her spine. If Jack wasn't going to share that he was being roasted at work, that was his problem. He'd always gone on about keeping their work separate from their private life. Everyone knew that a cop and a journalist were an unusual mix, and they had to be careful, but if Aiden had given him a grilling, surely Jack could have shared that with her. Wasn't that what being a partner meant? Being able to support each other?

She hoisted her backpack further up her shoulder and walked determinedly down the path, her eyes continuing to sweep the area for anything that looked unusual.

The other journalists from *The Prospector* were conspicuous by their absence. Surely, they would have heard the sirens and gone looking to see what had happened? Journalists were curious and nosy by nature, even if their paper was folding.

Zara certainly was. That's how she'd always been known. There only had to be the sniff of a story and she would be all over it, like a kid eating a cupcake.

There was something niggling in the back of her mind as she thought about Janelle Salter. The woman was hard to ruffle and it seemed to Zara that she had more experience with media than your average Joe.

Jack stepped out of the darkness across the street. Even if she hadn't known him, her eyes would have been drawn to his tall, lean frame. His wavy dark hair and the resolute expression on his face. The look was one Zara knew well. Determination. Resolve. Tenacity.

Her heart squeezed with a mixture of love and anger. God, he was frustrating!

'Zara?'

She turned and saw Jo pushing her way through the crowd towards her. Zara waved and turned back to watch Jack.

He was with a detective she hadn't yet met and they looked as if they were comparing notes.

Zara saw only the quiet confidence Jack was known for. He wasn't holding himself as if he had any animosity towards the man he was walking with and when she saw a throng of other police officers greet Jack, there didn't seem to be anything to concern her there either. Who had he hit? And why?

Maybe Sally had got her information wrong.

In the distance, she located the two women Sally had told her about, watching the happenings of the fire brigade and police.

'Come on,' she told Jo, who had reached her side. 'Let's go and talk to Janelle and Lou.'

'The wannabe pollie?'

'It was her office.'

'Shit!'

Zara caught snatches of the women's conversation as she got closer.

'Get in contact … insurance company.'

'I'll reschedule your …'

Their words were swallowed by the sound of the departing fire engine.

'Hi Janelle, Lou,' Zara said to the two women, who both looked at her in surprise, then at each other.

'Zara, hello.' Janelle seemed to recover herself first. 'I didn't expect to see you here tonight.' Her gaze slid over to Jo. 'But of course you are.'

'I didn't expect to be covering this type of event either,'

Zara said. 'I'm sorry this has happened to you. This is Jo, my offsider. Do the police have—'

'It's too early to know anything at this stage,' Lou said, interrupting her question. 'We really have nothing to say to you.'

Janelle shot Lou a look that said 'cooperate'.

'The police have only just finished asking us a few questions, so I guess they'll have to get inside and see if they can find out anything before we'll know anything,' Janelle offered.

'Were you expecting anything like this to happen? Did you get any threatening phone calls or similar this afternoon?'

Both Lou and Janelle shook their heads.

'Does it make you want to shut up shop?'

'Absolutely not!' Janelle whipped her head around to glare at Zara. 'I'm not weak or a pushover. Whoever did this might think I'll be deterred by their handiwork, but trust me when I say, I've been through much worse and it will take a lot more to dissuade me from continuing with my objective.'

'Would you like to tell me about those other times?' Jo asked Janelle.

Zara noticed she was holding her phone in her hand with the recording app on. That showed initiative.

'No. No, I would not,' Janelle said with a little huff, which sent a white cloud into the air. 'If you need a quote from me, you can say I'm devastated that someone would see the need to damage my property to get their own thoughts and views heard. We live in a democracy, and everyone has a right to their opinions and to be listened to, but never like this. My door is open to anyone who would like to talk to me.'

Lou put her hand on Janelle's arm. 'Come on, we need to look into the insurance policy.'

'One more question, if you don't mind,' Zara said. 'Do you know if the main street has CCTV?'

Janelle's eyes went to the streetlights and poles in the median strip, and she cocked her head to one side. 'I'm sure it does,' she said finally, still searching the street. 'I'm not sure where they're positioned.' There was a pause. 'I guess the police will look through the footage.'

'Again, I'm sorry this has happened to you,' Zara said. 'Please get in contact if there's anything more you'd like to say to the public.'

CHAPTER TWENTY-TWO

The bright fluoro lights flickering over his desk were beginning to give Jack a headache.

He rubbed his eyes and, out of habit, checked his watch straightaway. The numbers were blurry. Blinking a couple of times, he tried to refocus on the words in front of him, but they were fuzzy too. Pushing back the bank transactions he was trying to cross-check, he stood, putting his arms above his head and leaning from side to side. Two, three, four times each side. He jumped up and down on the spot.

His body was telling him it was time to go for another run but at this time of night there was no way he was doing that. A few good stretches would have to wake up him.

And a coffee. The machine was beckoning him. He checked the time again. Nearly 1 am. He'd regret having a coffee at this hour. Bed was looking like a very good option, especially after seeing Aiden's dejected face in the pub and knowing the reason behind it.

Lucas had gone home to his wife as soon as they'd finished tidying everything up and, really, that's exactly what Jack should have done – gone home to Zara.

She'd be asleep by now, even if she'd had a late-night call with her mum or a friend, which she did quite often when Jack had to work. Whether or not she would have written a story when she'd got home, he wasn't sure. Sometimes she did, but other times she liked to let it percolate while she slept and then got up early to write. She hadn't tried to get a statement from the police station tonight because Jack would have heard about it if she had.

One thing Jack did know was that even if *The Prospector* had folded, she would still pen the story and pitch it to different newspapers.

Still, she'd be asleep by now, so he could sneak in, shower and get into bed without having to speak to her and he really didn't feel like talking to anyone.

Pina, the technician analyst, had sent the whole team an email regarding something she'd found on Barry's bank account details. She'd highlighted four transactions that she couldn't cross-reference between all of their accounts, and they were so odd, they stood out like 'dogs' balls'. Pina's words, not his. Each one was $16,500, paid quarterly.

So instead of going home, Jack had laboriously filled in an Order to Produce for the court. He needed to speak to the CFO in Barry's place of employment. He also wanted to get a feel for the place. See if anything felt off. Like whether they might take bribes from crims.

Surely Barry wouldn't have been so stupid to take large sums of money and put them in his bank account, but Pina was right. Where was the money coming from?

'Jack, keeping late hours.'

A shadow crossed his desk and Martin stood in the doorway. He gave a tired smile.

'Want to get on top of a few things.'

Martin came into the room and without being asked, pulled out a chair and sat heavily. 'What a night, hey.'

Jack knew he didn't really expect an answer. 'Coffee?' he asked instead.

'I shouldn't. Have enough trouble sleeping during the day after I've pulled a night shift.'

'Same here, but it's a bit like putting your tongue on a nine-volt battery. You know you shouldn't, and it's going to tingle, but you do it anyway. To see how much charge is in it.' Jack was at the machine now.

'I've never thought about coffee like that,' Martin said with an astonished laugh. 'Go on then, I'll have one with you.'

The gurgling of the machine filled the room while Jack opened the fridge and brought out the milk. A few moments later, he was handing a cup to Martin and bringing his own to his lips.

Regret shot through him as soon as he tasted the strong liquid. He shouldn't drink this if he wanted to go to sleep before four this morning. He'd never learn! 'What did you make of tonight?'

'I'm surprised – but not. Can't really come into a town like Kalgoorlie and expect someone wouldn't take offence to what Janelle would like to do. At the same time, I've been caught off guard, because sometimes everyone ignores what's going on under their nose and gets on with life.' Martin gave a sigh and wrapped his hands around his mug. 'I guess I should have had an officer down there talking to her and making sure there hadn't been any threats made. Still, too late now.'

'Is there CCTV on the main street? Can we access it?'

Martin nodded, drinking deeply from his mug. 'Yeah. The camera room is in the next building, but we can get our hands on the footage from tonight. Guess that's what you're thinking?'

'Yeah. See who was on the street before the blast. Any chance I could get a look at it now or do I need an Order to Produce?'

'I'll make a call. You should be able to head over.' Martin paused. 'Do you need to do this now? Tomorrow would be soon enough.'

'Might as well do it while I can't sleep,' Jack held up his coffee in a cheers-like motion.

'What about the car accident, anything of interest yet?'

'Other than a million dollars' worth of gold being found? Not really. Just a few questions we need answered. I'm looking into it.'

Martin picked up his mug and crossed his legs, tapping his foot up and down. 'Are you liking them for theft?'

'Not really,' Jack told him. 'If it wasn't for these payments, I don't think we'd be looking at them at all. Everyone I've spoken to has told me that amount of gold is hard to come by. I don't think Barry suits the profile.'

'Has Jett ruled either of them out?'

'Not yet. We've got to do our due diligence. But none of us are that keen on them.'

'Of course,' Martin said, his eyes on the investigation board. He got up and went over, reading the timeline and looking at the photos.

'Have you heard that Aiden and his missus have split?' Jack asked.

'I hadn't,' Martin said. 'Shit.'

'He told Lucas and me tonight.' Jack paused. 'Might explain a few things. But, gee, it's out of the blue. Yesterday he seemed fine.'

'Hmm.' Martin rubbed his forehead. 'Well, thanks for the info, Jack. He was okay towards you today?'

'Yeah. No troubles.'

'Good to hear. Well, I'd better get on. The wife will be sick of keeping my dinner warm.' He checked his watch. 'Probably a crisp now anyway.'

'One more question,' Jack said, moving the papers around until he found what he was looking for. 'Kirsty rang the Gwalia mine site, and they told her they have security footage of the caravan park. They keep it for about six months longer than usual because it's related to a mine, apparently. What do we have to do to get that footage?'

'What do you want that for?' Martin asked.

'Information gathering really. We know from Carol and Jim that Barry and Jayne left Gwalia that morning. Might be a dead end. Thought we should try anyhow.'

Martin shrugged. 'You really think you're going to see someone attaching the lockboxes under their van?'

'Who knows? Maybe the boxes were already there. But maybe not.'

'Nothing surprises me,' Martin said, the weariness in his tone clear. 'Well, Jack, sounds like a longshot to me, but you do what you need to. Protocol is that you will need an Order to Produce, but Jett and the rest of the squad work closely with the management of all the mines in our area, so the top dog will probably give the footage to you without needing one. But one sniff there's something worthwhile on it, you'll need to get the paperwork through the court, quick smart, or you won't be able to use it as evidence.'

'Thanks,' Jack nodded. 'I'll get on it.' The information Martin had given him was what Jack had assumed, but he'd wanted to be sure. Working relationships between police and mines, or the community, would have taken years to build and Jack respected that.

Martin stood. 'Settling in okay, Jack?'

'Yes, no troubles now, boss.'

'And Zara?'

'She's fine too. The paper closed today, did you hear that?'

Martin raised his eyebrows. 'Can't say that upsets me. But what's Zara going to do now?'

'She's got a plan. Zara needs to be busy.'

'Good, good. Right, well, I'm heading home. See you tomorrow.'

'Night, boss,' Jack said. 'Can you make that call before you leave?'

'Sure. Head over there now and ask for Hugo. He'll make sure you're looked after.'

'Thanks.'

When Jack opened the door and stepped into the freezing night, the street was quiet. No cars, no explosions, no sirens.

There was a dog barking, though.

He walked the short distance between buildings and entered the pin code Martin had texted him, letting himself into the silent building. Another fluoro light shone bright, illuminating the council offices.

'Hello?' he called out. His voice echoed around the high-ceilinged room. 'Hello, it's Detective Jack Higgins.'

'Come on up,' a voice yelled from the floor above. 'Take the stairs.'

A small man with dark-rimmed glasses and a greying beard was standing at the top of the staircase.

'You must be Jack. Hugo. Come this way.' He spoke as quickly as he walked, which was much faster than Jack expected.

'Thanks for letting me in.'

Hugo shrugged. 'I often get phone calls at strange hours needing to see footage. No biggie. In here.'

He pulled open a door and Jack saw at least fifteen TV screens, all in black and white. The cameras were capturing a live feed; the one trained on the front of the police station showed the flags fluttering in the breeze.

Jack's gut constricted as he realised Hugo, or whoever had had yesterday's shift, would have seen the altercation between Aiden and himself. Wishing he could take back his reaction was moot. He could only learn from what had happened and make sure there was a different reaction next time, or even better make sure there was *never* a next time.

'This is what you're looking for, here,' Hugo said. He indicated to a desk in the corner with a small screen and a chair. A glass of water was placed near the mouse. 'I've cued the last twelve hours until the explosion. You can speed it up like this,' Hugo indicated to a button on the screen. 'And slow it down this way.' He demonstrated both actions again, then stood back. 'Anything else you need?'

'Nope, thanks for your help,' Jack said. 'I reckon I'll run it on fast to begin with.'

Hugo gave a snort of laughter. 'I'm sure it'll be riveting.'

'No doubt,' Jack grinned. He checked his watch again and imagined Zara curled up on her side, her hair drifting over her face. Jack could almost feel her warmth.

He should go home. Curl into bed alongside her. Slip his arm around her waist and pull her to him in the way she always loved. Tell her about Aiden, explain he didn't mind the scrutiny from his peers because he was in Kalgoorlie with her.

Jack checked the time and date stamp at the bottom of the screen, sat down and cued up the footage.

CHAPTER TWENTY-THREE

The sun had barely cracked the skyline and Ted was already out of bed and looking at the sky.

Her sleep had been restless, there was a swarm of bees buzzing in the background of her dreams. Except it wasn't bees.

She waited underneath the tree for three-quarters of an hour before she saw the drone high above her camp. A pinprick of red light glimmered as it flew back and forth in a grid-like pattern. The loud buzzing bee. Or wasp.

Ted had aimed her pistol at the machine, even as she realised the bullet wouldn't make the distance. Instead, she stayed where she was, out of sight, and watched.

Poachers tried all sorts of different ways to get on to properties these days.

Guessing they were checking to see if she had any new piles of dirt, Ted expected she might have visitors in the flesh tonight. Or next week. But next month would be too late, because they'd know she would have already processed the dirt.

It didn't matter when. She would be ready.

In her earlier years out here, she'd been lax with security, happy to take everyone at face value. That hadn't served her well. People she'd known and believed would never hurt her had stolen her first big haul.

Since then, her security had been high and she trusted no one.

Automatically she clicked her fingers, then shook her head, annoyed at herself. Zero wasn't here.

She threw more sticks on the fire and put the billy on.

With a cup of tea in hand, Ted walked the bush outside of her camp, searching for any sign of the drone.

Still, there wasn't much likelihood of it being up now. Grey mist was drifting through the bush, hiding everything a few metres in front of Ted. The sky was blocked out.

Ted watched the heavy moisture beads float through the trees. The air was dense but crisp as she breathed in and a Crested Bellbird warbled happily, somewhere deep in the bush hidden by the fog.

Large dew drops were playing a delicate balance game, hanging on to the tips of leaves before falling with a loud plop to the ground.

As she walked, Ted collected sticks for the fire. She'd have to put them under the van for a few days until they dried out. Wet wood made for a cool, smoky fire and all that did was smoke out her camp and give people an idea as to where she was; it didn't make her billy boil either.

Reaching around to the small of her back, she touched the pistol. The bush and isolation had never worried her. Nothing in nature could frighten her. Put humans out here, though, and everything changed. People scared her.

She would have to get another dog soon.

In the area she'd pushed up the dirt, Ted carefully surveyed the ground. The piles were pristine. Yesterday, as she did every day, she'd raked a wide perimeter around the mounds. If anyone turned up during the night, they would have no choice but to walk over ground that had been smoothed over.

The land was untouched.

Ted checked the trip wire she'd laid out, not expecting to see a problem. The alarm would have gone off in the van if someone had kicked it.

Seeing it intact, Ted nodded. None of the booby traps she had set up would be hard to get around or stop anyone from trying to steal her gold. All it would do was alert her that someone was on her tenement. She liked to know they were there.

Forearmed was forewarned and knowledge bore no weight. They were some of Vince's more sensible words.

Over the last four years, on average, five or six people a year had stumbled over her lease and found her camp. Some of them had a Miner's Right licence and some didn't. Either way, none of them should have been on her land, because she leased the tenement and prospectors weren't allowed on land that wasn't a pending lease. Still, the lure of finding that next big nugget was too much for some and they broke the law.

Dog eat dog.

Miner backstabs miner.

And in the good ole days it was miner murders miner. Bit harder to do without repercussions these days, but it still happened. Quietly.

That's the way it was out here.

The door of the backhoe creaked loudly as she reefed it open, climbing the few steps into the cab and checking the fuel. There was enough there for today, if she decided to go mining.

Ted pulled the dipstick and inspected the oil level, then walked slowly around her machine making sure it was operational. Every time something went wrong, it cost a bucketload to fix.

Inside her caravan, there were a few machinery magazines, telling her how much newer models cost. A few months ago, the idea of buying one had excited her. Yet what was the point? In reality, Ted was probably nearing the end of her mining life, and a new machine would see her well and truly out. Was there a reason to spend so much money?

Vince had told her she might need more money than she realised, later on. If she had to put herself in a nursing home or something.

Or something.

Ted imagined the washed-out brussels sprouts and poached chicken she'd have to eat, and the fact she wouldn't be able to see the sun or feel the earth, and she'd be stuck inside with people who were old in their minds and their bodies, not just their bodies. Ted would rather die alone in the bush than end up in a place like that.

Which meant she could buy the backhoe.

Bugger Vince and his bad ideas.

She tapped the mobile fuel tank, which she sometimes towed to town to refuel out of the bowsers. The hollow noise sounded the same as yesterday, another indication that no one had been on her land overnight. She'd need to refill it soon.

All checks done, she made her way back to the caravan and pulled her barbecue plate over the coals. A few minutes later bacon and eggs were cooking and a piece of toast was butter-side down, sizzling.

Ted never ate off plates. Dishes had to be washed, and water was limited out here. The region could go over a hundred days without rain. The old-timers had told her it could be longer.

She heaped the bacon and egg onto the toast and took a bite. Yolk squirted down her chin and back onto the barbecue. She grinned. Didn't need manners out here either.

A rumble in the distance made her look up. Firstly, she checked the sky, even though she knew that type of sound wasn't thunder. It was still blanked out by the fog.

Secondly, she reached around to the small of her back and took her pistol in her hand. The noise was getting louder and it was coming from her overgrown two-wheel track that led to the main road.

Louder still, and this time, her fear made itself known.

Quietly, she tiptoed over to the van and slid in through the door, feeling in her pocket for the remote control.

Dammit!

The controller for the booby-trapped bed was outside the van and she cursed herself. Usually, she was more organised.

Lack of sleep and being on alert all night had taken its toll on her brain this morning.

There was nothing to do but wait and listen. Those who didn't understand the bush didn't know how far clear noise could move across the land.

Ted took a deep breath and found her hands were shaking. That annoyed her. Fear had two meanings to her; forget everything and run, or face everything and rise.

She'd always faced everything.

The noise of the motorbike was almost on her now. She could feel the land vibrating under the tyres and the roar bouncing off the trees, the fog, the hills.

Getting into the caravan was the stupidest thing she'd done in a while. Out in the bush would have been safer. That way she could have dodged and weaved behind trees, slunk down into a mine shaft and made her way through the catacombs underneath the earth, the ones she knew like the back of her hand. She and Vince had marked them all out when she'd first moved out here.

Then suddenly, from the cover of fog, the motorbike appeared. It was inside her camp. A rider, wearing a full helmet and leather gear, brought the bike to a halt, spraying dirt across her fire and the remnants of her breakfast.

The driver looked around, revving the accelerator. The bike was angled towards the track leading to her mine. They revved the engine again and took off. It took only seconds for the motorbike to be swallowed by the low cloud, leaving Ted breathless and gathering herself.

Opening the door, she listened carefully. There were no other bikes behind this one. With any luck, whoever had been astride the bike was lost, looking for a way out. As much as she hoped that was the case, there was a prick in her brain that told her otherwise.

She knew people who liked motorbikes.

Reaching for her hard-bristled broom, she swept off the table, cleaning the sprayed dirt, then upended her chair, tipping the soil to the ground.

The billy had to be emptied, which she tipped into the growing potatoes, because nothing could be wasted out here.

She refilled it and stuck it back on the coals, all the while staying tuned for engine noise.

Maybe she could follow the tracks left behind.

They went along the well-worn path to her mine. From there, who knew and what would be the point? They might lead back to the firebreak road or take her in circles. Maybe whoever it was had been trying to draw her away from her camp. Well, they'd have Buckley's she decided.

Staying right where she was on her tenement and going about her daily business was exactly what Ted was going to do. They, whoever they were, weren't going to scare her away.

'Stupid old woman,' a male voice came through the mist. 'I can smell you.'

Ted let out a small screech and ducked in behind the closest tree. 'Who's there?'

The pistol in her hand was little comfort. She loaded a bullet into the chamber and fired it towards the sky without thinking.

'Go on, show yourself,' she yelled, sending another bullet towards the sun. 'You don't frighten me.'

Her voice bounced off the trees and back towards her, kept close to the earth by the mist. The fog was disorienting her and yet it shouldn't. She'd lived here for too long and knew every crevice, tree, plant and track. What was wrong with her?

Suddenly Vince broke into the clearing. 'Ted! Stop shooting! It's me, you mad old woman.'

Ted stared at him. 'Vince.' Letting herself sag in relief, she left her hiding spot behind the tree and headed towards him.

'In the flesh.' Vince clomped confidently towards the fire and grabbed a chair from under the van then set it up. 'God, look at you. Bad night? You look half dead. You sick? Dead?

I guess there's a possibility one day when I turn up here, you'll have carked it in your van. God, wouldn't that be a sight. All decomposed like a kangaroo in the bush.'

Trying to compose herself, Ted swallowed and put the gun away. 'What the hell are you doing here? Good thing you didn't get shot.' She glowered at him, crossing her arms over her chest. 'Was that you on the motorbike trying to scare the shit outta me?'

'You wouldn't shoot your own blood,' Vince said, poking the fire. 'What about a cup of tea?'

'You know where everything is.' Ted refused to hold anything. That would only admit her hands were still shaking. Bugger Vince! He should tell her when he was going to turn up out of the blue like this. Give her some warning.

'Bit of notice might be nice. You might find me in the bath or taking a crap.' Ted wiped her hands on her jeans and pulled out the other chair, as Vince got up and added more water to the billy.

'Get up on the wrong side of the bed this morning?' Vince asked, throwing a handful of tea leaves in the can.

'Visitors make me shitty. I've had two this morning. Two more than I ever wanted.'

Vince gave her the boyish grin that for so many years had made the girls flock to him. 'I'm glad to see you too.'

Ted hmphed.

'What do you mean two? And what motorbike?'

'Don't tell me you didn't hear it.'

'I didn't hear anything.'

She checked his face. When Vince lied, he had a little tic: his left eye twitched. He'd been so easy to read, ever since he was a little boy.

It was still.

'You can't be serious?' she replied, still standing.

'Well, I am,' Vince answered huffily. 'I drove out here. Only walked the last twenty metres. Thought I'd sneak up and see how good your hearing was.'

Ted thought about that. If he was telling the truth then he must've only just missed the bike by minutes. She supposed it was possible. The sound of his engine must have combined with the bike's.

'You alright, old duck?' he asked with uncharacteristic concern.

The billy started to bubble. Vince poured two cups of tea and handed one to Ted. 'You better get that into you. Want some brandy in it?'

She took the cup, regretting her sharpness. 'Don't be ridiculous.'

'Where's Zero?' he asked.

'What?' Ted looked up from the coals that had blurred in front of her stare. 'Oh, he died. Few months back.'

'Shit.'

'Bait. Gotta get me a new one.'

Sitting back down, Vince put his ankle on his knee and bounced his foot up and down as if he was thinking of something to say.

'What brings you out here?' she finally asked. 'Everything okay?'

'Can't a man visit his sister without a reason?' He took a sip of tea and smacked his lips. 'Can't make a cup of tea that good in town. Reckon the fire makes all the difference.'

Ted waited for him to answer her question.

He raised the pannikin and took a sip, keeping his eyes on Ted while he drank.

Uncertainty flickered in her now. God, that motorbike had really unsettled her.

'She's back.'

Ted pursed her lips and didn't take her eyes from her brother. The roaring in her ears started softly and grew to a crescendo.

'Back?'

'Yeah. Back in Kalgoorlie.'

CHAPTER TWENTY-FOUR

Zara didn't open her eyes, just slowly shifted her feet across the bed to tangle in with Jack's. His gentle, rhythmic breathing told her he was still asleep. She wanted to curl herself into him, absorb his warmth and steadiness and remember this feeling forever.

Then she remembered he hadn't told her about the incident with Aiden. Why had he hit him? She realised she was angry at him – for not telling her, not letting her in to his life, playing his cards too close to his chest.

It was as if Jack had breached her trust, yet she knew he hadn't. Jack rarely told her things that were going on at work, but he'd never been in a fight with a workmate before. If what Sally had said last night was true.

Or had he? Zara didn't know because now she couldn't be sure he would have told her.

Extracting herself from the bed, she got up and pulled on her trackies and a jumper.

In the kitchen, she waited for the kettle to boil and browsed through the online news. As yet, the explosion hadn't made it to any news feeds that she could see. Her story was almost complete, she only needed to finesse it then she could send it to one of her contacts in Sydney. They might pay extra if she was breaking news.

The thought of doing that filled her with excitement.

A noise behind her made her turn to see Jack standing sleepily in the doorway. 'Morning,' he said, rubbing his bare stomach. His boxer shorts were crumpled, and he oozed the warmth from the bed.

'Morning,' she said, pushing away her anger. Reaching for another mug, she wiggled it at him. 'Long one?'

'Mmm,' Jack pulled out a bar stool and sat on it. He ran a hand over his face and then smiled at her as she placed a coffee in front of him. 'Busy night. Sleep okay?'

'Yeah, not too bad,' she told him as she walked across to the kitchen table and opened her laptop. 'What time did you get home?'

'I'm not even sure,' Jack said. 'Late. Or early, depending on which way you're looking at it.'

'I didn't hear you come in.' She skim-read her article while sipping her coffee, checked for any errors, then sent a text to her contact at the *Daily Telegraph*, crossing her fingers they would be interested.

Zara headed for the shower. 'Are you going back in today?' she called out over her shoulder.

'Yeah, got a bit going on. What's your plans?'

Jack followed her into the bathroom and sat on the closed toilet lid while she undressed and stepped under the hot spray.

'Got a bit of research to do and another few stories to write. I'm fascinated with Janelle Salter.' She squeezed shampoo into her hand and scrubbed at her head, trying to wash away all the feelings from earlier.

'Why?'

'She's a bit of an enigma, don't you think? Have you met her?'

Jack didn't answer so she stuck her head out from behind the glass and looked at him. He raised his shoulders at her. Zara rolled her eyes and went back to washing herself.

'How's work?' Her question slipped out before she could stop it.

'Well, last night spiced everything up,' Jack said. 'You want muesli for brekkie?'

Zara took a breath. Deflection. 'Sure.'

Through the steamed-up glass she saw him leave the room.

Leaning her head against the shower wall, she watched the water swirl around the drain in a whirlpool of suds, wondering when he had stopped talking to her.

—

'Morning, Zara,' Nellie called out in a cheery voice. She was behind the coffee machine, banging and lifting the milk jug up and down as she made coffee for her customers.

Surprised at how nice it was to be called by name and welcomed, Zara smiled back. 'Hello. You look busy this morning.' She leaned her hip against the counter. 'Did you see the mess from last night?'

'I did,' Nellie whispered. 'I heard it was something to do with drugs. That she was selling drugs out of the office.'

'Did you?' Zara listened intently, knowing this was a small town and that gossip and fact needed to be filtered through and verified before she took anything as gospel. 'Who for?'

'I met Janelle a couple of times and I don't think she's the sort of person who would sell drugs,' Nellie said with a laugh. 'That story doesn't wash with me. Now if it was a mining company who wanted to close her down, I could understand that, but they'd do that all above board. Your usual? Are you wanting a sucking-up coffee for Percy again? I'll make you two.'

Zara paid, then leaned against the wall to wait.

Her phone dinged. An email notification.

Zara opened the app.

Janelle Salter.

Good morning, Zara. I trust you are well. I thought I would give you a quote in an email, so the wording was correct. Please see below. I believe you asked who owns the building. We lease the building from Ken Warner. Kind regards, Janelle.

Running her eyes over the words, Zara made sure the quote she'd taken down last night was the same as Janelle had written in her text. She closed the email, making a mental note to find out who Ken Warner was.

Last night, she'd googled Janelle Salter again. There had to be more to her story than what Zara already knew. Yet funnily enough, there was very little online about her.

She was mentioned in her university's website as a high achiever and then again in its alumni magazine, which said Janelle had decided to go into politics.

Zara searched anything to do with environmental policies, green industries and radical groups that Janelle might have been a member of, but there was nothing.

Janelle hadn't decided to run for the Greens, which confused Zara. It would have been easier to go with an already established party, rather than on her own. No need to reinvent the wheel, as her first editor, Lachie, would have said.

Her phone pinged with a message from Jo.

Where are you?

Getting coffee, she replied. *What's your order?*

While Zara waited for their coffees, she tried to work out which story was more important. The explosion or the gold that Barry and Jayne had attached to their van. She'd heard from the *Tele* about the explosion story just before she arrived at the cafe. They were taking it.

The door flung open and Jo ran inside.

'Zara,' she said breathlessly, dropping into the seat next to her. 'Have you got any more news on last night?'

'No, I haven't spoken to anyone, but I've written the story and I'm sending it through to Sydney.' She paused. 'That'll give us enough money to start a website.'

Jo jiggled her knees up and down with excitement.

'But we haven't got time to worry about that. We've got two active stories here and we need to work both. The gold and the explosion.' Zara pulled out her phone again. 'Do you have Sally's number?'

'Yeah.'

'Can you send it to me? Come on, let's get out of here and do some leg work. And we've got to drop this over to Percy.'

As they crossed the road, Zara put the phone to her ear and called Sally. She didn't answer.

The pawn shop sign was swaying in the ever-present breeze blowing down the main street. But something was different this time. The sandwich board sign that was normally near the door, proclaiming Percy bought gold, was not there.

Zara peered inside the darkened shop; the lights were out, and Percy wasn't in his usual spot.

She checked the door for a note and saw that he would be back in ten minutes. Maybe he'd slipped out for a bite to eat. She left the coffee on the doorstep.

'Okay, first off,' Zara said as they sat on a street bench, the wind whipping around their legs. 'Yesterday, we got distracted with the office closure, but really we should have followed up with Jim and Carol about Barry and Jayne to see what else they knew. I owe it to Jayne to work out what's going on and if she knew about the gold. I bet she didn't and we need to make some noise about the mobile coverage or lack of it. So let's go back to what we know.'

'Which isn't much,' Jo said.

'Might be more than you realise. You were the one who said Jack and Kirsty were on the Gold Squad, and you're dead right in saying that they don't usually investigate MVAs. So, what do we know? They came from north. Gwalia. What's at Gwalia?'

Jo shook her head. 'Nothing really. A museum of the old mine. There's a new operating mine there, but they don't do tours or anything.'

'What's the closest town?'

'Oh, well, Leonora is right there. Not five minutes away.'

'Gold mines up there?'

'Yeah. And further north too.'

'And we know it's a big lot of gold because of that conversation I overheard in Percy's shop.'

Zara's phone rang and she looked at the screen. With a grin, she answered it.

'Sally, it's Zara,' she said, knowing she hadn't left a message and that Sally wouldn't have her phone number.

A laugh came down the line. 'I thought it probably was. I'm not going to tell you anything.'

'Do you have anything to tell?'

'I'm not answering that question either.'

Sally's playful tone told Zara she wasn't put out with the phone call, which in time might mean she was willing to give up information.

'Look, all I wanted to do was touch base and see if there was any direction you could point me in,' Zara said. 'You don't have to tell me anything. I can do the hard work and digging, but a direction is always a good start.'

Sally was quiet now, probably considering her options. Next time she spoke, her voice was muffled as if she was talking into her shoulder. 'Look, I don't know much. I haven't been into the station since last night, and as far as I know, all is quiet, except for one thing.'

'What's that?'

Another silence. Zara knew better than to push.

'See if you can get in and see the CCTV for the main street. There might be something interesting there. Or not. I spoke to someone who watched it last night.' Her words held meaning. 'And another thing. Word is that the explosion came from Janelle's office rather than the reception area.' She took a breath. 'Now that's it.'

'Great, thanks, Sally. I'll see what I can do. And don't worry,' she promised, 'nothing has come from you.'

Sally had hung up before Zara had finished speaking, probably regretting what she'd just done. Still, she'd nurture that relationship now. Dipping her toe in the water for the first time was always the hardest.

'Can you get into the shire office and see if they'll let you watch the CCTV?' Zara asked Jo.

An expression Zara couldn't read passed over Jo's face. 'Maybe,' was all she said.

'Want to have a go?' she asked. 'I'm going to drive to Gwalia and see what I can find out.'

'That's over two hours away.'

Zara shrugged. 'That's what we do.'

CHAPTER TWENTY-FIVE

The caravan park at Gwalia was nothing but a gravel pad outside the entrance to the museum.

A large sign told visitors to enter through the reception area and pay the entrance fee, yet the double gates over the road were flung wide open and Zara was sure that many tourists walked straight inside without paying the charge.

She gathered her beanie and gloves and got out of her car, walking to the edge of the mine. Through the fence she could see the bottom; ledges the colour of bitumen wound down the side of the hole. Right at the bottom, the machinery was working and the roar of the engines rose to meet her ears.

The size wasn't a patch on the super pit on the edge of Kalgoorlie, but it was deep enough. Zara was glad she didn't get vertigo. She heard another car pull up and turned around. So far she'd counted eight caravans.

About a hundred metres away, small tin shacks had been fitted out as if miners from the 1800s were living in them. She'd poked her nose in to have a look when she'd arrived and seen water buckets, steel-framed beds with canvas covers and hessian bags as mattresses. Billies hung above the fireplace.

This was a living museum where visitors were allowed to immerse themselves in the exhibit.

She wandered over to the park, looking for someone to talk to, but most of the caravans were shut up tightly. Inside the office, Zara paid the fee and started to look around. Three people were looking at a horse-drawn hearse, complete with a coffin. She suspected that it had been used often.

'Bit grim,' Zara said to a woman reading the information plaque.

'Certainly a hard life back then,' she agreed.

'Where have you travelled from?'

'Oh, up north. We've had a bit of time at Karijini and decided to cut back down through the middle instead of going down the coast road. We're on our way home.'

'Guess you come across a lot of caravanners?'

'Sure do. You're not travelling?'

'No, I'm a journalist. My name's Zara. I'm writing a piece on van life.' She flashed a smile. 'Would you have time to talk to me?'

The woman seemed flustered. 'Oh, I don't know. I haven't really got much to tell.'

'I'm sure you do. How long have you been away for?'

'Only six weeks.'

'Where have you come from?'

'South Australia. We started at Port Augusta and went up the Stuart Highway to Darwin, then across the top to Kununurra. We really wanted to go across the Gibb River Road, so we did that, then Karijini and now here we are.'

Zara leaned against the corrugated-iron wall and looked up. Pinpricks of light were coming through the holes in the roof and dust-covered cobwebs hung in the rafters.

'What's the best thing to happen to you on this trip?' she asked.

'Maybe the waterfalls. They're stunning. And the colours of the rocks and land. It's like nothing I've ever seen before.'

'What's the worst thing?'

The woman seemed to pale and then looked over her shoulder. 'When we were in Darwin,' she told Zara, 'we were about to head off then a heap of police turned up and started to swarm all over the caravan parked next to us. We had to answer a lot of questions but we didn't know anything. The woman wasn't there, she'd been travelling by herself and she was found murdered in a toilet block down on the marina. It was terrible.'

'Oh no! What happened?'

'The police didn't say much, but I read in the paper she hadn't been sexually assaulted so they thought the attack was random.'

'Terrible,' Zara said. 'But, look, thanks for your time.' She handed her card to the woman. 'If you think you might have something more to add, give me a call. I'd love to talk more.'

She smiled at the woman and moved around the display, getting her phone out and googling: *caravan park murder*.

A few articles came up and she scanned them, getting the gist. A woman who had been travelling alone had been found murdered in the toilet block of the caravan park, not the marina. Her caravan had been trashed and the police were looking at a motive of robbery.

She tapped her pen against her forehead, thinking. She'd heard of another caravan death only recently.

A sign told her there was coffee and scones at nearby Hoover House and suddenly Zara had a hankering for more caffeine.

She sat on the verandah and the soft scents of roses she remembered from her mother's garden wafted towards her, touches of softness in among the harshness of rocks and flat earth.

The machines growled from the mine below, while chatter and laughter from travellers reached her.

Google was her friend right now. She typed in: *caravanners deaths*.

Her stomach turned as she read through eight different articles. All were from different states and by different journalists, all were only small stories, but all had the same theme.

In each, an unfortunate caravanner had died accidentally or was thought to have been murdered, or had been badly injured. There weren't any follow-up stories.

Sipping absent-mindedly at the coffee, which had appeared next to her hand while her attention was absorbed, she looked up the number for the Darwin police station and asked to speak to the detective in charge of the Sonya Myers case.

The phone connected and she heard a female voice. 'Detective Brooke O'Neill.'

'Hello Detective,' Zara said, and introduced herself. 'I wonder if I could ask you a few questions about Sonya Myers?'

'What's your interest?'

'Well, that's hard to say. I'm looking into the deaths of some caravanners here in Western Australia – different but similar to Sonya's, and I wanted to rule out what consistencies there are.'

'I see. What other caravanners?'

Brooke was going to be tough.

'Barry and Jayne Hathaway. They were involved in a single vehicle rollover and I was first at the scene of the accident,' Zara told her. 'Both died before being taken out of the vehicle.'

'And?' Brooke sounded bored now.

'And I found a GPS on the caravan, which was unusual. I've been trying to find out if there are other vans that have had the same thing. And if they do, why.'

Silence.

'I can't answer that question,' Brooke told her.

Zara was astute enough to know she just had. 'Okay, how about this one. Would it be unusual for caravans to have GPS units attached in strange places?'

'Look, Zara, was that your name? We don't answer journalists' questions. If you haven't got any information for me, then I'm going to have to hang up the phone.'

'Thanks for your time.' Zara felt her heart give an extra hard beat as she dialled a police station in Cloncurry and went through the same spiel.

'Yeah,' the rough voice of Charlie Hampson answered. He told Zara he wasn't a detective, but he'd worked the case. 'Don't have detectives out here. They gotta fly in from Brisbane and if they're busy we just do the best we can.'

'Did you find anything unusual on the van?'

'We sure did. There were three GPS units attached to the undercarriage. Not seen that in all my time of policing.'

'What injuries did the elderly man receive in the break-in?'

'He were real bashed up. Didn't die, mind you, just was gonna take a long time to recover. Lotta head injuries. They took to the poor codger with an iron bar. I reckon it was a golf club meself, but I haven't been able to verify that.'

'Sounds pretty rough. So it was a robbery?'

'Sure looked like it, but he swore black and blue he didn't have anything of value in the van.' He paused. 'But I never understood that either. If there wasn't anything of value then why was the van … why would he have worried to have GPSs on it?'

'Did you ask him?'

'Course I bloody did.'

'What was his answer?'

'That was the strange thing – he didn't know they were there.'

CHAPTER TWENTY-SIX

The park bench was hard underneath Jack's arse. He tried to huddle deeper into his jacket as he pulled his beanie down over his ears.

It was a delicate balance to get the beanie sitting exactly on his eyebrows, so it didn't cover his line of sight but was low enough to keep his ears warm.

Lucas sat at one end of the bench and Jack at the other. Their view was of a double-lane road and a caravan park on the opposite side. Kids' laughter rose above the high fence and floated to them on the wind, while cars swished past, loudly enough to make conversation difficult.

'That's interesting about the deposits into Barry and Jayne's bank accounts, isn't it? We haven't really had time to catch up since your interviews with Carol and Jim. Could they throw any light on anything?' Lucas asked, when the road was quiet.

He was watching the caravan park entry, where a dual axle twenty-two-foot van had parked, blocking the entrance.

'After speaking to Kirsty, I don't think either of them had too much information that's helpful. They met Jayne and Barry at Newman about two weeks ago. They took the same route, going from Newman to Meekatharra and turned off there to head east. Wiluna, Leinster, some free camping along the way, then found them again at Gwalia. They've leap-frogged over each other by the sounds of it.'

A truck towing two trailers rushed by, and Jack had to hold onto his beanie as the slip wind caught them.

'Where did they camp with each other? What towns?'

'Meekatharra and Wiluna. Carol stated they went to the art gallery together and then on to the laundromat. The next time they camped together was in Gwalia. Carol said Barry wasn't the nicest bloke. Gave Jayne a hard time about everything that wasn't suiting him.'

'I guess none of this really matters if we don't like them for stealing gold. Transporting – well, that's a different story.' Lucas's eyes hadn't shifted from the entrance of the park.

'Do you think they were doing that?'

'I'd find it hard to believe that they didn't know the boxes were there. Not saying they knew what was in them, but those payments still could be linked back to transportation, rather than knowledge.'

'I guess so,' Jack said. His gut didn't tell him that.

'Well, I've been running through the footage from the highway. I've found Jayne and Barry's car twice on the road from Newman and that's about all. Once we get the GPS data, I'm thinking a couple of us should retrace their trip. It would be a good opportunity for you to get on the road and see a bit more of our area.'

'Yeah, I'd be in that for sure,' Jack said, shoving his hands deeper into his jacket pockets. 'That wind is from Antarctica! You want to tell me why we're sitting here? I'm gonna lose my manhood if I've got to stay out here much longer.'

Lucas didn't seem to care about Jack's temperature, or dick. 'I've rung Gwalia and asked for the security footage of the caravan park, and they've sent that through. Interesting, there's been a journalist up there today, asking for the same thing.'

Jack closed his eyes.

'Zara will be following where Barry and Jayne came from,' Jack said. 'She'll be asking questions, probably working out where the mobile range cuts out. That really upset her, the lack of range.'

Lucas huffed. 'Upsets all of us.'

Jack wondered if there was any judgement in his tone. 'Did they give it to her?'

'No, but they said she was asking some pretty pointed questions. If they'd had caravanners who had been injured or robbed while they'd been camped there.'

Jack frowned. 'Burgled? Wonder what that's about.'

'Not sure.'

They sat shoulder to shoulder in silence until Lucas said: 'Thought you should meet Cas.'

Jack stayed silent – there was another car coming.

'Casper the friendly ghost,' Lucas clarified.

'Which buildings does he haunt?'

Lucas snorted. 'Believe in ghosts, do you?'

'Well, not yet, but I could be persuaded, depending on the evidence,' Jack said, deadpan.

'You'll see why we call him Casper the friendly ghost when you meet him.'

'Are you using my name in vain?' A quiet voice said from behind.

Jack turned and saw a thin man dressed in grey tracksuit pants, hoodie and sneakers. His beard was grey, and his eyes might have been blue once, but now they looked grey too.

'Casper, how's it going?' Lucas asked, without turning around. 'This is Jack. He's new.'

Casper was so soft-footed, Jack couldn't hear him walk to the front of the bench and sit between them.

'New is good,' Casper said, and folded his hands across his stomach, falling quiet.

'G'day,' Jack said.

Casper nodded.

There wasn't any conversation. Cars zoomed past and occasionally a kid on a bike rode along the footpath.

'Missy's been pinching jewellery again,' Casper said in a low voice, about ten minutes after he'd sat down.

Streetlights had come on and the car traffic had increased because it was the end of one shift at the mine and the start of another.

'Not again?' Lucas sounded exasperated. 'I only cautioned her two weeks ago.'

'She's not going to change.'

'Where?'

Casper jerked his head backwards. 'That-a-way.'

'Breaking in?'

'No. Door was left open, and it hasn't been reported because the jewellery had already been stolen from someone else.'

'Revenge.'

Casper raised one bony shoulder. 'More than likely. She'll hock it at the pawn shop, so you'll be able to pick her up from there, if you watch long enough.'

The tangled web of criminals.

'Heard anything about gold being stolen?' Lucas asked. 'As in bars.'

'They're not stealing bars, Lucas.' His tone was bemused, as if he really couldn't believe that Lucas had said something so ridiculous. 'Wherever it's coming from, the pieces will be small. They'll wait until there's enough for a bar and then melt it down and cast one. Geez, no one steals bars!'

'You know there's gold being stolen?'

'And that's another silly question.' Casper turned to Jack. 'One thing you need to know about gold thieves, prospectors or anyone who has got the fever, Jack. You can put ten thousand dollars in cash in front of them and they won't touch it. If you put gold on the table, they will have worked out how to steal it in three seconds flat.'

'Gold fever is real?' Jack asked.

'As real as you are sitting there.' Casper turned back to the road. 'Every man or woman who lives in a gold town has the fever.'

'And it's being stolen?' Jack repeated his earlier question.

'We're living in a gold town. Gold is made to be stolen.'

Jack had a million questions, but he couldn't ask any of them. He didn't know how Casper worked, how he talked, what information he gave. Patient was what Jack needed to be if Casper was going to be a source for him now, but the thrill that was sitting in his stomach didn't want to wait.

Putting his hands under his thighs, he bit his tongue.

Lucas wasn't saying anything either.

'Tab is the one stealing the cars from the mine sites,' Casper said. He stood. 'Tab and Gavin. But I don't have to tell you that. I'm sure you already know.'

'Got our suspicions.' Lucas pulled his beanie down a bit more. 'Serious question. Have you heard anything about grey nomads transporting gold?'

'No.'

Lucas nodded. He put his elbow over the back of the seat and half turned to Casper. 'Let me give you a hypothetical situation.' Lucas gave him the run-down on the accident and what they found. 'Now, is there anything you can tell us about that?'

'That gold will be coming from a mine site.'

'Can you tell me which one?'

'I don't know which one, but, again, it takes a lot of little flakes to make up five hundred grams, times by two. Unless a prospector is willing to wait years, that gold is coming from a concentrated area.'

'Just need to know where that concentrated area is.'

'I'm not here to do your job.' Casper said mildly. 'The explosion was interesting.'

The three men were silent. Again, Jack wanted to ask a million questions.

'The interesting part is why the woman is running with such strange policies.' Casper scratched his face. 'Don't know much about her, but I think she's worth looking into.'

'What makes you say that?'

'Have you looked into her history at all?'

'Only what we have access to. She's not known to us.'

'But maybe those who are close to her are. She has one consistent visitor. Really, Lucas, you don't keep your eyes open very well, do you?'

'I know you do that much better than me.'

Jack couldn't keep silent. 'At her office? The visitor comes to her office? I went through the CCTV footage last night and only saw one person entering the office. We've cleared her from our enquiries.' He felt a twinge as he said it. They hadn't even looked at Zara because she was ... Zara.

Yet that was the problem. Zara was Zara. Could she have done something so stupid and impulsive as to set a bomb so she could write a story about it?

Jack had been shocked at himself when the idea had popped into his caffeinated sleep-deprived brain last night and he had dismissed it, feeling disloyal.

But should he have rejected the idea so quickly?

'You might need to look harder then.'

'What are we looking for?'

'That's for you to work out, Jack.'

A bout of yelling started from the caravan park. 'I'm not paying you for the time I don't stay here, you bitch!'

'Dude,' came the reply, 'if you're living here full time, you have to pay, even when you're not overnighting here. Now cough up, or I'll call the cops.'

'Better than watching a soap opera,' Casper said, standing up and starting to walk off. 'You see every type of person in a caravan park. Every type. They could make a TV show of ridiculousness outta that joint. How many arrests you made there, Lucas?'

'Too many to remember, Casper. You were out here that night we had eight of us going in to get the bloke who held up the pharmacy, weren't you?'

'I'm the ghost for a reason. I move in silence, and no one knows I'm there.'

—

'Who exactly is Casper?' Jack asked, as they got into their car.

'We don't really know,' Lucas answered. 'He's been feeding us information for years. Everyone on the force, not just me. I reckon he and Martin might go back, somehow, but that's only my deduction, not gospel. Anyhow, he usually pops up at the station early in the morning says he wants to see someone. Usual spot out the front of the caravan park and at the usual time. Which is what it was today. Never seems to be worried about being seen talking to us. I'm still not sure how no one has worked out he grasses them up, but in all the years I've been here, nothing has happened to him. Not a beating or anything.'

'Must stay out of the way of the real crims,' Jack said. 'The bikies and such.'

'Not so sure. He's pointed us in their direction once before, during a murder investigation. But he likes to focus on the young kids who are standing at the fork in the road. He tries to get us involved so we can give them a talking to. Scare the shit out of them for doing something wrong and hopefully put them back on the right path. Trouble is it's hard for some of the kids to stay on the right side of the law, because of their circumstances.' Lucas flicked on the blinker and pulled into the police station car park. 'There's this one kid, Jamie. He lives on the northern side of town. Great kid. About six or seven. A bit cheeky, but nothing crazy, you know?'

Jack did.

'Anyhow, I've got to know Jamie because about once a month, over eight months straight, I had to visit his house. His father is a petty crim. It was the same every time I went to their joint. I'd knock on the door, call out who I was. The wife would answer the door, I'd go in and Jamie would be on the couch watching TV. I'd high-five him, he'd tell me about his day at school and then I'd go and caution his old man.' Lucas sighed. 'I reckon Jamie liked it when I turned up because he had someone to talk to and he had someone to listen to him. Tell me how that kid has got a chance.'

'See it all too often, don't we?' Jack replied as they walked inside.

Kirsty looked up and waved some papers around. 'Where's Jett?'

'On his way in,' Lucas told her. 'Give him ten. Got something?'

'Yeah, I'll tell you when he arrives so I'm not doubling up. Need any coffee?'

They both shook their heads.

'Okay. I'll be back in a bit,' she said and left the door ajar.

'Morning fellas.' Aiden walked in and tipped his head to both Jack and Lucas. 'Get everything tidied up?'

Lucas pushed out a chair with his foot. 'Take a load off.'

Aiden sat down and looked at each man, his hat in his hands.

'Morning,' Jack said, leaning forward.

'Listen, I just wanted to say, not too many people know about the missus leaving, okay? Wouldn't mind keeping it like that. Don't want anyone fawning over me.' He dropped his eyes to the carpet.

'Sure,' Lucas said. 'Not our news to tell.'

Jack nodded his agreement, wondering if he should let Aiden know he'd already mentioned it to Martin.

Still, Martin was a sergeant. He'd be able to handle information sensitively.

An uncomfortable silence began to fill the room.

'Anyway, that was all I came to say,' Aiden said at last. 'Under your hat.'

'No worries, mate,' Lucas said.

Aiden nodded and got up to leave.

Jack turned back to Lucas. 'I came across the name Ken Warner when I was searching property records. Seems he's the fella who owns the building that Janelle Salter is leasing her office from. Know anything about him?'

Lucas straightened up. 'He's the president of The Untouchables. Never had much trouble with him. He's a businessman. Owns his own camping gear store in town. His brother, Ray, is well known to most of the coppers around here, though.'

'Yeah, he's one nasty piece of work,' Aiden said. 'You'll find him at the skimpy bars most nights. Roughs up the girls if he gets the chance.'

'But would he own property?'

'Ray or Ken? Bikies own land and buildings everywhere. The legit businesses are how they launder their money from the prostitutes and drugs,' Lucas said. 'If Ken owns that building, we should be looking at him as well as Janelle Salter. Could be a retaliation thing. Christ, the last thing we need in Kal is a bikie war.' He looked at Aiden. 'Uniform know of any rumblings?'

'I haven't heard anything,' Aiden said. 'And you're right. We don't have enough police on the ground to cope with a bikie gang war.' He paused.

Jack's head swirled. 'Is there another OLMG?'

Aiden paused at Jack's words, then shook his head. 'Jack, mate, sorry about before, you know? Had a bit going on. Doesn't excuse my behaviour, though.'

'Forgotten already,' Jack told him.

'Cheers.' He kept his hand on the door and looked at them.

Jack wanted to ask if he was okay, but that wasn't how the coppers did it.

'Did you manage to get any info from the GPS?' Aiden asked. 'The one that Zara found. That was a lucky find.'

Jack focused on Lucas. 'Haven't heard anything yet, but Kirsty was working on it.'

'Speak of the devil,' Kirsty said, coming into the room with Jett.

'Morning, all,' Jett said. 'How's everyone pulled up?' Not waiting for an answer, he ploughed on. 'Kirsty, what have you got to tell us?'

CHAPTER TWENTY-SEVEN

'Check this out,' Kirsty said. She slapped some pages onto the desk.

Jack picked them up. 'The details from the GPSs?'

'Gold star for you! Firstly, can you tell me if there were any apps on either Barry's or Jayne's phones for this brand of GPS?'

Jack shook his head. 'Pina has managed to get access to the back-ups. Barry's phone was last backed up the night before the accident, and there weren't any apps relating to GPSs on there. So, unless it was downloaded after the back-up, then I'd say no.'

'Little ripper,' Kirsty said. 'These are the units that were used inside the lockboxes where the gold was found. As you can see, there's a serial number on the top of each. I've traced them back to their point of sale. First one was bought in Perth two years ago. Second one, Brisbane, six months ago, and the last one – now, this is interesting – was bought in Darwin only five weeks ago.' She looked around. 'If Barry or Jayne were keeping track of the units, they'd have the app on their phone right from the start. These guys are in the clear.'

Jack opened his mouth to mention a burner phone, but Pina would be all over that. There probably wasn't one.

'I've contacted the shop,' Kirsty continued, 'and asked if they have any security footage, and the manager's going to get back to me. They usually only keep footage for a week, but recently there's been a spate of shoplifting so they're keeping it longer. The other shops basically laughed when I asked if they had recordings from back that far. Which is understandable. I'm in the process of contacting the manufacturer to trace back the registration number to whoever bought it. They'll have a record. I'm ready with a warrant for the information but haven't managed to access the department I need yet. However –' Kirsty grinned '– we've been lucky, because both the GPS units in the lockboxes had a SIM card inside.'

She held up a map and then pinned it on the corkboard. 'These are the mobile phone towers that the GPS tracker pinged off. Now I'm going to assume that the tracker started pinging only when it was attached to the van. These types of GPS units are multipurpose. They search constantly and when they're in mobile range, they use the tower and when they're out of range, it searches for a satellite.'

'Clever,' Jack said. 'That would mean it was tracking the caravans all the time.'

'Exactly.' Kirsty nodded.

'And the pinging,' Jett said. 'Where did it start?'

'Wiluna.'

All four looked at each other.

'That's when the gold was attached to the van?' Jack wanted to make sure he was clear.

'Well, that's when the GPS was turned on. The GPS was in the lockbox, which was secured under the van, so it must have been put there before Barry and Jayne left Wiluna.'

'Gold mines in that area?'

'Yep, one. There're a few others around too. Mount Magnet, Meekatharra and more,' Kirsty answered.

'And the DNA sampling will help narrow it down as to which mine that gold came from?'

Jett nodded. 'Sure will. Can I bring up another point on the GPS units? They've been bought in three different states. And over the space of two years. This operation has been running for two years. Perhaps longer and it's pointing to being active interstate as well.'

'We could also assume that whoever is attaching the gold would choose an on-road van,' Kirsty said, 'because, again inside the criminal's mind, they would be trying to transport to a town, not further out bush. Those other trips are for experienced four-wheel drivers – well, they should be. God knows how many people we've had to rescue out there because they've snapped an axle or run out of fuel. That type of country is isolated bush and only appeals to a few. The Goldfields Highway, by contrast, is bitumen, an easy drive with lots of things to see along the way – and once you're past Leonora, there's only one way to go and that's to Kal. My hypothesis would be that whoever put it under the van would have arranged for someone to collect it in Kal. Or another spot. Perth or another capital city. Somewhere that's easy for them to sell it without being asked too many questions.'

'Not if the gold belonged to the van owners, though,' Lucas said. 'They'd just be driving where the mood took them, knowing the box was still attached because they had the GPS app on their phone.'

'Where's Barry's phone?' Jett asked.

'I tendered that into evidence too,' Aiden said. 'The newest iPhone there is. From memory it was pretty smashed up. Might not get too much out of it.'

'If we run with the hypothesis that it's not Barry and Jayne's gold, then we need to check all the spots where they camped en route to Kal,' Jett said. 'The last spot they stayed was Gwalia. That sounds like the safest place to find a ride for the gold and get it to Kal without tourists taking a turn.'

'Hold on,' Jack said. He turned to Lucas. 'Do you want to tell them what you know here?'

'Sure,' Lucas said, 'I rang the Gwalia museum today, looking for the security camera vision. Someone has already been there asking for it.'

Everyone's eyes flew to Lucas, then to Jack.

'Zara,' Jack confirmed.

'What the hell? What does she know?' Aiden burst out. 'This is what I was talking about!'

Jett stood up and walked over to Aiden. 'Enough, you should be on patrol. Thanks for your input, Aiden.' He ushered him out the door and shut it tightly.

Jack swallowed, the only noise in the room was the bare-faced clock with the bright-red second hand.

'What do you think she knows?' Jett asked Jack.

'I have no idea. I wasn't even aware that's where she was today. Lucas made mention of it when we were seeing Casper.'

'Lucas?' Jett swivelled around.

'Everything Jack told you. I don't know what she knows or why she's there. Only that there was a journalist asking for the footage. No name. We're only assuming it was Zara.'

'It'll be Zara,' Jack said.

'Okay, well, let's not worry about that for the time being. Someone needs to get hold of that footage and find out what the fuck is on it.'

Lucas sighed. 'I'm sure I'm not the only one in the state that wishes the gold price would go down,' he said.

'What?' Kirsty frowned.

'If it wasn't worth anything, no one would steal it!'

'Question,' Jack said. 'In previous cases of gold theft, who is the most common thief: organised crime or ...?'

'Really, it's anyone,' Jett said. 'You'll get the prospectors taking gold off other people's leases and trying to rip each other off, then there's the blokes who end up making the biggest mistake of their lives, working in the gold room by themselves and seeing the gold flakes on the floor after cleaning out the pipes. Good pour rooms have cameras in them, but no one cleans the lenses so they're filthy. Can't see stuff-all on the footage. Sometimes the temptation is too much if they're behind in their house payments or got a holiday coming up. They think that no one will notice five grams missing. Easy to hide inside a thermos or steel water bottle. Round figures, that's around seven hundred dollars in today's market. Grab five here and five a few weeks later, and perhaps another five after that – certainly gives them a boost. Then you've got the bigger fish. Organised crime. Bikies. Now they're up to their necks in this sort of thing and a couple of times before we've had some Mafia involvement.'

'If this is organised crime, then it will be across state borders.'

'Want me to put my feelers out in SA?' Jack asked. 'What are we looking for? Gold being transported by caravanners?'

'That's about what we're looking for, yeah,' Jett said. 'Let's make some calls.'

CHAPTER TWENTY-EIGHT

'Jo, we've got something,' Zara said over the phone.

'I've got something too,' Jo said, her voice coming through the car's stereo.

'What's yours?' Zara indicated to turn onto the Goldfields Highway, leaving Gwalia.

'I've seen the CCTV footage for the main street for twelve hours before the blast.'

Zara didn't ask how. 'And?'

'You're the only one who goes into Janelle's office. Not one other person. The only action is when Janelle leaves at …' Jo's voice faded off for a moment. 'Five fifteen pm. She stops in the doorway looking back into the office for a few minutes. Looks like she's talking, then she heads off. Lou comes out about ten minutes later, locks the door and then nothing.'

Zara checked her mirrors and made sure everything was clear behind and in front of her. The road began to clip by at one hundred and ten kilometres an hour. Not that she relaxed; she hung on to the steering wheel tightly and kept checking her surrounds.

'Nothing?' Zara replied.

'Do you get it? No one came in and out except Janelle, Lou and you.' She paused. 'You didn't leave a bomb behind, did you?'

'Shit,' Zara whispered. 'You think they set it themselves? Sally said the blast came from Janelle's office.'

'Oh no, wait on, I'm not saying that.'

'And you can see the front of the office clearly?'

'The camera is aimed almost right at their front door.'

Zara thought about this new bit of information. 'Well, we'd better do some more work on that tomorrow,' she said. 'I'll be home soon, but it'll be too late to go and question Janelle or Lou.'

The sun was still high in the western sky and her mind flicked to Ted. Maybe she'd call in there and see her.

'What did you get?' Jo asked.

'Well, the lady at reception told me I'd have to wait while she rang her supervisor, then an old battleaxe turned up and said unless I had a warrant or was the police, I wasn't seeing anything.'

'It sounds like she watches too many crime shows on TV.'

'She wouldn't be the first. Anyhow, I explained that I only needed to see if Jayne and Barry were on the footage and then she told me that it was an invasion of privacy. I wasn't going to get anywhere there.' Zara was still annoyed about the whole thing. 'On my way in, I spoke to a woman who told me she'd stayed in a caravan park in Darwin next to a van that got ransacked and the owner murdered.'

'Murdered?'

'That got me thinking, because my mate in South Australia told me she's interviewing another caravan park owner in Ceduna about a body they'd found.'

In her rear-view mirror Zara saw a car coming up in the distance. She checked her mobile range then made sure her car was steady on the road.

'That's sounding like a lot of dead grey nomads,' Jo said.

'That's what I thought. I did a bit of googling and found two more. The police in Darwin wouldn't speak to me, but the other one in Queensland did.'

Zara flicked her eyes to the mirror again as the car behind her turned on their lights. Good practice when driving on bush roads, but the action made her stomach turn for a second. Lifting her foot slightly, she slowed her ute, giving the car opportunity to pass when the time was right.

'An old bloke was roughed up in Cloncurry. And there were three GPS units on his van. Three! Jayne and Barry's had one I know about, but I'd bet my last pay cheque there were more. I think there's something there.'

'Was there any gold found?'

'Don't know. The Queensland copper said there wasn't, but if it had been taken by someone else, they wouldn't know. What he did say was that the old bloke didn't know the GPS was on his van.'

'Do we go to the police?'

'Not yet. We need concrete evidence and I don't want them to gag us yet. We'd have to get an agreement that we get first crack at the story if this is as big as I think it is.'

'Okay, what can I do?'

'Can you get a timeline together of all the reports of injured or dead caravanners over the last five years. Let's see if we can get some interviews and go from there.' She paused. 'This might be nothing or it might be huge.'

'Got it,' Jo said.

'Talk to you later, oh and good work on that CCTV footage. We'll line up another chat with Janelle tomorrow.'

Zara disconnected and noted she now only had one bar of mobile range. She wrote that down on her window and put on some music, before checking around her.

The car behind was still on her bumper.

The road in front was a long straight stretch, so Zara slowed some more.

'Come on, off you go,' she encouraged.

Without thinking, she hit Liz's number and waited for the ringing tone. Nothing. When she looked again, her phone was out of range.

Seriously, the government had to fix this lack of connectivity. If this story turned out to be nothing, she'd put all her efforts into getting the mobile range extended.

She tapped her fingers along to the radio, then checked her rear-view mirror again. The car hadn't budged. Still stuck to her rear.

Slowing again, Zara checked her speed. Less than one hundred kilometres an hour.

'Dude, just pass me,' she said.

Her eyes flicked between the road and the mirror. The car had moved closer to her and was still in her lane.

'What the hell?' She reached for her two-way and gave a call. 'Car southbound behind dual-cab ute, you're clear to pass.'

The car didn't change position.

Pushing her foot down, she sped up and the car stayed on her tail. She slowed down, and the car slowed too.

'Oh,' Zara said.

The car was purposely keeping pace with her.

'Oh shit.'

The numberplate wasn't visible because the car was too close. She sped up, trying to get a look at it in the mirror, but the car was quick.

Ted's driveway would come up soon. She'd call in there. Shake her companion that way.

'But what's the point in that?' she muttered. 'They could follow and there's no mobile range. Just keep going until you get range and then call Jack.'

Rounding a corner, she saw a truck coming towards her.

'Northbound truck,' Zara said into the handpiece. 'Got a copy? You're about to pass a white dual-cab ute. Got a copy?' She tried to keep the panic from her tone.

The radio stayed silent. The truckie either hadn't heard her or didn't think the call was for him.

'Northbound truck, got a copy?' She tried again. Truckies never turned off their radios.

Silence.

She sped up further, pushing over the hundred-and-ten-kilometre limit, her heart pounding. Who was behind her and why were they tailing her?

The truck rumbled by and she raised her hand in a panicked wave. The truckie didn't respond.

The road was long, straight and deserted. Just like where Jayne and Barry's accident had happened.

There hadn't been mobile range there either.

Her anxiety heightened along with confusion. What was the driver trying to do?

An orange flicker caught her eye and Zara let out a breath, giving a little self-conscious laugh.

'About bloody time,' she said as the car pulled out onto the right-hand side of the road. 'Idiot,' she chided herself.

But instead of passing, it held steady, right beside her. The windows were tinted so darkly she couldn't see anything inside.

Wait, was it moving sideways towards her?

Closer, and closer, until she had no choice but to put her left tyres onto the dirt.

'Fuck, fuckity, fuck,' Zara whispered. The drop-off on the side of the road was a good few inches.

She held her breath as her wheels dropped over the edge of the road and onto the dirt. They didn't grip straightaway and the car threw itself to one side then overcorrected.

'Oh my god!'

She leaned on the horn, hoping the noise would make the other car nervous and swing back to the other side of the road.

It didn't move, holding steady with two tyres over the middle white line.

There was little room for movement, from Zara's perspective.

Quickly she made a decision. She jammed her foot on the brake and the other car shot in front. But before she had time to exhale, she saw the brake light.

The car manoeuvred itself, so it was back driving in the middle of the road, its four tyres straddling the white line.

Grabbing her whiteboard marker texta, Zara looked for the numberplate and saw it was covered. Not in red mud or dirt, but deliberately draped with a piece of material.

'What the hell?'

Whoever was in that car wanted her off the road.

Fear flickered through her. Why would someone want to cause an accident with her? Because that's what would happen if they kept this shit going.

Zara wasn't sure what to do. Did she speed up? Did she turn around and go back towards Gwalia until she was back in mobile range? Or did she head to Kal and jeopardise getting home safely? She didn't want to end up like Jayne and Barry.

The road was empty of any other vehicles. The trucks Zara had noticed so frequently were non-existent and the grey nomads who usually frustrated her were nowhere to be seen.

They continued like that, with the car in front making sure Zara knew who was in charge. Occasionally their brake lights would come on and then they would speed up again for seemingly no reason.

Zara kept her ute at a steady one hundred and ten, refusing to slow when they did.

Cat and mouse. Zara was not going to be the mouse. She could be toyed with, but she'd never be eaten.

Twenty minutes later, a track off the main road appeared. The car jerked as it slowed down and wheeled around the corner without a flicker from its blinker.

Zara was too taken aback to follow its path with her eyes for more than a few seconds. She saw nothing but a two-wheel track leading into the bush. There wasn't a sign saying where the road led to.

The car disappeared almost instantly, and suddenly she was alone on the road again.

Letting out a breath, she put on her cruise control, concentrating on getting safely back to the outskirts of Kalgoorlie.

Was it kids playing a stupid game, she wondered, still checking her mirrors, or was it something more sinister?

CHAPTER TWENTY-NINE

Once the hands of the clock ticked past five pm, Jett suggested it was beer o'clock. Ten minutes later, Jack, Kirsty and Jett were at the door of their usual pub. Like everywhere in Kalgoorlie, it was a sea of high-vis and red dirt. Filthy faces and steelcap boots.

A roar went up as a woman in a bikini put her hands above her head and shook her breasts.

Three men at the bar held out hundred-dollar notes and she went to each one, letting them stuff the money into her bra, shaking her breasts after they did.

Another whoop from the men. More moved over to watch and the woman climbed onto a chair behind the bar. In her high heels, she turned slowly, allowing the men to get a good look at her body. She stuck out her hip, all with a sultry look and pursed lips.

'Ah shite,' Jett said, watching the woman parade her assets. 'When did they bring the skimpies in here? We'll need to stop drinking at this pub now.'

'Come on, love, you'd better get yer bra off for a few hundred quid!' Someone yelled out.

The skimpy didn't answer. This time she placed her hands on the back of the chair and bent over, wiggling her bottom.

Whistles and claps followed, the noise rising to another decibel.

Kirsty shrugged. 'They're in just about every pub. Can't avoid them all the time. What are you having?'

'Handle of dry, thanks,' Jett told her.

Jack thought a gin might have been a good way to end the day but took his lead from Jett. 'Same,' he told her. 'Do you want me to go instead?'

Kirsty's face lit up with a smile. 'Thanks for the offer, Jack, but I'm sure I can cope.' She nodded and disappeared into the raucous crowd.

Jett leaned in. 'You don't have to worry about Kirst,' he said.

Jack watched her stop and talk to punters before getting to the bar. 'Yeah, but she shouldn't have to look at the girls.'

'Why not?' Jett asked. 'She likes looking at them.'

It took Jack a moment to work out what Jett was meaning before heat flooded his face. 'Oh, shit. Right. Won't offer that again.'

Jett laughed and led Jack to a table as a chorus of disappointed cries went up. The skimpy had straightened up, given a little wave and blown a few kisses to the crowd. A bloke in high-vis was helping her down from the chair. She disappeared behind the bar and poured a beer for the first man who ordered.

Jack leaned back in his chair, watching the hyped-up crowd.

The doors opened again, letting in five more blokes, with Lucas following them in. Jack raised his hand and Lucas made his way over, smiling and waving to some people en route. Envy uncoiled in Jack's stomach. Lucas had been here so long.

Jack had a long way to go before he would know that many people in town and be accepted like his colleague was.

'Seems like this could be a pretty dangerous place for a woman to work,' he said.

Lucas shook his head. 'The girls are very safe. There's a woman, Josie, who organises their shifts. She keeps an eye on everything. One hint of trouble and she deals with it. And let me tell you, Josie is not someone you want to cross.'

Jett laughed. 'Josie's more frightening than some of the bikies we come across.'

'The girls don't walk home alone or anything and the skimpy house has more security on the outside than most banks. They're looked after well,' Lucas told him.

Now that the skimpy had returned behind the bar, the throng of spectators had started to move back and find tables to sit at, pool to play or a wall to lean against. It opened the bar up and made all the people much easier to see and evaluate.

Jack never stopped watching. He clocked Aiden over in the TAB section. He saw Kirsty give the skimpy an extra-large smile as she linked her fingers around four beers and turned back towards them.

Good manners made him want to help her, but the look on Kirsty's face suggested he stay in his seat.

'Here you go,' she said, placing the beers on the table.

'Cheers,' Jett said, reaching for a glass and raising it.

They all clinked.

'Last night's blast doesn't seem to have had too much effect on patronage,' Jack said.

'That's just where we live,' Kirsty said. 'Mostly everyone minds their own business until it becomes their business. People observe carefully. There's always undercurrents.'

Kirsty's words sounded ominous.

Jack glanced around again. He noticed a man with dark curly hair and a green John Deere hat sitting by himself at a table near the TAB section. His hands were in constant motion, flicking the drink coaster from edge to edge to edge, as he sipped his beer and watched the TV. On the table were three hundred-dollar notes and a folded newspaper. He was too far away to check but Jack would have bet his next drink the fella had underlined the horses he wanted to back.

It seemed that everyone else knew each other. Most were in groups of no less than four, which made the man in the hat, sitting solitarily near the TAB, even more obvious.

'Looks a bit out of place,' Jack said, tipping his head towards the man.

Swivelling his eyes but not his body, Lucas clocked him. 'That's Ray Warner. You know the fella I told you about from The Untouchables. He's bad news.'

Jack looked back at the man in the cap and memorised the parts of Ray's face he could see. Ray didn't seem to notice that he was being watched. His eyes were glued to the screen.

'Geez, there must be some money go through this place,' Jack said after a moment. 'Imagine if the government does what it wants to and tries to make us a cashless society. Kalgoorlie will fall over.'

Nodding, Jett leaned forward. 'Wait until the Kalgoorlie Cup. If you want to see cash, that's the place for it. Thousands of it folding in people's pockets. Then they go out to the two-up ring and win or lose out there.'

'I went out to the two-up ring last week for a look,' Kirsty said. 'The food van was out there and a few of the regulars.' She looked at Jack. 'You should go – you'll get to know who the regulars are pretty quickly and you'll find a melting pot of cultures and ethnicities out there. A lot of the rich blokes wear thick gold chains around their necks and wrists and they buy their wives the same sort of thing. How to tell everyone you've got money without telling them.' She took a sip of her drink.

'You can't get near the ring when the race round is on,' Jett said. 'The amount of cash is astronomical. Have to see it to believe it,' he reiterated. 'Hundreds of thousands. Cash is king in Kal.'

'And there's never any trouble out there?' Jack asked after a pause to take the words in.

'Hardly ever,' Kirsty said.

'That seems hard to believe.'

'Honour among thieves, my friend,' Jett said, clapping Jack on the shoulder. 'Once in a blue moon there might be a bit of an argument, but you can guarantee the person who caused it will be an out-of-towner. The regulars all trust each other … As much as crooks do.'

'When do they play?' Jack asked.

'Every Sunday,' Jett said.

'Ah, that's right, I'd forgotten. Aiden told me two-up was the place to be on a Sunday afternoon,' Jack said, wrinkling his brow.

Swivelling in his chair, he glanced at the TVs on the wall. One had the State of Origin match on, another was playing an AFL game; not any teams Jack was interested in.

'Yeah, a few of the uniforms like a flutter. Nothing illegal about that.'

Lucas looked around the bar. 'Looks like Aiden's on a good thing,' he said, nodding to the senior constable who had a plate of steak and chips put in front of him.

'Why's that?' Jack asked.

'Just collected five hundred big ones from the TAB.'

'Not bad for a night's work,' Kirsty said. 'Might have to hit him up for a loan.'

Jett drained his glass in one hit and stood. 'Better get going, the missus needs me to help with the kids tonight.'

Lucas glanced at his watch and groaned. 'Bugger it, me as well. Can you give me a lift, Jett?'

'Sure thing. Rest of you okay to get home?'

Kirsty gave them a wink. 'I'll be fine, fellas. I've got a hot date across the road in … ten minutes. Catch you tomorrow.'

—

Jack perched on a stool, resting his elbows on the bar, with a twenty-dollar note sitting in front of him.

The barman, who had introduced himself as Tom the previous night, finished pouring another pint and then tipped his head towards Jack. 'Same again?'

'Please,' Jack said.

Tom poured the beer then set it in front of Jack and took the twenty. 'You lot must get paid too much,' he said.

'Cheers,' Jack raised the glass. 'Why would you say that?'

'Well, I reckon you must be. Aiden over there turns up here most nights flashing big notes around, putting bets on the horses. Keeps losing but he just rocks up again night after night, money in hand. I know some big gamblers. Aiden doesn't quite take the cake, but he almost does for consistency.'

As they spoke, the door opened and a group of men walked in. One glanced around the bar before taking a table near Aiden.

'Does Aiden play big often?' Jack asked.

'Hang on, mate,' Tom said and went to take another order.

Pity swirled in Jack's stomach as he took another glance at Aiden. Another police officer's relationship bites the dust. Wouldn't be the last. Jack knew he needed to make sure he worked harder on his relationship with Zara so that never happened to them. And that meant going home about now.

But he wasn't ready to leave the pub yet.

'Sorry, mate, what did you want to know again?'

Jack refocused on Tom. 'Does he ever win big?'

'He's the worst gambler I know.'

'When did he last have large bets?'

Tom glanced over his shoulder. 'What is this, twenty questions?'

'Might be thirty yet.'

CHAPTER THIRTY

'Can't be that bad,' a woman's rough voice said.

Zara quickly wiped her eyes. She should've stayed at home this morning, but Jack hadn't come home until very late, smelling of booze and she hadn't wanted to talk to him.

Instead, grabbing her heavy coat, she'd walked to the park and had been sitting there for an hour or so feeling very sorry for herself. Her mum called this PLOM's disease. Poor Little Old Me.

Then the tears had started. She'd rather be alone so no one else knew about her moment of weakness.

The feeling of powerlessness was so fresh and real after her run-in with the car. Normally it would have been the first thing she'd told Jack, but when he hadn't come home she'd wrapped herself in the doona and gone to sleep.

Now the tears she always tried to avoid were trickling down her cheeks.

She felt a brush of air behind her, and then suddenly someone was sitting at the other end of the bench.

'I'm fine,' she said. Keeping her head down, she forced out the words. 'Just fine. Thank you.'

She ran her sleeve over her face again and started to stand, her back turned to the other woman.

'Well, that's good to know. I'm pretty sure young women cry in this park all the time and they're fine too.'

The voice was vaguely familiar.

Risking a sidelong glance, Zara's mouth fell open. 'Ted!'

'So rumour has it.'

Ted had her elbows hung over the back of the bench. She was half turned away and staring out across the park as if she understood Zara didn't want to be seen in a vulnerable state.

She was dressed in jeans; these ones were cleaner than the first set Zara had seen her in. Her shirt was crinkled under an overlarge duffle coat, which had streaks of red down the back. Her hair, plaited and wound up in a bun on her head. And she had a pile of library books next to her. Zara was amazed that there were still duffle coats in existence. 'What are you doing in town?'

'This and that. Always go to the library to get some reads. That's the library there.' She nodded towards the white brick building, which was just behind them.

So many questions, but none she wanted to ask. Not while Ted was sitting here, quietly, almost as a comfort. Not without being intrusive and not without risking the fragile relationship she was in the process of building.

'I haven't written your story yet,' she blurted out. 'The paper has shut down, but don't worry, I'm going to find a home for it. I don't think it will be hard. Plus, I need to talk to you some more. Get some stories from you.'

Ted didn't answer, only raised one shoulder. It didn't matter to her.

Zara tried to sniff quietly, then ran her hands over her face again. 'Guess I'd better leave you to it. I'm sure you've got things to do.'

'Well, maybe I do,' Ted said but didn't move.

Zara looked at her, waiting.

'I had a visitor. Someone on a motorbike turned up at my camp uninvited. And the night before that there was a drone. Not that any of this is useful to you, but it might be worth filing away in case you hear of it happening in other places.' She looked at Zara. 'Don't usually give journalists the heads up, but there's too many people getting around on land that's not theirs and taking things which they don't own.'

Zara's journalist instinct kicked into gear. 'Drones and motorbikes?'

'Singular. One bike.' Ted scratched her arm and wiggled on the bench, before slipping into a slouching posture. 'Damn wood is so hard, it makes my arse go numb,' she said.

'Did you recognise the rider?'

Ted seemed to think about this, then shook her head.

'What did they do?'

'Nothing. Rode up, stopped at the camp for a few seconds, did a couple of three-sixties, working up the dirt, then disappeared out into the bush. No point in following out there. Too many places to hide.'

'What do you think they were looking for?'

'Anything that's not theirs, I reckon.' Ted paused. 'Gold, most likely.'

'Do you have any for them to steal?'

Ted smiled vaguely. 'There's always gold. You just have to find it.'

A flicker of excitement replaced the anger Zara had been feeling. She sat back down and faced Ted, her face alight. 'Do you know who was flying the drone? Has it happened before? Why are you telling me?'

'Better take a breath, you might hyperventilate,' Ted said.

Zara laughed, her earlier tears forgotten. 'Sorry.' This woman had confidence oozing from her and Zara wanted to absorb it every time she was near her.

'No matter.' Ted turned to her. 'I don't know anything except a drone was flying over my lease. I wouldn't normally mention it. We all keep everything close to our chest out here, but I was in town and saw you sitting here. Thought you might be able to make use of the information. Anyways,' she said, getting to her feet, 'I'd best be getting on. See you round, Crow-eater.'

'Crow-eater,' she whispered to herself. 'Why are South Australians called that? Wait,' she called out. 'Can you stay a moment?'

'Don't come to town for chitchat.' But she stopped and turned around.

'Why'd you move out into the bush all those years ago?'

'Who wouldn't want to live in the bush? No nosy people interfering with your business.'

Zara took that jibe on the chin and kept going. 'What's the real reason?'

'You saying I tell fibs?'

'No. But I think there's more to your history than what you've told me.'

'Do you?'

'Uh huh.'

'And what are you going to do with that, now your precious paper has closed?'

'I'm going to start my own.'

Ted smiled. 'Good girl.'

Zara felt her face flush.

Ted lost her smile quickly and seemed to think. 'Sometimes things happen that make people distrust all of humanity. That's all.' She paused. 'I tried town once. Used to go out to the block just to prospect then come back in. But I didn't like it. Too many arseholes. My brother helped me move out there. Like I told you, after Mum died. I never left.'

'What makes you love the bush so much?'

'When there's no one else around, it's easy to see who is sneaking up on me.'

Ted started walking away and this time, Zara knew she wouldn't be able to keep her.

'I'll come out and visit you again,' Zara said to her departing back.

'Hope you're better prepared than last time.'

Then she was gone.

How bizarre that Ted had found her at the exact moment that all the despair in the world was taking over. She was the last person Zara had expected to see near the main street of Kal.

She thought about the drone and the motorbike rider. What was she going to do with that information? Every second person owned a drone these days. Wouldn't be easy to find out who was flying over Ted's lease. And the bike? Could be anyone as well.

She got up and wandered along the footpath, feeling a strange sense of freedom. Not since she'd left uni had Zara not worked for a company.

During uni, she'd freelanced to cover some of her fees.

Lachie had been her first real editor, at *The Farming Journal*. That's where she'd cut her teeth, writing pieces on agriculture, grazing systems and profiles on farmers. She'd loved that work, but there had been more exciting stories to find.

Ben had been the next – that's when Jack had moved to Adelaide from Barker to do his detective course and she had followed him. Then she'd freelanced.

Being employed by the large media group twelve months ago had given her the security of employment and the community of journalists she'd missed while freelancing.

Now it looked like she was going to be freelancing again. Or at least for the immediate future.

She kicked at a leaf blowing down the street and tugged her jacket around her. From the other side of the road, a couple of kids called out, running to catch up with their friends. A woman walked out of a shop and watched them, her arms crossed, until they turned the corner.

It was only a few minutes later, Zara found herself out the front of the pawn shop.

She'd seen a guitar in there on her first visit. Her fingers automatically curled around an imaginary neck of a guitar, and she heard strumming in her mind. The first song she'd learned was 'Take Me Home, Country Roads'. Would she recall the chords? God, that had to be nearly twenty years ago, didn't it?

She opened the door. As expected, the bell jangled as she walked in.

Percy didn't look as if he'd moved from the stool behind the Perspex barrier since she'd been in there last.

'G'day,' he said, not looking up.

'Hi,' she replied. 'Quiet in here today?'

Percy checked his watch. 'Yeah, give it time. It's still only early.'

As if on cue, the bell tinkled again. A man entered first, glancing around the shop, then he held the door open, and a woman entered.

Zara noted the nervousness on the man's face, yet the woman was almost bouncing with excitement. They looked to be in their early sixties.

'Hi!' the woman said with a huge smile.

Zara smiled hello and moved towards the back of the shop where the guitar was still on display.

'How can I help yer?' Percy asked.

'Um, my wife and I, we've found some gold,' the man said.

'Oh, we did!' his wife said. 'We found gold, can you believe it?'

'And we'd like to sell it. But we don't really know what to do.'

'Not an easy feat, finding nuggets,' Percy said. 'I can buy it from you, though.'

The wife glanced at her husband and then at Percy. 'We were prospecting out of Wiluna. Not sure where exactly. It was so exciting. I was using the new detector and then suddenly there was all this squealing in my headphones and Walter had to come and find me because I let out such a screech! You thought I'd fallen down an old mine shaft, didn't you, love?'

'Certainly happens,' Percy said. 'Mine shafts are dangerous bits of gear.'

Walter nodded, letting his wife continue speaking.

'I wouldn't fall down a shaft! Surely, you'd see it before that happened. Wouldn't I?'

'Don't be so sure. Often, they're under bushes or drilled into the sides of rocks. Bloody unsafe if you don't know what you're looking at. Anyway, how much have you got?' Percy held out a plastic dish for them to drop the nuggets into.

Digging into her handbag, the woman drew out a small glass jar, undid the lid and tipped its contents into the tray.

'They're a couple of nice pieces,' Percy told her. 'Looking at about six grams, I guess. Got your ID on you?'

'Oh, yes, sure.' The woman dug around again in the depths of her large bag.

'I'll do it.' Walter opened his wallet and handed over his driver's licence.

'Nice to meet you, Walter Bergman,' Percy told him. 'And you, love?'

'Oh, I'm Mary. Mary Bergman.' She gave him another brilliant smile and bounced a couple of times more.

'First time over this way?'

Zara heard the clatter of nuggets onto the scales.

'Yes, first time in Kalgoorlie. Gee, it's cold here, isn't it?'

Zara reached up for the guitar and took it down from the display. The wood was smooth beneath her fingers.

She sat on the floor, cross-legged, and rested it over her knees, fingers curled, thumb touching the strings.

'There we are, that's a nice tidy sum. Five hundred and three dollars.'

Zara heard a cash drawer open and Percy counting out the money.

'I can't believe it! Just like that, we have five hundred dollars in our hand,' Mary said.

'Beginner's luck,' her husband replied, taking back his ID and putting his wallet into his pocket.

'While you're feeling lucky, you should try the two-up on Sunday,' Percy said. 'You going to be in town for a bit?'

Walter laughed. 'Don't you think we should quit while we're ahead?'

'Not if you're on a lucky streak. There's the chance of winning a lot more than five hundred bucks at two-up.'

Zara tuned out while Percy ran through his tourist sales pitch. Finally, with the decision made, she stood, guitar in hand.

'Thanks for helping us out,' Mary called, zipping up her handbag. She squeezed her husband's arm happily as they walked towards the door. 'That's so thrilling, honey,' she told Walter. 'We need to go back out there and have another go. I really think we should, don't you?'

The door closed behind them, shutting out their voices as Zara held up the guitar. 'Can I buy this?'

'Sure can.'

'Do you take card?'

'Rather cash.'

'Oh, I'll have to go and get some out.'

'I'll hold it for you,' Percy said. 'No trouble. The ATM's next door.'

She raised an eyebrow. 'Somehow I don't think the guitar is going to sell in the next ten minutes, Percy. Looks like you've had it on the floor for a while.'

Percy ignored her cheekiness and Zara left the shop.

The ATM. A note on it told her it was out of order.

'Bugger.'

Searching the street, she saw a bank over the road, but the queue was out the door. It was pension day.

She joined the line and waited her turn.

Finally, thirty minutes later she pushed the door to the pawn shop open again, cash in hand. 'I've got it,' she called as the bell heralded her arrival.

Raised voices met her.

'I won't buy any more from you, mate. Told you that last time you were in. You're gonna get me in trouble and ...' Percy broke off as he looked past his customer and recognised Zara. He glared at the man in front of him. 'Get a move on. I've got real customers to deal with.'

The man picked up something from the counter and shoved it angrily into his pocket. 'This won't be the last you hear about this,' he said.

Zara stepped out of the way as the man stormed by. She drew in a breath.

Andrew? No, but something like that. Adam? They'd met before.

Well, whatever his name was, he'd been trying to sell something to a pawn broker.

The door slammed.

'Didn't get what he wanted,' Zara said, pushing the money under the Perspex barrier.

Percy counted it slowly. 'Most people want more than their item is worth,' he told her. 'Sometimes it's worth nothing. No point in arguing with them, I just give them the goods back if they don't take what I offer.'

'Does that man come in often?'

Percy glanced up at her. 'All of my customers come in often.'

Zara took the hint and changed the subject. 'Do you know Ted Upton?'

'Why would you be asking about her?'

Shaking her head, Zara couldn't help but laugh. 'My god, everyone in this town is so bloody secretive. What's that all about?'

Percy unlocked the door next to the counter and came out holding the guitar. He handed it to Zara. 'Because we don't mind other people's business here. Anyone can come to Kalgoorlie and slip right in. We don't care who you are, why you're here or where you've come from. Just don't interfere with our business and we won't interfere with yours.' He smiled and went back behind the counter, locking the door. 'And thanks for the coffee.'

CHAPTER THIRTY-ONE

'Janelle, we've got a few questions for you,' Jack said.

'Ask away,' she said, as she swept behind her desk. 'The police said we were able to clean up the office, so I hope that was the correct information?'

Jack assessed the woman. Her hair was tied up in a ponytail and her sleeves were rolled up to her elbows. She didn't seem to be afraid of hard work.

Lou was washing the walls and had black soot all over her face and arms.

'That's fine,' Jack said and glanced towards Kirsty who was looking around the office, her hands tucked firmly behind her back.

'So, what questions would you like to ask?'

'I've watched yesterday's CCTV footage,' Jack told her. 'I wanted to clarify what appointments you had on during the day.'

Janelle stopped sweeping and looked at Lou, who dropped the sponge so quickly that Jack thought she might have been looking for an excuse to stop work.

'I've got Janelle's calendar on my phone, hold on,' Lou said.

She flipped through a few apps before finding the right one. 'Okay, Janelle had a phone appointment with the manager of Happy Valley Mines at ten am and another meeting at three pm. The rest of the time, we were putting together our policy for the phase-out of mining and oh, yeah, at four forty-five pm, Janelle rang the local Telstra office to see if she could get some information on mobile phone tower positioning. A journalist had come in and mentioned that north of Kalgoorlie is a bit spasmodic. She was involved in an accident and couldn't get help for the people in the car apparently.'

Jack nodded. 'So did you have any visitors in the office or was that day all about phone calls?'

Lou checked her phone again.

'I haven't got any appointments noted here and the journalist was our only visitor. Unfortunately the visitors' book I always get people to sign was burned in this disaster.' She spread her hands out indicating the mess.

Kirsty spoke up. 'You will have noticed the damage is mostly to your office, Janelle. Not to the reception area. We think the explosion happened in here. The damage to the wall makes it obvious. Did you have a wall safe or something that might have exploded unexpectedly?'

'What? No!'

'Have you had any lost property in the office? Did anyone accidentally leave something in the office, which was out of place? Maybe a handbag or shopping bag?'

Lou looked at Kirsty and crossed her arms. 'Why are you asking these questions?'

'We're trying to establish what happened,' Jack said. 'This explosive was packed with nails and screws. On the surface, that makes the explosive look like it was intended to hurt people. But interestingly, it didn't have the fuel to blow it too far, so it really wasn't to hurt people. More attention seeking.'

'Attention seeking,' Janelle said, rubbing her hands over her face. They left black streaks on her skin.

'And there is something on the CCTV that we don't understand.'

Kirsty walked over and stood next to Jack. 'We've watched the CCTV footage, Janelle, and other than the journalist, the only two people who we can place in this office on the day of the explosion is you and Lou.'

Lou scoffed as Janelle threw down her broom. 'You are the second lot of people to ask about that. Some reporter came in here this morning asking the same type of questions.'

Jack stilled. That wasn't Zara; he knew.

'So why do you think he or she might have done that?' Kirsty asked.

'Because *she's* barking up the wrong tree, the same as you are,' Lou snapped.

Outside, trucks and four-wheel drives covered in yellow reflector tape rumbled past.

'Could someone have come in when you were away from the desk, Lou?' Jack asked, trying to smooth the situation over.

Janelle glanced across at Lou.

'I suppose so,' she answered. 'I don't usually leave my desk unattended, but if I have to slip out, I lock the office door.'

'As I said, forensics have told us the blast came from inside your office, Janelle. Do you have an insurance policy?'

'What, now you're thinking I tried to blow up my own office for a payout? You're unbelievable,' Janelle said. 'I love what I do. I believe in the end game.'

'And I do too,' Lou said.

'Sure, but a bit more attention wouldn't hurt, would it,' Jack pushed. 'Your party goes against everything Kalgoorlie stands on. I'm sure you're getting rebuffs in the street, or people ringing up and telling you to get out of town.' He refused to think about the words he'd just said in relation to Zara. Because the same could be said for her. Needing a big story.

Janelle glanced at Lou now, who shrugged. 'You might as well tell them,' Lou said.

Jack's eyes slid from Janelle to Lou and back again.

'Tell us what,' Kirsty asked.

Janelle threw her hands up. 'It's so minor I'd forgotten about it. A couple of weeks ago there were phone calls that suggested something like this could happen if we didn't pull out of the election.'

'And did you report these phone calls?'

'If I came running to you every time someone said something nasty, I'd never leave the police station,' Janelle said. 'You've got to have skin as thick as an elephant's to be in this game.'

'But surely this was a threat?'

'I didn't take it as anything out of the normal.'

'Do you record your phone calls? Is there any way to verify this?'

Janelle looked at Lou, who again shrugged a shoulder. 'No, we don't,' she said. 'Maybe we should start doing so.'

Jack made a note to pull the phone records, even though he wouldn't be able to verify what was said during the call.

'How are you funding your campaign?' Kirsty asked.

'Donations,' Janelle said. 'I can supply you with a list of people who have already handed over substantial sponsorship. I've already told you this!'

'Yes, I believe we mentioned we would need that,' Jack told her, closing his notebook. 'Listen, we'll be back with more questions, but in the meantime, if anything untoward happens, please contact us and ...' He paused. 'Not meaning to sound dramatic but do either of you have plans to leave town for anything? Meetings in Perth or ...'

Janelle scoffed. 'Are you telling us not to leave town? How ridiculous! But don't worry, we have no intentions of leaving town. I'm here for the long haul.'

Back out on the street, Jack inspected the scorched cement. 'They're convincing,' he said, as they set off for the police station.

'If they didn't have anything to do with it, how did the bomb get planted inside the office? We can't place anyone else at the scene,' Kirsty answered. 'Except Zara.' She grimaced and looked at the ground as she said: 'We should talk to her.'

Jack paused, wondering if he should share his concerns. Loyalty and worry churned in his stomach.

'One hundred per cent,' he finally said when he realised Kirsty was looking at him. 'I'll give you her phone number and you can call her in for an interview if you want.'

'Are you sure, Jack?' She'd stopped walking now.

'Of course I'm sure. Sorry, I was just thinking things through.'

They started to walk again. Jack rubbed his hand over his hair. 'Have we gone back over enough days? How long can a bomb sit in one place waiting to be detonated, especially if it's on a timer?'

Kirsty stopped and spun around. 'What if it wasn't on a timer?' she asked. 'What if it was activated by someone with a mobile phone or some type of device? They wouldn't have to be near the front door. They could be across the road, in the pub. Just so long as they were in range of the radio transmitter. That would explain the back office. I remember a case I investigated in Geraldton. Bikies put a bomb in the wall of the clubrooms in case they ever needed to destroy evidence.'

'Really? Did they ever use it?'

'Bloody oath they did. We were looking at one of their members for a murder. When they set it off, they killed two of their own.'

A roar of engines drowned out Kirsty's voice as four bikies pulled up at the stop lights. They were riding two abreast, their leathers bright blues and reds. One of them had a sticker on the fuel tank promoting a charity ride to raise money for the children's hospital in Perth.

'Fuck, they are ruthless, aren't they?' Jack said. 'And what evidence would The Untouchables need to get rid of in Janelle's office?'

'Guess that's up to us to find out, if there is a link.'

'Okay, let's go back further. Maybe over the last week. See who goes in and out.'

'Pina might be able to do that for us,' Kirsty said. They walked up the stairs into the police station, just as Sally came running down the passageway.

''Scuse me,' she said, as she ran towards them.

Aiden was following her. 'DV call-out,' he said on the way past.

Jack and Kirsty stood against the wall until they passed, then pushed open the door to the squad room.

'I found something,' Lucas said when they walked in. 'Have a look at this.' He swung the computer screen around. 'Watch this bloke,' he said, pointing to a figure on the screen and hitting play. 'This one. In the hat. I've slowed the images right down and I think this is our purchaser.'

'Is this the CCTV for the GPS units?'

'Yeah, this is the shop in Darwin.'

A man handed over a box to be scanned and paid with cash. He waved away the receipt but took the bag that was offered. As he went to leave, he stopped and glanced up at the walls as if he was looking for something.

'I know it's grainy, and there's not a clear image of his face, but I just got off the phone from the retailer. I had them go back through the till receipts.' Lucas tapped the screen again. 'I'm waiting for them to email through the transaction details. That, my friends, is one of the GPS units we have here.' His face was alight. 'I think we have him.'

'Play it again,' Jack said. He leaned in closer.

There it was, clear as day. A man in a hat, handing over cash for a small rectangular box. No image or brand could be seen, but the transaction was obvious. An email ding sounded from Lucas's computer, and he clicked it open. 'Ha! There we go.' The printer whirred and spat out a sheet of paper. Lucas jumped up, snatching the page and pinning it to the board.

'Good work!' Jett said from his desk.

'Cash sale on top of that,' Kirsty said.

'I haven't found out who registered it yet. If we can do that, then that'll help, but now we've got an image of who bought it.'

'Let's hope it's not registered under a false name,' Jack said.

Another email dinged into an inbox, and everyone checked their computer screens.

It wasn't Jack's so he turned back to Lucas. 'That's good work, finding that bloke,' he said.

'I'll run an image search to see if I can come up with something.'

'Good idea—' Jack's words were cut off as Jett slammed his fist on his desk.

'Get a load of this!' he whooped, jabbing his finger at his computer screen. 'The gold is consistent with the Wiluna mine mineral count! It's been stolen from that mine.'

'Serious?' Kirsty asked. She took a couple of steps closer to Jett.

Jack joined her as they stood behind Jett and read over his shoulder. Kirsty smiled and clenched a fist.

Jack was confused by the numbers, ratios and percentages. 'What am I looking at?' he asked.

Jett ran his finger under the summary paragraph. 'This is all you need to worry about for the moment. You'll have time later to read all of the figures and make heads or tails of them. But these little words – *are consistent with gold already obtained from the Wiluna area* – are the ones we're looking for. So!'

Lucas had the adrenalin-charged look of someone closing in on their prey. His eyes were shining as he held up an index finger. 'Point one. We now have confirmation that the gold is from around Wiluna.' His second finger went up. 'Point two. We know that the GPS was put on a van in the same area.'

Jack's phone started to ring. 'Higgins,' he answered.

'It's Pina,' she said.

'Hi, have you got something?'

'Two things. Those payments into Barry's account – the quarterly instalments – are from his daughter. He'd lent her money for a house deposit and she was paying him back.'

'That clears that up then,' Jack replied. 'And the second thing?'

'We've broken through the code for the second GPS,' she said. 'Turns out the one at the front of the van started pinging at a different time from the one we've already checked.'

Jack looked up at his colleagues and motioned for them to be quiet. 'Hold on, Pina, let me put you on speaker. Jett, Lucas and Kirsty are here.'

He jabbed at the touch screen and Pina's voice came through loudly.

'I was just saying the second GPS, the one at the front of the van, was placed there at a different time from the other one.'

'On the same day at a different time or a completely different date?' Jett asked.

'Different date. One that matches with the time they were at Gwalia.'

CHAPTER THIRTY-TWO

Zara and Jo leaned towards the map of Australia that was pinned to the library wall.

'This accident, in Queensland, was last year and the one in New South Wales was early this year,' Jo told Zara. 'I haven't been able to talk to the police there yet. I've put in calls, but no one has returned them.'

'Did you find anything on the one in Ceduna?' she asked.

'There's a short news article in the local paper about a man who had been found next to his caravan – it was reported as natural causes.'

Zara nodded. 'But it can't have been, because otherwise why would Liz have been going there to investigate? She told me that he had defence wounds and it looked as if he had been strangled. I don't think the story has gone to print, because I haven't seen it come up in my Google alerts. Liz must still be looking into it.'

Jo folded up the map. 'What do you think?'

'That we've got work to do. Was there anyone we could interview in regard to the Queensland accident?'

'Yeah, Duncan Predure. He's the old bloke who was beaten up with an iron bar. I've got his number here.'

'Okay, let's give him a call. But before we do, I did some research on Ken Warner. He's the owner of the building that Janelle Salter leases.'

Jo looked up. 'Geez, isn't he the president of The Untouchables?'

'That's the one.'

'His brother is in that gang too. From memory, I think his name is Ray. I heard Bruce talking about them a while back. Some court case, I think, but it's been a while and I'm a bit hazy.'

'Yeah, you're right. The explosion was in Janelle Salter's office so on the surface you'd think it would be related to her and the No Mines campaign. But what if it's something else? Like someone trying to get at Ken Warner? There's a couple of newspaper articles on his son, which Bruce wrote. The son was arrested for smuggling drugs, only the prosecutor couldn't make the charges stick, so he was let off.' Zara grabbed her phone and pulled up the article. 'And there's another one only in recent months. Listen to this: *Today, Kalgoorlie detectives intercepted eighty thousand dollars' worth of methamphetamine when they pulled a vehicle over for a licence check. At the wheel was William K Warner, son of president of the Outlaw Motorcycle Gang The Untouchables Kenneth Warner. He was bailed and is expected to appear in court on the* ... blah blah blah.'

'That's right,' Jo said. 'Caused a bit of a ruckus because everyone knew he'd transported the drugs and they wanted him away, but he had such a slippery lawyer it wasn't going to work. It doesn't explain why Janelle and Lou were the only people in the office before the bomb went off, though.'

'I think we need to look harder. The Untouchables have

lost a shipment of drugs. That's the way the club makes their money, so they're going to be needing another option. They need to recover that money somehow. What would be the best way to do that?'

'They're not going to get that kind of money from the insurance on Janelle's office,' Jo said.

'I know,' Zara said. 'I can't help thinking there is more to Janelle's office, though. Make a note, Jo, we need to see if The Untouchables have links to interstate gangs.'

She scratched out a note then asked: 'Did you find anything more in Gwalia yesterday?'

Zara leaned back in her chair, wondering whether to tell Jo about the company she'd had on the way home. Not wanting to frighten her, she shook her head. 'Nothing that I haven't already told you.' She pulled her phone out and put it on the table. 'Got Duncan's phone number there?'

Jo read out the number for Zara.

Her call went straight through to his message bank, and they listened on speaker as an elderly man's voice told them to leave a message. As it ended, a female voice could be heard telling him to push the red button to finish recording.

'Right-oh, let's go to the newspaper office and see if our keys still work,' Zara said. 'We might need to do some old-fashioned research by reading old newspapers.'

They gathered up their things, thanked the stern-faced librarian and started the trek to their old office.

As they turned onto the main street, they could see action around Janelle's office. The windows had already been replaced and now a painter's van was parked out the front. Fast work for something that had only happened two nights ago. Especially considering it was a crime scene.

Zara found herself wondering about the bikie link again.

Janelle and Lou were out the front, leaning over the bonnet of the van, looking at something.

'Good morning,' Zara said, as she and Jo walked up to them.

They looked up from a colour chart but didn't smile.

'Sorry, we can't talk,' Janelle said. 'We're busy.'

'Janelle,' Lou reproached her boss quietly.

'Made a decision yet?' a man came out of the office, in splattered overalls and with paint caking his hair.

'Yeah, this one,' Janelle said, tapping on a sample. 'Antique white.' She turned to Lou. 'You googled that, didn't you? It's a calming colour?'

'If you want calm, you'll need to go with a light blue, green or beige,' Lou answered her. 'And none of them are going to blend nicely with your purple logo, so you'd better go with the white. Plus, I think that's more professional.'

'Fine,' Janelle told her. 'Yes, let's go with that white. Thank you.' She moved away from the van.

'Got the tradies quickly,' Jo said. 'I thought they were pretty hard to come by, with all the building that was going on during Covid.'

'The owner of the building has organised it all,' Lou told her. 'We're lucky. I'm hoping that we don't have too many down days. There's only one hundred and ninety-two days before the election and we have a lot of work to do.'

Zara's focus sharpened. 'That would be Ken Warner? That's handy he's got people on call. Have you met him?'

'Not in person, but I've spoken to him on the phone.'

'Do you know he's the president of The Untouchables?'

Janelle's eyes shot to Zara's, then she gathered herself. 'I don't care what he does in his spare time. That's nothing to do with me. I lease the building, pay my rent on time. It's purely a business arrangement.'

Jo leaned forward. 'Most people would say that arrangement was setting you up for a fall – a politician with links to bikies.'

'What?' Janelle was incredulous. 'I don't have any links to bikies; I lease an office.'

'But how do you prove that's all it is?'

Janelle looked as if she was going to lose her temper, so Zara intervened. 'We're only asking questions the police will ask,' she said.

Zara's phone rang. 'I really have to take this call,' she told them. 'If you want to talk, call us. Jo and I are starting our own newspaper. *The Prospector* shut down a couple of days ago, so feel free to advertise with us, or get in contact if you need something put out there. Okay?'

'Thanks for your time,' Lou said automatically even though they had met on the street.

'Hope you get your office back up and running as soon as possible,' Jo said.

Zara's phone stopped ringing as she and Jo walked away from Janelle and Lou. 'We need an office,' she told Jo. 'Somewhere we can make uninterrupted and private phone calls.' She guided them to a seat underneath a large gum tree and looked around. For once, there wasn't any traffic on the street, nor kids playing in the park.

'Can you take notes?' Zara asked Jo, who nodded.

Zara put an ear bud in and gave the other to Jo.

A wavering, elderly man answered the call. 'Hello?' he said.

'Thanks for calling back, Duncan,' Zara said, after she'd introduced herself. 'I'm a journalist looking into the people who have been attacked in caravan parks. I wonder if you'd answer a few questions?'

'A journalist? Well, I'll be. What could you possibly want with me?'

'Answers to a few questions about the, ah, problems you had with your caravan. Would you be open to that?'

'Well, yes,' Duncan said, 'but I don't think I can tell you much. I don't remember a lot.'

'The police I spoke to said there was a GPS attached to your van. Did you put it there?'

'No, I did not. I was as surprised as the next person when that policeman told me about them. You know, I asked my children about that when I got out of hospital. I wondered if they'd decided to keep track of me, but they promised they knew nothing about it either.'

'And you didn't have anything of value in the van that you needed to keep track of?'

'I live simply. I have nothing of value.'

'Where were you staying before you were attacked?'

'I was at a little place called Fig Tree Camp. There's hardly anything there, but I like camping like that. I camp simply and don't go bush to be surrounded by people.'

Zara indicated for Jo to google the location.

'Were there any other campers there?' she asked Duncan.

'Yeah, just one. A younger woman, travelling on her own. But she stayed out of my way and I stayed away from her. I know most people like to chat, but I like the silence.'

'Had you seen the woman before?'

'I wouldn't have thought so,' Duncan answered, sounding bemused. 'I hardly saw her, just knew she was there. I don't think I'd remember her if I tripped over her in the street.'

Jo turned her phone around to show Zara where the camp site was.

'Fig Tree Camp is near Bania National Park?' Zara asked.

'That's right,' Duncan said. 'Near the Mount Rawdon Gold Mine. I like to do a bit of prospecting, see. Not as much as I used to, mind you. My legs give out a bit more easily than they did ten years ago, but—'

'Hang on,' Zara interrupted. 'You were camped near a gold mine?'

'That's right.'

Jo found the mine site. It was active.

'And then you went on to Cloncurry where you were attacked?'

'Took me a couple of days to get there, but that's where I was headed.'

'And did you have any intentions to come to Western Australia during that trip?

There was a silence. 'Not this time. My niece lives in Western Australia and it would have been nice to visit, but the drive is too far for me these days.'

'Duncan, did you find any gold?'

'No, ma'am, not this time. I have before. Only enough to pay for the fuel I've used, but it's always a help. Going for a swing gives me something to do during the day, you know. As much as I enjoy camping and being by myself, sometimes the days get a bit long.'

'Sure, and just going back to the GPS, did the police suggest that it had been planted there?'

'There's no other option, but I don't know why anyone would.'

'Well, look, thanks for your help. Can I call you again, if I have any more questions?'

'Course you can.'

Zara hung up and looked at Jo. 'You know what the common denominator is here, don't you?'

'Gold. Transporting gold.'

'Yeah, and they're using grey nomads to shift gold around the country or get it to Kalgoorlie. That's why they attach a GPS, so they can track the vans. The question is where are they putting the gold so the occupants of the caravan don't know it's there? And why?'

—

Zara was glued to her computer screen. Between searching for gold theft reports and trying to get more information on Janelle Salter, she felt as if her eyes were square.

Janelle had said her funding was coming from donations, but Zara had only been able to find that the original seed funding had been put up by an anonymous individual twelve months ago. Individual donations could be made without disclosure to the Commonwealth if they were under eleven and a half thousand dollars.

There were ten individual donors who, unsurprisingly, had supplied eleven and a half thousand on the nose. Surely that should have warranted further investigation by the regulator.

When she googled the Advisory Board for No Mines, there wasn't one.

Zara sent a text message to a bloke in Canberra who had previously been a source, but when she didn't hear back from him straightaway she suspected she wouldn't at all. Then again it didn't seem as if her number had been blocked.

She couldn't do anything more on the gold transportation by grey nomads yet because she really didn't know where to go with that. She'd told Jo she'd think about that overnight.

Which had brought her back to Ted. Because Ted was fun and she was at a bit of a loss with the gold.

Google had failed when searching for Ted.

Chewing her thumbnail, Zara poured herself another glass of wine and looked out the window. The sky was dark now, and all she could see was her reflection and the wall behind her where's she'd hung a photo of her and Jack.

She took a sip of wine and picked up her phone to text him. *All okay?*

They never asked each other what time they'd be home. That wasn't how they ran their relationship. Yet she'd hardly seen Jack since the night of the explosion.

Zara hadn't even put the phone down before there was a reply.

Yep, working a lead.

That was all Zara needed to know. She might see him in five minutes, five hours or tomorrow morning.

Reorienting her thoughts back to Ted, Zara opened up Facebook.

Social media was such a great place to look for people. Zara was constantly amazed at the information that people – women, in particular – put up for strangers to see. Her friends were always posting photos of their kids proudly holding up Merit Awards, which also happened to include the school's name.

Nothing that a predator would find interesting there. Not.

Then there were the people who plastered their European holidays over Instagram, advertising for the world to see that their house was empty.

And the ones who told everyone in a video that their ex had left them, they'd lost twenty kilos and were ready for that brand-new relationship. Two seconds later, they'd be posting photos of themselves all loved up with some random and then a further two seconds on there'd be tears over another breakup.

Eye-rollingly boring, uninteresting and annoying.

Both Jack and Zara rarely used socials. Zara had been more on LinkedIn for professional use rather than the social media sites like X, Facebook and Instagram. TikTok, to Zara, was only a noise that a clock made.

She typed in *Ted Upton* and was unsurprised that Ted didn't have a profile.

Closing her laptop, she rested her elbows on the table and flicked through the notes she had taken as she'd sat by Ted's campfire.

There was engrained dust on the page of her notebook and a splash of tea. She rubbed her hands over the page, feeling the grit of the dirt, remembering the heat of the fire and terror when the scarecrow had popped up from the bed, then the gun in her back.

Edwina Upton.

What a unique woman. The sort of woman who would have sorted those bastards who'd frightened her on the way back from Gwalia with their car and shitty driving, forcing her from the road. Unlike Jack, who didn't seem to be at home at all at the moment, which meant she couldn't even tell him about them.

CHAPTER THIRTY-THREE

'Bastards,' Ted hissed, walking around her freshly dug-up dirt.

Someone had come in while she'd been in town. They had sifted through everything she had dug up over the last week.

Dirt was spread out, there were footprints and dig holes and, to add salt to the wound, they'd used her backhoe to dig up a few more buckets of earth and been through that too.

There was no way of knowing if they'd found any gold, because even though Ted had found nearly three hundred thousand dollars' worth of nuggets in the same area, how could she know if she'd got them all?

How could anyone have known she'd had a find like that? Ted had told no one except Zero. He'd been alive when she found the first one and it was unlikely he could have passed it on through doggy woofs.

It had been a huge ripsnorter of a nugget that weighed just over five ounces. Well, that's what Vince would have called it, a ripsnorter. The word, to Ted, was crass and uneducated, and neither of them were that. Vince, however, had fallen into the rough and tumble of Kalgoorlie, perhaps forgetting his upbringing.

Ted, on the other hand, stayed up to date with news and politics, was widely read and listened constantly to the radio and, just recently, she had even graduated to podcasts, with the new phone that piece of gold had bought her.

Kendall had bought that first nugget, and because it had been valued at just under four thousand dollars it hadn't had to be reported to Austrac.

Over the next few months, she'd carefully sifted through the ground and found more gold. Her hiding place had been in the ground under her caravan. No one would have thought to shift her van out of the way.

Every time she went to town, she took her latest find into the bank and stored it in the safe deposit box.

Every so often she cashed in a smaller nugget for her shopping. Didn't have to touch her bank account that way so the nest egg she'd worked so hard to build wouldn't be touched.

Now this. Poachers, gold thieves or stealers, call them what you will, but they had mined *her* land.

Ted could hear her mother's voice in her mind.

A lesser woman would cry, but, Edwina, you are not that. You are an Upton and we are strong, capable women.

Sinking onto the ground, Ted dug her hands into the earth, keeping them there for a few minutes, then let the sand drift through her fingers.

Who knew? Why had they invaded her lease?

Perhaps they had hoped she'd been on a run. Maybe it was a stroke of bad luck.

But Ted didn't think she believed in any type of luck, bad or otherwise.

Could she report it to the police? Did any other prospector report a theft like this? She could almost hear the cops laughing.

'How much gold have you had stolen, Ms Upton?'

'I'm not sure.'

'You're not sure?'

'I don't know what was in the ground.'

Trespassing, yes, but who was the witness and how would the police find who had … Ted let out a loud, frustrated groan. All the pent-up anger of her life came out. She pounded the ground, then picked up the closest thing and hurled it across the land.

The shovel she'd flung hit the backhoe and bounced off the tyre back onto the ground.

'How dare you,' she yelled.

The words echoed back at her and around the cleared area.

How dare you, how dare you …

Finally with all her energy spent, Ted lay on the ground, looking at the darkening night. A blush of blues, pinks and soft oranges spread over the clouds and sky. The cold crept in as the sun slipped below the horizon, and she could hear the Boobook owl making its first call.

Tonight, she wouldn't set the booby traps or alarms. She didn't care. The poachers could come again, and she wouldn't try and stop them. If they wanted her gold, they could take it.

She gathered herself together and walked dismally back to camp.

Not bothering with food or stoking her fire for the night, she went into her van and climbed into bed, fully clothed. Drawing the sleeping bag up to her ears, and making sure her beanie was on tight, Ted stared into the dark, listening to the wind speaking to the trees and the owls calling to each other.

The poachers wouldn't come. They'd already been and left nothing behind, so she was safe to sleep.

—

Ten the next morning and Ted was walking through the sliding glass doors of the police station. The front desk area was busy. Three people were waiting in line and a police officer was standing at the doorway beckoning someone over so she could speak with them.

Ted ran her hands down her jeans and took a breath.

She chanted her mother's words over and over. *A lesser woman would cry, but, Edwina, you are not that. You are an Upton and we are strong, capable women.* How funny, she thought, as she sat on a plastic chair to wait, that from so long ago – and from the grave – her mother could still have an influence over her emotions.

A heavy woman sat down beside Ted, circled in the smell of cigarettes and garlic. She gave Ted a glare as if she was in the wrong place then angled away from her.

Ted ignored her. She'd never set eyes on the woman before so her reaction didn't matter.

Again, she ran her hands down her jeans and then touched her bun. She really wanted out – especially when two uniformed officers dragged a kicking and yelling man into the station. He was fighting, twisting and turning, trying to get away from their grip, while an officer held open the door leading to the cells.

'Fucking pigs,' the man yelled. 'He touched my missus's bits. Her private bits, you know! How would you like it if a bloke did that to yours? You should be arresting him for that, not me. I was just protecting my woman.'

'Yeah, mate, we understand. But breaking someone's nose, no matter the reason, is plain assault,' one of the officers told him.

Ted wished she was anywhere but here. She half rose to leave, but as she did, a new resolve swept over her, and she straightened up.

She was an Upton, she'd already faced trauma and heartbreak and she'd healed herself from that shit. As much as she could. The poachers wouldn't get away with what they had done.

Taking a breath, she went up to the officer behind the desk.

'How can I help you?' he asked.

'I'd like to make a complaint – or whatever this needs to be – about trespassing on a gold prospecting lease.'

The officer looked over the rim of his glasses. 'On a prospecting lease, you say?'

'Yes. Yesterday while I was away, someone has come in and gone through the dirt I had dug up ready to mine.'

A smile played around the officer's lips as he tried to stay professional, yet he knew the outcome.

Ted knew it too and pre-empted his words. 'Yeah, look, I know there's two chances of finding who did it: none and zilch. But if we don't start reporting things like this, whoever is doing it is just going to keep doing what they're doing.'

The officer's smile faded. 'That's true,' he told her. 'I'm surprised. You prospectors are a secretive bunch, and I don't think I've ever taken a trespassing complaint in the whole seven years I've been here. Wait here and I'll get someone from the Gold Squad to come and talk to you. What's your name?'

'Ted Upton. Edwina Upton.'

He indicated for her to take a seat again and picked up the phone.

Ted nodded to herself as she went back to the horrible, uncomfortable plastic chairs. Standing up for herself felt good.

Liberating. Empowering.

She checked to see if anyone was looking at her, in her worn-out clothes and dirty shoes.

Everyone was caught up in their own world of turmoil. The woman who'd been next to her was now telling the officer behind the desk that her daughter had been missing for three days and it was high time someone did something about it.

'Bonnita hasn't run away, mate, I'll tell you that. She's a good girl.'

Ted watched the distressed woman, a long-forgotten feeling of anxiety starting in her stomach.

Moments later, an officer came from the bowels of the station and approached the woman. 'Kay, do you want to come back with me?' she asked.

Ted assumed the woman was known to her.

'No, I bloody well don't,' the woman snapped. 'You should be out there looking for my daughter. Why won't you look for her?'

'Come on out the back, Kay. We can chat about Bonnita there.' She put a hand under her elbow to guide her to the door.

'You need to find Bonnita,' the woman said and started to cry.

Taking a deep breath, Ted tried to stop listening. She *missed* her daughter. And hated the bastard who'd convinced her that her mother wasn't good enough for her.

'I know, love,' the officer said gently, 'but do you remember? Bonnita died three years ago. She's in the cemetery.' The officer's voice faded away as they went through the door, but the woman's howls didn't. They were so full of pain that even the hardened cop at the front desk glanced up and took a deep breath.

'Edwina?'

Ted wasn't used to her real name being used, so she almost missed the tall man in plain clothes who had come to the door.

She rose. 'Yes, that's me.'

'Come through. I'm Jack Higgins.'

Ted gave him a small nod and gathered her tattered handbag to her chest as she followed him through the door.

'You've had a bad experience,' Jack said as they sat down in the small interview room.

Her heart jumped at his words. God, she hated authority and being in a place like this.

'That's one way of putting it,' she answered, her heart giving a couple of extra hard thumps.

'Would you like to tell me what happened? Your tenement is to the north of Kalgoorlie?'

Putting her bag on the table but still holding the leather strap, Ted nodded. 'Yeah, if you've got a map, I'll show you where it is.'

'Tell me what happened first and then we'll get to that.'

'Few nights ago, it started,' Ted told Jack. 'Something like this happens every few years. You know you get people wandering around in places they shouldn't be, but the other night was different. I knew they were casing the place.' Ted looked at him, speaking clearly.

'How so?'

'They sent a drone. Just on dusk. I guess it had some type of night vision thingy. I'm not up with all that new technology but I've heard about it on the radio. It must have been able to see something at night because it spent three or four hours in bursts flying around in the pitch black.'

Jack nodded and made a note. 'Ever heard or seen the drone before?'

Folding her hands in front of her now, Ted formed careful words. 'Don't think so.' She paused. 'Then there was the motorbike.'

'The motorbike?'

'Yeah, it turned up the morning after the drone. Came in from the direction of the road, stayed a few moments at the camp and then shot through into the bush. It rode off towards where I'm mining now.'

'Okay, and did you know the rider?'

Ted had spent hours thinking about this. She'd known someone who rode a bike once, but that was years ago. 'I don't think so. Hard to tell with all the leather get-up they wear.' She brought out her mobile phone. 'Here, I took some photos of the tread on the tyre.' Fumbling with the apps, she sighed. 'Not too good with this stuff.'

'That was forward thinking of you.'

'Yeah, well, I almost didn't come in. Seems stupid to report something I haven't necessarily lost.' She turned the phone around and slid it across the desk.

Jack picked it up and looked at the photo.

Watching the detective, Ted thought he was chewing the inside of his cheek. Nerves? Maybe he hadn't been here long.

'Have you had a big find lately?'

Raising her chin slightly, she gave a nod. 'Been a while since I did. Not something we miners talk about.'

'I understand. How long ago?'

'Maybe twelve months.'

'Who else could have known about it?'

'I've been asking myself the same question. I can't think of anyone who would have known. I put the nuggets in my safe deposit box at the bank and I've only sold small ones. Even if there was someone looking over my shoulder, they haven't had much to see.'

'How far do you live from Wiluna?' Jack asked.

'Wiluna? That's a bloody long way from where I am,' she said. 'How far?'

'Geez, I don't know. I've never been there. Small town built on mining, north of me. Maybe four hours, bit more, perhaps.' She leaned back, keeping her eyes on Jack. 'You not from around here?'

'I'm new, but don't worry, I'm getting the hang of things quickly. Sometimes I need to get my bearings. What about Gwalia?'

Ted nodded, a little feeling of wariness inside her now. 'That's closer. A whole heap closer.'

'Where were you yesterday? I'm guessing you weren't on your lease if they came during the day?'

'I come to town once every couple of months. Get supplies and stock up on books from the library. Got home late yesterday afternoon and found it like it was. Here.' she took back her phone. 'I took some more photos.' She flicked the photo over to another one. 'There's a few, go ahead and have a look through.'

Jack took the phone, looking at the photos. She noticed he zoomed in on the footprints and then on the mound of dirt.

'Is it easy to get a vehicle into this area?'

'You'd have to know the landscape. The track to my place is off the main drag and is reasonably well hidden. It's got a teddy bear strung up high on a tree to show the turn-off to people who I want to visit, which isn't that many, mind you. So they would have had to have looked carefully because the bushes cover the first part of it. But if they've put the drone up or used some of that satellite technology I've heard about, I guess they could see it from the air.'

'And do you know if they found any gold?'

Ted put her elbows on the table and looked at Jack. 'Only those bastards will ever know that. This is why I was hesitant to report what happened. I can't know. Yes, I've found gold in that area. A lot. But was there any still to be found?' She shrugged.

'Needle in a haystack,' Jack said.

'Might even be smaller than a needle,' Ted said with a wry smile. 'Let's try a pin.'

'One last question before I get the map,' Jack said. 'Do you have any security cameras or the like? Anything that could help identify who was there?'

'I booby-trap the place, the way the old fellas taught me to. Nothing new out there, including me and the caravan. Look, Jack, you said your name was?'

He nodded.

'Jack, what happened is strange. Yeah, we get poachers, but this isn't poachers. They were organised. Knew how to use my machinery and my water plant. After fast money, I reckon, and they thought they'd find it at mine.'

'You're a woman by herself out in the middle of the bush,' Jack countered.

'I'm also very well known for not being afraid to use my gun.'

The detective chewed the inside of his cheek again. 'I won't ask about licences and storage for that gun now, Ms Upton, but I would caution you about using it.'

Ted flicked his words away. 'I'll do what it takes to protect me and my gold,' she said.

CHAPTER THIRTY-FOUR

'I've found some video footage for you,' the caller told Zara.

Zara checked the Bluetooth screen on the dash of the ute for the phone number. It was a landline and the phone said it was from Gwalia, but neither of the women she'd spoken to at the mine museum there had wanted to help her. 'What did you say your name was?' she asked, as she looked for a safe area to pull off the highway.

'I didn't. But, look, I want money for this. I've risked my job and I think I've found what you're wanting. I have to get paid for my trouble.'

Zara cocked her head to one side, thinking quickly. Before she could speak, the voice spoke again.

'I could just take it to the police. They're investigating this too.'

'You could,' Zara agreed, 'but they won't pay you. You'd be doing your job as a good citizen.'

'That's why I've come to you. Two thousand dollars and I'll email you the file.'

'Two thousand?'

'Take it or leave it.'

She thought about her dwindling bank account. 'I'll take it, but I have a question.'

'Shoot.'

'Why are you doing this?'

'I told you, I want the money. I'll text you my account details and you can put it in there. As soon as I see it, I'll email it through.'

Zara shook her head. This was the crudest blackmail offer she'd ever had. Jack would be wild at her taking the option, but she was going to do it. If worst came to worst, she had this person's bank account details and they could trace her that way. 'How can I trust you?'

'You've got no one else to trust.'

That was a fair statement.

'Go on, send them through. I'll get half the money transferred now, and the other half when I've seen the video. See if it's useful to me,' Zara said, finding a parking bay and pulling over. She'd been on her way to visit Ted this morning but whatever was on the film needed to take precedence.

The woman didn't argue.

Moments later her phone pinged and Zara checked the message. Nothing but numbers. This woman clearly had no idea what she was doing.

Withholding her name didn't give her anonymity. Zara had her phone number and her bank details and could find her identity in two seconds flat.

Taking a breath, Zara transferred the money and then sent a screenshot of the payment confirmation.

The minutes ticked by.

Zara checked her emails. Nothing there. She refreshed her text messages.

Still her phone remained silent.

'Come on, come on,' she whispered.

Then her phone rang. Liz.

'Question,' Liz said. 'You mentioned something about finding a GPS at the crash site you were at the other day. Do you know if there was any gold found in the caravan?'

'Why do you ask?' Zara's stomach fluttered. Had Liz found out what she had?

'This old bloke I told you about – there was a GPS on his caravan too. Don't ask me how I know. I just do. When I hit the police up, they wouldn't answer the questions, so I did a bit of research. Last year there were two caravan accidents, one in Queensland and the other in the Northern Territory. Both had GPS trackers attached to their vans.' She paused. 'Both caravans had been ransacked. I think they were looking for something that the drivers were transporting.'

Zara's phone dinged again. She checked and saw it was from the unknown number. 'Liz, I'll call you back, okay? I'm following something up and I'm about to go out of range, so hold that thought. I'll ring you back as soon as I can.'

Her car was buffeted by wind from a passing truck. She should get off the road a bit more. Or find a better parking spot. She also needed to wee.

Checking her mirrors, she did a U-turn and drove back towards Kalgoorlie until she found a parking bay that had some surrounding bush.

The wildflowers were stretched out like a carpet and the branches of spindly looking trees scratched at her shoulders and arms as she hid from the traffic.

Once she was done, she put her roll of loo paper back in its usual spot in her car door.

Always be prepared, she could hear her mother telling her.

Back inside the ute, she got out her laptop and connected it to the hotspot on her phone then opened the email.

Clicking the attachment, she held her breath, hoping but not really expecting to see anyone she knew on the footage.

The video had been zipped to make it easier to send. It was five minutes long.

She recognised the gates, which could be closed over the road. The sign told her where the entry was.

A line of cars were parked along the fence, although she couldn't tell their colours because the footage was black and white. Couples walked through the gate, pointing at the mining equipment. Their lips moved, but they were silent; the video was without sound.

A man went through the gate, with a large dog on a lead. The dog looked like a goofy one, its tongue lolling out of its mouth and its large head nodding from side to side as it walked.

Zara picked out Carol before she saw her face. There was something about her body language and shape that was familiar. She was walking alongside a woman, smiling and waving her hands around.

Jayne! A very alive Jayne.

Shock slammed into her stomach before a wave of nausea swept over her as she remembered holding the woman's hand and lying to her about Barry.

Jayne pointed away from them and Zara followed her finger. In the distance was a ute and caravan, hooked up and facing towards the road. There were two figures next to the van.

Zara hit the rewind icon to go back thirty seconds.

Barry's body language was uptight and jerky. Like he was in a hurry. He stomped away from his van towards the two women, who were in the foreground of the footage. He stood in front of them both, arms crossed, then he shook his head.

Carol smiled, touched Jayne's arm and walked on. She was out of their eyesight when she looked back at them and shook her head sadly, before walking on and disappearing out of the frame.

Barry's arms were now waving, and he put his hand on Jayne's arm and tried to steer her towards the van.

Zara stared out of the windscreen, thinking about what she'd seen, then she rewound the footage and watched it for a third time.

This time she focused on the person talking to Barry at his van.

Female, blonde, thin.

Zara could only see her back. She was indicating to the van and Barry was shaking his head. Asking questions maybe?

What she wouldn't do for some sound!

She rested her head on her palm, with her elbow on the window edge, and ran her fingers through her hair. What was she seeing here?

Three trucks following each other thundered by the parking bay, then the road was empty again.

The engine noise continued into the distance.

Zara rewound the footage yet again.

Barry dismissing the woman near the van. She turned and half of her face was caught in the frame.

Zara hit pause.

She leaned in closer and tried to zoom in on the image.

Blinking, she traced the image.

'Holy hell,' she whispered.

CHAPTER THIRTY-FIVE

'Thanks for coming in, Ted. We really appreciate the information you've given us,' Jack told her at the door to the police station. 'We'll do our best to come up with something, but as you've said, it'll be like searching for a pin. Unless we can find some footage that the drone has taken, and we can link it back to someone, we're a bit hamstrung. That doesn't mean we won't try, though.'

Ted nodded. 'It'll be tricky, for sure. If you do come up with anything, or I can help in any way, let me know. I don't go far.' She nodded again and strode off down the street, her duffle coat flapping out to the sides.

Her body felt lighter and Ted guessed it was the relief.

Surprisingly it had been a help to tell someone what had happened, and for them not to dismiss her or laugh. That young copper, well, he was a nice chap. Maybe too nice for Kalgoorlie.

Just like Zara. She was too nice for Kal too, Ted thought. The poor girl was so topsy turvy. Ted could tell she'd been hurt badly and was trying to get over what had already happened.

Ted knew what grief was, and Zara was shrouded by the aura of sadness and anger, even though she tried to hide it.

Her heart ached for a moment, as a long-forgotten maternal muscle memory tugged at her. Looking at the sky, Ted judged it to be about eleven in the morning. Too early for the Tatts bar, and too late for coffee. Where would she find Vince? Probably in a pub somewhere. Or in the back shed of one of his mate's places playing gin rummy or another card game that they could bet on.

Her phone was in her pocket and she got it out, debating whether to call him. Old bastard would probably drop dead if he saw her name on his phone screen.

There was no point anyway. What would they do? Sit at a bar somewhere and talk about the old times?

That sounded like torture to Ted. Nope, she'd just go home.

Or maybe she'd swing by the pound and see if they had a dog who needed rehoming. Now, that idea filled her with much more pleasure than sitting in a smelly bar or cafe.

Instead of heading straight for her ute, she walked aimlessly along the path, watching the traffic. Even though the pavements were empty, there was always movement on the roads. A shift change at the mine made the street busy, the men cramming into a pub for a beer before going home.

She stopped as she came to a smoked-out office. That was an unusual sight. A skip bin was on the street and a trail of dirty footprints led from the office to the bin.

Ted checked around to see if anyone was watching. Across the road, a woman pushed a pram and there was laughter coming from the cafe down the street.

Hoping no one had seen her, she put her phone back in her pocket then put her hands on the rim of the bin and hoisted herself up until she could see inside. There would be something worth pinching, for sure. People these days were so wasteful, always throwing out furniture when it could be refurbished.

The remnants of a sign lay underneath a broken chair and bookshelf.

Janelle Sal ... That's all she could see of it.

A young man hauling a water-damaged coffee table clattered through the door and stopped as he saw her. 'You right there?'

Startled at his words, Ted dropped back to the ground, probably looking ridiculous, she thought.

'Oi, granny, you okay?' The voice was louder this time, as if he was unsure whether she was hard of hearing or ignoring him.

Ted blinked.

My god, don't tell me I'm that old, she thought.

'Just seeing if there was anything of use in here,' she told him. She watched his face break into a smile.

'This is all just shit in here, granny,' he told her. 'Or maybe I should call you Magpie instead?'

The cheeky little sod!

'You mind your manners,' Ted told him. 'Whose office is it?'

'Here you go, ask the lady herself,' he told her, nodding over her shoulder. 'And stay away from the bin. I don't want to have to fish you out.'

Ted turned away hiding a smile, but her expression froze when she saw two women walking towards her.

'Oh.' She reached out to grab hold of the bin and yanked in a breath.

'You alright?' the young man asked as he threw the table over the top.

From inside the bin there came a crashing sound and the tinkle of glass.

Vince had warned Ted she was back, but there was no way Ted had expected to see her walking down the street.

'Hey, lady, seriously, are you alright?' This time the man got up in her face and she pushed him away. 'Okay, okay, I was only checking on yer. Fuck me sideways. What is it with women? One minute nice and the next a raging lunatic.' He stomped away, leaving Ted with only seconds to spare.

Seconds to give her a chance to gather herself before she was face to face with her daughter.

She watched as her daughter's eyes flicked to her, away again and then back, pinning her to the spot. Her mouth formed a perfect O.

'Jesus! What are you doing here?' her daughter exclaimed.

'Divine intervention,' Ted said. She cleared her throat. 'Guess I could ask you the same thing.' Ted adjusted her jeans and tucked her hands into the pocket of her duffle coat.

'I heard you were back,' Ted said, ignoring the intake of breath. If they all continued in that vein, there wouldn't be any air left in the universe for the rest of the population. 'This your office? What happened?'

'Still nosy, I see.'

'I wouldn't want to change.'

The contour of her daughter's chin and cheekbones were as familiar as if Ted had seen her yesterday, not eighteen years ago. The thin lines around her eyes were new, though, as were the expensive-looking clothes.

Ted's arms ached to reach out and smooth her hair and worry lines.

'No chance of that.'

Then her daughter spoke. 'Come on, we've got things to do. We haven't got time to stand around talking.' The two women walked inside.

Ted smiled somewhat sadly. There had been too much damage, too much hurt for them to make amends. They had probably already known that, but here was confirmation.

CHAPTER THIRTY-SIX

'Jett,' Jack said, his face serious, 'I want you to have a look at this.'

Lucas's head shot up as did Jett's. 'What have you got?'

'I had a phone call from Danny, an investigator I worked with in Adelaide, telling me about a man who was found outside a caravan in Ceduna. He's sent me some photos,' Jack handed over the printouts. 'Defence wounds here and here –' he pointed to the marks on the dead man's hands '– then you'll see the ligature marks here. There's similarities in this case to our grey nomads, mostly that there was a GPS involved and they've found gold bars.'

'Trafficking gold too?'

'Yeah, so I've gone back through our records. Spoken to a detective in Darwin. Brooke O'Neill.' Jack's face was solemn. 'She investigated another death. At first, it looked like a rape in the ablutions block of the caravan park. A woman's body was found underneath running water.'

'Geez, she was murdered?'

'Yeah. Brooke has sent me these photos.' He handed another lot around. 'Anyhow, obviously no DNA on the body, because of the water, yada yada. But when they found her caravan, it had been turned over. They thought it was a burglary or someone taking advantage of the fact it was empty.'

'That wasn't the case?' Kirsty asked.

'The wall cavity had been ripped open. No one could really work out why, and then they found a GPS under the van.'

Jett gave a snort. 'There was gold in the wall?'

'We've got no way of knowing because it's not there anymore, but I reckon that would be a safe assumption. I've trawled back through the woman's movements as best I can. It's a bit harder because it's over twelve months ago and all the roadside footage has been wiped. Anyhow, I've tracked her to Kalgoorlie, going north past Wiluna and then on her way to Darwin.'

Jett stood up. 'Let's get an employee list for the mine at Wiluna. Let's see if there's any POIs on it. Or someone who's already been charged before. Kirsty, you and Jack get on the road and head up there. Talk to everyone, threaten them with death if they don't talk to you.'

'Hang on, there's a bit more,' Jack said.

'Going back to the Ceduna bloke – Danny's crew has been through the van and found a lockbox in a secret compartment in the side of the van. Between the inside and outside wall. Quite ingenious really. But the interesting thing is that this isn't something that could have been done in five minutes. To cut the wall, insert the cavity and make a door would have taken time. So we've got two vans that they've had to smash up to get at something. Presumably, this wasn't working for the crims. Too much noise, effort and chance of being caught, let alone having to get rid of the occupants.

I bet they were worried that the bodies were beginning to pile up and someone would put two and two together.'

'How come we haven't?' Jett demanded.

'Because they've been in different states with time apart between the incidents,' Jack said. 'We need to get in contact with other states and see if they've had any similar incidents. Maybe they were trying something new with Barry's vehicle. The lockboxes under the van might take two or three minutes at most to set up. There's no damage to the van and you just wait until everyone has either shot through sightseeing or gone to bed. Slide under the van, clip the lockbox to the base and get out. Easy. And vice versa for getting it back.'

Lucas got up and went to the computer. 'Here's the employee list for the Wiluna mine,' he said, handing out copies.

'We'll get on the road,' Jack said, taking his copy. 'Call through anything you find.' He yanked open the door and almost tripped over Aiden.

'Sorry, mate,' he muttered.

'All good,' Aiden said with a glance towards him.

'Did you need anything?'

'Nah, mate, I was on my way to the crapper.'

Jack paced away from him.

They now knew how the gold was being transported and where it was coming from. They only had to work out how it was getting off the mine and who was stealing it.

Jack stuck his head back in the room. 'Can you find out who is in the gold pour room?'

'Yeah, already done it. Just running the names now,' Lucas waved his hand, not taking his eyes from the computer screen.

'You ready, Kirsty?' Jack asked.

'Yeah, let's go.'

Jack grabbed his wallet then followed Kirsty out. As they passed the toilets, angry voices reached them and Jack stopped.

'Okay?' Kirsty asked over her shoulder. 'Come on, we need to get a move on.'

'Wait a sec.'

He knew Aiden was in there, and he also knew Aiden's temper.

Putting his ear to the door, Jack listened.

'I just overheard them talking,' Aiden was saying.

Pause.

'Yeah, they're onto the South Australian one. And I think I heard something about Darwin too. We're out. What's worse is that bloody journalist has been snooping around Gwalia looking for the security footage. I don't think anything would have been on it. Hayley is too clever for that, but who knows.'

Pause.

Jack quietly let himself inside and took out his phone, switching it to video mode. What he took now wouldn't be admissible in court and it could be enough to get him kicked off the force, but he was willing to risk it.

'I heard them talking, man. The dees. They know the old fella in Queensland had been tortured. What the fuck happened there? He was supposed to end up dead. No witnesses, remember?' Pause. 'Doesn't matter now. The dees'll call the other states and all the caravanners that we stuffed up will be found. They'll work out we've been doing the mines over so that's it. We're done. It's time to get the fuck out of here. I'm leaving now.'

Another pause, this one longer.

'I don't give a fuck. You pull Hayley out now. No more gold, okay? It's too dangerous. We just need to lie low until we can start it up again.'

Aiden's voice trailed off as Jack stepped around the edge of the toilet cubicle and held up the phone. He saw Aiden's face turn from angry red to shocked pale in two seconds.

'Shit, Jack, what the hell? You gave me a fright. Can't a man take a slash in peace?' Aiden blustered.

'Who are you talking to, Aiden?' Jack's voice was steely.

'Pull Hayley out now,' he said into the phone before tossing it into the bowl of the toilet.

'Who's Hayley?' Jack demanded, still recording. 'Want to fish that phone out of the toilet?'

'You can get fucked.'

'Be better if you cooperate. You know that. Come on, man, get the phone out. I'd really like to talk to you about the other mines and the other caravanning accidents. You seem to know quite a bit. And I'm incredibly curious as to who Hayley is.'

Aiden reached down to get the phone but hit the flush button instead and turned, catching Jack off guard.

'Oomph.' Aiden laid a footy tackle into Jack and knocked him to the floor. Jack's phone spun out of his hand as he tried to get himself back up onto his knees and catch his breath.

The door slammed open, and Aiden was gone, jogging down the hallway.

Jack knew that wouldn't alarm anyone. Police ran everywhere when there was an emergency.

He tried to call out, but there was no breath in his lungs. With enormous effort he grabbed hold of the basin and pulled himself upwards, starting to hyperventilate as he attempted to get extra air into him.

The door swung open again and Lucas walked in whistling as he unbuckled his belt.

'Shit, Jack.' He raced to his side and put his arms under Jack's armpits. 'What the hell?'

'Aiden,' Jack managed.

CHAPTER THIRTY-SEVEN

Zara locked her ute and walked down the track towards Ted's caravan.

The information she'd seen on the film could wait until she had a chance to show it to Jack at home, but for now, she wanted only to talk to Ted. She could answer the questions Zara had.

And questions she had, because when Zara had changed her Google search to Edwina Upton, Kalgoorlie, Western Australia, she'd found a newspaper article on the historical website Trove.

Edwina Upton and her daughter, Hayley, attended the Kalgoorlie Christmas pageant on the 23rd of December.

There was a photo of a very young Ted with her arm around a girl of about two, waving at Santa's sleigh that was being pulled by a piece of mining equipment.

That had made Zara search the daughter.

Hayley's name had come up with a photo from a graduation at the University of Western Australia. Hayley, the article had said, had been dux of the class. A blonde woman, slight, with a pretty face.

Now Zara knew who her mother was, she could see the similarities between them. Their eyes were a similar shape and blue.

Zara also knew the woman's face, but her name wasn't Hayley.

'Ted!' Zara called out as she got to the fence. 'Hello, Ted, are you here? It's me.'

This time when she heard a screech like someone dying, Zara didn't flinch. The scarecrow next to the caravan leapt from its bed as the door of the caravan cracked open. Ted poked her head out, book in hand.

'Didn't scare you this time, Crow-eater?' she asked. She jumped down the steps, pulling a jumper around her shoulders. 'I was hoping for at least a small yelp.'

'I was ready,' Zara said with a smile. 'Are you up for a chat?'

'Just got back from town,' Ted said, not answering her question. 'Did you find out anything about the drone or the bikes?'

'No, I haven't yet. Have you?' Zara pulled up a chair near the campfire and waited.

'Bastards came in while I was away in town and threw over the place.'

'Threw it over?'

'Went through all the dirt I'd dug up. Took any gold, if there was any. Hard to know if there was any there. Bastards.' She placed a few sticks on the ashes and waited until they caught, flames licking around the edges of the wood, before she put on some bigger sticks, then logs.

'I've got a question,' Zara said. 'It's a bit personal, though.'

Ted grunted. 'Like that would bother you.'

'I was doing some googling last night.' She watched Ted before adding, 'You know what Google is?'

'What do you take me for? A bush hick? Just because I don't use this stuff doesn't mean I don't know what it is. What'd you look up?'

'You.'

Ted's head shot around. 'What the hell for?'

'Thought it would be fun.'

Ted grunted again.

'I found out you have a daughter.'

'So does most of the population.'

'True, but not all of their daughters change their name.'

'Not my issue what she calls herself.'

A noise like a shot echoed through the trees. Zara tensed, then looked around and laughed. 'Look, if you don't want to talk about it, you can just tell me. You don't need to try and scare me …' Her voice trailed off as Ted stood upright, her eyes darting everywhere.

'Get over here,' Ted whispered. She reached behind her back and drew out her pistol. 'Quick, under the van, so they won't know you're here.'

Zara shook her head. 'Not this time, Ted. You've caught me once; I don't scare easy a second time. Don't you want to talk about Hayley?'

'Stuff Hayley for the moment. I'm not bloody joking.' Ted's voice was low and held the slightest hint of panic. 'I wasn't sure it was them, but I am now. We're in trouble.'

Ted's words made Zara search the wooded area, her heart slow to catch up with what she was seeing. Movement from the trees. A figure, tall, dressed in black, holding a gun in the crook of his arm.

'Oh god, what is this?' Zara leapt towards the caravan, panic searing through her.

'Too late, Ted,' the man said. His tone was whiskey rough, as if he'd dragged his words through gravel. 'And you,' he told Zara. 'Stop right there.'

Zara took in a sharp breath as Ted turned the pistol towards the voice.

His muscled arms were bulging as he held the gun trained on Ted's chest, eyes narrowed almost daring Ted to move so he could shoot her. On his head was a John Deere hat.

'Jesus.' The word slipped from Zara's lips. He looked like a fucking mountain.

Ted on the other hand was doing a beautiful job at feigning nonchalance, but Zara could see the tightness in her posture.

'For fuck's sake,' Ted said, sounding bored. 'What—'

'Sit,' he commanded, swinging the gun towards Zara. The barrel stayed trained on her head. 'Or the hack'll get it. Surely you won't want her death on your conscience, Ted.'

Ted stayed quiet, her gun still aimed at him. Zara wanted to yell at her to put one in his knee. Didn't she know there wasn't any way to get help quickly out here!

'You sit down there, little journalist, and shut the fuck up. If you're charmed, you'll get out of here alive. If you're not, well ...' He gave a shrug as if Zara's life didn't matter to him.

Her heart was now pounding and sweat slicked across her palms, as she buried her hands into the dirt. It seemed like her only weapon. She was too far from the wood heap to grab a log and belt him around the head. Could she fling the dirt far enough that she could get some in his eyes? He was too strong for her to even consider overpowering him; she had to work smart.

'I knew when she came back that you lot were going to turn up here,' Ted said finally. 'You're all as predictable as the rising sun.' She sounded annoyed rather than fearful. 'How about you just fuck off.'

'You've still got attitude, I see,' the man said with a cocked eyebrow. 'Nice to know you've missed me.'

Zara's eyes flitted between the two of them now. They knew each other, old friends by the sound of it.

Ted clicked her tongue against the roof of her mouth. 'Tut tut. That ego of yours always did get you into trouble. If only you could understand that you've barely crossed my mind since.'

Since what? Zara wanted to scream.

'Ah, Ted, so spirited. I always loved that about you.'

'The feeling isn't mutual,' Ted retorted. 'What the hell do you want, Ray? I told you when you and that bastard brother of yours turned my daughter against me to never come back.'

Easing her phone out of her pocket, Zara checked the signal. It was flatlining, not even the tiniest hint of range to make an emergency call.

She started to shuffle slowly towards the bush, in the hope of getting behind a thick trunk of a blackbutt gum.

'Stay right where you are.' This time Ray's words were aimed at Zara.

She felt his eyes on her face and froze.

Ted didn't. She walked towards Ray seemingly unafraid.

'Ray, get the fuck off my land,' she said. Casually, she lifted her arm skywards and let a warning shot off.

Zara couldn't help it, she squealed and hit the ground, her hands over her ears.

'Now, now, Ted,' Ray said. 'That's very antisocial of you.

I would've expected your hospitality to be much warmer given our history.'

From her position on the ground, Zara saw Ray's fingers tighten around the gun. His left eye narrowed as he looked down the barrel, Ted squarely at the end of it.

Ted let off another shot, then brought her pistol down aiming at Ray's heart. 'Would you? Well, I don't do hospitality for the likes of you and your lot. Hear me? None of you.'

'Sorry, no can do, the gang's on their way. Aiden called it about half an hour ago, musta got sprung when he was trying to warn us. Our game's up and we're coming here to hide until everything calms down and we can get out of the state.'

They both had their guns trained on each other now. From Zara's point of view, it would be the one who was quickest on the trigger that would get out of this alive.

'See, that's the good thing about you living out here,' Ray said. 'Hardly anyone knows where you are, and you know the bush so well, you'll be able to help us get across the border. We're here for your help.'

'Over my dead body,' Ted snapped.

'That can be arranged,' Ray told her, an arrogant smile playing around his mouth.

'Was it you bastards that threw over my dirt?' Ted demanded.

Despite her fear, Zara was in awe of the way Ted was handling the situation. She just kept dishing smartarse answers back to Ray, but something was going to blow. Very soon.

The smile dropped from Ray's face. 'Don't accuse me of being a thief,' he snarled.

'Why not, that's what you are. I know you took my first lot of gold. You and that rotten brother of yours. How else did he get his start? Gotta hand it to him, though, he did better than you did. Doubled what he stole, then doubled it again. You on the other hand have always been useless with money. Still, you can't help it if you've got fewer brains.'

'Being bitter doesn't become you,' Ray said. Colour had risen in his cheeks.

'That money get you into the bikies, did it? Tell me, Ken gonna turn up here today too?' Ted was goading him now.

Zara wished she wouldn't. If she just put a bullet in his knee … Then she refocused. 'Ken Warner?'

'I'm already here,' another voice said. A man with a similar build to Ray strolled into camp, hands in his pockets and a large smile on his face. 'So nice to see you, Ted, after all this time. You look well.'

'Well, welcome one and all,' Ted said without breaking stride. She turned her gun to him, then put it straight back onto Ray. 'We could have a reunion.' Her eyes flicked over Ken. 'Few more grey hairs than you had years back.'

Zara thought her face softened for an instant, but the hardness was back before she could be sure.

'A reunion, what fun,' Ken said, sitting in a chair next to the fire. 'Thanks for having us here, Ted. Things are a bit hot in town, and I'm more of the type who likes the cold.'

'Don't remember sending the invitation,' Ted snorted.

Zara pulled her knees up to her chest, her phone on her thighs. Watching Ray and Ken, she tried to tap her security code in without them noticing her. If she could hit the record button …

Ken ignored Ted and turned to Zara. 'You better come over here, love,' he said. 'Don't want you over there by yourself. Here.' He patted the ground next to him. 'Come and sit next to me.'

'Leave her alone,' Ted said. 'She's got nothing to do with anything. I don't want a part of whatever harebrained scheme you've got going. You promised me when you shot through last time that you'd never come back. Doesn't look like you're keeping that promise.'

'I asked him to come.' This time it was a woman's voice. From deep within the trees.

CHAPTER THIRTY-EIGHT

'You as well.' Ted sounded resigned now.

'He's my dad, so he should be here.'

The woman from the Gwalia caravan park footage came into sight. Zara's mouth fell open.

'My biggest mistake,' Ted muttered. 'Not you, Hayley; your father.'

Ken looked at Ted, with a smile on his face, then got up and went to Zara, yanking her up by the collar of her jumper.

She yelped.

Her phone fell onto the dirt and Ken kicked it away.

'Fix that up, will you, love?' he said. 'Better not leave anything to chance. I know what journalists can be like.'

Zara saw Hayley raise her boot and bring the heel down onto the screen. She heard it shatter.

Spurred into action now, Zara thought quickly. Diving her hand into the earth she grabbed a fistful and flicked the sand into Ken's eyes, before he had a chance to react.

'Fucking bitch!' he barked. Still holding her collar with one hand, he used the other to claw at his eyes. Zara tried to twist away, but Ken slapped her across the face. He pushed her into the dirt and held her there facedown, his knuckles pressing into the back of her skull. Yanking her up, he gave her only seconds to take a breath before he ploughed her back down, this time harder, with short sharp movements. Each time, he held her long enough to force her further into the sand, squashing her chin and nose.

Forcing her to breathe in the sand.

It hit the back of her throat and she gagged, gasping for air. One breath in brought sand, the breath out made it stick to her airways.

She wanted to scream, but she wouldn't give him the satisfaction.

'Zara, oh, dear god! Jesus, Ken. Let her go. She's got nothing to do with this. Nothing!'

Feeling his grip loosen at Ted's words, Zara clawed at her mouth, coughing until she almost vomited. Tears and dirt blurred her sight. She spat the grit out of her mouth and looked up to see a fuzzy image of Ray coming towards them. Blinking, she tried to clear her eyes.

'Stop,' Ken commanded him.

Ray dropped back instantly.

Oh god, oh god, she thought. *Jack, where are you?* Then she decided to emulate Ted. 'Get your hands off me,' she screeched with what breath she had, trying to twist away.

'I told you to leave her out of it,' Ted snarled. But she didn't move or shift the gun from Ray.

'Just stop,' Ken told Zara. He dragged her to the fire and made her sit down at the foot of his camp chair, keeping a hand grasping her jumper. 'You're not going anywhere.'

Ken looked at his daughter. 'Were you followed?'

'Can't be sure,' Hayley said, 'but I don't think so.'

Ken kicked Zara's leg. 'I guess you'd love to write a story about this, wouldn't you?' He motioned to Ray to get hold of Ted. 'Better cable-tie her hands, and ankles. She's just as likely to leg it. We'll never find her if she does that.'

'Pig's arse,' Ted said. 'You forgotten I've got a gun?'

Ray shot a questioning glance at Ken. 'She'll use that pistol again if she can.'

'You should use yours on her,' Hayley said to Ray. 'Wouldn't be any great loss.'

Zara saw Ted raise her chin even further and knew the words had stabbed deep inside her psyche. Ted was too proud to show them she was hurting.

Hayley turned to Zara. 'If you'd kept your prying bloody questions to yourself, life would have been much simpler for you.'

'Well, tell me what's going on,' Zara said, channelling Ted's courage. 'I might be able to help.'

Ken crossed his legs and seemed to regroup, brushing off some dust. 'Don't say a word to her.' He looked around. 'God, Ted, I could have given you a much better life.'

'I wanted nothing from you,' Ted spat.

'And I want nothing from you,' Hayley said to Ted.

'And yet here you both are.' The gun wavered only slightly.

'Hey,' said Zara, trying to create a distraction. She was still spitting the dirt from her mouth. 'I already know about you, Hayley. I googled you last night. You went to uni and studied to be a mining engineer. I know you graduated at the top of your class and went out to mine sites and started work.' Zara took a breath, hoping her revelation wasn't going to get her murdered. 'And I know your shot-firer husband was killed in a mining accident underground. And now here you are, working for a politician and calling yourself Lou.'

Ted scoffed. 'Is that what you're going by now?'

'You know I could help you, right?' Zara continued. 'I could tell your side of the story. Hold the mining company accountable. Public scrutiny is heavy pressure.'

Hayley's eyes narrowed and she took a step towards Zara, but Ken put his hand on her arm.

'Ten out of ten. You've been doing your homework,' Ken said. 'Aiden said you were a nosy little bitch. I guess you know that the mining company didn't pay any compensation to Hayley, nor did they change their methods and policies to make sure this couldn't happen again?'

Hayley and Ken locked eyes and Zara saw unresolved fury.

'That mining company ruined my daughter's life. There is nothing worse, nothing, than watching your daughter suffer and not being able to take that pain away.'

'Nothing worse than having your daughter's father turn your only child against you either,' Ted put in.

Ken ignored her.

'It's got to stop,' Hayley said. Her eyes were manic and wild, glittering with anger. 'I need to stop it. All of it. Everywhere. People die. And the companies get richer and richer and the families don't. They lose people they love. And the mines. Don't. Care.' Her fists were clenched now, and her eyes glazing over. She was losing herself in her outrage. 'Do you know how many people die each year through accidents on these sites?'

No one answered.

'Do you?' Hayley screeched, this time. She was breathing hard. 'There are men and women who don't go home to their families at the end of their shift. My Harry –' her voice broke '– he was one of them. He never got to know I was having our baby.' Her face changed again. 'And then I miscarried. First they killed Harry and then they killed our baby.'

Ted shook her head and looked down, perhaps hiding the same sadness that Zara was feeling after that revelation.

'The public should know about this, Hayley,' Zara tried again. 'I could get national coverage if you'd let me try.'

A gust of wind came from nowhere and then a loud crack from overhead. Ken whipped around to see where the noise came from.

Falling silently through the air, a branch landed on the ground.

Zara looked up and thought she saw, above the trees, dust billowing in the sky. Hope flared. Maybe the cops had managed to get a chopper up.

'Jack,' she whispered.

But the bush was silent. The hope that had so quickly arrived faded.

Maybe they weren't coming.

'I never understood how you could stand back and watch our daughter struggle.' Ken's voice was hard. 'That's when I lost all respect for you, Ted.'

'And that's when I started to hate you,' Hayley told Ted.

'Oh, it was well and truly before then, my girl,' Ted said practically. 'You seem to have forgotten that your father—'

'He did everything!' Hayley yelled. 'He found me money to get No Mines going, he found me money to help me live when I didn't have anything and you did nothing! He found me and picked me up out of the gutter and you did fuck all.'

Ted drew herself up straight. 'I took you to the doctor. That was the most important thing to do. You were having delusional thoughts and hallucinations, trauma-induced psychosis.'

'Absolutely not,' Ken shook his head. 'There is nothing wrong with my daughter except grief and if working to shut the mines helps her heal, then my brothers and I will do everything we can to support her. The Untouchables are family.'

'That's a load of shit and you know it.' Without warning, Ted pulled the trigger.

A balloon of dust went up next to Ken's leg.

Zara screeched and Hayley laughed. 'Not so clever now, are you?' she exclaimed. Then as Ted's action sunk in, she turned her fury on her mother. 'Don't you dare hurt him.'

'Ah, Ted, you gotta be a better shot than that.' Ken seemed unfazed at the stray bullet but Ray's face had coloured purple with anger.

He took a few steps closer to Ted. 'You can't have many rounds left in that chamber, *love*,' he said in a low voice.

The tension between them all was electric. Zara could see that nothing would make him happier than to take out Ted. She had to do something. 'Tell me about the gold. Is that you too?'

Ray spun around to look at her. 'You keep your fucking nose out of this,' he said.

'Why? Maybe I want to help you.'

'Maybe you don't,' Ray snarled. 'Maybe you just want to live.' He looked down at his gun and smiled. 'Guess I might be in charge of that.'

Ken's eyes widened and then he yelled. 'You're a fuckhead, Ray. The cops know about the gold and how it's being transported, it won't be too long before they work out who's behind it. They're going to work out where all the bodies are buried and you want to leave another one?'

Another strong gust of wind blew through the camp, throwing dust into the air. Zara's heart bottomed out. The dust she'd seen before had been the willy-willy, which was blowing through now.

Hayley turned to Ray. 'This is all your fault!'

'Hey, I did what I was told.'

'No, you didn't,' Ken said. 'I told you to always make sure no one's around when you and your buffoons collect the gold from the vans. You fucked up in Queensland just like you fucked up all those other times. How many times do I have to tell you not to leave witnesses?'

'Well, what else were they going to do?' Ray blustered. 'They got interrupted so they couldn't finish the job.'

'I can finish this job.' In one quick motion, Ken reached underneath his coat and pulled out a gun. It took only seconds.

Ray's face registered the action and he put his hands up, trying to stop the inevitable.

A blast echoed through the trees with surround sound.

Spurting blood, a fountain of red blew into the air.

This time it wasn't only Zara who screamed. It was Ted too. Her face and chest had red seeping across them.

'Ted!' Zara screamed. 'Ted!'

'Jesus, Dad!' Hayley was wide-eyed, her hand over her mouth.

'Dead wood,' Ken said calmly, aiming his gun at Ted now. 'Too much at stake.'

'Your own brother,' Ted whispered, spitting blood from her mouth. Her gun had dropped by her feet and she reached to pick it up, but Hayley was quicker.

Ted was left standing, staring at her own daughter, who was holding a gun to her heart.

'Come on,' Ken said to Hayley. 'I need a hand. There's plenty of mine shafts around here we can toss him down.'

Ray's leg was twitching in the after-throws of life.

Zara needed to scream. She needed to get out of here, fold herself into Jack and move somewhere that was extra safe. Where she could see everyone coming.

'Hayley, come on,' Ken said. 'You don't want to go down, do you? Get your shit together. You knew the risks! Let's go.'

Hayley gathered herself and nodded.

Ken moved to Ray's body, keeping his gun trained on Ted. 'Show us where the closest mine shaft is.'

'No.'

Zara looked from one to another and took a chance. 'Hayley?' she said. 'Why were you stealing the gold?'

'Don't answer her,' Ken snapped, and brought out a zip tie from his pocket. In two steps he was towering over Zara, reaching for her hands.

Zara linked her fists together and swung them around hitting his arm, causing him to teeter off balance.

'Slut,' he snarled, grabbing her hair and pulling her backwards to stretch out her body before he rolled her over.

Zara breathed in more dirt and started to cough as it hit the back of her throat and lungs. She felt the pressure of being pushed further into the ground. Just like before. There was nowhere clear to breathe. Every time she tried, she took in another lungful of sand. She kicked her legs out and tried to wrench herself back over, earning her another shove into the ground.

'Ken!'

Ted's voice.

Then there was another, closer to her ear.

Hayley's.

With her eyes and gun still on Ted, she'd squatted down next to Zara.

'Of course we're stealing from the mines,' she said. 'But No Mines is not all we're stealing for. It costs money to run a bikie chapter. And you gotta have money to make money.'

In the background, Ted was yelling, then there was silence. There were black dots swimming in front of Zara's eyes now. She tried twisting and turning, anything to get away from him, but Ken held her head tightly to the ground. She was going to suffocate.

Hayley spoke loudly, so Ted could hear her too. 'We need to fund the No Mines party in every state, somehow. I won't stop until I get revenge for Harry's death. Janelle is a small cog in a big wheel. Replaceable. If she goes, I'll just find another one like her. Nothing that money can't buy. It bought her. She's a monkey on a string, and it wouldn't take long to get sitting members to vote the way we want them to if we can just wave a few cool mill in front of their noses.'

'Delusional,' Zara tried to choke out.

'Dad needs to fund the bikies. Easiest way to do it because the penalty for stealing gold is less than trafficking drugs or weapons. Gold buys drugs and drugs buy credibility in the bikie world.'

'Police!' A voice rang out, echoing through the bush. 'Put your weapons down! On the ground. On the ground!'

'Hayley, get behind Ted,' Ken yelled.

Ted shook her head. 'God, it's nice to know that the father of my only child is happy to use me as a human shield. You're a fuckhead.' She shaped her hand into the sign of a gun. Defiant. 'Don't touch Zara.'

'Gonna stop me?' Ken yanked Zara up.

Her head was spinning, she was coughing and needing to drag in clear air. Her legs buckled and suddenly it was only Ken's strength holding her while her head tumbled forward. Trying to raise it, she grunted. Her eyes were caked with grit and she spat out dirt with each outward gasp.

Jack, she thought. *Jack will be here.*

Hayley crouched to the ground, running crablike to get behind Ted, who was trying to get in behind the camp chair.

Ken now held Zara in front of him with his gun pointed at her sagging body.

'Don't come any closer,' he yelled. 'I've got a hostage.'

'On the ground,' the voice yelled again. 'Police! You've got to the count of three. One. Two. Three.'

Through the slits of her eyes, Zara tried to work out where everyone was.

A warning shot fired over their heads and Ken ducked. Zara saw that Ted was now pointing a pistol to the sky. She must've been carrying a second piece. Probably because of the appearance of the drone and bike, then whoever had thrown her lease over.

Jesus, so many guns, Zara thought. *No one is going to get out of here alive.*

'You mad fucking woman,' Ken screamed at Ted. He reached around to his back and brought out another hand gun then turned it in the direction of the police. 'We're not putting fuck all down.'

Hayley stared at Ted, and the two sized each other up.

Another shot. Ken moved the gun from side to side and covered where he thought the police were. 'There's more where that came from.'

'Weapons down,' a voice screamed. 'On the ground!'

Somehow, when Zara looked again, Ted was lying arms outstretched, next to the camp chairs, new blood covering her forehead. *Who was bleeding? No, no, no. Not Ted. Not Ted!*

She opened her mouth and expected to hear her own fearful scream. But there was nothing.

Ken fired off another shot.

Zara couldn't hear anything. She could see the dust from the scrabbling and bullets, Hayley's mouth moving, the blood vessels in her throat standing out as she screeched at Ken.

Ted on the ground like a rag doll.

No noise. Only a shrill piercing ringing in her ears.

People dressed in black combat gear stormed through, guns raised, masks covering their faces.

For a moment, Zara couldn't be sure they were the police.

Hayley went down. There were sprays of red, landing on the ground and mixing with the dirt. Men surrounding her, talking into their radios. Handcuffs out.

Ken facedown.

Ted, was she alive?

Again, she tried to call out, but there was a man bearing down on her. A faceless, masked man. Zara tried to curl away from him. Turn her back and roll into the foetal position.

She couldn't. When she moved her legs, her stomach erupted in heat.

Blinking again, needing to clear her eyes. The man disappearing behind another cloud of smoke.

It was hot. So hot. Her stomach felt as if it was on fire.

She smiled because once she'd been told the Kalgoorlie summers were like a furnace. It must be summer.

And in summer she could strip off her jumper and swim in cold water. Float in the deepest, coldest sea, which would be lovely because her body was burning with fierce heat. A deep sea would always be freezing.

Or a dam, or even under the ground in a cold, cold mine shaft. She could press her stomach into the chilly rock and cool down.

The masked man was alongside her, hands under her head now, talking frantically into his radio.

Somehow he morphed into Jack. Jack, who was cradling her head, saying her name. She could make out his lips moving. Then he looked like he was screaming.

Zara tried to reach up and touch his face. But she couldn't reach the dirt smeared over his checks. He didn't need to yell. She was right here. She was always right alongside him.

Her hands fell back on the boiling sand. The sand that somehow was streaked over Jack's cheeks and it must have been raining because his face was wet. So why was it so hot?

'It's okay,' she tried to say.

Someone would come.

They always did.

Someone would come.

And then there was a deep dark abyss of black.

CHAPTER THIRTY-NINE

Jack sat next to an empty hospital bed, his head in his hands.

He'd cried too many tears – more tears than he'd ever thought he could hold in his body. There had been a steady stream of police and nurses checking on him. Asking if he was okay. Could they get him anything. Stupid questions and ones he'd asked of others before. There was nothing anyone could do. Well, the doctors, but they hadn't been convinced they could save Zara.

'We will do everything we can,' the kindly doctor had told him under the bright fluorescent lights of the corridor as an orderly wheeled Zara towards the operating theatre.

The sheet was stained with her blood. Her hand, which hung from the side of the gurney, had a bandage wrapped around it where the ambos had tried to put in a cannula.

'How're you holding up?' Jett asked from the doorway. Lucas was behind him.

Jack shook his head, trying to clear the image. 'Fine,' he said. A ghost of a smile crossed his face as he remembered a conversation he'd once had with Zara about the word 'fine'.

She'd said that you could assume a woman was not fine if she described herself that way.

His smile dropped as he remembered how he'd thought Zara had set the bomb in Janelle Salter's office. What type of a dickhead had he been? 'Did you get them all?'

'Every single one of them,' Jett said, coming into the room and taking up a position next to the window. He glanced towards Jo, who was sitting on a chair by the bed, her face red and blotchy from crying. 'I've cleared it with media relations. You can write the exclusive, Jo, but not until we've authorised the timing. Okay?'

Jo gave a nod. It didn't look as if she cared whether she wrote the article or not.

Jett turned back to Jack. 'And Ted will be okay. They're keeping her in for observation. Ken took a bullet to the shoulder, but the doc said he'll be fine to stand trial by the time that comes around. Hayley, well, she's not saying anything and is still in the interview rooms. I'm going back there shortly.'

'Ask her who set the bomb in the office.'

'It was Ken. Aiden caved in like a badly cooked pavlova,' Lucas added. 'Turns out he's been used by Hayley, just for info, so there's no love lost there. Ken used to go in early every morning. I went back through the footage and found him on every single day for the last month. Four am going into the office. He'd stay about twenty minutes then leave again. Course, being the owner of the building he had a key, so he came and went as he liked. At this stage I don't have anything to prove this, but I think he was leaving Hayley information about where the gold was being taken from and left so she could attach it to the caravans. I'll get it out of Aiden or Hayley.'

'Genius, really,' Jett said. 'Who's going to be suspicious of a single woman in a caravan park? Plenty of people travelling by themselves these days.'

'True,' Jack said. 'What about moving the gold?'

'They were using the grey nomads to transport it. The bikies figured no one would ever suspect them or stop them and with the GPS units attached, they could track them anywhere. Aiden reckons there's eleven of the poor buggers who have been injured or killed when they've tried to get the gold back. Hayley is denying everything. When she does speak at all.'

'Were they all tracked with the GPS?' Jack asked, standing and starting to pace the room.

'Yeah. The gig has become more sophisticated over time. Said they lost a lot of gold the first few times they tried it. Boxes fell off, or they lost the mules.' Lucas leaned against the doorframe, his arms crossed. 'All because they didn't want to shift it themselves. There were too many risks – they'd be stopped, we'd be watching, which of course we do.

'They waited for the caravanners to transport it somewhere safe and then they'd whip in during the dead of night and collect it. Trouble was not all of the caravanners played their unknowing part the way Ray and Ken wanted. They were awake or woke up. Came home late after a few beers at the pub. The bikies must have been using idiots to collect the gold because they stuffed it up so many times. I don't quite understand why they took the risk, but, in another way, I do. We've always got eyes on the OLMGs.'

Kirsty came into view behind Lucas. 'Finished it,' she said quietly to Jett.

'What?' Jack asked.

She was holding a computer, and set it down on the tray table next to the bed. 'Going through the list of employees. There was no one on there of interest. Out of all the thousands who work up there, not one had a criminal record.'

'That's good,' Jett said. 'Their checks and balances are working.'

'Then I tried to work out who else could be going on site and might be able to leave with the gold.' She looked up.

Jack was trying to concentrate but it was hard with Zara in the operating theatre.

'Jack?'

All three of his colleagues were looking at him.

'Sorry, what did I miss?'

Kirsty hit the play button again.

He watched the grainy black and white images on the screen of a fuel truck entering through the checkpoint of the mine. The driver touched the tip of his finger to his forehead to give the security camera a wave. He knew that his face would be streamed back into the control room.

Kirsty switched to a new video file. It showed the same man getting out of the driver's seat, thick rubber gloves in hand as he undid the couplings and attached the heavy hose to pump out the diesel into tanks.

Again he smiled for the camera.

'Are you serious?' Jack asked.

'He knew we were going to get him,' Lucas answered. 'In the end.'

Now Jack's attention was squarely on the screen.

The next video was of the driver pulling up at the office and handing something through the window. In return, he was handed a large, square-mouthed thermos.

'For his trip home?' Jack asked.

'That's not coffee in there,' Kirsty said. 'The contents are worth a whole lot more than a caffeine hit.'

'Who is this guy?'

'A minion. He's a member of The Untouchables, but very low down. Does what he's told. Might not have even known what was in there. Probably thought it was drugs. He's been arrested too and charged with trafficking stolen goods.'

Jack shook his head. 'Stealing from the mines so they can shut them down.'

'And that was only Ken and Ray funding that part. The rest of the gold went back into The Untouchables.'

'What would they have done if the mines actually did get shut down?'

'Never would have got through parliament,' Jett replied. 'Money talks.'

'And bullshit walks,' Jack said.

The doorway into the ward darkened and a tired-looking doctor looked in. His face was serious. 'Mr Higgins?'

Jack looked up from the screen, butterflies spinning in his stomach. He schooled his face to deadpan. He stood, as did Jo, and took a few steps forward. 'How is she?'

'I won't beat around the bush,' the doctor said. 'The next twenty four hours is going to be touch and go. The surgery went well, but the rest is up to Zara.'

'What?' he whispered. 'What do you mean?' He felt Kirsty's hand on his shoulder.

'Zara is young, fit and healthy, but the bullet has pierced her liver. There is considerable damage.' He spoke gently. 'I am hopeful, but one can never be one hundred per cent sure in operations like these.'